"Beautifully imagined, beautifully crafted."
—SANDRA GULLAND, author of
Mistress of the Sun

"The three central, compelling women of
In Need of a Good Wife are each, in turn, terribly
lost and deeply brave. I adored them and rooted for
them in their struggles."—KATRINA KITTLE,
author of *The Blessings of the Animals*

"Graceful prose and historical settings that shine with
vitality...unforgettable."—KRISTINA RIGGLE,
author of *Keepsake* and *Real Life & Liars*

"You will fall in love with the brave, resourceful
women in this utterly captivating novel...McNees
writes with warmth, drama, humor, and tenderness
of love, loss and hope."—STEPHANIE COWELL,
author of *Claude & Camille*

Praise for

In Need of a Good Wife

"*In Need of a Good Wife* is as wonderfully candid as it is epic. Kelly O'Connor McNees creates unforgettable heroines (and anti-heroines), and infuses dreams of the American West with fresh spirit, humor, and yearning. I love this novel so much!"
—Wendy McClure, author of *The Wilder Life*

"You will fall in love with the brave, resourceful women in this utterly captivating novel—some beautiful, some worn but not defeated, all amazingly resilient—as they travel across nineteenth-century America to a small, dingy town in Nebraska to marry strangers and make better lives for themselves. Kelly O'Connor McNees writes with warmth, drama, humor, and tenderness of love, loss, and hope, and how happiness can be found in the most unlikely situations if you open your heart."
—Stephanie Cowell, author of *Claude & Camille*

"The three central, compelling women of *In Need of a Good Wife* are each, in turn, terribly lost and deeply brave. I adored them and rooted for them in their struggles, worrying about them when life forced me to set the book down to eat, work, and sleep. I found it deliciously satisfying that the redemption I wished for each of them arrived in completely unexpected ways, taking both me and the characters by surprise."
—Katrina Kittle, author of *The Blessings of the Animals*

"Life kicked 'Bixby's Belles' in the teeth, but they got back up for another round. Their determination inspires as their story captivates. With graceful prose and historical settings that shine with vitality, *In Need of a Good Wife* is unforgettable."
—Kristina Riggle, author of *Keepsake* and *Real Life & Liars*

continued . . .

"Rare is the book these days that captures my undivided attention, but this story enchanted me, reminding me of a time in my life when reading was a comforting adventure, and my hope was to fall in love with a book and its characters. Painting vivid images of the poverty of post–Civil War Manhattan City and the harrows of Destination, Nebraska, McNees weaves a hopeful, compelling story of love and resilience so engaging it is impossible to put down."

—Robin Oliveira, author of *My Name Is Mary Sutter*

"Reading *In Need of a Good Wife* is like going on a great adventure into the past. As you turn the pages, you'll find love, imagination, and a kind of charm I didn't know existed anymore. It's a wonderful book—sturdy and delicate all at once."

—Rebecca Rasmussen, author of *The Bird Sisters*

"*In Need of a Good Wife* is a beautifully wrought story, every page bursting with poetry and adventure. McNees sweeps us west with such hope and excitement that we ache and rejoice, celebrate and cry as Clara Bixby's band of mail-order brides leaves behind the bustling streets of New York City to search for new beginnings on the flat Nebraska landscape. A simply gorgeous book that will stay with you long after you read the last word!"

—Susan Gregg Gilmore, author of
Looking for Salvation at the Dairy Queen and
The Improper Life of Bezellia Grove

"Anyone who grew up on *Little House on the Prairie* will instantly fall in love with this book. Kelly O'Connor McNees brilliantly captures the hope and hardships of the American West and has created a story destined to be a classic."

—Tasha Alexander, author of *A Crimson Warning*

"Vivid, generous, funny, and often quite moving, *In Need of a Good Wife* casts light on a little-known corner of American history—and the women (and men) who struggled to make their way in an unforgiving world."

—Joseph Wallace, author of *Diamond Ruby*

"*In Need of a Good Wife* is a thoroughly charming novel, written with a gentle, wry humor and an eye for detail I found delicious. Clara, the gutsy heroine, is delightful, as are a number of the other characters, the good and the bad alike. Beautifully imagined, beautifully crafted: I absolutely loved it."

—Sandra Gulland, author of *Mistress of the Sun*

"Kelly O'Connor McNees has written a warm, generous story of women who leave everything behind to take a chance on a better life halfway across the country. She combines vivid historical detail with such emotional accuracy that I was convinced I, too, needed to escape grimy post–Civil War Manhattan and make the long train journey to Destination, Nebraska, where 'even the name of the place suggested plenty: *Nebraska* sounded like *basket*.' *In Need of a Good Wife* is a richly drawn portrait of a uniquely American experience; this novel is an absolute treasure."

—Nancy Woodruff, author of *My Wife's Affair*

Berkley titles by Kelly O'Connor McNees

THE LOST SUMMER OF LOUISA MAY ALCOTT

IN NEED OF A GOOD WIFE

In Need OF A Good Wife

Kelly O'Connor McNees

BERKLEY BOOKS, NEW YORK

THE BERKLEY PUBLISHING GROUP
Published by the Penguin Group
Penguin Group (USA) Inc.
375 Hudson Street, New York, New York 10014, USA

Penguin Group (Canada), 90 Eglinton Avenue East, Suite 700, Toronto, Ontario M4P 2Y3, Canada (a division of Pearson Penguin Canada Inc.) • Penguin Books Ltd., 80 Strand, London WC2R 0RL, England • Penguin Group Ireland, 25 St. Stephen's Green, Dublin 2, Ireland (a division of Penguin Books Ltd.) • Penguin Group (Australia), 250 Camberwell Road, Camberwell, Victoria 3124, Australia (a division of Pearson Australia Group Pty. Ltd.) • Penguin Books India Pvt. Ltd., 11 Community Centre, Panchsheel Park, New Delhi—110 017, India • Penguin Group (NZ), 67 Apollo Drive, Rosedale, Auckland 0632, New Zealand (a division of Pearson New Zealand Ltd.) • Penguin Books (South Africa) (Pty.) Ltd., 24 Sturdee Avenue, Rosebank, Johannesburg 2196, South Africa

Penguin Books Ltd., Registered Offices: 80 Strand, London WC2R 0RL, England

This book is an original publication of The Berkley Publishing Group.

This is a work of fiction. Names, characters, places, and incidents either are the product of the author's imagination or are used fictitiously, and any resemblance to actual persons, living or dead, business establishments, events, or locales is entirely coincidental. The publisher does not have any control over and does not assume any responsibility for author or third-party websites or their content.

PUBLISHING HISTORY
Berkley trade paperback edition / October 2012

Library of Congress Cataloging-in-Publication Data

McNees, Kelly O'Connor.
In need of a good wife / Kelly O'Connor McNees. — Berkley Trade paperback ed.
p.   cm.
ISBN 978-0-425-25792-0 (pbk.)
1. Mail-order brides—Fiction.   2. Businesswomen—New York (State)—New York—Fiction.
[1. United States—Social life and customs—1865–1918—Fiction.]   I. Title.
PS3613.C58595I5 2012
813'.6—dc23
2012004002

PRINTED IN THE UNITED STATES OF AMERICA

10 9 8 7 6 5 4 3 2 1

To RAM and WJM.

"They had three in the family, and that's a magic number."

There is a saddle horse especially for me and a little shotgun with which I am to kill sage chickens.

—Elinore Pruitt Stewart, writing to a friend about her new life on the prairie in *Letters of a Woman Homesteader*

Fall 1866

Clara

The oak planks in the floor of Rathbone's basement tavern, Clara knew, were lined with invisible cracks. The men who drank at the tavern brought the filth of Manhattan City in on their boots, manure from the street and muck from the floor of the omnibus, and the men's careless steps ground the dirt into the floor. If Clara didn't whisk it out quickly enough with her broom it would lodge in the cracks, and the planks would split down the middle. Mr. Rathbone would have to replace them—an expense that might make him think twice about how badly he needed a barmaid on his payroll.

The thought straightened Clara's back and she stretched it, the long fingers of her right hand clenched around the handle of her broom, before resuming her chore. It worried Clara, the possibility of losing the job, and, in losing that, losing everything—the money she made only just paid for her room and board upstairs at Mrs. Ferguson's with scarcely enough left over to keep body and soul together. Of course, if her father were still alive, things would be different. But he wasn't—he had died in debt back when the tavern was known by his name, as Wilson's, and Mr. Rathbone had bought it for a song.

Clara supposed she should be glad for it. It wasn't easy making a go of it in these times. Rathbone had already lost what meager business they could muster to the new place across the street, the Eagle Tavern, which sold ale at half price for the first hour of the evening rush each night. The roughs lined up around the block, the very same roughs who had previously done their drinking at Rathbone's long walnut bar. Clara had no love for any of them—in fact, she detested drinking in a man, thought it made him weak and womanish—but what did fate hold for Rathbone's without them? Here it was, the middle of the noon meal and there wasn't a soul in the place. Each morning, as Clara polished that bar, its burled grain like marks left in the sand by the waves on Long Island Sound, she prayed that come evening, Rathbone's would be full of men either too happy or too full of dread to go home. She didn't care which it was, as long as the men kept sliding coins toward the till. Of course, Clara indulged in using a little too much wax from time to time, buoyed by the thought that she could make the surface slick enough to yank the men's hands out from under their sorry jawbones, send their chins crashing down onto the hard wood.

Clara's survival depended on the loyalty of fool drunks, and she did not take kindly to this fact. But the drunks didn't scare her either. She had stood up to plenty of them in her time, once separating a pair of scuffling men by clobbering the bigger one in the back of the head with her rolling pin.

At half past one, two men dressed in black came in and took a small table by the window. One was lanky and tight-lipped and the other was fat, with a wide face like a camel's. His smile seemed to stretch all the way from one ear to the other. He rubbed his hands together as if to warm them, but it was, Clara had noticed when she descended the stairs from her room at Mrs. Ferguson's that morning, a perfectly pleasant October day.

"Miss?" said the heavy man, waving Clara over with his hand. She took her time leaning the broom up against the wall and making her way across the room to them. As she walked, she recognized something in her own slow amble and realized it was a memory of her mother, who had walked this way, seven balky children underfoot and a husband with a temper like a festering sore. Mrs. Wilson lived long enough to see three of her children make it to adulthood, Clara and two sisters. Maura had run off with a prospector six years back and hadn't been heard from since. Frances was hit by a streetcar the following year. Once there had been nine Wilsons, but now there was just Clara.

"If there is any justice in this world our Creator made, Reverend Potter, they will be serving a chicken pie," the fat man said. "I've heard it's the best in the city." *Well, there you have it*, Clara thought. *I pray for customers and the Lord sends me a couple of holy rollers. I'll be lucky if they order coffee.* Truth be told, Clara *was* a bit flattered to hear them talking up her pie. She had been the one to suggest to Mr. Rathbone that the tavern should serve a proper meal at midday. Their competitors served only hard-boiled eggs and pickled herring on crackers—a pauper's meal.

Reverend Potter, his fine hair precisely combed and oiled, glanced skeptically at the small, grease-clouded window that looked up to William Street. Pigeons shuddered by, and the broad hems of pedestrians' skirts passed like great gray ships on the sea. "I'm not convinced anything good can come," he said, "from a kitchen with a rat's-eye view of the world."

Clara cleared her throat to ensure that this Reverend Potter knew she had overheard his remark. "Afternoon, gentlemen. What may I bring you?"

"Good afternoon," the heavy man said. His gaze lingered on her face a moment. "What handsome eyes you have, miss."

Clara pressed her lips into a line and raised an eyebrow. She knew very well that she had plain eyes, deep-set, with stubby lashes. She was tall, for a woman, and slender, with a neck that could be, on its best days, swanlike, provided she was in a well-shadowed room. Clara prided herself on that neck, her uncomplaining disposition, the pie. These were her good features—not her eyes.

The fat minister's spirits were not dampened by her poor reception of his compliment. "And what are you serving for dinner today?"

"You're late for dinner, but as luck or the Lord allows, we have a few chicken pies left," Clara lied. Behind the door to the kitchen, a dozen pies sat lukewarm in their tins, still lined up where she had left them when they came out of the oven at eleven. The food would be long lost to the mice by now if it weren't for the tavern cat, on patrol around the perimeter of the stove. He was an ornery tom, orange and slinking and just about full up of scathe for this plagued world.

"Thank you. We'll have those." Clara turned to go. "And an ale for me. Reverend?" He looked at his companion.

"Milk," Reverend Potter said. "Cold."

Clara nodded. In the kitchen she asked Bessie, the only person in this world taking orders from Clara, to warm the pies, and the girl slid them into the range on her flat wooden paddle. Behind the bar Clara drew the ale slowly, careful to keep the foam from rising over the rim of the glass. The Right Reverend ought to have his ale drawn properly, even if his friend took his God-fearing a little too seriously. Clara sighed when she heard the words echo in her mind. The *Right Reverend*. That was just the sort of thing George was fond of saying, in his signature tone of false deference. Without fail, his cheek earned him a laugh from his friends: the feather in his cap. And, as for Clara, well. She feigned exasperation, but to be the girl George had set his sights on—to be on his arm, walking up Broadway past a bevy of laundresses standing in an alley, their cheeks pink from the steam, even in January, their ravaged arms red up to the elbows—was a marvel. Those girls were sucking on so much jealousy and longing Clara liked to think it made their teeth ache.

Clara was George's *girl*. She would have settled for being George's hat. And when he used his poker winnings to buy her a ruby ring, and took her down to the Trinity Church to rattle off those vows, he never once broke into a smile—not even when the minister uttered the word *chastity* in the presence of her swelling belly. Clara thought of what they had done in the gallery of the Bowery Theater, behind the peach velvet drapery with gold braid fringe that skimmed the floor in time with their exertions; Clara had imagined the drapery was the most exquisite bed curtain in the finest mansion in town. That three nearby couples heaved in their own syncopated rhythm mattered not a whit to Clara. They were flies buzzing against a window pane. She had believed, for once in her miserable life, that with George the profit outweighed the loss.

But if George could float you on the air in the palm of his hand, he could tie you to an anchor and turn his back while you plummeted to the depths. New girls came through Mrs. Ferguson's parlor in flocks, looking fresh and pink, without a care in the world for such a thing as hanging on to a *husband*. The word was still new on Clara's tongue, tart like a berry. It wasn't long before George took up with this one and that one, parading them around just to hurt Clara, it seemed, for there was no one else to notice. She knew all about the roving and insatiable longings of men and would have been willing to tolerate a great deal, if only George had allowed her to retain at least *some* dignity.

He had his reasons, of course, to seek solace outside the walls of their room five months ago, when they had been forced to bear the unbearable. For the baby had not survived. In times of sorrow, Clara had come to understand, women turn inside themselves. Men inch away, like worms. If that doesn't get them far enough, they stand up on their legs and run. And so it was that George was gone, poof, in the night, with a little dark-haired garlic-eater named Lucia. People said he had taken a job at a brickworks in Buffalo.

"Miss Bixby," Bessie called from the kitchen. "Them pies is up."

"All right," Clara called. "Thank you, Bessie." *Miss*, everyone had started calling her again, but *Bixby* was George's name. Clara supposed it was a well-intentioned attempt to offer her a clean slate. She was no longer George's wife, but neither could she go back to the young woman she had been before, Miss Clara Wilson. She was something new altogether: *Miss* Bixby.

As if she were merely George's spinster sister instead of the woman he had once vowed before God to care for all of his days.

Clara carried the pies on a tray from the kitchen to the bar and lifted them onto the plates. At the table, both ministers were reading newspapers. Reverend Potter, nearly blind it seemed, held his about an inch away from his right eye and moved the page back and forth, keeping his head still.

"Reverend Arthur," he said. "Did you read this story about—let's see now . . . where is it?—this town of Destination, Nebraska?"

Reverend Arthur folded his paper and laid it on the table. "No. What an odd name for a town."

"Indeed, it is." Reverend Potter read.

Two men died Saturday after their destructive rampage claimed their lives, as well as the lives of two reliable workhorses—and caused thousands of dollars of damage. Samuel and Terrance Young, brothers and veteran inebriates employed at Drake's Brewery in Destination, population now down to 105 from 107 including the town and its outskirts, managed to set fire to their own shoes, and, in attempting to outrun the flames, spread them across a dry field and inside a barn that contained two tethered horses and a cow. The building was quickly consumed with the men and horses inside, though the cow made an ambling escape. This is the third such incident in this beset frontier town in as many months. While a handful of the original settlers brought wives and sisters with them, all those women died or returned to eastern cities long ago and the town is now populated almost entirely by bachelors. The only fair faces to be found are those, besmirched with rouge and sin, belonging to the fallen women who live together in a house of mirth at the edge of town. Said Destination's mayor, Randall Cartwright, regarding the debauchery of Destination and the death of its citizens, "I mourn the loss of those men only inasmuch as I didn't have the chance to hang them myself from the only tree in town."

Reverend Arthur shook his head. "My word."

"It's true what the reporter says," Reverend Potter told him. "This town *has* been in the news before. I recall it distinctly. Do you notice they don't even mention a church— probably haven't gotten around to building one yet."

Clara brought the plates to the table and the ministers put their newspapers under their chairs. "Enjoy your dinner, gentlemen," she said, setting the pies down.

"We thank you, miss." Reverend Arthur unfolded the white napkin and draped it across his knees. "For two confirmed bachelors such as ourselves, a tavern pie is the closest we come to a home-cooked meal." He pierced the pie's crust with the tines of his fork and a cloud of steam rushed out. "Now, Reverend Potter, *this* is divinity."

The ministers bowed their heads and Arthur said an impassioned grace. Potter gave Arthur's *Amen* a disdainful glance and set about what was for him, a man dubious of all human pleasures, the grim task of eating. Clara returned to her broom, glancing occasionally at the tavern door, attempting to will another customer or two into existence. What would her father say if he could see his tavern and her in this lowly state? Clara felt she had sunk as low as it was possible to go—the only job left was laundress, but she vowed she would die first. One had to preserve a little dignity, no matter what the cost.

At the table, the men continued their conversation. "This is what I try to impress upon my congregation, though they are deaf and dumb to it," Potter said. "A godless man has no compass. A town of godless men is bound for destruction. This Destination is obviously well on its way." He was getting excited, his voice beginning to squeak like a hinge.

Clara glanced at the door once more and saw the portly Reverend Arthur nod in response to his companion's comment. But his eyes were on Clara. She turned sideways to avoid his gaze, but it asserted itself as if it were a physical thing, a lurid hand tracing the outline of her figure. The longer he leered at her, the harder she clenched her jaw. Dr. Calumet had told her to keep a calm disposition, that agitation could bring on the crippling headaches that had plagued her since the baby died. Of course, Dr. Calumet didn't have to work in Rathbone's tavern.

Potter creaked on. "Destination, Nebraska, is like so many places in this land. What that town needs is religion. Don't you agree, Reverend Arthur?"

"What that town needs," Arthur said, scraping the last of the chicken gravy from his plate and licking it off the fork with considerable relish, "is some women."

When the men finished their meal, they placed a stack of coins and a pamphlet about redemption on the table.

"May the Lord continue to bless you," Reverend Arthur called to Clara.

She waved from the far side of the tavern. "If he does, he'll keep you out of my sight," she muttered as they climbed the stairs to the street.

Not another soul came in after them, so Clara sent Bessie home and straightened up behind the bar. The newspapers under the chairs caught her eye—she had not seen them when she cleared the men's dishes. Clara crouched down to sweep them up and, standing, struck her head on the underside of the table so hard the room went white for a moment. She sighed as she rubbed the rising knot with her fingertips and remained there on the floor, resting her brow on her knees, then willed herself up and into the chair where Reverend Potter had sat.

His newspaper was still folded open to the story on Destination and Clara skimmed it. She had seen the newspaper ads and brochures: "Cheap farms! Free homes!" and "Great inducements to settlers with limited means!" She had heard the talk—many people who had very little here in New York wanted to make a go of it out west. After all, they had practically nothing to lose. But Clara was skeptical. Could it really be as easy as all that? At one time, she had almost gone herself, but there was always something keeping her in New York; first her parents' care before they died, and then George. She supposed both of the ministers were right in their assessment of the town's needs. God was an essential tool in keeping men from behaving like animals, it was true. Clara felt that the Lord had done very little for her personally, but she didn't begrudge him that; instead she took it as a kind of compliment. She was weathering her own storms all right. She didn't need or expect his intervention.

But Reverend Arthur was onto something when he said that the town needed women. For how else did men come to God if not through the influence of their mothers first and then their wives? Men needed women—that was a fact. This rooting around in a public tavern for a hot meal was a shame, and Clara truly believed it hobbled a man to have to concern himself with these mundane tasks. A man with a wife could be and do anything if he knew his hearth and home were in order, with a strong-shouldered woman at the ready. When she had first met George he was doing just fine on his own, but under her care he became his better self, more vigorous, cleverer, full of ideas. And all because she believed in hot food, cold baths, thick wool socks, feather beds, fresh air, and church twice a week, and every night after dinner she asked George to read novels to her as they sat together in front of their tiny hearth in their room at Mrs. Ferguson's. And Clara hung on his every word, full of love for the way he stumbled along, flubbing the pronunciations but selling his flub as if the makers of the dictionary were wrong not to have consulted *him* beforehand. There was no doubt in Clara's mind that she had been a devoted wife. She hadn't *driven* George away, the way some people said. They didn't know everything, didn't know that he was trying to outrun the sorrow that nipped at his heels, a son born and buried in the same week.

She glanced again at the article. It was a funny sort of thing to try to conceive of, a town with no women. Imagine being the first one to go! Who would want to do it? She had heard about some of the things men had tried to entice women to the West. The "heart in hand" catalogs made a sad little stack of hopes and dreams on a wire rack in the post office, pages and pages of three-sentence advertisements by marriageable men and women. But did lasting matches actually result from these connections? The system seemed fraught with potential problems. For one thing, how could a woman know if a man was telling the truth about himself? No man was going to pay a penny a word to announce to the world of eligible ladies that he was a *Weak-willed man of 40. Will drink too much and treat you poorly, while you break your back working in my hovel.* Clara chuckled at the thought of this ad drawing a response from a beleaguered woman who respected that, at the very least, this prospective husband was honest. How low their sights were set, the women who had endured the long and terrible war of rebellion.

And yet any place that wasn't Manhattan City, wasn't teeming with drunks and piles of garbage and endless noise, held quite an appeal. Lately, Clara had caught herself daydreaming of a small white cottage where she might live alone, taking in sewing. She must have seen a picture of it somewhere, in a magazine or an old book, and it wasn't located anywhere in particular, just somewhere far from William Street and the room at Mrs. Ferguson's still haunted by everything that had happened there. The cottage was a place apart. A family of birds lived in a tree nearby and she imagined that she could leave a pail of water out for them to splash in. She would scatter stale bread in the grass for them too. The roof of the cottage sagged slightly and the trim around the windows needed paint, but it was quiet and tranquil and plain, and for that it was beautiful.

Clara shook off the vision and pushed herself out of her chair, setting the folded newspapers on the table by the door in case someone else wanted to read them this evening. The last thing she needed was Mr. Rathbone catching her sitting down when she was supposed to be working. Just as she was coming around the bar she heard his steps creaking down the stairs outside and the bell over the door jingle as he pushed it open. Mr. Rathbone was a barrel-chested man with a beard so dense and sleek it seemed at times like a mink stole wrapped across the lower half of his face. His smile was a surprise of pink in that mass of darkness.

"Afternoon, Clara," he said. "Have we done a good business today?"

Her breath caught as she remembered the pies lined up on the butcher block in the kitchen, all that flour and lard and good chicken squandered. She had forgotten to wrap them up, to send some home with Bessie, a few others to Bill—the lunatic who sat on the corner bench all day long, one good leg and one stump wrapped in wool, singing the "Battle Hymn"—anything to get those pies out of the tavern. Mr. Rathbone would know when he did the books that they were losing money on food, but he didn't have to see the waste laid bare like this in his kitchen. *Blast those ministers*, Clara thought, *for distracting me. For making me think about George.*

She didn't have time to stop Mr. Rathbone from stepping into the kitchen, and when he did he stopped short. She came in behind him and for a moment the only sound was the door flapping on its hinges, like a hand, already waving her good-bye.

"Ah, my girl," Mr. Rathbone said as he swiped his hand over the back of his neck and massaged the fold of skin at his hairline.

"Yes, sir—I know it," Clara said, anxious to take the burden of what he had to do off his hands. She didn't begrudge him the need to make his living.

He looked at her and sighed, the corners of his eyes bending like twin frowns. "Mrs. Rathbone has a niece outside Albany. She is just fourteen but has been working her father's farm since she was knee-high. Tavern work will be nothing for her."

Clara nodded.

"You *know* I want to keep you on, but this child will live with us. She'll work for nothing."

"I understand, sir."

"I hate to do it," he said. She followed him back out of the kitchen and behind the bar. He opened the till and counted out two weeks' pay.

"I can't take any more than what you owe me, sir."

"Yes, you can. Now, come on." Mr. Rathbone pressed the money into her hand.

"No, sir." Clara shook her head. "I couldn't."

"Don't be stupid, girl." His voice was sharp and he worked to soften it. "Think of what your father would say. Please take it. I feel bad enough as it is."

Clara hesitated a moment longer. "All right," she said, putting the money in her pocket.

"If you need anything, anything at all, you come to me—you hear?"

She nodded. Mr. Rathbone knew all about George. Everyone did. Clara could see the guilt digging a line across his forehead. He was as good as turning a widow out into the street. Right before the start of winter. Clara felt the pain begin to thrum at her temples, but she shook it away. This was the way life had been for a long time now: The world shoved her off her course and she pushed back against it, too angry or foolish to give up. She'd find another way to get by, though at the moment she wasn't sure how.

He shook her hand. "You'll find another position. I know you will."

"Yes, sir," Clara said, and she meant it. She turned toward the door.

"Wait—you should take a few of these pies."

Her hand was already on the knob. "No, thank you, sir," she said. God help the next blasted chicken pie that came into her sight. Her eyes grazed the room one last time and rested on the newspaper. She plucked it up and tucked it in her apron pocket as she stepped up into the daylight.

I t had been years since Clara had been out in the middle of the day with nothing to do. She didn't want to climb the stairs to her empty room just yet, didn't want the truth of what had just happened to penetrate her mind. So instead she started walking.

William Street was crowded with carriages and market carts. Men with broad shoulders hoisted wooden crates and shouted to each other as they carried them down the stairs to the cellars below the shops. In front of Libby's a bevy of dancing girls gossiped and pointed at a man across the street who tipped his hat low and scurried around the corner, hoping no one would see him. All the girls wore long red feathers in their hair that wavered in the breeze, and their makeup was thick and garish on their pocked skin. Clara walked a few blocks farther north than she usually did—she realized just how small the scope of her everyday life had become over the last few years. She turned left and walked up a quieter block toward the park. The few trees were red and gold, their leaves not yet ready to fall. The chill in the air made her rub her hands together, and she longed for something hot to drink.

"Clara Wilson, is it you?"

A woman in an expansive dove-gray dress put her hand on Clara's elbow. Clara peered at her.

"It's Bitty Lathrop. From Sunday school. Don't *tell* me you don't remember!"

"Bitty!" Clara exclaimed, a little embarrassed. "Of course I remember you! You caught me lost in thought." But Clara wouldn't have known this woman from Eve. Bitty had once been, well, a great deal smaller than she was now.

"How *are* you?"

"I'm well, thank you," Clara said. A group of children shoved past them, chasing a hoop as it rolled down the street. They stopped to steal some apples from a tree, its heavy boughs drooping over the fence around a yard at the end of the block. "And you?"

"Oh, just lovely," Bitty said. "I'm married now, with four children. My Charles works at City Hall."

"Oh, that's marvelous," Clara said. She recognized Bitty's smile now, and it made her think of her sisters, gone so long. They all had played together, whispered and giggled in their pew at service.

"And *you* must be a schoolteacher now," Bitty said, glancing at Clara's plain dress. "I always knew you would be."

"What do you mean?"

Bitty slapped Clara playfully on the arm. "You don't remember the way we used to line up our dolls on the bench after class and play pretend lessons? You took it awfully seriously, Clara. I can still see the way you held that ruler, like a weapon!"

Clara laughed. She felt a little pang remembering the cold room at the church, the minister's wife who taught them about Noah's ark and Lazarus raised from the dead like some kind of magic trick. The woman had a tiny whisper of a voice that made every Bible story feel like a secret. "That was such a long time ago."

"So I have it wrong, then?" Bitty asked. "You aren't a teacher?"

Clara shook her head. "I've been working in my father's tavern for the last few years." She didn't see any reason to tell Bitty that it didn't belong to her father anymore.

"Oh," Bitty said, trying to cover her disappointment. "Well, isn't that nice of you to help him."

"I suppose," Clara said. "Though lately I have been thinking it might be time to find something new to occupy my time."

Bitty smiled. "Well, I have no doubt you will find something interesting to do. Of all the little girls in that class, you always were the smartest one."

"I was? I can't *imagine* that's true."

Bitty nodded solemnly. "But it is! We all thought that, if anyone did, you would be the one who would . . . do something special." Clara could see that Bitty felt awkward finishing the sentence, which sounded a little like an admonishment.

Clara *had* loved school. She remembered that now, though

it had been a very long time since she'd allowed herself to think about the things she once loved. "It's very nice of you to say that, Bitty," Clara said. "And perhaps you're right—perhaps it isn't too late to make good on my potential."

"We were all so proud to know you, Clara." Bitty took her hand. "*Still* proud. You just never know what might happen. Look at me. Would you ever have thought I'd have a husband?"

Clara smiled. "Well, of course, Bitty." But the truth was, Bitty had been a homely girl, with a sallow complexion and teeth like a jackrabbit.

Bitty shook her head and winked at Clara. "You're just being kind. But it's all right. A matchmaker found him for me, if you want to know the truth. My daddy paid her a pretty penny too."

Clara stared at her a moment. The sudden idea Bitty's story gave her—a way to leave Manhattan City for good, a way to claim that little white cottage from her daydream—seemed to hang in the air right before Clara's eyes, like one of those apples on the tree at the end of the street. She had no right to it, to the promise it held. And yet it bobbed there, red and full, waiting to be plucked.

Rowena

Rowena rose early, determined to respond to the invitations and have it over with. She dressed in her room, stepping into her lavender gown, and lifted one sleeve at a time high enough to push her arm through. Between the steel crinoline and the layers of cotton petticoat and satin flounces, the ensemble was almost too heavy to lift. Life had been easier when Hattie was here to help dress her, but that was back before the war.

She passed into the dark upstairs hallway and descended the stairs, her hand trailing along the banister. Though she felt her fingertips grow grainy with dust, she willed her mind to ignore it. The morning sun shone through the long narrow windows that flanked the front door of the row house. The promise of a new day, brisk and bright at the height of autumn, should have filled her with hope, but all Rowena could see was how threadbare the carpet in the front hall looked in the unyielding sunshine.

The invitations sat in a neat pile on her writing desk in the study. The lacy calligraphy on one urged her to join Celia Birch and Eliza Rourke for a tea given in honor of the new

Mrs. Lindley, Eliza's sister-in-law. Mr. Lindley owned three homes in Manhattan alone, not to mention his country house in Riverdale, where the stabled horses probably ate finer food than anything Rowena had seen lately. The second square of fine cream-laid stock promised dinner and dancing at the home of Mr. and Mrs. Channing of Madison Square. Louise Channing had lately made something of a project of Rowena. Along with the invitation, she had slipped a personal note in the envelope, promising that her nephew Donald was willing to escort Rowena, if she had no one else in mind.

Rowena got angry all over again at the thought of it. Donald Channing! Who spoke with a lisp and had what Rowena could only conclude was some kind of fungus growing out of his ear. She had spent one interminable evening with him and Mr. and Mrs. Channing a month back, after Mrs. Channing had told Rowena at a luncheon that it had been long enough since Richard's death.

That was how the woman said it: long *enough*. As if Rowena were a child wrung out from a tantrum who needed the stern hand of a disciplinarian to set things right. The wisest, noblest man Rowena had ever known, the man who carried her very own heart in his haversack, walked out on the battlefield at Cold Harbor and got shot by a Spencer repeating rifle belonging to a man from his own company. All the blood drained out of his chest and down into the dark Virginia soil, where, in digging their trench, the men had found the decomposed remains of soldiers who had died there three years before. But never mind all that. It was high time, according to this old cow, for Rowena to start looking for someone to replace Richard. Mrs. Channing nattered on about overhearing women spreading rumors at the draper's: Rowena Moore, left with nothing after Richard *chose* to go to war when he could have hired someone to fight in his place.

"My dear," she had begun, her withered hand clutching Rowena's wrist. Her voice dripped with such exaggerated sympathy, Rowena could have choked. "I know it's difficult to hear the words of these cruel gossips, words which can't *possibly* be true, but I am only thinking of you. A widow, however grieved, must think about her future."

And so Rowena had agreed to the dinner out of sheer weariness. But after two stultifying hours of conversation about Donald's button factory and his collection of antique candlesticks, she had nearly leapt from her chair when a member of the Channings' army of maids whisked her empty ice cream dish away. Rowena muttered her good evening and scandalized all three of them by insisting that she would find a carriage home, alone. Outside it was pouring rain, and water gushed in rivulets through the mud in the street. Rowena tried to open her umbrella, but the ribs were stuck—it had been ages since she'd actually needed to use it—so she tucked it under her arm and hurried on, the sides of her soggy bonnet sinking against her cheekbones. She imagined that with each sure footstep, each clack of her heel on the cobblestone, she was breaking one piece of Mrs. Channing's limitless bone china, until the woman would have to suck her soup out of her nephew's sweaty hat.

Rowena's anger kept frothing up inside her as she passed through the square onto Broadway. Suddenly, her heel caught a rough stone and she slid and fell, landing hard on her backside with a splash. The world halted for a long moment. She felt a roiling then in her lungs like nothing she had ever known, and she took a breath, then stood and screeched like a banshee. All the couples who were hurrying home from the theater scattered like a horde of mice. Rowena hauled back with her umbrella and pummeled it against the lamppost with all her might. "I will sell my *body* to the *sailors* at South Street," she shrieked at everyone and no one, whacking the base of the streetlamp over and over until the glass lantern swung dangerously from one side to the other, "before I marry that dull, yellow-bellied"—she whacked and whacked and tried to think of what else he was—"*festering-eared* Donald Channing!"

"Miss," a man said, approaching her carefully. "Do you need help?"

She looked at him, her big doe eyes wide and wild. The things she knew she should say—*No, thank you, sir, I'm fine* or *Yes, sir, I need a whole lot of help indeed*—flashed through her mind like the words painted on the banners soldiers carried into battle. But instead she opened her mouth and let out a twisted wail so beastly it seemed to curl the hair at his temples. His mouth dropped open and he stood staring stupidly at her. She lifted her umbrella straight up in the air as if she intended to clobber him over the head with it, a near impossibility, since Rowena was barely five feet tall, and he shrank away and turned a corner, his eyes on the ground as he ran. Seeing how easy it was to get rid of him coaxed a rippling laugh from her chest. But the laugh turned down on the end, into a sob, and she sank down in the gutter and cried for a full ten minutes before scraping herself up and walking the rest of the way home.

Rowena now understood that there were particular sorrows one would never get over. She no longer saw her existence as an ascending march toward happiness; instead, it was a stasis to be endured, a clanging and sputtering machine that produced nothing.

Miraculously, as far as Rowena could tell, the Channings had not heard about her outburst just a block away from their home. Rowena shook her head, wondering if this was providence or a curse, since, if Mrs. Channing *had* seen the incident with the umbrella, Rowena would be saved from worry about being invited to anything ever again. She picked up her pen and pulled a leaf of paper from the desk drawer.

Dear Mrs. Channing, she wrote. *Thank you for your kind invitation. Since our last visit I have longed many times for the opportunity to spend time with you and Mr. Channing, as well as your*—Rowena paused, inhaling a steadying breath through her nostrils—*charming nephew, so it is with great disappointment that I must decline, due to a prior commitment. You will be in my thoughts and I hope you will enjoy a jubilant evening.* Rowena signed the letter and folded it carefully, as if neatly matched corners could disguise her disdain. Next she declined the tea, for she did not have a single afternoon dress she would dare to be seen in, and the draper had refused to extend her credit until she settled last month's bill.

Even if she had found something to wear, Rowena had lost her taste for parties. Before each one came to a close, the guests always started chattering about who would host the next one, and eventually, Rowena knew, she would have to take her turn. *Wouldn't it be something*, she thought, *to see their faces when I rose from the head of my own table to bring a tray in from the kitchen and serve them myself?* A fine menu of buttered bread and the carrots Hattie put up last summer, before Rowena had had to let her go. Butter was her one luxury, and if there was a single thing on this earth those shrill and contemptible women could be sure of, it was that Rowena wasn't going to waste one speck of it on them.

She pushed back her chair from the writing desk and placed both letters on the table next to the door, then opened it. A cold gust of wind swept the front hall and lifted the edges of the paper. Slamming the heavy door shut, she turned to the wardrobe in the front hall. Fall really was here and she'd need her wool cloak. She took it off the hook in the back and shook it out, debating over whether it needed to be brushed. Rowena shook her head. She knew she was stalling for time, putting off the task she dreaded a thousand times more than responding to Mrs. Channing's invitation: Saturday was the day she visited her father at the asylum on Wards Island.

"Let's get on with it," she said aloud, her words echoing in the hall. She tied her bonnet strings and plucked up the letters she planned to post on her way. On the corner, a rough-faced Irishman stood smoking a pipe in a patched jacket. The neighborhood wasn't what it had been.

Rowena's father, Randolph Blair, had to her knowledge never once in his life raised his voice until the year 1863. He had a sheaf of wiry white hair that stood straight up on his head, and the same lively, round eyes as his daughter, but his voice was a soothing baritone, more vibration than sound. Mr. Blair was one of Manhattan's finest attorneys and made a name for himself in business law. He was not by any means a wealthy man, even at the height of his career, but favors and goodwill helped him build the row house near Bond Street. He was well respected enough to have brokered a marriage between his daughter and the equally upstanding and under-funded Richard Moore, whom, to his great satisfaction, his daughter seemed genuinely to love. Mr. Blair lived life in a kind of hushed caution, carefully considering his every word and choice, no matter how small, looking for chinks in the armor. His own father had crossed the gulf to insanity in his sixties and Mr. Blair knew chances were fairly good that the same fate awaited him. He would often tell Rowena that if he lived to fifty-five with his mind intact he would count him-self fortunate to be sure, and then lie down in front of the Bowery streetcar.

But he didn't make it nearly that long. Shortly after Ro-wena and Richard were married, Rowena's mother came down with the fever and died, leaving her widowed husband alone in the house. Rowena went over to check on him each day, her nerves tight as a fiddle string as she observed him for signs of mental distress. She needn't have feared missing anything. There was no subtlety to the Blair family brand of insanity. The pans, he told Rowena, were clanking together in the cup-boards all night long. So he threw them out in the snow in the front yard. Marguerite, the housekeeper who had practi-cally raised Rowena, got on the first ferry up the Hudson on her way back to Montreal when Mr. Blair dumped his full chamber pot on her head while screaming that her hair was on fire.

Hattie had assessed the situation in the kindest way possible when Rowena asked her to come over to see with her own eyes what was going on, to help Rowena decide what she should do. "Miz Moore," Hattie said, putting her rough hand over Rowena's and patting it like a small child's head. "Your father's still sewing, but his needle don't got no thread."

Rowena had no idea of the extent of her father's financial troubles until the bank stated its intention to take back the Blair family home. She had believed her parents owned it outright, but it seemed her father had borrowed a great sum of money against it, which he proceeded to burn in a bonfire.

"Why?" Rowena screamed at him as she hurried around the side of the house and slapped his hands away from the flames. "*Why* are you doing this?"

"My dear, that money was filthy, filthy, filthy. *You* should be thanking *me*."

"What do you mean, 'filthy'?"

"Infested. Diseased. That money could have made all of us sick."

She knew then, *knew* what she would have to do with him, and she felt her heart crack open and slide down the back of her sternum.

"Papa," she'd said. "Oh, Papa."

Clarity flashed briefly across his face as he recognized Rowena's expression—the very same expression he had directed toward his own father many years ago—and that was when he bellowed for the first time in his life, long and low. "Nooooo." He repeated the word three times, like a tugboat's plaintive warning in a fog.

He was blessed, in a way, Rowena thought. A new hospital had just opened on Wards Island, a place for people like him, with nurses who combed his hair and comfortable clean beds. There was even a little stretch of beach where he could sit on a bench and watch the ocean steamers coming into the harbor, full of immigrants hoping to start anew in America.

Rowena felt something sour rising in the back of her throat. *Blessed.* That was a word she had used to make *herself* feel better. What a terrible lie. No man was blessed who couldn't be left alone in a room without the risk that he might use his wife's sewing shears to cut holes in all the drapery. The hospital's existence made *Rowena* the fortunate one, she knew, for now she could rest easy, knowing her lunatic father was hidden safely away from the eyes of Mrs. Channing and her friends, whose little black hearts pumped liquid gossip instead of blood.

There was only one problem: Rowena had spent nearly every penny Richard had left her when he died, and there hadn't been so very many pennies as she would have expected. She owed the draper money, along with the grocer and the carpenter who had fixed her front steps. But, worst of all, she owed the asylum money, a good deal of money, and she didn't have a clue how she was going to continue to pay for her father's care.

She was almost to the ferry dock when she saw the poster, nailed to the trunk of a tree.

Weary of the Miasmas of Manhattan City?

Miss Bixby seeks spinsters or widows with no children, of attractive appearance and good character, to consider travel and potential marriage to men of good standing in Destination, Nebraska, God's own country. No cost to you—all travel expenses paid. Find out more at our community meeting, Friday, November 2, 6:30 P.M. in the sitting room above Rathbone's Tavern.

Elsa

The room was crowded with forty or so women by the time Elsa arrived. Women gathered in groups of three or four on chairs and sofas in the large sitting room, and Elsa recognized two of the girls from the Channing laundry. All week the girls had spoken in urgent whispers about this meeting, how it could be the beginning of their escape from a life of drudgery at the washtub. Elsa, forty-five years old with twenty-nine years of that drudgery in the Channing laundry behind her, felt she had far more reason to be here than they did. The competing conversations were so loud that they drowned out the sound of Elsa's footsteps across the floor at the back of the room. A line of women stood along the window, their wide skirts and stiff petticoats making it impossible for them to sit down with any dignity. Most were handsome or had the rumor of something beautiful in their faces. And each and every one of them was young.

Elsa clutched her hands behind her back and leaned against the wall, then allowed one of her thick fingers—her grandmother had clucked over them, telling Elsa she would never play the *Klavier*—to trace a tiny circle on the scrolling yellow wallpaper. It was all she could do not to turn around and walk back out the door.

Just then a tall woman at the front of the room dragged a bench in front of the hearth and stepped up on it. She clapped her hands and the women's conversations died down to a murmur.

"Ladies, ladies," the woman said. "Good afternoon. Welcome. I thank you for coming on this blustery day."

Elsa watched the women in the front row nod demurely as they clutched their hands in their laps. They were already auditioning for a part they knew nothing about. Relentless, always, the competition among women.

"How many of you are here because you saw one of my posters?" Several hands went up. The woman nodded. "And how many of you are here accompanying a friend?" A few others raised their hands.

"Well, let's see—where to begin. My name is Clara Bixby, and this is my operation. That's what you need to know, right from the start. If there's some part of you that's right now thinking you might like to find a way to make it *your* operation, might like to find a way to take the reins, I will tell you once and only once: There's the door." She pointed at the entrance, right next to where Elsa stood in the shadowed back half of the room, and forty faces turned, suddenly, in her direction.

Clara clapped her hands again. "Now then. That's settled. So." She took a big breath. "Why are we here? I'll begin with a letter." She took a paper out of the pocket of her dress, unfolded it and read:

Dear Mayor Cartwright,

Sir, we are not acquainted, but I hope to change that. It has come to my attention through the New York Herald *that your fine town, made up of the best sort of God-fearing men, loyal to our Union, so devoted to this country's expansion and development that they are willing to forge new paths in the West, has fallen on hard times. If you will forgive my presumption, I would like to propose a solution to the problems of your town.*

As you well know, Manhattan City is full at this hour with unmarried and widowed ladies whose lives were forever changed by the war of rebellion and its long-term effects. Plenty of men died on the battlefield, but plenty more have been ruined by drink and sickness upon their return home, leaving the women they were married to, and the women they might have married, had they been well and strong, in the lurch. And though the righteous side prevailed in this conflict, sir, there is a sadness over us all here in the East when we live each day with the heavy price we had to pay to set things right.

In each American, whether born on this soil or fresh off the boat from another land, there burns a desire for challenge and opportunity, for new vistas and the promise of what the soil can yield. I believe, Mayor Cartwright, that should you and I organize our efforts, we would find a cheerful and willing wife for any of the men in your town who wants one. And I'm sure I don't have to tell you of the civilizing influence of a good Christian wife.

Now, it is only fitting that your men pay the expenses of importing their brides as well as a small fee for my efforts. I'm sure you agree. But you may be wondering how they might regain those funds. There is one last element of my proposal that may convince your most pragmatic of men. The land office is at this time allowing unmarried women to file a claim for the same 160 acres as men, adjoining any parcel of land they choose. In this way, your bachelors could double their holdings at the time of marriage to one of my girls.

Please do think it over, sir, and I will await your response. In the meantime I am

Yours sincerely,
Clara Bixby

"So, ladies," Clara said. "How long do you think it took him to reply?" She scanned the room as the women glanced at each other, no one bold enough to wager a guess. "How long?" She pointed at a woman in the front row wearing a yellow dress, her inky hair coiled in a snood. "You there—how long do you think it took him to reply?"

"Two months, ma'am? This town sounds quite remote." She said this with a little trepidation and looked to her friend for support. The friend shrugged, and the woman in the yellow dress glanced out the sitting room window at the street, as if to confirm that Manhattan was still there and that they were still in it, its teeming population, its noise and food and history offering the security of a place established.

Clara shook her head. "In fact," she said, "Mayor Cartwright's letter took only seven days to reach me. I can only conclude he replied that very day. Since receiving the mayor's enthusiastic endorsement of my plan, I have received letters from eight men describing the sort of wife they've been praying for. And that is why you are here today. If you have the providence to match one of these descriptions, you will begin to correspond with a bachelor and, come late spring, travel with me to Destination, Nebraska, where you will begin your new life."

A wave of excitement passed through the room, evidenced by the quivering hair arrangements and clasped hands Elsa could see from where she leaned against the wall. The girl in the yellow dress stood and slipped down the side of the room and out the door, leaving an empty chair in the front row. Her friend whimpered and wrung her hands in her lap.

Clara shrugged. "Anyone else feeling a doubt should take her leave now. This is an opportunity for those who wish to see it that way, but I have no interest in convincing the unwilling. Each of you who leaves makes my job easier."

A lone girl in the center of the room stood and called boldly, "Thank you, ma'am," then worked her way out of the row and closed the door behind her.

Clara gave the woman a forthright nod of her chin, then motioned to Elsa. "Miss, standing in the shadows, here is a chair for you." She pointed to the empty seat in the front row. Elsa felt all eyes in the room turn to her for the second time since the meeting began, and to calm her nerves she picked up the thread of her unending silent conversation with God.

Lord, what have I done to offend you this evening? Elsa asked. She felt at once his reply, a dry patch spreading in her throat, a cough exploding from her lungs in one short burst. She turned her back on the ladies in the room and put her hands to her mouth in case she should cough again. A moment passed and her throat regained its moisture. *All right, Lord, I will listen. Not talk.*

She made her way to the front of the room, where Clara stood patiently, her steady hand still pointing toward the chair. Elsa was suddenly aware of her clothes, the cotton dress, once dove-gray, now the color of leaves laid bare after the snow melts. Her hair was wiry in its simple bun and silver around her temples, the colorless strands threading through the yellow blond. Most of all, Elsa was aware of the space she occupied in the narrow aisle between the wall and the last chair in each row. She had to turn her hips slightly to move through without bumping the shoulders of each woman she passed. When she was a young woman, her size had shamed her, but life had worn her vanity like water on rock. It had been years since Elsa had given any thought at all to her appearance. She was the shape of the container into which she was poured. It wasn't a fact on which to linger.

When she passed into the light, she saw Clara's eyebrow lift slightly, wondering, Elsa knew, if Elsa was old enough to be the mother of most of the girls in the room. Of course, she was. There was nothing she could do about that.

Elsa settled into the chair and Clara turned her attention back to the room. "This brings me, ladies, to the matter of requirements. You simply *must* be at least twenty-one years of age—I will consider no exceptions to this rule. And you must provide a certificate from a physician of your fitness to travel. Winter in Nebraska, I am told, is a good deal colder and longer than the one we have here in Manhattan City, and

I'd be surprised if this town has a doctor. Those of you with fortitude are the ones who will be chosen."

A few potential brides shifted in their seats, and Elsa found herself hoping they would follow the other timid women right out the door. She was bewildered by how suddenly fierce her desire was to secure one of the spots. The feeling had come on as if out of the blue. *So I'm to go then, Lord?* Elsa shook her head in surprise.

She wasn't a bit afraid of a place without medical care—of that she felt sure. A physician had examined Elsa only once in her life, in the steerage deck of her ship when it first touched North America at Grosse Isle in the St. Lawrence River. There had been reports of illness on board. The immigration officials would quarantine every passenger, ensuring that those who were not yet ill would contract the disease, if they found even one confirmed case of cholera.

The physician had lined up the children first, the girls and boys together, and made them strip to their underclothes. Twelve-year-old Elsa stood with her arms crossed in front of her, her fingertips pressing into the ample flesh that ringed her ribs. She felt the eyes of the boy on her right skim her freckled shoulder. He was less than half her size. Elsa stared straight ahead, afraid to look in the doctor's direction to see what he was doing to the other children. Her hair was the whitest blond then, parted down the center and scraped into tight braids by her Tante Gretchen's comb. As the immigration physician made his way down the row, Elsa felt a crease forming in her forehead that pulled painfully on the strands of hair at her temples.

She had had no English then. The doctor's words had the pinched and severed sounds of her own *Deutsch*, the *ein* and *eck* and *ach*, but the content made little sense. When he finally reached Elsa, he put his icy fingertips on either side of her jaw and lifted her face. He looked from one eye to the other and back again, but never into them, then pinched the skin on her shoulder and watched to see how quickly the impression of his fingertips subsided. She could feel breath shudder in and out of her lungs, as if it consisted of a sludge of mud and pebbles instead of air. The doctor slid his hand over her collarbone then and down inside the front of her shift. Elsa felt hot tears well around the lower rim of her eyes. She knew he was feeling for her heartbeat, but he ran his rough knuckle over her nipple one too many times, and even at her age she knew there was something wrong. He grunted once, quietly, as his fingertips moved over the little knob, hard in the freezing cold of the ship, then pressed the heel of his hand into her chest and looked at the ceiling, listening.

"It beats very quickly," he said.

Elsa blinked at him, understanding none of his words, and released tears in two slick ribbons down her cheeks.

"Please complete and return this form to me as soon as possible," Clara said, snapping Elsa back to the present. "Do the best you can to describe your physical attributes and any abilities you have that you believe will make you a competent wife. Include a likeness if you are able. And don't forget to provide an address where I can reach you. Good day, ladies."

A rustle of papers made their way to Elsa's end of the row. She took one of the forms for herself and tucked it in her pocket.

As she walked up Broadway back to her quarters at the Channing mansion on Madison Square, Elsa thought about what she should say on the form and how she might say it. It certainly was no use manufacturing a story about her beauty or youth or musical gifts. Any man would soon learn of the truth, and anyway, Elsa never told lies and she didn't plan on starting now. Any man who was going to want her would have to want the qualities set down in her being by the Lord. *Bavarian-born spinster*, she thought. *Healthy, strong, unafraid of hard work. Devoted to the Lord and Savior first, Martin Luther second. Currently employed as laundress. Can also cook, scour, sew, knit, and spin.* She would save the object of her fiercest pride for last, render it in bold letters: *Reads and writes in English.*

Clara

In the five years Clara had been living at Mrs. Ferguson's, she had done her best to make the room into a home. She was proud of how neatly she kept the hearth swept and stacked with wood. Next to it she had arranged her little kitchen—nothing more, really, than a narrow table and a small iron kettle for tea or beans when she didn't feel like taking her meals in the dining room downstairs. She kept her bed stacked with quilts and the bed key handy to keep the cornhusk mattress off the floor. Mrs. Ferguson's was known for its particularly large and aggressive brand of mice, three parts vermin and one part Satan, George always said.

Under the window Clara had set up a table and chair for writing letters or reading books. Just outside was a streetlamp, and starting at dusk it offered her light well into the evening so she could save her lamp oil. She sat there now, her chair pushed slightly back. She had the sense of deep responsibility tinged with fear. What she had proposed to Mayor Cartwright had raised the hopes of a lot of lonely people in a town with a strange name, and they were all counting on her to follow through.

The matter of the town's name sparked so much curiosity among the prospective brides that Clara finally wrote to Mayor Cartwright to ask for an explanation. After she sent the letter off, she worried that her question might have caused offense, but the mayor replied in the charmingly aggravated tone she was coming to know. Mr. Cartwright took no responsibility, he explained, for the actions of men who had come before him. Especially when those actions were of the foolish variety. The story went that a group of men intending to homestead set down on a rude map the plans for their journey west. As much of the country through which they planned to travel was unsettled, locations known by their landmarks— the site where a river split in two, or a peculiar cluster of tall, skinny trees—were known by these descriptors only. There were no towns to speak of and certainly no towns with names. One of the men marked with an X the place on the map they planned to go, and next to the mark he wrote *destination*, for that was what the X signified. Someone else borrowed the map, forgot to return it, and then passed it along to some other equally uninformed soul. Before long, people took to calling the place *Destination*, as if that were its name. "Confusion begot confusion," the mayor explained. "As it so often does."

Clara marveled at the two stacks of paper before her. Just a few weeks had passed since her meeting with the prospective brides. On the left were eight letters from lonely bachelors on the cold prairie, plus one from a man who wanted only a housekeeper. On the right, she had twenty-two applications, just about half of the women who had attended the meeting.

Clara had calculated the cost of train and ferry tickets for each bride, plus what they would need for food and lodging along the way. She added her own travel costs, for she would journey with them to ensure that they reached Nebraska, and a profit of fifteen percent per bride, which seemed like a fair wage considering the work she planned to put in to making careful matches. Clara knew that even with all the care in the world, two or three women might have a change of heart. Fifteen percent would allow her to sustain that loss and still end up with enough money to establish herself in a nearby town, Omaha or Des Moines—she hardly cared where, exactly. Only that it be somewhere far from Manhattan City, with a little white cottage for rent.

The first step was to figure out just what the men were looking for.

Dear Miss Bixby,

I am a gentleman of twenty-five years employed as a porter and postmaster at the train depot. I am seeking to correspond with, and, if mutual adoration results, marry a refined young lady who could make my home a paradise.

. . . .

Dear Miss Bixby,

I am a bashful man who has terrible luck with the fairer sex. I am not bad-looking, but I suppose my nose is rather large, my eyes rather small. I don't drink at all, miss—not a drop—and I swear that I am kindhearted and honest. If a lady would only give me a chance, I think I could make her happy.

Dear Miss Bixby,

I am in want of a wife. Requirements: Educated brunette, amiable, musical, and knows her place. No fat women, no teetotalers, and no Irish.

. . . .

Dear Miss Bixby,

I run the butcher's shop and am a widower with five children. I'm in desperate need of a wife. She must be able to manage these children plus a large garden and cook us all three squares a day. Send along two if you can spare them.

Clara paused and read this last letter again, then heard her own sharp laugh cut through the room. *What woman in her right mind would agree to* that *arrangement?* And that was when the true challenge of this endeavor dawned on her: A good portion of these men were bachelors for a reason. They had very little to offer a woman. Some of them knew it and some of them had deluded themselves with the notion that it was merely the paucity of women in town keeping them single. Clara saw that she could bring the horses to the water, so to speak, but she couldn't make them marry men too foolish to make a good case for themselves.

If she was going to earn her money, she would have to do more than make travel arrangements. She would have to broker these marriages, take these men's words and turn them into something a woman would respond to. It would be difficult, but it was work she could feel good about. Helping lonely people find each other seemed a much more laudable goal than serving men liquor in a tavern.

Clara's thoughts were interrupted by a soft knock at her door. She pushed her chair back, its legs scraping the floor, and stood up. Standing in the hall was a tiny raven-haired woman in a gown of blackberry-colored silk.

"Good afternoon, Miss Bixby," she said. "I've come to return this." She thrust an envelope across the doorway at Clara.

Clara looked the young woman over. "You could have left it with the proprietress downstairs," Clara said irritably. She suspected that this applicant wanted to come in person so that Clara could lay eyes on her, so that she could show off this gown, her thick, dark hair. She knew of a certain Italian Jezebel named Lucia, with hair that color and the same penchant for fine clothes, and look what had come of that.

The woman nodded, but her attention was on Clara's room. With her mouth twisted in a disdainful sneer, she took in the bare floor and undressed window, the wardrobe with a broken door handle. A moment ago the room had seemed respectable, a single woman's tidy refuge from a world that no longer had use for her, but now Clara felt she was seeing it for what it was in this woman's eyes: a shame, a mark of her poverty. Clara felt exposed, and angry for it. "We have many applicants, Miss . . ."

"Moore," the woman said. "*Mrs.* Moore. I am a widow."

Clara chewed her lip. Well. Probably this little thing had fleeced an old man for his money. "*Mrs.* Moore," Clara said, then stopped. She meant to chastise the young woman for disturbing her at home but now hesitated. The silk dress was more tattered than it had seemed on first appearance. Clara's eyes skimmed the hem, darker than the rest of the skirt, and she realized at once that Mrs. Moore had blackened it with boot polish to disguise its fading.

Mrs. Moore seemed to be making some observations of her own. Her gaze lingered on the hearth, and without turning back to follow it, Clara realized what she saw: George's worn slippers on the shelf, a little dusty, truth be told. The blood rose in Clara's cheeks. *That I should have to explain myself to this . . . child.*

"Are *you* married?" the widow Moore asked. Her shoulders were square, her voice an impertinent taunt.

They stood eye to eye a moment. Clara felt she would wait all day for this woman to back down. A realization dawned: In brokering these marriages, Clara had stumbled on a kind of power she had never known. She was determining the path of these women's lives. Their future happiness—or lack of it—depended on Clara. Finally Mrs. Moore's gaze flicked to the floor and Clara smiled at her victory. She wouldn't be made to drop her eyes in her own home, no matter that this young woman supposed she resided several rungs above Clara on the social ladder. "No, I am not."

"Look," Mrs. Moore said. "I will speak plainly. You know as well as I do that I am more beautiful than the other women who came to your meeting, *and* of higher standing. You seem like an intelligent woman, even if your sense of fashion leaves a great deal to be desired." She cast a haughty look at Clara's plain dress. "I would think you would understand that you *need* me."

Clara narrowed her eyes. "I hardly think that is the case. Manhattan City is *full* of beautiful women."

"Yes, but most of them don't need *your* help to find a husband."

"So why do you?"

Mrs. Moore laughed. "I don't. I'm days away from a proposal and could get plenty of others if I tried." She paused and pressed her lips together, as if she were considering her words carefully, wondering how much of herself to reveal. Finally she shrugged and waved her hand as if to dismiss everything around her. "But I am sick to death of this city."

Now Clara laughed. *Only beautiful women have the luxury of boredom*, she thought as she opened the envelope and unfolded the application. *Rowena* was her Christian name. *Pretty*, Clara thought. Rowena had included a tintype. Clara glanced between it and its inspiration. A lovely likeness, but in person the girl was stunning. Of course, everyone knew it was quite unnecessary for a pretty woman to be clever.

"I see you play piano," she said.

Rowena nodded.

"You play it well?"

"*Quite*," Rowena shot back. She had begun to tap her foot. "I'd be happy to demonstrate my abilities on the piano downstairs."

Clara held up her hand. "That won't be necessary." Where had this pert little thing come from? Clara was surprised at how much venom she felt for Rowena. This girl was just what was wrong with the world, another of the dozens of frivolous girls streaming into the city on a lark, another Lucia, with no purpose, no responsibility, not a thought for the damage done by their little adventures. They all felt entitled to a certain kind of life, but they didn't want to earn it by making an honest match. Instead they felt perfectly justified in taking things that didn't belong to them, things they didn't deserve.

"I do not think," Clara said, handing the papers back to Rowena, "that your disposition is suited for this endeavor. I'm sorry. These men need dutiful wives to bring peace and comfort to their homes."

Rowena raised one eyebrow and leaned close to Clara, clearly unaccustomed to being denied what she wanted. "And were *you* a dutiful wife? To George Bixby? Is *that* why he ran off?"

Clara felt her jaw go slack.

"Yes," Rowena said with a cruel smile. "I know about him. Everyone does." She seemed to be taking a great deal of pleasure in turning the conversation around on Clara.

Clara stood paralyzed for a moment, her anger bubbling up. As she regained her composure, she saw a pathway opening that would serve to put this girl in her place much better than rejecting her application outright. *Much more beautiful in person*, Clara thought, knowing she would write the line in her letter to the bachelor.

"Perhaps I was a bit hasty," Clara said, her tone suddenly sweet. "Now that I think on it a bit more, I believe I *do* have a gentleman for you." She picked up the butcher's letter. "Mr. Daniel Gibson. A businessman."

Rowena's eyebrows lifted and she held out her hand. "May I read it?"

Clara pressed it against her bosom and shook her head. "I'm sorry. It's confidential. But I can tell you that he writes well. He is an educated man looking for a beautiful wife. I will tell him *all* about you—you have my word."

Rowena nodded, her eyes shining with satisfaction.

Savor it, girl, Clara thought. *Savor that smug feeling while it lasts.*

"You can expect a letter from him sometime in the next few weeks."

After Rowena left, Clara turned back to her work. She read through each man's letter, then leafed through the stack of applications from the women. She set aside several of them right away. Two girls listed their ages as eighteen, seemingly oblivious to Clara's instruction that all applicants must be at least twenty-one. Another seemed too frail, given that she mentioned that it was her "dying wish" to see the Missouri River. A few seemed illiterate and a few more were clearly too lazy or strange or dim-witted to be considered.

Hannah Darby, for instance, seemed wholly preoccupied with the presence and abilities of Indians.

Dear Miss Bixby,

Is Nebraska the place where they have the Soo injuns or is it the Comanchey? My sister Lizzie says she read that the braves are stronger than three white men put together and that they ride horses but without saddles because their legs are so strong and they can do black magic. Lizzie says every single one of them is handsome and because they are godless heathens they can take as many wives as they please. Is it true, miss? She also says that every white man is afraid of them. Do you think the white men in Nebraska are afraid of them? If I were well-

protected I should very much like to see one of these braves
riding his horse and see his long hair in the wind. Lizzie says
they can talk to animals too. Tell me, miss, is any of this true?

Sincerely,
Hannah Darby

Clara rolled her eyes as she tossed Hannah's letter into the bin. She was beginning to wonder if any of these applicants would make fit matches.

Fortunately Kathleen Connolly's application surfaced next. She was Irish and Catholic, which limited the options, but Amos Riddle had said nothing about religion, only that he needed a sturdy woman who could do her share of the work on his land. Kathleen seemed to fit that description. Her application went into great detail about her experience with carpentry and livestock.

Molly Zalinski and Deborah Peale had fastened their applications together in the top left corner and begged to be chosen "both or neither," for they did nothing in this world but what they could do together. Their bond charmed Clara, and both of them seemed earnest and bright, ready to take on the challenge these marriages posed. The porter, Stuart Moran, had asked for a "refined" lady, and Deborah promised that she could bring along a silver tea service. Molly seemed to come from humbler circumstances, and her expectations would be fittingly realistic for the wife of a farmhand like Nit LeBlanc. He would have to work hard to earn her trust, however. Molly explained that she planned to write to him under a nom de plume until she was sure his intentions were pure.

Anna Ludlow might very well become the minister's wife, for she could weave and he kept sheep, and they both stated that "reading the Scripture" was a pastime. Clara felt a little satisfaction on behalf of the town that it had proved that mole of a man Reverend Potter wrong—Destination *did* have a church after all. Two, in fact.

The bashful brewery worker Walther Luft would appreciate Bethany Mint's claim that she "didn't care a thing about her husband's looks." Cynthia Ruley seemed to fit the curt list of requirements given by another brewer, Bill Albright, since her tintype showed her to be slender and, according to her description, she was a talented violinist. Lucretia Blackstone might do for Jeremiah Drake, the brewery's owner and the only man who seemed entirely fixated on hair color. She was a blonde.

By morning, Clara had written a short reply to each man's letter, introducing her suggested companion. It was nothing to Clara to stay up all night long. She preferred short, intermittent dozing to the danger of submitting to true, deep sleep. In sleep, Clara's dreams were full of the memories she spent her waking life trying to evade.

All the time she worked, she waited to feel remorse for concealing from Rowena the tiny fact of Daniel Gibson's five children, but the remorse never came. The bachelors, not the brides, were Clara's customers, and it was the bachelors' happiness she had been hired to tend. If a presuming creature like Rowena learned a little humility in the process, well, so be it. Clara couldn't lose sight of the purpose of all her hard work; on the backside of one of the discarded applications, she sketched the outline of the little white cottage in the center of a meadow, not a single tavern or glass of ale in sight.

Elsa

The maids' quarters of the Channing mansion occupied the east side of the garden level of the house, which was partly underground with small, high windows looking up toward the daylight. There were ten narrow rooms, each containing a cot and a row of hooks on the wall. The Channings were considered the most generous of all the wealthy Manhattan families. It was a lavish thing to give the maids their own rooms. At the west end of the floor was a large open room lined with laundry tubs and wringers. One long table for folding, ironing, mending, and knitting occupied the center of the room.

Half the maids worked upstairs serving in the dining room, bringing weak tea to Mrs. Channing in her bedroom late at night and whisking the silver tray away a half hour later without waking her up, opening the drapes each morning and washing the glass with vinegar water, pulling the drapes closed at night. The other half spent their days in the laundry room. Elsa was one of them.

Each week the laundresses washed linens for twelve bedrooms upstairs and tablecloths and napkins for three meals a day, along with the family's underclothes, towels, and Mr. Channing's numerous shirt collars. They lived in a cloud of lye-tinged steam, and it was for the good of their lungs that the doors and windows remained opened to the back garden all day long, whatever the weather. In winter, a laundress could be at once flushed in the face from the heat and numb in her fingers and toes from the cold.

In the garden was a bench where Elsa liked to take her midmorning break to rest her swollen feet. Today, she pulled a letter out of her boot—it was no use keeping paper in her apron pocket when it was perpetually damp, along with the front of her heavy linen dress, and, beneath that, her shift, and, beneath that, the skin of her abdomen, rubbed red and always covered in rash. Now the paper felt wonderfully crisp against her fingertips. She had picked it up first thing in the morning at the post office and savored her anticipation of reading it.

Only one other time in her life had she received a letter with her name on the envelope. Elsa had no need for letters from her employer, as she lived under his roof, and nearly everyone else she had ever known was dead. Last year a girl, Lucia, who worked alongside her in the laundry room, took up with a brickworker named George and moved with him to Buffalo. She had written with news of her new life. Lucia had vowed to stay friends after she left—Elsa hadn't even known that they *were* friends until Lucia said the word on her last day. Elsa didn't talk much while she worked, but she supposed she had listened to Lucia's continuous narration, about her mother, about her beau, about the merits of Buffalo over Manhattan City, with some interest and Lucia had appreciated that.

Well before dawn on the morning Lucia was to leave, Elsa went above stairs to the kitchen before the maids awoke. She felt a strong urge that she should make something for the woman to take on her journey, something warm and soft and filling. It had been a long time since Elsa called one of her grandmother's recipes from her memory. But she found that the knowledge was still there, waiting patiently for her return. Quietly, carefully, Elsa added wood to the fire, then skimmed flour from the bin and heaped it in a mound on the board. She cracked eggs into a bowl and mixed them with butter and sugar, then folded them into the flour with her hands. Three fragrant plums, chopped into bits, studded the *Kuchen* and she slipped it into the range, praying that the sweet smell would not wake the house. When it cooled, just as the maids were filing in, she tied it in an old handkerchief and slipped it into her apron as she descended the stairs.

Lucia was glad to receive the gift, but then she had left. Elsa would have liked to have a friend, if she had known that was what Lucia had become, but the realization came too late. Lucia was gone now, her life changing and Elsa's staying the same.

Just as Elsa unfolded the letter and smoothed the creases with her palm, she heard Mrs. Channing's shoes clacking over the slate floor of the laundry room. The laundresses snapped to attention and Elsa stood from the bench, crouching quickly to slip the letter back in her boot and scurrying down the stairs to join the other workers.

"Ladies, I have come down to tell you myself," Mrs. Channing said, full of false humility over her willingness to go below stairs, "how very important it is that everything be perfect for the party this evening. We expect the whole of society to be here. That means every inch of linen must be pressed twice over, every bit of lace starched. I am counting on you."

She moved her eyes slowly along the line of women, nodding at each one as they said, "Yes, ma'am."

"Very well." Mrs. Channing turned for the stairs but then paused, stepping back down. "There is one other thing. I have heard talk amongst some of the society ladies about this Clara Bixby and her proposal to take women to the West."

A few of the girls, some, Elsa noted, whom she remembered seeing at the meeting above the tavern, looked down at the floor.

Mrs. Channing raised a crooked finger and pursed her lips. "I want you all to know that I disapprove profoundly of this woman and her scheme, on matters of propriety *and* safety. The western towns are full of criminals and wild men and Indians, and no respectable woman would volunteer to put her own life in jeopardy by traveling there. Just today, the *Times* warned that our city's surplus of maidens will be ruined by this venture. I wouldn't be surprised if they ended up in brothels." The old woman was working herself into a lather. "Why, Manhattan City is full of perfectly good, hardworking men of all classes, and I should think your time would be better spent looking to make a match here."

Elsa shifted her weight from one foot to the other, feeling the stiff corner of the letter press into her ankle. She had only ever laid eyes on Mrs. Channing a handful of times, and each time she was struck by how little the matron resembled the women who worked for her. Even Mrs. Channing's smooth, carefully pinned hair and alabaster skin seemed the characteristics of an entirely different species of woman, a woman who bore no marks of the world's rubbing up against her: no calluses, no scars from childhood burns, no broken teeth or limp or deafness in one ear. The experience and significance of luxury was something Elsa had been able only to imagine, despite living right below it for the last twenty-nine years. When she saw Mrs. Channing, whose pristine tatted shawl hovered around her shoulders like spun sugar, whose collarbone was draped with three strings of garnets, Elsa felt as baffled by her as she might have felt seeing a zebra prance down Broadway. In truth, she felt only pity for the woman. *Woe unto you that are rich, for ye have received your consolation.*

"Heed my word, girls. I can't stop any of you from pursuing this dangerous course. But you should know that, should you try and fail to find happiness in Nebraska, as you no doubt will, do not come back to the Channing residence looking for a position, for we shall not take you back. We have no use for your sort of women around here."

Mrs. Channing was defensive now, though no one had challenged her right to speak her mind on matters of the management of her own home. She stomped out of the room in a huff and up the stairs.

So that would be it, then, Elsa thought. *It may already be, if any of these girls start whispering about who was at Miss Bixby's meeting.* It suddenly mattered very little to her what the letter in her boot contained. She was going to go to Nebraska, for Mrs. Channing's disdainful speech had made plain what Elsa supposed she had known for a long time: There was nothing *for* her here.

She had come off the boat as a girl and lived in one cluttered room with her *Tante*, helping with the sewing Gretchen took in and washing dishes in the rooming house kitchen for their board, until the homesick woman died in her sleep. The landlady found Elsa hiding under the bed when they came to take the body out. She gripped the girl's shoulder, stood her up and brushed the dust out of her hair, and said, "You'll go to work for Mrs. Channing."

Elsa was sixteen. Since then she had washed every article of clothing that the wealthy woman wore against her bare skin, and yet Mrs. Channing had not once called Elsa by name. For twenty-nine years, Elsa's stunted life had played out in the basement of this mansion, and it had hardly occurred to her to feel something as presuming as dissatisfaction. This was the only life she had ever known; what other life could there be?

But something was changing in Elsa. Her age had begun to make her impatient. The previous winter she had contracted a fever that didn't subside for a week, and though she finally did recover, she realized that she might not have so many years left. She didn't care to spend them here. Mrs. Channing's warning to the workers made Elsa feel something so unfamiliar it took her a moment to name it. Anger. The wealthy woman's withered fingers were reaching just a little too far into the private sphere of Elsa's imaginings of what her life *could* be. And Elsa saw now that she simply wouldn't allow Mrs. Channing to do it.

Later, when the day's work was done, Elsa closed the door of her chamber and moved quickly in her bedtime preparations: pulling on the wool slippers, smoothing the blanket on her lap, lighting the nub of candle on the bedside table. Finally, finally, she opened the letter, bracing herself for anything, repeating her resolution in her mind that she *would* go, no matter what.

The first line took her by surprise as she read, *As I believe Miss Bixby explained to you, I am seeking a housekeeper–cook, not a wife.* Miss Bixby had explained no such thing.

This was one thing Elsa hadn't expected and she let it wash over her, considering what it meant. A blessing, she decided. There was no need to worry now over the matter of her appearance, her plump physique. Though at one time she had prayed earnestly for a husband, it was not to be, and many years ago she came to peace with her life as a spinster. It was a difficult path, being in the world alone, but Elsa couldn't imagine it changing now. Knowing this man wanted something she was sure she could provide—competent housekeeping—was a comfort. Elsa read on.

> *I am an old man with no time for foolishness. You need not be pretty, for I don't plan on looking much upon you. Rather you should be the sort of woman who looks as if God made her for something. I spend all day in the field. You only must be hearty enough for the winters on this farm. Oh, and if you are one of those women who chatters like a hen, tell me now and save yourself traveling all the way here only for me to send you back to New York. I like a quiet, orderly house. I have worked hard for what I have and I don't believe in getting something for nothing at all, the way the children seem to now. I am very glad I never had any young ones myself. Children are nothing but a vexation.*
>
> *I am glad that you are Bavarian too, for I will expect you to cook our sort of food. I am glad to see you are neither a*

*Catholic, nor a Methodist, which I have come to believe is
even worse. I don't see how it's any business of the Reverend's
what I take to drink with my meals. If you go in for all that
bombast in a revival tent, don't set toe on that train is all I
can tell you.*

*I am not a rich man but I can promise that you won't
want for anything here. I can offer room and board and a
small wage. Quite small, mind you, but around here there isn't
much to spend it on. You will have the second floor all to
yourself, including your own sitting room, as I keep to the
first-floor bedroom because of my rusted-up knees. I have a
cow, two horses, and a chicken coop, along with 100 acres of
wheat and barley, and my neighbor keeps pigs and barters. I
also have 3 ewes and a spinning wheel around here
somewhere. It belonged to my late wife. She was the best
knitter in Dodge County, and you won't hear that only from
subjective parties such as myself.*

*My understanding is that the other women are going to
apply for land before they marry. If that is what you want to
do you'll need to find another gentleman, for my farm is
already too big for me to handle and I figure I've got about ten
years before I keel over in the field one day. I could just as
easily ride over to Omaha and find a housekeeper there, but
the fools in this town can't stop talking about Miss Bixby's
belles, so I thought I would throw my hat in the ring. I came to
Nebraska from Manhattan City too, and I suppose I like the
idea of helping someone from home. As I said, I never had any
children, so you'll only have to worry about me. I don't believe
I am too much trouble.*

As you can see, my English is very good, no accent to speak

*of, and I expect that yours will be too. We'll see when you
write back. Tell me if you are interested in this scheme and
what sort of household supplies you need. It has been a long
time since I had a woman in the house. Most days I eat canned
beans for dinner, and they are awful. I await your reply. Until
then, I am*

Yours sincerely,
Mr. Leopold Schreier

Elsa closed her eyes in an attempt to slow her mind, which
was racing ahead to paint a picture of what could be. She
saw the farmhouse on a plot of land so flat you could flick a
marble across it and it would roll on forever without stopping.
She saw rows and rows of wheat bending in the wind like a
woman stretching this way and that before rising from bed,
saw a cow and heard the low clank of its bell as it ambled over
the clover. A room—rooms!—of her own, not in the bowels
of the house but *upstairs*, with, perhaps, a window or two
through which she could watch the sun rise as it smeared the
sky with color. Though she now spoke English well, Elsa re-
tained a foreigner's insight into the language, the ability to
see words from the outside, and she thought now that even the
name of the place suggested plenty: *Nebraska* sounded like
basket, something you might fill with food.

But, still, Elsa hesitated. To allow herself to want a thing,
even a thing so small as a housekeeping position on a western
farm, was dangerous. Because in wanting, Elsa had come to
believe, one separated herself from the Lord. Longing revealed a lack of trust, posed an impertinent question: Had the

Lord thought of everything, or had he forgotten to account in his plan for this particular servant? Who was Elsa to suggest to God what he might do for her?

She wrote back to Mr. Schreier on the blank back side of his letter. In tiny, careful script she thanked him for his offer and asked for a broom, two washtubs, five cakes of soap, and a good wire brush. Her pen hovered over the page as she thought about what else to say. He wanted to know that she spoke English well and she wanted to show him. So she continued by writing,

> *I came to America in 1833 with my mother's sister, after the death of my parents. Our ship was held because of fear of cholera (though it was never found on board) for six weeks in Quebec. This delay would have been unbearable but for an Englishman on board who brought with him a trunk full of, not linens or clothing, but books. This man was very kind to the children. I believe he was a teacher or minister of some kind, and he organized a little classroom for those people who wanted to learn English. I hope you will not think it prideful of me to say that learning came easily to me, for I believe glory for all that is good in the old and new worlds belongs to our Lord. By the time the ship finally arrived in New York Harbor I could write very well and speak a little. My teacher presented me with an English Bible as a gift when we disembarked, and I keep it with me always.*
>
> *Yours in Christ,*
> *Elsa Traugott*

Elsa put the letter in her boot, carrying it with her for three days before she could make up her mind about sending it. The way she saw it, she was sinning on at least two fronts. It was prideful to believe that she could manage Mr. Schreier's household better than any of the other women Elsa imagined must be clamoring for the position. But worse still was the dark thing unfurling its tentacles inside her. She *wanted* desperately to leave New York and start again in this new place, wanted to claim the fresh air and open space for herself, for her own comfort and enjoyment. Surely the Lord was closer at hand in the wide-open wilderness of Nebraska than he was in Manhattan City's crowded and filthy streets. Without Miss Bixby's help, Elsa couldn't imagine how she might make such a journey. Yet if this longing wasn't the sin of avarice, Elsa couldn't imagine what was.

Was it wrong to mail the letter? She felt she should let the Lord decide, but neither action, mailing the letter or not mailing the letter, seemed neutral, each one promising to initiate an effect. The longing clanged on in her chest like the bell that swayed beneath the neck of Mr. Schreier's cow, and when she could no longer bear to wait, she posted the letter.

Rowena

Rowena recognized her father from behind. His fan of stiff white hair was unmistakable. He sat very still on the bench gazing out at the water, where a flock of gulls plunged toward the surface in a symmetrical formation, then scattered suddenly to contentious, screeching independence. Rowena cut a wide arc around the side of the bench to approach her father from the front and give him time to notice her arrival. She didn't want to startle the man, and she held out hope he would recognize his daughter.

"Hello, Papa," she called, and waved.

His gaze flicked to the brim of her bonnet and he stared as she approached. Then his eyes drifted back to the water. When Rowena sat down beside him, the man flinched and pulled his arms into his chest, crying out.

"Who are *you*?" he asked anxiously. "Did *you* take my hat?"

He was getting worse. "Papa, it's me. Rowena. I am your daughter. Remember?"

He narrowed his eyes at her. "My daughter is a little girl. She is playing in the back garden with that awful kitten. What is his name? He is *not* to come in the house anymore."

"Beelzebub," Rowena whispered.

Her father looked up at her, surprised. "Yes, that's it. Are you a neighbor? Has he done something to your garden? I'm so terribly sorry."

"No, Papa. *I'm* Rowena. *I* was a little girl playing with the kitten in the back garden, but time passed and I grew up. Don't you remember? You were there for it all. My birthdays, my wedding. *You* were the one who introduced me to Richard."

"Say what you will about that cat—he is the best mouser in lower Manhattan."

Rowena took a breath and laced her fingers slowly in her lap, left thumb, right thumb, forefinger, middle finger, ring finger—now bare—pinkie, then clutched her hands together until the knuckles blanched.

"You remember, don't you, Papa, that Richard died?" She looked at him but he didn't reply. A broad maple tree stood near the bench, its leaves brown and curled and missing in patches, like a demented man who had yanked out fistfuls of his own hair. The wind off the river was chilly and Rowena shivered. She turned her body on the bench to face her father, put her hand on his elbow, then moved it slowly up to his neck, the liver-spotted rim of his ear. "Are you cold, Papa?"

"Yes, my dear. I am." She stood and helped him up, knowing she would run her mind again and again over that *my dear* on her way home, as if it were a charm, an omen that she had chosen rightly. She took his arm and led him back to the asylum's entrance. The building had been under renovation since Mr. Blair had come to live there a few years before. There was a satisfying proportionality to the structure; if it had been a drawing on paper, a child could fold it in half and both wings of the building would match up precisely. They passed through the foyer into the large open sleeping quarters the nurses called "the chapel," for that was the room's original purpose, back when the building had been an immigrant hospital. Under an archway on the far wall, they had set up an altar with a white tablecloth and wooden candlesticks, always lit beneath the cross that hung on the wall. There was symmetry, too, Rowena noticed, in the cross. *What is it about this balance in a shape that holds such innate appeal?* she wondered. *Why do we expect life to take the form of action and reaction, gift and reception, when it is so often out of balance?* Two long rows of beds stretched out between the door and the altar, and at the foot of each was a rocking chair.

"Papa, let's get you comfortable," Rowena said. "And then I have something to read to you."

He grunted but didn't protest and Rowena helped him over to his bed, about halfway down on the left-hand side, and eased his overcoat off his shoulders. She draped it over the back of the chair, then pulled his blankets back, taking a knitted shawl from the foot of the bed, one that had, in fact, belonged to her mother, and opened it over his shoulders. In the windowpane behind her father's head was an image of his perfect double.

"The nurse will bring your tea in a little bit." Rowena sat down on the edge of the bed and pulled the letter from her dress pocket. "Papa, I want you to hear this," she said.

Dear Mrs. Moore,

I am very pleased to make your acquaintance in writing and look forward to the time when we shall meet in person. I

cannot help but praise your beauty. Miss Bixby speaks highly
of you and assures me that your sights are set, as mine are, on
matrimony. She also tells me she has relayed to you the details
of my situation and you remain undeterred by the prairie
winter, among the other challenges. I see already signs that you
are just the sort of steadfast woman I seek. Perhaps I should
tell you a little more about myself and my home that might
help you make your mind up.

The Gibson manse is a hectic place, as I'm sure you've
gathered. The dining table is never empty, with at least the
usual five guests at every meal. Conversation is lively, full of
stories of adventure on the prairie such as rattlesnake hunting
and wars with the Indians—though just between us I must
admit that I suspect some of these tales are slightly exaggerated.
Nonetheless, the storytellers make good company, and they
have gotten better about remembering not to bring their guns
to the table. Since our one young lady is learning to play the
flute, we have music and sometimes, when the celebrants
behave themselves, costumed tableaux in front of the hearth.

Rowena stopped and looked up at her father, who stared
blankly at the empty wall. She smiled, genuinely pleased by the
description so far. "Doesn't it sound wonderful, Papa?" she said.
"Dinner parties with five or more guests every night! I can only
imagine how many maids Mr. Gibson employs." She turned
back to the letter to see that the man did have a few concerns
about the company he had been keeping, and rightly so.

But on the whole we are out of balance, each of us in need of
the influence of a refined lady's manners and speech. I lament

*that only half of them have yet learned to read and am
counting on your education and abilities in this regard.*

Grown men and women, *illiterate*—what a scandal! *Well,*
Rowena thought, *it won't be long after my arrival that I set* that
right.

*As for myself, I suppose some folks have called me handsome. I
work hard to maintain this household and what I need most in
the world is a partner's help. I am*

*Ever yours,
Daniel Gibson*

"Well, Papa, what do you think?" Rowena tucked the
blanket on either side of his hips, unable to look into her father's face. "Daniel Gibson," she said softly, then cleared her
throat, trying to wrestle the emotion out of her voice for what
she had to say next. "Papa, I am going to have to go away for
a while."

This harnessed his attention for a moment and he made
true eye contact with Rowena for the first time since she could
remember. "What's that?"

She gave him a weak smile and wondered if any of his
strange behaviors were put on, to convince her or the nurses
that he had given up trying to rein himself back in. If a man
was only half crazy, people might expect things of him. The
danger of breaking into tears seemed to have passed, like a
cloud crossing over the sun, and Rowena spoke now in a firm
voice. "I have to go to Nebraska, Papa, so that I can marry

Daniel Gibson. Aside from you, there's no one left for me here in New York. Once I get set up there in the town, Destination, I will send for you. It sounds as if there is plenty of room in the house."

Rowena's father watched her without saying a word, then folded his hands the way she had when they were outside on the bench, one finger at a time. "If you are the one who took my hat," he said, "I would like very much to have it back now."

"I didn't take your hat, Papa," she said, standing and kissing him on top of his head, then smoothing his unruly hair. "I won't be leaving until the spring, so you will just have to put up with me until then."

Each time she left a visit with her father at the asylum, Rowena had to turn abruptly on her heel and walk straight for the door as quickly as possible, without turning to look back at him. Turning to look back was far too dangerous.

On her way out of the building she had to pass the office of the asylum's head clerk, Mr. Harrison, who stood waiting by the door.

"Mrs. Moore," he said, stepping toward her. "I was hoping chance might lead our paths to cross today."

Rowena sighed. "Well, there is only one way out of this building and you have been planted here for some time. I don't believe we can credit fortune for our meeting."

He smiled as if he were highly amused by her remark. "Mrs. Moore, we must discuss the balance of your account."

Mr. Harrison was the worst sort of man to owe money, and Rowena owed an awful lot to all sorts of men, so she should know. She preferred the terse, impersonal collectors, with their firm deadlines and strongly worded letters, to a man like this, who feigned patience and compassion when what he was really doing was figuring out how to punish you for your transgressions.

"Yes, sir, we must." Rowena pressed her heels together and planted them into the floor, straightening her back. She imagined she was a tree climbing up, up, up out of this place.

"As you know, we are deeply honored to count such a respected man as your father among the people we serve."

"I'm not sure, Mr. Harrison, that he is so respected anymore. I have yet to see a single of his former colleagues come to visit."

"The insane are . . . well, a troubling group of people for those who don't understand them."

"They are a troubling group for those who *do*," Rowena said, then softened her voice. "I don't blame them for not wanting to come."

"You father is more fortunate than some, in that he has a devoted daughter who comes to him each week to oversee his care."

Rowena bit the inside of her cheeks to keep the bitter laugh inside. She didn't want to think about how they might neglect her father if they didn't know she would be there, faithfully, every Saturday. What would happen to him after she left New York?

"But, as I'm sure you understand, Mrs. Moore, the level of care we provide here is very costly." Rowena appraised Mr. Harrison's suit: rich brown wool, a gold Albert chain, freshly polished.

"Oh, I understand very well where all the money goes."

Mr. Harrison narrowed his eyes. "I am going to ignore

that rude remark because I am a man of *beneficence*. It is what makes me so good at my job. The fact is, Mrs. Moore, that you have not responded to our requests for payment that is long overdue. I would hate to see your father's care suffer because his daughter was capricious with his money."

His money, Rowena wanted to scream, *is in the fire pit in the backyard*. The idea that Mr. Harrison, through orders to his nurses, might take his angst out on her father was more than Rowena could bear. But instead of screaming, she conjured once again the image of a tree, swaying just a bit in the wind. Rowena reached into her pocket for the thick envelope of banknotes and handed it to Mr. Harrison.

He blinked at it in surprise, then lifted the flap and counted. "Well, very good, Mrs. Moore. We are settled then."

"For now," Rowena griped, buttoning her cloak and pulling the hood up over her hair. Outside, sleet had begun hammering on the diagonal. It would be a long and treacherous walk home over icy cobblestones.

"Godspeed, Mrs. Moore," Mr. Harrison said from the doorway of his carpeted office, where twin fireplaces on either side of his desk warmed the room and a silver pot of coffee steamed on a tray.

Rowena felt her jaw tighten. "If you could refrain, sir, from speaking to me anymore, I should *very much* appreciate it."

She stepped out into the weather, feeling relief tempered by an eerie recognition that, once again, the world's sense of balance had asserted itself over disproportion. For who would have guessed that the value of her gold wedding band was exactly, to the dollar, the amount she owed Mr. Harrison?

The Letters

Dear Lucretia,

How strange that I have come to think of you as "my own" when I have never laid eyes on your person! Is your hair fair? Since I was a boy I have stood firm that I should never marry unless the girl was very blond indeed. Until I receive your reply, I shall write to no other lady.

Ever yours,
Jeremiah Drake
Owner, Drake's Brewery

. . . .

Dear Mr. Drake,

I will ask only one more time that you stop writing to me. I have changed my mind about this whole thing. Desist, sir.

Cordially,
Miss L. Blackstone

Dear Kathleen,

You say you are skilled in caring for cows and pigs. How about goats? Specifically, I am wondering what to do about this billy who continues to find his way inside the house, though I can't be sure how since I have bolted all the doors. He smells the way I imagine eternal damnation smells, but stronger still, and let me tell you that it is nothing pleasant to be jabbed in the leg by his horns. As I write, he is staring at me from my easy chair, where he is currently in repose. What am I to do, Kathleen? I pray for your arrival and for deliverance.

Beseechingly,
Amos Riddle

. . . .

Mr. Riddle,

What you must do is walk the nanny goat back and forth in front of the open door. If that doesn't get him out, you can always shoot him. I'll be there soon.

Yours,
Kathleen

My dear Anna,

Though we have never had any acquaintance, I feel since reading your letters that we are intimate friends. I am so glad to know that you are fond of novels. I believe we will get on very well. I know that some men believe, clergymen in particular, that a novel will pollute a woman's mind and encourage her to linger on our earthly tromp instead of loftier matters, but I disagree. What harm may come from a good story? Though Mr. Dickens at times lingers on scoundrels, should we not understand better from meeting them on the page why they turn away from God's law? I have never spent better evenings than the ones in which I've followed Mr. Copperfield's adventures.

Your thoughts on Wesley's concept of prevenient grace are heartening, too, as I concur that it is surely a better rendering of Christ's compassion than strict adherence to Calvinist doctrine. I have long hoped for a wife with whom I could examine and debate our theology.

I close hoping this letter may find you with the rose tint of good health glowing in your cheeks. Will the spring never come?

Yours,
Rev. Prentis Crowley

Dear Cynthia,

*I wanted to tell you before it slips my mind that I have
never consumed a beet in my life and don't intend to start
now. If you are determined to cook beets, please stay in
New York.*

Regards,
Bill Albright

Dear Mr. Jeremiah Drake,

*Sir, I would describe the color of my hair as closer to an
auburn, but it is a light auburn and lightens a great deal over
the summer if I am working outdoors. I have enclosed a lock
with this letter and await your opinion.*

Yours,
Lillyann Martin

. . . .

Dear Miss Martin,

*I am sorry but I must insist on a woman with <u>blond</u> hair,
for what are we without our principles? This lock is darker*

than I hoped for. Please write to me if New York has
a particularly sunny spring and your circumstances
change.

Apologies,
Jeremiah Drake
Owner, Drake's Brewery

Dear Miss Peale,

I wonder, is your father originally of the Baltimore Peales? I
ask because I too am interested in gas lighting using the
horizontal rotative retort and should like very much to speak
with him about a modification I have been working on for a
few years now.

Fondly,
Stuart Moran

....

Dear Mr. Moran,

Yes, those very Peales are my relations; however, due to a feud
between my father and his uncle over the dispensation of a
collection of spoons after my grandmother's death, we no longer

*speak to that branch of the family. I wish I could offer you
assistance.*

Deborah Peale
....

Dear Miss Peale,

*What a terrible disappointment. I suppose you may still make
the trip west, if you like.*

Stuart

Dear Mr. Luft,

*Truly, sir, as I have said, it is not a man's appearance but his
character that matters. The beliefs in his heart and soul. That
said, I should like to know just a little bit more about the
problem with warts you mentioned in your previous letter.
Have they spread completely across your face? Have you
considered seeking medical advice? It is your safety and health,
foremost, that concerns me, of course.*

*Sincerely,
Bethany Mint*

Dear Mr. Drake,

To be honest, though as a child my hair was so fair as to be nearly white, it has darkened some in recent years. I hope that won't be a cause for concern. I am a steadfast, honest woman, willing to do whatever I can to establish a happy home and a partnership based on mutual adoration and care.

Affectionately,
Mary Rousseau

....

Dear Miss Rousseau,

Am I speaking Greek? I requested a blond wife, and you are not she. I am starting to wonder how so many of you can be so dim-witted.

—Drake

Dear Lonesome Winters,

Have my letters not convinced you by now, miss, to tell me your true given name? For I should very much like to know it.

How can we speak truly of our feelings when you are to me a mystery still?

In faith, I shall wait for you here.

Nit LeBlanc,
Hand
Schreier Farm

Winter 1867

Mayor Randall Cartwright wrapped the wool muffler around his face and neck, then took up the empty crate and tramped through the snow to the woodpile stacked against his uncle's sod house. The wind cut through every worn patch of his clothes and his eyes stung. His left-hand glove had developed a hole in the join between the thumb and index finger. The tender web of skin there was chapped and peeling, as if it had been burned. But it was only the effect of the unrelenting cold.

Back inside he pushed the door closed and shoved it into the jamb with his shoulder. Randall's dog, Sergeant, woofed from his burrow under a pile of moth-eaten horse blankets.

"Must be nice," Randall said. Sergeant pulled his head back into the warm cocoon so that only his snout was visible, but when he heard Randall tearing a piece of salt pork into bits and placing it in a bowl, he snapped to attention. When the dog had shown up on the front step last year, one of his ears was missing. The fur had grown over the scar where one eye used to be, and he held his right front paw curled up to his chest. The paw eventually healed enough to walk on, but Sergeant limped like a man with a peg leg. He shambled over to his place under the table.

The banked coals woke up and blazed flames up the wood in the stove. A. J. Baumann charged a hefty price for a cord of firewood in his store, since it had to come all the way from eastern Iowa by train, but it was worth every penny on these cold January mornings. It wouldn't take long for the room to heat and the melting icicles to stream down the walls and form puddles on the floor.

Randall's uncle Lambert Kellinger built the soddy when he first came to Destination on his own, about ten years back, with the help of Leo Schreier and some hired men. They plowed an acre of buffalo grass, then cut the sod into strips with spades and stacked them like bricks in alternating lengthwise and crosswise rows. The soddy was bigger than some, with a small sleeping alcove separated by a curtain, and two doors, one off the kitchen and the other off what Uncle Kellinger called the "front room," the house's sad excuse for a parlor. Randall slept there on the sofa each night, his long legs hanging over the arm, the blood draining out of them until they were numb. In order to turn from one side to another, he had to sit up and shift himself back against the cushions. His shoulders were too wide to roll and he risked falling off with a heavy thud. It was uncomfortable, but it was better than sleeping on the cold dirt floor.

At the small table Randall cracked the skin of ice on the milk and poured some into a shallow pan. He tried slicing the stale hunk of bread on the board but it was as hard and dry as a brick, so he broke it in half and swept the crumbs into two bowls. When the milk steamed, he poured it over the bread. He heard Uncle Kellinger swear and cast off his blankets.

"Took you damn long enough to get the fire going this morning," he said as he threw himself down in his chair in disgust. He yanked one of the bowls toward him and milk sloshed over the side.

Randall nodded. He knew better than to respond to the old grouch, to tell him that the fire was up at the very same time it had been the day before, and the day before that. Uncle Kellinger took pride in the fact that he was a caustic son of a bitch. Anyone who tried to get in the way of that was a fool.

"That dog should be out in the barn."

This too was a familiar exchange. "Uncle, it's too cold at night for him to stay out there without a fire. Would you have me spend double on wood to keep the barn stove going at night?"

Uncle Kellinger grunted.

Randall took the last bite of soggy bread, then tipped the bowl against his face and drank the last of the milk. He wiped his hand over his beard where some of it had dripped. "Well, I've got work to do out in the barn."

He stood up and put his gloves back on, thinking that he would need to stop in at Baumann's later in the day to get some salve for his hand, then pulled his wool hat down over his ears and wrapped the muffler across his face.

"Work," Uncle Kellinger snorted. He sat back in the chair in his thin nightshirt, untied at the neck. His wool socks were pulled up to the knees, like a woman's stockings.

At the threshold, Sergeant hesitated when he saw the depth of the snow and whined a little, looking up at Randall.

"Let's go," Randall said in a low voice. "Unless you'd like to stay here with him."

On the way out to the barn, Randall tucked another load of wood under his arm. The wind lashed at the tender skin of his neck beneath his beard. His nose was running and he wiped it on the back of his glove before the snot could freeze in his mustache. Inside, he dumped the wood in the crude stove he had fashioned out of a big kettle the brewery had discarded and a long, bent pipe that did little to redirect the smoke outside. It was enough, though, to warm the room while he worked over the winter and to keep him from going crazy cooped up in the house with his uncle.

It soothed Randall's nerves to see his tools laid out in two rows on the table where he had left them the day before. His latest project was a kind of automatic broom that could be used to sweep a carpet. He had taken a cylinder of wood and affixed the bristles from four hairbrushes to its surface, then built a lightweight box around it, just big enough so that the cylinder could spin. When he pushed the broom over a piece of fabric covered with broken hay, the bristles collected the hay and the box kept them from spilling back out again. With a pole attached to the top of the box, he could stand up and push it along the ground. There was no need for a dustpan. This invention—which he had yet to quite accomplish, for the box leaked and the bristles quickly became clotted with debris—was a useless success, since no citizen in town owned a carpet, and Randall had little hope of getting a prototype to Chicago or St. Louis and finding someone willing to manufacture it. But he didn't let matters of practicality deter him. Randall loved the puzzle of the thing, the possibility of solving a niggling problem in a novel way. He loved the prospect that he might be of use.

For what was a man if he couldn't be of use? Randall felt that if anything mattered in this world, *duty* must matter. He had tried to be dutiful, even as a young man in St. Louis, when, as his parents' only child, he cared for his mother through her long illness and slow death. After she was gone, he cast about for a summer, drinking great quantities of ale with his friends and roaming the lanes by the river looking for girls. The powdered décolletage, the cloying perfume that came from New Orleans—it just about drove him into a mania. He reveled in its hold over him but feared it too, and he was forever grateful when one evening his father grabbed him by the back of his collar just as he was about to walk out the door once again and sat him down in a chair. Randall would find something useful to do, his father said, or the old man would cut him off.

So Randall wrote to Cyrus McCormick in Chicago, who had developed a reaping machine that promised to change the practice of farming forever, though some farmers were still skeptical. Randall explained that he was good with his hands. He could solve problems. He would work hard and he didn't expect much pay if McCormick would take him on as a kind of apprentice. He never received a reply to the letter, and later it occurred to him that McCormick probably received dozens of letters like his each week. Eventually Randall found work at the levee in St. Louis, unloading ships, and he spent fifteen years there. He was satisfied at least that he had a place to go each day, honest pay at the end of the week. He was bad at saving money, though, and barely kept his head above water. His father died; the ale-drinking friends moved away or married or died too. St. Louis, the city in which he had lived his whole life, began to seem like a foreign place.

Then the war of rebellion came, and if ever there was a clear path to duty, this was it. Randall was agnostic on the politics. Slavery was, unquestionably, an abomination, and Lincoln was a leader for the ages to be sure—Randall grew his beard for the first time when he saw an image of the president's noble profile. But there was a whiff of hypocrisy in the speeches of the stiff-backed abolitionist blowhards way up in Massachusetts. Randall doubted that, given the opportunity for the immense wealth and fertile land to which the Georgians had access, the Yankee farmers wouldn't take it, and the free labor that came along with it, in a heartbeat.

But the cause of keeping the Union together was something Randall could get behind, and he heeded Lincoln's call to sign up. He was shattered when the recruiting officer took a look at his birth certificate and shook his head. Randall was nearly forty by then and he realized that though he wanted very much to be of use, the United States of America might not have much use for him. He followed the news of each battle with a heavy dread in his gut, and he considered forging a new document but feared that the gray sprouts at his temples might give him away.

Restless, directionless, he drank himself into oblivion for the whole of December, then came down with a fever that nearly killed him. When the spring came, Randall was desperate enough to leave St. Louis for good. He was driven to write his mother's rancid-hearted brother to ask him whether there was a way he might be of use in Destination, Nebraska.

Around noon Randall's stomach was growling, but he dreaded going back inside. He decided to go into town instead, stopping at Baumann's store for the salve and then going to the tavern for dinner. Uncle Kellinger lent his horses to Leo Schreier over the winter, since that man seemed to have a use for them and a warmer barn that would keep them from freezing to death. Since November, Randall had been making the half-mile walk into town on snowshoes. He pulled a small sled behind him for the provisions he would bring back; when no one was looking, he let Sergeant ride on it. The snow was deeper than the dog was tall, and it made for slow going. What Sergeant really needed was his own set of snowshoes—an idea that set Randall to thinking for most of the cold walk.

Baumann had shoveled out a path to the entrance, a poorly hung door that slapped closed behind him on a spring. Two thick blankets had been tacked to the door frame to keep out the wind. Randall pushed them aside and stepped into the store. Sergeant shook the snow off his back and trotted toward the hissing stove in back.

"Afternoon, Cartwright."

"Is it?" Randall said. "The sky's so dark all damn day, it's hard to tell."

"It's enough to drive a man insane," Baumann said.

The store was sparsely stocked this time of year. All business pretty much shut down from November to April, except for the absolute essentials. By October, anyone with half a brain had put up all the food he would need: vegetables preserved by Omaha housewives, sacks of barley and flour and beans, dried meat. Eggs and butter could be had on barter, and the occasional chicken. The butcher, Gibson, had yet to slaughter the handful of animals ready for it. No one knew what was taking him so long. Some of the men hunted rabbits and even prairie dogs, but Randall never had taken to the ropy meat. Baumann said he stayed open to sharpen tools and sell firewood, but mainly he just needed the company.

"You got anything that can help me with this?" Randall asked, gingerly pulling off the glove and showing Baumann his raw hand.

"This is all I've got." Baumann pulled a tin out of a drawer behind the counter. "It works if you can stand the smell."

"Hm." Randall opened it and lifted the container of goo to his nose. It smelled like lard and beeswax. "I'll try anything."

"You should bandage it too," Baumann said, handing him a length of cotton. "It looks pretty bad."

Randall scooped a bit of the salve out with his index finger and spread it on his hand, then wrapped the bandage tightly around his palm. He squeezed his fingers into a fist. "Have you had your dinner yet?"

Baumann patted his stomach. "Shepherd's pie today, heavy on the potatoes. Mrs. Healy is worth her weight in gold, and then some. I hope spring will bring a few more like her."

Randall grinned, though he felt like cringing. "We'll see, won't we?" He paid for the salve and whistled for Sergeant. The dog reluctantly left his warm place by the stove. "I thank you, sir."

Baumann waved as Randall slipped past the blankets hanging over the doorway. "Don't freeze your balls off out there. There's no salve that can help you with that."

As Randall crunched across the snow, he ruminated on Miss Bixby and her brides. He was uneasy about the entire venture. It wasn't that he objected to the idea of more women in town—*that* they sorely needed—but Randall was afraid he hadn't done a very good job describing Destination to Miss

Bixby. Everything she knew came from that confounded newspaper article, which sought to sensationalize the town's troubles purely for the entertainment of its readers. For one thing, Destination wasn't completely bereft of women. Mrs. Healy, the widow who owned and ran the tavern, lived among them, though she had made it clear that at fifty years old, she wasn't interested in marrying again. And some of the homesteaders ten or twenty miles out had wives, but they came to town only once a season.

It *was* true that Samuel and Terrance Young were drunks, and they *had* burned down Gerhard Gade's barn. Those two had been causing trouble since the first day they arrived in town. But the sense of chaos those men were purported to represent just didn't exist. The riffraff had moved west with the railroad. Most of the men who remained worked themselves half to death just to survive. Yes, they drank and played cards. Fights broke out on occasion, but the men of Destination weren't unlike the men one might find in any town. Just a little more bored and lonely. There wasn't much more to it than that. But Randall supposed the truth made a far less interesting article. He worried that Miss Bixby, and therefore her coterie of brides, expected pandemonium and perhaps had too inflated an idea of what they might need to do, how drastic a change they might have to make.

On the other hand, he also worried that these city women didn't know what they were getting themselves into out here. It was hard to understand just how remote Destination was until you arrived. The town didn't really even have a doctor, though Augustus Owen put the word after his name. Women brought with them all kinds of mysterious ailments Randall—

and Owen—knew nothing about. They would be wanting the foods they were used to. They would be needing new dresses eventually, and those funny buckled shoes. Not to mention real beds and kitchens and dining tables, which few homes in this town could offer. How would Destination accommodate them?

Randall pulled his sled up onto the front porch of the tavern and leaned it against the wall. He unhooked his snowshoes and knocked the snow off his boots, then opened the door, letting Sergeant hobble through first, called to action by the smell of the kitchen. Word had spread about the shepherd's pie, and the dinner crowd was unusually large. Dr. Owen was there, speak of the devil, sitting at a table with Wyndham Ross, who homesteaded on the other side of town, and Albert Wessendorff, the grocer with nothing green to sell.

Randall sat down at an empty table. Mrs. Healy waved to him from behind the bar and went into the kitchen to get him some food. Randall settled back in the chair and took off his hat. His thick hair was damp with sweat and melted snow. Just as he was beginning to relax, he realized that the man with his back turned at the next table was Jeremiah Drake. But it was too late to move.

"Mayor Cartwright!" Jeremiah said as he turned in his chair, a glass of ale in his hand.

Jeremiah was one of the few men in town who ever called him *Mayor*, and when he did he meant it as a taunt. When Randall had arrived in Destination, the town didn't have a mayor. Jeremiah steamrolled the other men in every important town matter, doing whatever he pleased and whatever benefited his profits at the brewery. Randall had talked the rest of the men into giving him a chance to govern, promised that he would be an impartial representative and put the needs of the entire town first. This had resulted in the title and a small room in the town hall where he went to answer correspondence once or twice a month. Nothing else came of it. It was Randall's fool need to be of use asserting itself all over again, he knew, and in the end no one gained much of anything.

"Just the man I was looking for," Jeremiah said.

"That so?" Randall tried to keep his irritation at bay. Mrs. Healy brought the pie over and set it down in front of Randall, along with a small empty dish. He spooned some of the meat into the dish and put it down on the floor by his ankle. Sergeant sighed with pleasure as he jammed his face into the bowl and moved it around in a circle on the floor. Randall couldn't blame him—it smelled like heaven.

"Now, would you look at that sorry excuse for a dog?" Jeremiah said, pointing his hat at Sergeant. The dog's one good ear perked up. "I can't believe somebody hasn't just gone and shot him."

Randall paused with his spoon halfway to his mouth and turned to glare at him.

Jeremiah grinned and held out his hands. "Only kidding," he said as he slapped the mayor on the back. "Listen, the boys and I here"—Jeremiah gestured to the porter, Stuart Moran, and the dim bulb Bill Albright, who worked for Drake at the brewery—"were just talking about these women we've got coming in the spring. Moran hasn't yet asked for a likeness of his bride and I was telling him he is a fool."

Stuart shifted in his chair. He was always the first to talk about another man's business when he was out of earshot, but when the focus shifted to him, he squirmed. "I can tell from her letters that she is fair. She sounds coy. Only good-looking women can act that way."

Jeremiah turned to Bill. "You got a good look at that letter. What do you think?"

Bill shrugged. "I can't get past the fact that this embarrassment of a man called her his 'prairie flower.'"

Jeremiah slapped the table and their dishes jumped. "God help you, man. She may turn out to be a prairie dog instead. This is why I made my demands known up front. I won't settle for less than precisely what I want."

"And how's that working out for you?" Randall said too quickly, challenge creeping into his tone. "Has anybody fallen in love with you yet?"

"Plenty have," Jeremiah said, staring Randall down. "But I've yet to be impressed."

"What about you, Cartwright?" Stuart asked. "You set all this up—"

"I wouldn't say that," Randall interrupted. "Miss Bixby wrote to me and asked if she could bring some brides west. You all said you wanted them. I'm just the messenger."

"Fine, fine," Jeremiah said. "But what he wants to know is who is coming for *you*? You must have saved the cream of the crop for yourself. I know I would have."

Randall waved the comment away. "Oh, I'm too old for all that," he said, knowing that he and Jeremiah were about the same age.

"Boys, some men's blood runs hotter than others, if you know what I mean," Jeremiah said. Randall knew exactly what he was getting at, and it took all his composure not to haul back right there at the table and break his nose. "I can't go another winter without a woman. Maybe our mayor can."

Bill and Stuart looked at Randall to see what he would do, but he ignored them. He scraped the last bite of his dinner into his mouth and looked over at the bar. Mrs. Healy was watching the exchange anxiously. She was hardly the sort of rough woman one expected to be running a tavern in the middle of nowhere. She dreaded the inevitable fighting, the drunks making a mess. Fate had dealt her a bad hand, to be sure, when her husband was killed on the train while they were en route to California. She found herself stranded in Nebraska, a place she'd probably never even thought to wonder about.

"Mrs. Healy," Randall said, walking over to her and pulling some coins from his pocket. "Could you wrap up three more of these for me, please? My uncle sends his regards."

"Be happy to," she said. He nodded good day to the men, who seemed satisfied that they had won the little competition they had invented for themselves. Sergeant was waiting by the door when Mrs. Healy brought out the food.

Randall pulled the pies home on the sled with Sergeant lying curled around them like a kitchen towel, greedy for their warmth. If Drake was trying to get under Randall's skin, he was doing a pretty good job. That slippery bastard cherished acting as ringleader to his little band of fools. "I thought maybe he was like this because of losing his wife last year," Mrs. Healy had told Randall once. "But everybody says he's always been this way. If that's true, I'd say his wife is lucky to be in her grave." Now Randall felt sorry for the unlucky young lady Miss Bixby would find to be Drake's second wife. He felt responsible, but he wasn't sure what there was to be done about it.

Back at the soddy Uncle Kellinger was hunched in an armchair next to the stove reading a newspaper. Sergeant dived straight for the horse blankets as Randall carried in the pies.

"Took you long enough," his uncle said. Randall set one pie on the table and put the other two in the cupboard for tomorrow's dinner. He put the coffeepot on the stove but didn't wait for the water to boil. Let the old man fix his own cup for a change.

"I've got more work to do in the barn," Randall said. What difference did it make lying about what he planned to do? His uncle wasn't likely to come checking on him. Sergeant leapt up when he moved toward the door, but Randall shook his head and pointed toward the blankets.

"You've got to stay here this time." He leaned down and lowered his voice. "And stay out of his way."

Back out in the snow once again, Randall strapped on the snowshoes and retraced his steps about halfway, to the western edge of town. It was well after three o'clock and the sky already seemed to be darkening toward evening. It was getting colder out, if that was even possible, Randall thought glumly.

As he knocked on the oak door of the only house in town nicer than Leo Schreier's sturdy wood-frame home, Randall recalled the words from the New York paper's article. "A house of mirth," it had called this place. The phrase made him chuckle. He unhooked his snowshoes and stacked them on the porch.

A grandmotherly woman in a modest black gown opened the door. "Good afternoon," she said.

"Hi, Jenny Lou." Randall stepped inside and pulled his muffler down off his face.

"Mr. Cartwright—it's you." She hugged her arms and shivered. "Oh, it's cold out there."

"You'd never know it from in here," he said. He took off his coat and hat and hung them on the cast-iron tree next to the door. The house had a proper hearth, and an enormous fire blazed inside. Several pairs of slippers sat warming in a line on the stone floor in front of two overstuffed armchairs. Pairs of armchairs dotted the rest of the parlor, each one covered in a different pattern of silk or satin. No one knew who owned this house, though they hadn't tried very hard to find out. If there was one thing everyone in Destination agreed on—except, perhaps, Reverend Crowley—it was that the ladies of the log house should be left alone to do as they pleased. Whatever man was behind the operation took good care of them. The furniture was new, the pantry well stocked, and a real doctor brought in on the train from Chicago whenever one of the ladies needed him.

"Would you like a whiskey?" Jenny Lou asked.

"No, but I thank you for the offer. Is Mariah about?"

Jenny Lou nodded. "Oh, yes. She is expecting you."

Randall made his way down the hallway. The fourth door was ajar, the low light of a lamp casting its glow into the hallway. He knocked softly and Mariah called for him to come in. He closed the door behind him and laid the money on the table by the door.

"Hello, love," Mariah said from where she sat on the bench in front of her vanity. Half of her thick, black hair—some of it false, Randall suspected—was twisted and pinned on top of her head in a lush bundle dotted with silk roses. The rest trailed down her back in a braid with a pattern that reminded him of the scales on a fish.

"Is that a new dress?" he asked. It was blue silk molded to her tiny waist with a flutter of white around the neckline, square like a picture frame.

"Do you like it?" She stood up and came over to him, then took his hand and led him over to the bed. It was high and soft, three husk mattresses and a feather bed stacked on the bed frame. He nodded and sat down. The room was warm. On the stove in the corner a pan of water and cinnamon sticks simmered, giving off a spicy-sweet smell.

Mariah stood in front of him and he put his hands on her hips, pressing the soft flesh next to the bones in her pelvis with his thumbs. Randall had been coming to her for more than a year, since the first day he saw her get off the train at the depot and walk toward the log house clutching her small leather case. Mariah combed her fingers through his bushy hair and he closed his eyes. His hands looked so large against her tiny frame that he felt like a beast and a little ashamed of it. He moved them to the small of her back, over her rump, down the back of her thighs.

"You look tired," Mariah said. "Is everything all right?" She kissed the top of his head and he opened his eyes. Her lips were full and red, her eyes bright. "I've missed this big wolfy beard," she said, tugging playfully on it with her fingers, then bringing her breasts to his face. The hooks at the back of her dress were undone and he pulled it down easily while she untied the corset and stepped out of the plain cotton shift. She was naked except for the gold locket she always wore. He had asked her once what was inside but she would only shake her head. Her outline in the dim light made his heat rise; when she pressed her hand into his lap he moaned softly. Mariah giggled and shoved him down on the bed.

Randall wasn't fool enough to think he loved her, or, even more naïvely, that she loved him, but he didn't mind that she was kind to him in addition to everything else he paid her for. After she had worn him out they lay in the bed together. She rested her cheek on his chest and he wondered whether she did this with everyone, afterward; he pushed the thought away. He had been in a dark mood all day, he realized. Randall visited Mariah because it made him feel good. He didn't want it to become one more thing that depressed him.

"Are you ill, sweet love?" she whispered. "You're awfully quiet."

Randall shook his head, pulled her closer. "I'm fine. I'm better now." He glanced lazily around the room. A painting of two lovers on a riverbank hung on one wall. In the corner opposite the stove was Mariah's armoire, stuffed with dresses and bonnets far too fine for any social event in this town. He knew very little about her, only that she was twenty years old and from Detroit. She meant to go to California someday. She didn't put milk in her tea. Randall felt the old nagging questions bubbling up. How had he come to be here, in this town? What had he really *done* with all his useless years?

Mariah stood up and gathered her garments from the floor. She padded over to the armoire and hung them up, then took a dressing gown from the hook and shrugged into it, tying it at the waist. When she padded back to the bed, her footsteps silent, Randall bolted upright.

He pointed at the floor. "You got a carpet!"

Mariah seemed pleased that he had noticed. "It was a gift."

Randall laughed and stood up. He threw on his clothes, his mood brightening. "I've got to go, Mariah."

She giggled. "Well, what's gotten into you?"

"Until next time, my dear."

She waved from the bed as Randall slipped out the door. He buttoned his coat as he rushed down the hallway, then fumbled to get his snowshoes back on outside. In the barn, the puzzle of the broom sat in pieces, waiting to be solved. And now it could be of use.

It was late in the season for butchering, but Dodge County had just passed through one of the warmest falls on record, and it made little sense to slaughter a cow until it was good and cold.

At least that was what Daniel Gibson told himself, but the truth was that he simply hadn't done it yet. Daniel kept wondering if he was lazy. It seemed a strange question to ask himself since, if he really was lazy, wouldn't he also be the sort of man to make excuses about it, to deny that the fundamental problem resided in his own disposition? On the other hand, Daniel really *didn't* believe laziness was the problem. It wasn't that he felt unwilling to do the work; he simply felt frozen, as inert as that cow would be a few minutes after he slit its throat. Wyndham Ross asked him about it again after Sunday service—when should he bring over his cow?—and again Daniel muttered a litany of excuses to keep the farmer at bay. His son Dag had been sick, and this being the first winter his wife was gone, Daniel had his hands full. There was a leak in his soddy's roof that needed repair. He had sent his knives to Omaha for sharpening.

"All right, then," Ross said. "But I really can't wait too much longer."

He was right, of course. Nobody else had asked Daniel about beef this year, but there were plenty of pigs to deal with, salt pork and sausage to make, hams to smoke out behind the shop. Any misfortune could befall a town—drought, plague, war—but hunger never deserted a human being until his life was over. They always needed Daniel to do his work and until now he had never failed to perform it.

In the shop on a Tuesday morning, Daniel wiped down all the clean surfaces once again. The empty barrels were tipped upside down against the wall to keep out the dust. Once he butchered a few pigs he would fill these with layers of salt and pork, then cover it with a strong brine and a brick to hold the pork under its surface.

Daniel heard the door and looked up to see Amos Riddle. Could there be a man less well suited to homesteading? Small and bespectacled, Amos had pale, white hands that flipped nimbly through the pages of books in his parlor in Philadelphia, but they hadn't ever done much else until he arrived in Nebraska. Everyone in Destination knew he was bright—probably the brightest one in town, possessed of a university education bought with a little family money—but he'd never held a hammer or saw or rifle before he claimed his land. Daniel suspected Amos had read about homesteading in a boys' adventure story, or a volume of soaring poetry, and gotten his chest puffed up with romantic notions.

"Morning, Amos," Daniel said. The man was scarcely keeping the fire going through the night, much less raising livestock out there on his plot, so Daniel didn't think he had to worry about another order.

"Good morning. I am wondering if you can help me with my goat."

"What kind of help do you need?" It was highly unusual for a man from these parts to *eat* a goat, but Amos was an unusual man.

"I'd like to have him slaughtered."

Daniel nodded slowly. "All right. Can't say as I've ever butchered a goat, but it's all the same to me. Bring him in and I'll take care of it."

Amos looked down. "Well, I'll be needing help with that too."

"What do you mean?"

"I can't get him out of my house."

Daniel stared at him a moment. "Well, how in the hell did he get *into* your house in the first place?"

"Don't ask," Amos said. "All you need to know is that he's there now, and I want to make a stew out of him. Will you help me?"

Daniel couldn't help but laugh. He hoped it didn't sound mean-spirited. Whatever was between Amos and the goat seemed contentious and personal. In a way Daniel admired Amos for sticking it out through the winter here all alone, when he could be just about anywhere else, doing anything but breaking his back on work he knew nothing about. "Sure, I'll help you," Daniel said. "Why don't I stop by later this afternoon?"

Amos nodded and tipped his hat. "The sooner, the better."

With that, Amos left and Daniel got back to work. Around two, he pulled the collar of his wool coat up over his ears and went a few doors down the main road to the tavern. He liked to wait until most everybody else had come and gone and the tavern was quiet. Mrs. Healy always kept a bowl of stew warm for him.

"Mr. Gibson," she said when he came in. "I was wondering whether I'd see you this afternoon. Thought maybe you finally let Mr. Ross bring in his cow."

"Let me guess—he was just here talking about that very thing." Daniel sat down at the bar and took off his hat.

"Indeed," Mrs. Healy said. She went into the kitchen and came out with his stew and a plate of corn bread. "He seems a little perturbed, if you want to know."

"Well," Daniel began, as if he were going to say something else on the matter. But how could he explain it to her, the strange lack of confidence he suddenly felt in his knife, the way he would grip the handle tighter and tighter but still imagine it slipping out of his hand at the wrong moment and clattering to the floor? His palms grew damp all the time now. His fingers shook.

Mrs. Healy gave him a worried glance. "Is everything all right?"

"Oh, yes—fine. Just hungry I suppose."

"Good. Now, tell me how your children are doing." Oh, the children. Daniel fought the urge to put his head in his hands. Four boys with their cuffs up around their shins, outgrowing everything they owned and nobody in the house who knew how to sew. His one little girl was nearly feral now from lack of attention and he had not the faintest idea how to talk to her. The children missed Mother's food, they cried. They missed her singing voice, the little plays she helped them put on. Why did she have to die?

"It's such a shame, what happened to you," Mrs. Healy said.

Daniel gave her a knowing smile. "Well, there's enough tragedy to go around in this town, isn't there?"

Everyone knew how Mrs. Healy had ended up here—she and her husband had decided to start again in California after their grown son died of the fever, but her husband was killed by robbers on that train, and all their money was gone. Nobody knew why she stayed. Even at her age, it puzzled Daniel why, at the very least, she hadn't set her sights on another man by now. It had to be awfully hard for a woman to be on her own out here. He knew it had been hard on Greta, so hard it played tricks on her mind. Sometimes she looked at Daniel as if she didn't recognize him. The children too. About broke his heart to see one of them tapping her on the back of the hand, saying, "Mother? Mother, won't you talk to me?" And Greta standing up and walking over to the window. After the spring came, the prairie shot through with wildflowers in pink and yellow and white, they were living without her.

It was why, when Mayor Cartwright told them one night in the tavern about the letter he'd received from New York, Daniel decided on the spot to pay the fee, whatever it was, and send for any woman who would have him. He didn't want to think about how these children would fare through another year alone. He had no notion of love, though, admittedly, hope stirred a little when he saw how pretty Rowena was in her tintype. How young and clear-eyed. Daniel was lonely, but in truth he wasn't any lonelier than he had been when Greta was still with them, shut up tight in the world inside her head. It was a blessing that he didn't have much time to think about any of it.

"Do you have a wife coming in the spring?" Mrs. Healy asked as she rubbed a rag in circles on the end of the bar. She wouldn't meet his gaze as she asked the question. Everyone in town knew about Daniel's troubles, but they didn't like to pry.

"That's what they tell me," Daniel said. He decided then, on impulse, that he wouldn't tell Rowena about how he earned his living for fear the nature of the work would trouble her and she would decide not to come west. Besides, by the time she arrived, he might not be a butcher anymore. He might not be anything.

He finished up his food and screwed his hat back on his head, then left to keep his promise to Amos. Daniel kept his wagon on runners through the winter and his horse pulled it easily over the ice-crusted snow, out to Amos's small plot of land. If his mind and hands were working right, Daniel would slaughter the goat when he got there and hang it in Amos's sorry excuse for a barn to drain. A few days later Daniel would go back out and bring the carcass to the shop in his wagon. He had looked up goats in the butcher's guide that came from the knife company in Chicago and learned he could salt the meat Amos didn't want to use right away, just like pork, in the big barrels he kept in the cellar. He wondered how it would taste.

Amos was sitting on an overturned crate in front of his soddy when Daniel pulled up.

"What the devil are you doing out here?" Daniel said,

squinting against the glare on the snow. "You're likely to freeze solid."

Amos just shook his head. "Come on and see for yourself," he said, walking toward the door and gesturing for Daniel to follow. "But I'm warning you—it's pretty bad in there."

The first thing Daniel noticed when Amos opened the door was the smell. It took his eyes a moment to adjust to the darkness inside the house, but when they did, he wanted to turn around and head right back out the door. The floor was dotted with dark pellets of feces and puddles of urine. In the kitchen, the small cupboard door had been pulled off its hinges and broken jars lay on the floor in front of it. One kitchen chair leaned to the side and Daniel could see it was because half the leg had been chewed away. The sofa was dented where the stuffing had been pulled out. In the corner by the window the goat sat and stared at them, its horns curling up like question marks.

Daniel turned to Amos openmouthed. "How long has it been in here?"

"About a week," Amos said. "This time."

"It's been in here before?"

Amos nodded. "He comes and goes as he pleases." He pointed to a ladder on the other side of the room that led to a blanket up in the sleeping loft. "And I've been spending most of my time up there."

Daniel kept his gloves on. He moved toward the goat, its waste squishing under his boots. It trotted over by the stove, out of reach. When Daniel followed it there, the goat slid behind the sofa, then back into the kitchen. It scraped its horns on the cupboard door and bleated at them. "Damn it," Daniel said.

"Believe me—he can do this all day," Amos said. The goat charged suddenly, straight for Amos, but he was practiced at stepping quickly out of the way. His hip hit the table beside the armchair, and the oil lamp crashed to the floor. The goat trotted over and began to lick at the oil. Amos shook his head and looked at Daniel, holding up his hands.

Daniel knew they could just shoot the animal, but it wasn't a bright idea to fire a gun inside the house. They needed to get the creature outside. Daniel went back out to the wagon and brought back a length of rope. He tied a slipknot on the end and crept up behind the animal.

"Oh, he doesn't like rope," Amos cautioned.

"Shut up, if you're not going to help."

Daniel got close but the goat bucked its head and a horn stabbed Daniel's palm. He pulled his hand back, then opened it wide as the goat slid behind the sofa again. His palm was bleeding but the cut wasn't deep. Daniel took a deep, angry breath, his molars clamped down. His whole life felt this way lately; he barely knew what he wanted, but whatever it was kept eluding him. He crossed the room to the sofa and yanked one side away from the wall with a swift motion. The goat turned in a half circle, then made a low staccato sound. Moving quickly, Daniel came at it from the side with his knee, knocked it hard off its back legs, and pressed its hindquarters down on the floor. It kept still long enough for him to slip the rope over its neck.

Daniel stood up, his pants slick with shit, and let the goat right itself. He pulled it out from behind the sofa and Amos hollered with delight. Daniel cut his eyes at Amos and he quieted, then shoved his hands into his pockets.

The goat pulled mightily against the rope, but its hooves couldn't gain traction and it moved backward like a skater toward the open door as Daniel pulled on the rope. Out in the snow, the daylight was so bright Daniel's eyes teared up. He held the rope with one hand while he swiped his sleeve over both eyes. His nose was running. He pulled the goat over to the wagon, reached in with one arm to open the case that contained his knives, and pulled one out. Daniel had meant to put the goat down inside the barn so there wouldn't be such a mess out in front of the house, but he wasn't going to take any chances with the animal getting away now.

Amos stood in the doorway watching. *I'm going to charge that son of a bitch double for this job*, Daniel thought, breathing through his nose. He gripped the knife in his right hand, so tightly he could feel the skin stretching over his knuckles, then pulled the rope taut so that the goat was looking straight up at the sky. The white slope of its neck waited. Daniel hadn't killed anything, not a chicken, not a rabbit, since the spring. Even his own children had been eating beans, thin soups of vegetables and rock-hard salt pork at least a year old. Here was the work he had been trained to do—take the animal a man raised and help that man make it into food. There was nothing nobler, nothing more essential. The world had shifted under Daniel's feet with Greta gone, had changed forever; still, there were things to be done that only he could do. Daniel took a breath. With a steady hand, he pushed the blade against the goat's flesh, and he nearly laughed because it was so easy, the way the vein split open and the blood rushed out, hot on the frozen ground. It was so easy.

He had a bride coming in the spring. Eight of the men did, even Amos. Things would change again, this time for the better. Now all he had to do was wait.

Spring 1867

Clara

Clara sat down on a bench and pressed her fingertips into her eyes, trying to get at the pain that crackled in the center of her skull like a wick. In three days, she and her flock of brides would board the New York Central to begin the long trip west, and a few things remained unresolved, to say the least.

Among her myriad concerns, chief was the matter of the ladies' health. Clara had insisted on medical evaluations for each one of them, and with good reason. They would be spending the next several days in very close quarters, and if even one of them was ill, the whole lot could arrive in Destination green and feverish. It wasn't a recipe for getting these grooms to fall in love. But a doctor's examination was costly, Clara knew, and a good portion of these girls didn't have a penny. When the letters certifying their good health trickled in, it was clear some of them were forged. Many of the women had seen Dr. Calumet, a man who by default had become physician to the downtrodden women south of Houston Street. He had cared for Clara herself in her darkest time after the baby's death, though she scarcely remembered anything from those days.

She decided to pay him a visit and try to discern whether his opinion of the girls' good health should be trusted. His examination room was on the first floor of a building everyone knew around the neighborhood as Libby's.

Dr. Calumet, it seemed, owned the building and leased it to Libby and her employees. Though he claimed never to climb the stairs to the satin-strewn chambers of the nighttime ladies, he did, out of pity, he told Clara, help them with the ailments common in their line of work—poxes and sores and the occasional bruise, not to mention the unwanted reminder, nine months delayed, of nature's actual purpose for the couples' secret collisions.

Clara stood on Dr. Calumet's doorstep now, knocking on the door with her gloved hand. After a moment he came to the door wearing a woman's apron soaked with a red liquid. His sleeves were rolled up to the elbows.

Clara gasped. "My *God*, sir."

Dr. Calumet glanced down at his torso, then laughed. "Ah, no—it's paint, my dear. I am working on a series of battlefield images. Come have a look."

Clara let out a breath and felt the rancid foam in the back of her throat recede. On a second glance at his apron she saw three paintbrushes poking from the pocket, bristles up. She remained planted on the doorstep. "No, thank you. I am late to an appointment. I've come to talk with you about a few women you have examined on my behalf, brides planning to travel west for marriage."

"Maidens, all, miss—I assure you."

Clara felt the pain in her head surge hard this time, and she placed her palm on the door frame for support. After a moment passed, she opened her eyes. "That is not my concern, for I take them at their word." *Knowing full well*, Clara thought, *that at least a few of them are lying.*

"Are you all right, Mrs. Bixby? You seem to be in pain."

Clara waved his comment away. "Just one of those headaches, brought on, as you know, during times of distress, and I am distressed, indeed, sir, today. It is very important that I should know whether any of these women are showing signs of illness. The journey to Nebraska is a long one, and we do not have the time or funds to procure medical care along the route." She closed her eyes again as another wave of pain washed over her.

"Please, come at least into the anteroom and sit down for a moment. You should have a drink of water."

Clara nodded and followed him inside. In the corner was a bench and she sank down onto it and leaned her head back against the wall.

"If anyone is unfit for travel, it is you, Mrs. Bixby," Dr. Calumet said. "Are you sleeping? Do the headaches still come on very often?"

Clara shook her head. "I am not here to talk about me. Would you please just do something to assure me of the health of my brides?"

Dr. Calumet sighed. "First, you must try a dose of this headache tonic." He went to a cabinet and removed a narrow vial and a glass tumbler. He held the brown liquid up to the light, swirled it around, then filled the glass to the brim.

"Drink this down," he said. "I'll bring you some water."

Clara considered the potion for a moment, then decided to take it to appease the doctor. Nothing she had tried for her headaches—cold compresses, vegetable mash, steam treatments, citric acid—had ever worked to alleviate the pain, and she didn't expect this tonic to work either. Calumet had once offered her the brown glass bottle of laudanum, but she had refused, though Clara felt sure the tincture would work. She had seen plenty of women at Mrs. Ferguson's who made liberal use of the "twenty drops" dosage until their desire for it took them over completely. Clara never wanted to fall under its spell. She tossed back Calumet's newest concoction; the sludge tasted terrible, like coffee grounds and pickle brine, and when the doctor handed her a mug of water she drank it down in three long gulps, then concentrated on trying not to vomit.

Dr. Calumet nodded his approval. "Now to your brides—lovely ladies, Mrs. Bixby, and I congratulate you on that fact. I saw no signs of illness in any I examined. Of course, there are some who could benefit from an improved diet and more fresh air. Others have taken the fear of warm-water baths to an extreme, for I am of the opinion that bathing does the body more good than harm. But on the whole these women are as healthy as any other in Manhattan and will be all the healthier when they get to the clean open air of the western territory."

Clara put her palms on the bench on either side of her hips and pushed herself to a standing position. It was torturous not knowing when the headaches would come on. Clara felt she should have known they would reappear at the least convenient time. All winter long she could have endured them in her bedroom, blankets over the window to block out the spearing daylight; but no, they would come on now, when she had a list as long as her arm of things to do before departing. *But this is how the world replies*, she thought, *if a woman has the gall to assert her existence and upset its plan.*

"I thank you for your time, sir," she said, "and for the tonic."

"I sincerely hope it helps you, Mrs. Bixby. Please take care to get plenty of rest before your journey."

She stepped into the street, her jaw clamped down like a vise against the pain. Rest did not have priority at the moment. She pulled the list of brides from her pocket, determined to visit each one and confirm that she was packed and ready to leave. This proved difficult. Kathleen Connolly's father told Clara his daughter was not in, though when Clara glanced up at the second floor from the street, she saw a flash of red hair, then heard the house-shaking thump of a sturdy Irish hip attempting to knock down a locked door. He might not want her to go, Clara thought as she walked away, but heaven help the man who stood in that girl's way. Deborah Peale, Rowena Moore, and Bethany Mint did not answer their respective doors.

At the Channing mansion, Clara took the footpath that ran along the east side of the house to the elevated back garden and the steps that led to the scrubby yard outside the laundry. Two sets of windows were open wide, connecting the dark work space inside with the open air of the yard. A few women in gray uniforms and white aprons were hanging bedding on long stretches of clothesline. The late-morning air still held a chill and Clara's knuckles ached when she thought of how cold the wet linens must have been.

She glanced around for—she checked the list again—Miss

Elsa Traugott. Though Clara had only a vague memory to go on, she knew this was the plump, quiet woman from the meeting above the tavern. Curiously, Miss Traugott had given only the address of the nearby post office on her application, but the postmaster had told Clara that she worked in the Channing laundry. Two women nearby were beating a rug as fiercely as if they suspected it had Confederate sympathies; when one of them stopped for breath she looked up and spotted Clara, then whispered something to her companion. They seemed to recognize her.

Clara approached them. "Do you know where I might find Miss Traugott?"

The laundress's eyes widened. "You're here for *Elsa?*" She glanced at a cluster of women working at the long table inside. "Are you certain?"

"Why wouldn't I be here for her?" Clara asked, her eyes challenging the girl to give voice to her thoughts.

The laundress dropped her gaze to the ground, stalling. "I, ah, I thought she was already married. That's all, miss."

Clara nodded. "Well, she isn't. Not that it's any of *your* concern. If you know her, please point her out. My time is worth something to me, and I shouldn't like to waste it in talking with you."

"That's her over there." The laundress pointed rudely. "With the gray hair."

Clara held her gaze and opened her mouth to reprimand the girl, then thought better of it. *Let her be her own undoing.* She started toward the door to the laundry room.

Elsa looked up from her mending and froze, then set it

down carefully and glanced around. She rose from her chair and walked toward Clara.

"Miss Bixby," Elsa whispered. "What are you doing here?"

"I came to confirm that you are prepared for the departure on Saturday. Are you trying to hide from me?"

Elsa shook her head. "No, miss, but please—let me come to you later this afternoon. I can't talk here."

"Well, why ever not?" Clara felt the sparkle of pain behind her eyes, stars in a dark sky.

"My employer does not approve of the Nebraska venture."

"But why should you care what she thinks, when you will leave soon anyway?"

"Because I want my last week's pay, and she will withhold it if she knows why I'm leaving. And any one of these girls might tell her if they need to earn her favor."

Clara nodded and remembered that Mr. Rathbone had been a kinder employer than most. "Forgive me for intruding," she whispered. "I will be in my room at Mrs. Ferguson's this afternoon." Clara raised her voice then and said dramatically, "My apologies. I can see I am looking for a *different* Miss Traugott. Good day." She strode across the yard and back down the footpath to the street.

Her final stop before returning home was the dressmaker's shop. Mr. Rathbone, out of equal parts kindness and guilt, had arranged for the woman to make new collars for each of Clara's dresses, along with a new fur-trimmed cloak and traveling dress. She was grateful for this gesture. Her wardrobe was in a terrible state, and it was foolish to go west without the proper attire. But she hadn't wanted to spend any of what little she had collected from the men so far. She had intentions for her profits.

The headache had subsided and she left the shop with the new case full of clothes feeling refreshed. But the feeling would not last.

"Why, hello, *Mrs.* Bixby," a voice said. Clara turned to see a familiar man poke the brim of his stovepipe hat with his umbrella. "You sure are looking lovely today."

Clara could scarcely get her tongue to work. "George? I thought you were in Buffalo."

"I was for a time," he said. "Breaking my back firing bricks in a kiln. But then I ran into Mac Stanley, visiting relatives there, and he mentioned how well my Clara was faring back in Manhattan City. Starting some kind of travel business. So I came to see for myself."

Clara's mind snagged on *my Clara*; the rest of George's words slid by like raindrops on a window. And there it was again, the flowering pain.

George appraised her dress, charcoal gray gabardine with white piping and a high collar, just right for a middle-aged woman traveling unaccompanied by a man, but still very finely made. The price of one yard of the gabardine alone had been higher than what she had usually spent on entire dresses in the past. "I see that Mac was right—it seems you are faring very well indeed."

"I can't believe you're here," Clara said. He had left without a word and never sent so much as a letter in all these months, leading her to wonder if he had ever existed at all. And yet here he was. She waited for her surprise to harden to anger, but it didn't come. Her headaches were nothing compared with the chronic illness that was her love for this man. She wanted so much to muster hatred for him, to turn haughty and give him a piece of her mind, then leave him standing in the middle of the street. But the mere sight of him, not to mention the sound of his voice, had drawn the fight right out of her. How *lonely* she had been, surrounded by his slippers and abandoned shaving kit. "What do you want, George?" she asked, weary.

He smiled. His cheeks were pink from his time working outdoors, and the ruddiness suited him, made his eyes seem brighter. "Why, what kind of a question is that for a wife to ask her husband? I want to come home. I've missed you, Clara."

Don't be stupid, girl! she shouted in her mind. And yet when George reached for her gloved hand she let him take it, let him bring it to his cheek. She had felt the rub of his jaw on parts of her body she was too shy to name, even in silence, and she would be lying if she denied that she longed to feel it once again.

"What about your little Papist?"

"Lucia? How could you even think of her? She never meant a thing to me, my little filly." This nickname had proved an effective tool in the past, a loving reference to Clara's long thin legs and knobby knees, over which she had lamented as a young girl. She would never have the curving womanly shape of a cello, but George had praised her limbs so well she had come to believe in their beauty. For a time. In truth, she knew she looked less like a filly and more like a well-dressed scarecrow.

Clara formed the hard lump in her throat into words. "I'm not taking you back, George." She felt she was one compliment away from total collapse, and she realized her only hope was to get back to Mrs. Ferguson's and shut herself in the room with a chair propped under the doorknob. She turned east and started walking, the leather of the new boots still stiff around her ankles.

George followed at her heels. "Clara, you know I love you. I'll never stray again—I give you my word."

This made Clara laugh, and the laugh seemed to shift the conversation in her favor. George's flirtation had soured into a kind of pleading. He doubled his steps and caught up to her, walking swiftly at her side, but she refused to turn her head and look at him.

"I have no use for your word, George. Let me be. You wanted your freedom and now you have it. What I do with my time is none of your concern." At the entrance to the rooming house, Clara stopped and steadied herself for the words she'd never had the chance to say when her husband had vanished the previous summer. "Good-bye, George."

His arm shot out and he grabbed her wrist. "Clara. Maybe you misunderstand me. I am not asking your permission to come home. I am telling you that's what I'm going to do. Perhaps you have forgotten that we are still married in the eyes of the law, not to mention the eyes of God."

Clara scoffed. "Fancy *you*, worrying about God."

"What's thine is mine, my little filly. We swore it."

Of course he wants the money, she thought. *Of course.* Clara felt her hands clenching into fists. "George, if you try to come through this door, I will holler like the dickens."

He raised his eyebrows. "Well, look what a little money will do to make a woman uppity!" He seemed to consider his options and chose, as he usually did, strategy over temper. "Very well, wife. I have no desire to cause a scene. You'll see— I'll convince you in time. I hear," George said, "that you will soon be departing for the West. When do you go?"

Clara hesitated. "We have been delayed by a few weeks, at least," she said. "I can't imagine that we would go before the end of June." He would uncover the lie soon enough, but it might buy her enough time to shirk him, at least for a while.

"All right, then," George said. "Plenty of time for you to have a change of heart." He tipped his hat and turned, swaggering away. This swagger had undone Clara many times, and it threatened to do so again if she let down her guard for even a moment.

Why the cursed, blinding plague of love was let loose on this world, I'll never know, Clara thought as she watched him walk away.

Elsa

Elsa pressed closed the door to her chamber, then pulled off her mud-caked boots and set them on the mat of tied rags next to the door. She could almost feel her ankles swelling without the tight laces there to constrict them. Elsa exhaled a long sigh of relief. Miss Bixby seemed to have convinced the other laundresses that she had come seeking her by mistake. As far as Elsa knew, no one had gone to Mrs. Channing with the gossip. Only a few more days now and she would finally be free of this place.

Elsa appraised the room. Miss Bixby had told the brides they were permitted to bring a single trunk of belongings. This was more than enough for Elsa, who could fit nearly her entire life in the tattered linen-covered chest that sat at the foot of her bed. She knelt down on the floor and opened the hinged lid. Removing the contents to two large piles, she began to rearrange the articles in order of necessity. The boiled-wool blanket would certainly come in handy, as would the warming silk underclothes she wore beneath her work uniform all winter long, soaking them once a week in a small tub of boiling vinegar water. Elsa owned three dresses and two shawls but only the one pair of boots, so she didn't expect the clothing to take up much space. She would leave room for her Bible, of course, and a tablet of paper and a fountain pen— for writing letters, she told herself, though of course she had no one to whom she could imagine writing.

A few items of sentimental value had been lurking at the bottom of the trunk, and Elsa hadn't touched them since boarding the ship in Bremen thirty-three years before, so afraid was she as a girl of the power they held over her emotions. Later, in the storm and stress of life, she forgot about their existence. Now was the time, Elsa supposed, to face them and decide what to do with them once and for all.

As a child, Elsa had been fond of sketching, a fact she had all but forgotten until she saw the little bound book nestled on the floor of the trunk. Inside were the rough and wavering likenesses of her parents: first there was a drawing of her mother sitting in an armchair, her cheekbone resting on her knuckles and a long wisp of hair swaying in front of her eye. Next Elsa had drawn her portly father, grim with his pipe clamped between his molars, his attention on a stack of papers on his desk. Elsa remembered the day she drew him this way. She had been such a quiet mouse of a girl that he hadn't even known she was there in the room. If she could have turned the sketchbook page to reveal what took place after the image of the man working quietly at his desk discovered his observer, the next drawing would have revealed a man in motion, flying to his feet and the gruff words: *Raus hier!* Get out of here.

When she ran, it was to her grandfather's cottage, into the kitchen where her grandmother spent each morning kneading dough for bread. The fine hair at her temples curled, damp from the heat of the oven, and she hummed old hymns no one else seemed to remember. Methodically, she taught Elsa to crack an egg with one soft blow that broke the shell into two intact pieces, never complaining that a dozen were wasted until Elsa mastered the technique. Currants could be soaked in rum to plump and sweeten them. Sugar and butter would turn to caramel, as if by magic, with the right amount of heat and time and patience. You could know a cake was done baking if you paid attention for the moment when its sweet-butter scent crested, then eased. Elsa took all this in with the carelessness of a child who couldn't understand that someday soon all she would have left of her grandmother would be the recipes.

At the bottom of the pile of linens in the trunk was the Traugott family's christening gown, used by Elsa's father and his siblings, as well as Elsa's brother Johan, who died in it, and Elsa herself. Despite her Lutheran convictions against imbuing objects with divinity, the garment seemed to Elsa a holy relic, steeped in all the memory and hope and sorrow it had clothed and endured over the years. In the throes of fever, Elsa's mother, knowing she would soon die and that when she did Elsa would depart for America with Gretchen, urged her daughter to keep the white lace gown among her most precious things. To save it for the day when she would have a child of her own.

Elsa lifted the delicate garment by the shoulders. The linen was so fine she could see the outline of her fingers through the fabric. The collar tied with a narrow silk ribbon and the skirt was edged with torchon lace, her great-grandmother's specialty, it was said among the family.

On most matters, Elsa put her trust in the wisdom of the

Lord, but on this, the absence of a child from her life, her heart lingered, plucking at the wound, refusing to let it heal. *Hope deferred maketh the heart sick.* She would have been a good mother, she thought, risking pride. A patient, careful mother who took solace in the simple routine of bathing and feeding a child, rocking her to sleep, teaching her about the promise of the risen Lord. Elsa would have felt it was her sworn duty to prevent all harm coming to that baby. Each day she saw so many women in the streets of Manhattan City who did not heed the duties of this calling, who were careless and hard to their children, and it pained Elsa to see it. Why had she been overlooked?

Elsa stood up, one of her many strategies for clearing an infecting thought from her mind, and nodded once. *Enough.* There was plenty to do in the here and now to keep her from worrying over such unanswerable questions. She folded the gown and placed it back in the trunk. It was merely an object with some use left in it. It could be cut up for handkerchiefs; the lace could be used to trim a window dressing. If she was seeking a trial with her foolish reverie, she had found it, for now Elsa had to coax her boots back on over her swollen ankles so that she could call on Miss Bixby.

Elsa crossed Mrs. Ferguson's parlor to the stairs, where order had long been restored since the meeting the previous fall. Then it had been full of ladies, but now it was full of men, some holding their hats on their laps, others smoking thick cigars and laughing over a deck of cards. Elsa kept her eyes on the carpet, willing her body as she often did to remain invisible. At the top of the stairs she turned left, then knocked on the door with an embroidered sign that read *Bixby* in cross-stitched letters.

For a moment there was no reply. Then Elsa heard a shifting of furniture and a croaking voice call out, "Who's there?"

"It's Elsa Traugott, miss. I've come as you asked."

Another spate of silence passed and the woman called, "Come in."

Elsa opened the door and found that the room was cloaked in almost complete darkness, despite the efforts of the afternoon sun. Miss Bixby lay in the narrow bed with the blankets pulled up to her chin, her bent arm cast over her face.

"Miss Bixby," Elsa said. "Are you ill?"

"Please . . . whisper," she said. "If you must talk at all."

A quilt had been tacked over the window with a nail and hammer, Elsa saw, as her eyes adjusted to the dim light of the room.

"Miss Traugott, I'm sorry you came all this way. I only wanted to confirm that you are prepared for our departure on Saturday."

"What ails you, miss?"

Miss Bixby waved her hand without uncovering her eyes. "Oh, it is one of my headaches. They have never been so dreadfully bad as this. But it is only because I am trying to thwart my miserable destiny." She opened one eye as if to test her endurance, then squeezed it shut. "Well, I shall not be deterred, whatever the pain."

"May I try to help you?" When the patient didn't reply, Elsa pulled a chair up to Miss Bixby's bedside, carefully straightened the woman's arm, and put it down at her side.

Then Elsa placed her fingertips on Miss Bixby's brow. At first the woman stiffened, but as Elsa moved her fingers in slow circles over the skin, following the arches of Miss Bixby's eyebrows, then spiraling out to the temples, where her hair was matted and damp, Elsa felt her relax.

It was the lot of hired women to be intimate with strangers. Elsa never balked at any of it; she simply began, in her measured way, the task at hand. When she was still a young woman, Elsa had washed the blood from the cotton batting she used each month. When Mrs. Channing labored far too early and birthed a tiny, lifeless child, it was Elsa who had scrubbed the fluid-caked blankets as the woman's sobs echoed through the house.

"What do you mean by your 'miserable destiny'?" Elsa whispered. She rose and stepped to the hearth, where a kettle of water steamed, then dipped a towel in it and wrung it out. She moved quietly, folding the cloth, and placing it on Miss Bixby's head. The woman sighed, tension falling away from her mouth.

"That would be another name for my husband, George."

"Forgive me, Miss—*Mrs.* Bixby," Elsa said. "I did not know that you were married."

"I'm not sure that I am, or I wish that I weren't. I am happy to be called *Miss*, if you don't mind. He ran off with another woman—well, he ran *around* with a henhouse full but ran *off* with just one. But now that I have made something good come into my life, some way of providing for myself that gets me out of that tavern, he has turned up once again to plague me."

"I am so sorry to hear it, Miss Bixby," Elsa said, her heart aching for the woman. There was no perfect life, married or not, mothering a child or nursing a child's absence. In wealth or poverty, there was no stretch of time in life that passed without trial.

"We just have to get on that train before George figures out that I've gone." Miss Bixby peered at her nurse with suspicion. "I suppose you think now that he has come back I ought to thank the Lord and take him in. I suppose you think that I should submit, or *cleave* to him, or whatever it is the Scripture decrees."

Elsa contemplated this question, for she wanted to give an honest answer. It was true that in marriage a wife *was* meant to submit to her husband's will, for the children were under her, she was under her husband, and he was under God. Such was the order of things established when Eve was conjured out of the rib. And, yet, to whom did a woman submit when she was *unmarried*, as Elsa was unmarried, fatherless, basically alone in the world? Elsa understood the answer to be that the woman should submit directly to the Lord.

"Well?" Miss Bixby said, annoyed. "Have out with it. Tell me how I have sinned."

"Just a moment," Elsa replied. "I am thinking."

If an unmarried woman submitted to the Lord, with no man to intervene between them, then all of God's commandments and comforts that seemed, in the Scripture, to apply solely to men might apply to her too. But what of Miss Bixby, *un*happily married—not only that, but *deserted* by a man who disregarded the duties of his position as a husband? Did this not mean that Miss Bixby too was, in a way, unmarried? If Mr. Bixby had returned, not to take responsibility for his obligation but to claim money that he had not earned by the work of his own hands, was that not a greater sin than Miss Bixby's refusal to take him back? *If the unbelieving depart, let him depart.* There was nothing in the verse about taking him back.

All the while Elsa pondered this, she continued to sweep her fingertips over Miss Bixby's brow, then dunked the cloth back in the hot water and renewed the compress.

"You have worked a miracle—the pain is subsiding," Miss Bixby said with astonishment in her voice. "You must have been told this before: You have a calming presence."

Elsa shook her head, feeling a swell of satisfaction. "No, miss. No one has told me that. But I haven't nursed very many folks. In fact, not even one, really, except for my aunt. And that was a long time ago."

Miss Bixby moved to sit up but Elsa put her hand on her shoulder. "Please—keep still awhile longer. Your body needs rest." Miss Bixby sighed but submitted to the warning. "I should like to quote some Scripture to you, with your permission. I think it applies well in the matter of your husband."

Miss Bixby pursed her lips. "Let's get on with it. Shall I be stoned for my ingratitude? Compelled to worship at his feet?"

Elsa sat very still. *"Come unto me, all ye that labor and are heavy laden,"* she said. *"And I will give you rest."*

Elsa did not believe, as she had been told Papists and pagans did, that the word of God held mystical power, as sorcery or the words of a spell, to transform one thing into another, an afflicted spirit into a spirit at peace. The power of these words to stun and humble grew from two simple things: their *existence*, that they had been recorded in history and passed from parents to children through so many generations and made plain, so that even one so lowly as a washing woman could read them; and their unadorned *truth*.

Miss Bixby lay very still as the words washed over her. After a moment, she lifted her arm from the quilt and felt in the dark for Elsa's hand, then pressed it into her own.

Clara

Later, Clara would reflect that she should have viewed the weather as a sign that this would be the first of several very bad days. The rain began around midnight, falling in sheets against the windows and flooding the gutters. The roof at Mrs. Ferguson's leaked; in Clara's room alone, five pots of various sizes caught the drips and *plinked* musically through the night, keeping her awake.

But Clara would have been lying awake anyway. It was May eighteenth, the day the brides would depart for Nebraska. The trip was nearly seven months in the making.

She dressed slowly in the gray gabardine dress, smoothing her thick hair into braids and coiling them at the back of her head. With her small trunk packed and waiting by the door, Clara swept her room for the last time and cast the gathered dust into the fire, now almost gone out. It felt impossible that she wouldn't be coming back here, but if this venture in Nebraska went as she hoped, then it was true. The room seemed too small to contain both the great joy and the great sorrow she had known in the last few years. George had carried her over this very threshold on the evening of their wedding. They were both drunk on champagne, and late in the night after spending hours in bed, he tied Clara's apron over his naked form and fixed them both a cup of tea. She had laughed so hard at the sight of the apron strings trailing down his bare behind, she had cried, wiping the tears with the back of her hand. A few months later in this bed she had birthed her son; in this bed, her heart went out of her body when he died.

Clara shook off the memories. Today was about the future, the massive, unbesmirched expanse of time that stretched out before her, the chance to start again and leave all her sorrow behind. Clara wouldn't let herself forget it. She shut the door and said her good-byes to Mrs. Ferguson, arranging for her trunk to follow her to the train station.

When she got there, she found the platform busy with travelers coming and going to points up and down the East Coast as well as the western cities. The first leg of the journey would take the women by train from Manhattan City to Buffalo, up the line of the Hudson River and then west along the path of the Erie Canal. The following morning, a ferry would take them to Detroit, and they would navigate a series of trains farther west, to Chicago, Rock Island, Des Moines, and beyond. It would be six days before they arrived in Destination.

Rowena Moore appeared first, dressed in the blackberry silk gown and a new bonnet, her ribbons pressed, her boots gleaming. She had followed the letter but not the spirit of Clara's edict regarding luggage. Her single trunk was enormous, more than half as tall as she was. Rowena stood next to it, likely waiting for someone to carry her onto the train atop a goose-down pillow.

If I have to kill her somewhere around Chicago, Clara found herself thinking as she glared at the trunk, *at least I'll have a place to stash the body*.

"Good morning, Miss Bixby," Rowena chirped with false sweetness. "I trust the train is on schedule."

Clara nodded. "As far as I know. We should arrive in Buffalo near midnight."

"What a long journey we have ahead of us. No doubt we'll be ragged by the end."

"Let's just pray we make it there in one piece."

"Indeed." Rowena stood with her hands clutched behind her back, her pert nose in the air. It irritated Clara to have her hovering around as the other brides arrived. Kathleen Connolly nodded good morning and stepped up onto the train when Clara pointed to the car they would all be sharing. The soon-to-be minister's wife, Anna Ludlow, and Elsa Traugott came next, each with a solemn look on her face that hinted at a mind full of pious thoughts.

Clara glanced at the large clock on the platform. Only fifteen minutes left until departure, and she had yet to find a seat for herself. Intimate friends Deborah Peale and Molly Zalinski arrived then, walking arm in arm as they had each time Clara had seen them since the fall. They wore matching red gloves and giggled as they waved in unison. Once inside the car, they pressed up against the windows, waving at the people walking by, without a bit of embarrassment that all of them were strangers. They were little more than girls, although they claimed to be twenty-one. Clearly, they had no idea of what lay ahead of them.

The train's engine started to huff, and noise on the platform increased. Clara glanced at her list. Three brides had yet to arrive. Just then, Cynthia Ruley and Bethany Mint came running, clutching their bonnets to their heads, the cases bouncing against their hips. Clara checked their names off the list; each was set to marry a man from the brewery. Porters began loading the trunks, and the crowd on the platform thinned. One more, Clara thought, and where could she be? She looked to the clock again.

"Miss Bixby!" a voice called from behind her.

Clara spun around. "Miss Bernard, thank goodness. The train is about to leave." Pauline Bernard was the fifth woman to correspond with Jeremiah Drake, and it had taken a letter from Dr. Calumet certifying her hair color to convince the man that she was a true blonde. When Clara saw Pauline's face, she closed her eyes. "Why are you crying?"

Pauline shook her head and pressed several dollars into Clara's hand. "I just can't do it."

Clara stared down at the coins and sighed. "Couldn't you have told me this a month ago? A week ago?"

"I tried to make myself go through with it. I really did. It all seemed like such a good idea until I really thought about the distance. You'll explain to Mr. Drake, won't you? I fear he is going to be very disappointed. He seemed so pleased with me."

Clara shook her head. "I'll try, Pauline, but you have to promise me you'll write to him yourself. Explain your situation."

Pauline nodded. "I promise. I wish I could pay you all the money back, but that's all I could scrape together." It wouldn't even cover the fare to Buffalo, much less the rest of the tickets Clara had purchased on Pauline's behalf.

"All aboard!" a porter shouted. The noise from the engine was deafening.

Clara stared at Pauline a moment longer, then shook her head and shoved the money into her pocket. She could cover this loss, but she dreaded having to deliver the news to the mayor and Mr. Drake. After all that extra work trying to find a woman to satisfy him. *I should have charged him double*, Clara thought. The porter yelled again.

"Pauline," Clara said as she patted the whimpering girl's shoulder. "It's all right. I understand. It was good of you to come and tell me yourself. But I have to go."

Sixteen long hours later, the train pulled in at Buffalo. The women filed sleepily down onto the platform and gathered in front of the depot while Clara paid a man to take the trunks to the dock where they would board the ferry first thing in the morning.

At the inn across the street, a long white building with black shutters, a lamp burned in the window and, mercifully, the innkeeper was expecting them. It was a mark of their exhaustion that no one, not even Rowena Moore, made a fuss about which room she should have. They doubled up based on who was standing nearby and climbed the stairs, barely pausing to say good night.

Only Molly, who ended up in a room with Clara, felt in the mood for a conversation.

"My, it's warm in here," Molly said, unbuttoning the back of her dress. She cracked the small window and the cool night air flooded the room.

"I think it's chilly," Clara said. She slipped out of her boots and dress, then got quickly under the covers. Her head throbbed. "Could you turn down the lamp?"

Molly sat down on the bed. Her cheeks were flushed. "It must be this wool dress." She hummed as she stepped out of it and hung it over the back of a chair. "Miss Bixby, would you believe Deborah is no longer speaking to me?"

"Molly, I'm very tired."

"And all because I told her that she really shouldn't write letters to Tom anymore, now that she's going to be married to someone else. Tom was her beau in Manhattan City. I think he's an absolute cad, but Deborah loves him. Even after he told her right to her face that he would never marry her."

"Molly, aren't *you* tired? It's been such a long day."

Molly turned the lamp down and slipped into the bed on the other side. "I feel strange," she said, putting her palm to her brow. She sighed. "It just seems awfully silly to me to go all the way to Nebraska if you aren't willing to leave Manhattan behind. 'This is an adventure, Deborah!' That's what I tried to tell her. 'We are at the beginning of an adventure.' But she just huffed and puffed and moved across the aisle from me."

Clara opened one eye and glanced at Molly.

"Do you feel ill, Molly?"

"Oh, I suppose not," she said. "I'm just worried about Deborah."

Molly lay on her back with her eyes wide and glistening in the dim light that came from a streetlamp in front of the inn. There was so much hope and excitement in her face, and it filled Clara with dread. So far Clara's life had been full of disappointments, but they were only her own disappointments. She had never felt responsible for another person's happiness before. It seemed she had been terribly presumptuous about what she could do for these women and men.

"I hope Deborah isn't still cross in the morning," Molly whispered.

"She won't be," Clara said softly. "Try not to worry."

Rowena

Rowena sat in her seat and felt the gentle sway of the train on the rails as it moved west out of Detroit on the third day of their journey. After the previous day's interminable and chilly ferry ride, it felt good to be back on solid ground. Outside the windows, the city passed away. They traveled through an orchard where the trees were just breaking into blossom, the temperature yet too cool to coax the bees out of their hives. Rowena's eyes felt heavy.

The day of departure hadn't come soon enough to save her from one last humiliation at the hands of her former social peers. Around noon on Monday a knock on the row house door had called Rowena from her writing desk, where she was calculating with a pen and paper just how much money she still owed her creditors.

She dropped the pen and sat up straight, her mind galloping; she hadn't heard a knock on that door in more than a year. Rowena stood, smoothing the wrinkles from her worn-out day dress. She had used it to teach herself how to do laundry—an unwise decision, it turned out. Too much soap made caustic wash water and damaged the fabric in places. Ironing it had been an equivalent disaster. In the front hall she opened the door just wide enough to peer out.

"Who's there?"

"Why, Rowena, it's Eliza Rourke."

"Oh, Eliza," Rowena said, allowing the door to swing open another couple of inches, but not nearly all the way. "My goodness, what a surprise. I wasn't expecting you." Rowena felt her heart break a little over the pale blue of Eliza's ribboned cap.

"Forgive me for popping by unannounced, dear. But it seems the only way I could get to see you, as you've declined the last three of my invitations, and answered none of my letters."

Rowena sighed. "I am sorry about that. I have had so many other engagements, you see. . . ." *Would anyone believe such a lie?*

Eliza raised an eyebrow. "Is that so?"

Rowena nodded.

"Well, then, I suppose you are faring better than I suspected." Eliza glanced down at Rowena's tattered skirt. "Still, might I come inside for a short visit?"

"Eliza, now is not really a good time."

"Please, Rowena—just for a moment? I've been worried about you."

Rowena sighed again and opened the door. "Please, do come in."

Eliza stepped inside, the skirt of her apricot silk walking dress sweeping the door frame. Rowena held out her hands to take Eliza's shawl. She turned to the wardrobe as Eliza took a few steps into the front hall. As Rowena turned the knob on the door, a strange impulse came over her. She glanced at

Eliza, then turned to the wardrobe again. With her fingers hidden under the expensive wool, she pinched the clasp on Eliza's diamond brooch and slipped it into her pocket.

Rowena hung the shawl on a hook and turned immediately, so that she did not have to see the look on Eliza's face as she gazed around at the nearly empty house. Rowena led her to the parlor and gestured to one of two remaining chairs on either side of the hearth. The sofas and the grand piano that had once made the parlor a lovely place for a party were gone, along with the game table and its ivory chess pieces, the china cabinet and its contents, and the bronze birdcage. Rowena had even traded the rich velvet drapery in for fabric and fashioned simple muslin curtains for the front windows.

Eliza faced her friend, her jaw slack. "Rowena," she whispered. "What's happened?"

"Whatever do you mean?" Rowena asked, stalling for time.

Eliza wrung her hands. "What do I *mean*? Your house is empty! Oh, I had heard rumors, but never in my wildest imagination could I have thought things were this dire for you."

"You make too much of it. I've only sold a few things to settle some matters related to Richard's passing."

"A *few* things?"

Rowena gave her a warning look and Eliza glanced away, changing the subject. "How is your father's health?"

"Improving," Rowena lied. "He has gone to live with a relative of my mother's. I wanted to take him in here, of course, but she insisted."

Eliza nodded, the awkwardness hanging between them. "Well, that's very kind of her and surely a comfort to you."

"Indeed, it is." Rowena straightened her skirt, folded her hands together in her lap.

A look of relief washed over Eliza's face. "Did you hear about the tea for Mrs. Wellington? The *frock* that atrocious Hannah Wallace chose to wear? A true horror of chartreuse lace. I tell you, it was the color of a small child's vomit."

This was what they had done together, Rowena realized. The basis of their entire friendship. Talking over the details the following day had always been more delicious to them than the party itself—how the soup was wrong, the glassware incorrect. Rowena and Eliza both believed in rules and their unbending application. Eliza was trying, Rowena could see, to reclaim their old common ground. But the truth was that Hannah's dress, however ugly, was finer than anything Rowena owned, than anything she might ever own again. She looked down at her lap.

Eliza responded with a tragic sigh. "Oh, Rowena, this is madness! I can't keep quiet on it. Why didn't you tell me you needed money? John and I would be happy to help you with—"

"I don't need money." Rowena felt her neck and ears grow pink. To be shamed this way, in her own parlor, was more than she could bear. She felt the beast rising in her chest.

But Eliza was not bright enough to heed the signs of imminent explosion. "Why, John was saying *just* this morning that it's time we found a governess for the children. My garden society meetings keep me away from home quite a bit these days, and, of course, things are going *very* well for John at the bank. You would be simply *perfect*—my Amelia could learn such fine manners with a real lady as her teacher."

Heaven help me, Rowena thought, as she felt the first wave of rage crash to the shore. "Your children," she said slowly, standing up to signal the end of the visit, "are *fat* and *dim* little creatures, just like their mother. Even the best governess could do nothing about that."

"Rowena!" Eliza screeched, leaping from her chair. "What is *wrong* with you?"

"Get out of my house." She pointed at the door, stomping her feet like a toy soldier. *"Get. Out. Of. My. House."*

Eliza stared at her a moment, stunned into silence, then shook her head into action. "Gladly," Eliza spat as she headed toward the door. She yanked it open and stepped outside, turning back to yell, "Mrs. Channing will be distressed a great deal to hear about your appalling behavior."

"Mrs. Channing can go to the dogs," Rowena shouted. "Right along with you."

Indeed, Rowena thought. *What* is *wrong with me?* There was once a time when she had been a model of composure and refinement; she could host a party of twelve guests or more and, with careful seating arrangements based on this one's love of music or that one's love of wicked gossip, keep the pairs and trios happily tucked in for hours. Rowena delighted and charmed every man who crossed the Moore threshold, but never so much that he should mistake her for a flirt. All of it only increased the collective opinion of Richard Moore, that he should be so dignified and clever a gentleman as to have secured the affections of this woman. They had envied him. *How far one can fall*, Rowena thought. Now, scarcely a day passed without one of her fits. The only hope for her was to leave this place, to start anew in Nebraska.

She had awoken long before dawn on the day of departure, determined to lock up the row house for the last time before the sun came up and illuminated the heart-wrenching task. She had found a tenant through the university, a man coming from England to study in New York. He would pay a modest rent in exchange for promising to keep up the place while she was gone. Of course, she could stay in New York and sell the house to generate some money for her father's care, but then where would she live? The money from a sale would last for a time, but not long enough. Marriage was the only permanent solution to her troubles, and marriage *outside* Manhattan the only tolerable arrangement. Rowena knew the truth, that she probably never would come back to New York, but saving the row house *just in case* offered a slight bit of reassurance.

She wasn't sentimental about belongings. After all, she had sold nearly everything of value in the house. Certainly every gift Richard had given her in their brief time together— a cameo necklace, a beaded shawl, an inkwell engraved with her initials—had been dispensed with long ago, turned into salt pork and flour.

But she had indulged in bringing along the one letter Richard had ever sent her, written in haste in a makeshift tent on some battlefield about three months before he died. Rowena had waited a long time to hear from him, worried constantly that he had been shot or come down with the flux or a fever. There were so many more ways a man could die than ways he could survive. Thinking on the litany was enough to drive her to the next bed over from her father in the asylum.

But despite all her disciplined effort to keep the ugly fantasies at bay, to focus on the image of Richard walking up the path and opening the front door, he'd died *anyway*. No prayer, no thought she held on his behalf had made a lick of difference. *My own little wife*, the letter began, the words burned so clearly in her mind she didn't even have to unfold the letter to recall them.

As you know, I am no man of letters. Expounding on the sorrows and glories of this world is better left to the poets for I can do neither justice. But will you think me unmanly to say, Rowena, that when my heart thinks on you it pretends to be something a little like a poet, with a poet's wistful sighs?

Now that we are separated, everything on which I gaze has a vacancy. I try to boil my blood to do the work a soldier must and though I do hate my enemy I pity him too, just another man, wrongheaded in every way of course, but separated from his beloved as I am separated from mine. So much death as I have seen here seems to me utterly senseless when all of us at the last only want to get back home.

I must quit ere long for it is nearly bedtime, but if we were together, my own, it would be to bed perhaps, but not to sleep! Oh, Rowena, thinking of you in the blankets, your rose cheek on the pillow, calls my whole being into action. I will get home to you or die trying, of that you can be sure. Until then I remain your affectionate husband,

Richard

It was a good letter. She felt proud of him and a little bit sorry that there was no good reason, ever, to show it to anyone else. To have shared a conspiracy of love with another human being, to have created between the two of you a private world, full of words with double meanings, expressions and postures indicating something only the two of you could interpret—to have shared this and then to have the only person who shared in it with you taken away was a strange thing. Suddenly, Rowena was the sole resident of that little island, with no way, no desire, to reach the mainland. And yet, given enough time, she would die there, alone. The desire to be loyal to Richard and the instinct to fight for her own survival were at war within her, even as the train rushed west, its motion a constant reminder that she had already made her choice. The hardest thing in the world, she knew, was to know you had something marvelous *while* you had it. But that had never been Rowena's problem. She had known it very well all along.

They arrived in Chicago that evening, the train slowing to a crawl on the causeway tracks that passed beneath the brick archway of Central Depot. To the east, white-tipped waves rolled across the surface of Lake Michigan, nearly pink in the glow of the evening sky. On the other side of the train a stagnant lagoon bordered a narrow green strip of a parkland, and beyond the trees the wide stone walkways of Michigan Avenue bustled with pedestrians. Chicago possessed a fresh and deliberate order. There was an ingenuity to this growing city, a tirelessness that was missing in New York. Rowena's mother had a cousin who had settled here about five years back with her husband. Rowena knew she should have written to tell the cousin she would be passing through, but the stop was brief, and she really didn't want to have to explain what she was doing on a train bound for Nebraska.

The seven brides, plus Elsa and Clara, filed off the train and lined up in the anteroom of a dining hall on the upper floor of the station, sputtering and sighing and adjusting their gowns like a flight of doves on an eave. The proprietor looked up from his newspaper and grinned, then moved his eyes down the line of them, one by one, to find the prettiest face, as men could always be counted upon to do. Rowena nodded at him when his eyes lingered on hers, then glanced to either side to see whether the other woman had noticed her victory. She couldn't say for certain.

Miss Bixby stepped forward and told the man how many were in their party, then passed a handful of notes to him when he told her the price. He held the money pinched between his fingers and used the same hand to gesture to a waiter standing on the other side of the room. The man wore a crisp white shirt and black cravat and stood as straight as a post. He nodded politely to the women and led them to a long table at the back of the room. They were serving a choice of beef ragout or quail, he explained, pea soup and milk rolls.

Rowena lingered at the back of the group, watching the proprietor. He turned back to his station near the bar, where his newspaper lay draped over his tall chair. Walking around to the back side of the table, he crouched down to remove a small box from an interior shelf and slid the money inside, then replaced the box on the shelf. Easing into the chair, he snapped the paper open. Rowena pressed her lips together, considering. Despite the optimistic tone she had taken while discussing the marriage with her father, Rowena knew chances were Daniel Gibson would be awful, and then what would she do? Little by little—Eliza's brooch, a man's pocket watch in Detroit, a bit of the money in that box, perhaps—Rowena was amassing insurance.

"Sir?" She worked an airiness into her voice, an admiring singsong. "Forgive the interruption."

He lowered the paper, then cocked his head to the side when he saw to whom the voice belonged. "Why, miss, it's my pleasure to be of service. What may I do for you?"

"If it's not too much trouble, might I ask for a hot towel?" Rowena touched her face, miming embarrassment. "We have been traveling for so long, and the dust in Michigan was unbearable."

He stood, adjusting his suspenders to account for his shifting belly. "Of course. Let me speak to one of the chambermaids. I will return in just a moment."

"I appreciate your kindness, sir," Rowena said. She tipped her chin down and looked at him through the top row of her eyelashes. She could practically see the saliva pooling in the corners of his mouth.

"Yes, just a moment," he said again, then turned to the hallway.

Rowena moved closer to his side of the table and clutched her hands primly at the front of her dress. She glanced back at her traveling companions. They had been served their soup in porcelain tureens with delicate handles. A column of steam rose under each woman's chin. They engaged in a quiet conversation, a few giggles occasionally rising above the din. As each second passed, Rowena took an imperceptibly small step toward the back of the table, where the metal box shone on its shelf.

When they first married, Richard had said that her hands reminded him of two butterflies, with their constant fluttering motion. The buttons of her dresses astonished him as he fumbled to unfasten them in the dark of their bedroom, but Rowena needed no light to slide the pearls through the slits and back out again, to press the pins into the intricate twists of her hair arrangement, like a coil of sleek black moss. Her winged hands whispered over the bones of his pelvis as she pulled him toward her and inside. They whisked the hair from his brow, tickling down the cobblestone line of his backbone. He had clutched her fingers to stop their undulations for a moment, had brought them to his lips.

Those hands dipped now toward the nectar inside the metal box and skittered across the notes. In one smooth motion she had folded the money inside her fist, then locked the box and returned it as she pushed the banknotes up into the tightly buttoned cuff of her sleeve. Just then the proprietor returned with the hot towel perched in a bowl, and Rowena used it, smiling, to wipe the deed from her hands.

After supper they descended the stairs back to the platform and filed into their rail car. Rowena thought the group seemed sparse, and a glance at Miss Bixby confirmed she was thinking the same thing.

The woman rubbed a circle on her temple with two fingers.

"Miss Connolly," she said to the ginger-haired girl who wore a cheap lace collar under her shawl. There was no refinement whatever in the Irish, Rowena thought. Both the men and women were all bluster and utility, no grace. "Have you seen Cynthia Ruley and Bethany Mint? They were with us at the restaurant."

Miss Connolly shook her head. "They got on another train."

"What do you mean?" Rowena watched the lines in Miss Bixby's forehead deepen as she replied. "There *is* no other westbound train."

"Detroit-bound, back to New York. They said those soup tureens at the dining hall convinced them. They didn't want to live anywhere they wouldn't have fine china."

"Are you having a lark with me, Miss Connolly?" Miss Bixby asked. She seemed to be making an enormous effort not to glance at Rowena.

"No, I am not. I'd have liked to box their ears. I'm sorry to have to be the one to tell you."

Deep lines of worry marked Miss Bixby's forehead. "I don't believe it. Did they leave a note for me? A message? *Anything?*"

Miss Connolly shook her head again. "They said they weren't cut out for it."

"Obviously not," Clara said, wringing her hands. "But what am I going to tell their gentlemen?"

That was two more gone. The seven remaining travelers—Kathleen, promised to the homesteader Amos Riddle; Anna Ludlow, who was meant to marry the reverend; Molly Zalinski and Deborah Peale, bound for matrimony with a farmhand and the depot porter; plus Elsa and Clara and Rowena herself—settled back into their seats and the train lurched to a start. Two rows up a duet of giggling cut through the peace of the car. Deborah and Molly were hunched over a magazine they had bought from a newsstand outside the train station in Chicago. From their frequent gasps and the shrill sound of their laughter, Rowena supposed the magazine contained pictures of women in various states of undress. One of them, Deborah or Molly, had come down with a cold and her laughter broke down each time into a fit of dry coughing. It only seemed to make them laugh harder. "Really," Rowena muttered under her breath. They had no composure, took no pride in the visage they presented to the world, and they seemed an awful lot more like girls than women.

Rowena glanced at her umbrella leaning up against the seat and felt a tiny bit of relief. She knew she wasn't above taking matters into her own hands.

Clara

The next morning, Clara finally lost her fight against the hypnotic rhythm of the train as it neared Rock Island, Illinois, and fell into her first deep sleep in days, perhaps weeks. After waiting so long for this opportunity, her mind wasted no time in springing the latch on its trunk full of dreams. The images cascaded out like a collection of costumes backstage at a theater: fur and peacock feathers and masks, silks of black and red, boots and slippers and shawls. Benign things that would lull her into believing this dream would be a pleasant one. All of these fluttered before her eyes, and then the set shifted and Clara was climbing the stairs at Mrs. Ferguson's. Each soft thud of her boots on the threadbare carpeted stair echoed within her chest. The sleeping Clara ached to cry out to the walking version of herself in the dream, to tell her to stop, but it was no use. The long trip down the upstairs hall was agony.

Clara watched herself open the door. Inside, a third Clara lay on the bed. She was yellow and gaunt with childbed fever, restless and, herself, dreaming of another place and time. She looked at the walking Clara, and the dreaming Clara watched them both. There was a strange unreality about everything in the room, the way one feels standing between two mirrors that reproduce an imagine into infinity. The Clara in the bed turned her face to the wall, so that only the other two—the walker, who was unprepared, and the dreamer, who knew with deepening horror what was to come—saw George approaching the bed with the inert bundle blanketed in his arms.

His mouth was wrenched wide in panic. "Clara," he moaned, falling to his knees. A corner of the blanket fell away, and the tiny foot broke free. One imagines that a newly born infant's features will be indistinct somehow, as unformed as raw clay, but in fact the wrinkled arch of the lip, each knee and finger, contain all the complexity they ever will, only in miniature, and a baby comes into the world weary, as if he has already lived one long, tiring existence somewhere else. The bottom of this foot was pale, the white flesh giving way to blue. George touched his palm to the toes and hung his head.

"Clara. I think he's gone."

Clara's long, low keen silenced the train car. But what woke her was the sensation of air rushing into her lungs just after she let the sound loose. She opened her eyes and leaned forward in the seat, panting. Molly and Deborah crossed the aisle and kneeled at her feet.

"Miss Bixby," Molly said, her hand on Clara's shoulder. "Are you all right?"

Clara waited a moment before sitting up, then opened her eyes and blinked at them. All the horrors went back into the trunk and she slid the lock into place. She nodded. "Yes. It was just a dream," she said. *A dream of a memory*. But how real could a thing be if no one else in the world, besides George and Dr. Calumet, of course, knew that it had happened? Clara had kept the pregnancy a secret, had kept the baby's death a secret too, for so long that she sometimes wondered whether she had conjured him solely in her mind and not out of her body. Clara felt thankful she had awoken on the train before the part where George went away and came back, drunk as she had ever seen him, with a tiny casket under his arm. "It's all right, girls," she said. Clara smoothed her skirt and focused on her breath.

She turned to look out the window. Up ahead what looked like a low fog obscured the trees and sky. *How odd*, she thought, for in Chicago it had seemed too cool for fog. Then she heard the hissing of something making contact with the exterior of the train, like a box of straight pins tipped over on the floor.

The train slowed. A man in a navy blue uniform entered the car and clapped his hands.

"Attention, please. We have crossed paths with a hailstorm, as you probably can hear." The man had to raise his voice above the din, and the train continued to slow as he spoke. "It is very dangerous for us if the rails become icy, so we will be delayed for a while as we assess the strength of the storm."

A few women groaned with frustration and others began whispering speculation.

"Ladies," the man said, holding up his hands. "There is nothing to fear. You are in good hands." He seemed to take a little too much pleasure, Clara thought, in imagining himself to be their rescuer. She began to calculate how much the delay would cost her.

On the fourth night of the trip, they stopped in Rock Island, arriving late because of the hailstorm. Clara found a farmer's wife willing to host them for less than what the town's only boardinghouse charged. If there was any benefit to the group's diminished size, it was that accommodations were easier to come by.

The woman had a large pot of soup waiting for them, along with a plate of hard biscuits and a stack of tin bowls. Unlike the disinterested innkeepers in the cities, she was eager to know everything about the reason for their journey.

"So, you're *all* to be married, then?" the farmer's wife said.

She wore a simple yellow kerchief over her hair and glanced around her table at them, astonished. The brides nodded as they dug hungrily into the soup. The trip was beginning to wear on everyone. The white cuffs on Kathleen's dress were dirty and frayed. Molly's eyes were ringed with dark circles, and Deborah had hardly giggled at all for an entire day.

"What a trusting bunch!" she said.

"Not all of us," Elsa said. Clara realized she and Elsa had barely spoken since leaving New York. She seemed even more coiled in on herself than usual, contemplating everything but saying little. The journey must have been hardest on Elsa, given her age, but Clara hadn't once heard her complain. "I'll be working in a man's house."

"And I'm responsible for this whole endeavor, come what may," Clara said.

The farmer's wife shook her head. "My, my, my. Well, the least I can do to help is to see that you get a good night's sleep. I don't have many extra rooms, but there is a sofa in the parlor, and I've laid out some blankets in the pantry. I do have my daughter's room upstairs, with her off on her honeymoon."

"Miss Bixby should take that." Kathleen spoke up, shoving the last spoonful of her soup into her mouth and reaching for another biscuit. She glanced around the table and dared anyone to disagree with her.

Clara smiled at her. "No, it's all right."

"After the day you've had? You need sleep, Miss Bixby." The others nodded.

"Well, I'll take the room if Molly stays with me." Molly glanced up at Clara, her eyes glassy, and coughed in response. "I don't think her cold is getting any better."

At dusk they scattered throughout the small house. In the morning they would take a ferry across the river to Davenport and then the Mississippi & Missouri rail to Des Moines. As big as any of them had ever pictured this country, it had turned out to be bigger. The traveling felt numbing, endless. Clara's exhaustion was made worse by anxiety about what would happen when they finally arrived in Destination. In her mind, she tried to rehearse what she might say to the men whose brides had backed out, but the words wouldn't come. She knew she needed sleep.

A moment later, sleep, too, became impossible. As Clara helped Molly up the stairs, the fatigued girl stopped and glanced at a framed portrait on the wall. It was of the farmer's daughter in a gingham dress, standing next to her horse. "Oh, how pretty," Molly exclaimed. She stiffened suddenly, then lifted her hand to touch her shoulder. "Oh, my neck," she said, swaying on the step. "It's so stiff." She winced, trying to turn her head, then collapsed and fell down the stairs.

Clara's cry roused the house, and Kathleen and Deborah rushed to help Molly back through the parlor to the sofa. The farmer's wife touched Molly's brow.

"This child is burning up," she said.

Deborah began to wail. "Oh, Miss Bixby, she's had a fever for days and days. Since before she left. She made me swear not to tell anyone. She *made* me swear."

Clara's mouth hung open. How could she not have noticed? She felt frozen in place. "Oh, Deborah."

"She needs a doctor," Kathleen said.

Elsa appeared at Molly's shoulder with a bowl of water and a cloth. "Get her shoes off," she said quietly to Anna, and they went to work. Molly came to and asked what all the fuss was about. She tried to sit up but Elsa pressed her shoulders firmly into the cushion. The farmer's wife recruited Kathleen to come with her to call on the doctor, but he lived a mile away and there was no telling whether he would be in. "And he works mainly with horses," she said, "so I don't know what good he will be."

After they left, the women fell asleep one by one clustered around the sofa, some sitting up, some lying on the floor. Clara sat in a chair by Molly's head, stroking her hair as she slept. A clock on the mantel ticked loudly in the silent room and Clara prayed. When Kathleen and the farmer's wife came back an hour later, alone, Clara's face fell. There was nothing they could do but wait.

In the morning, though, Molly seemed better. She barely remembered her fall the night before, though she had bright purple bruises on her knee and shoulder. Elsa brought her a mug of cold water and she drank it down, then ate a biscuit spread with jam. Clara sat back in her chair watching her.

"Miss Bixby, I feel fine now," Molly said. "Really. I'm so sorry to have given you all such a scare."

Clara shook her head. "You may feel fine, but I don't think we can go ahead until you've had another day of rest and we can get the doctor here to see you."

"Oh, please," Molly said, her eyes filling with tears. "We've come so far. We have to keep going."

"Don't be foolish, Molly." Deborah sat beside her on the sofa and took her hand. "You need to get well first."

"I'm well. I really am! What do I have to do to prove it to you? Do you want me to eat something more? Do you want me to dance a jig?" Molly stood up and twirled, giggling.

"If she says she's well, she's well." Rowena stood next to the table, with her hands on her hips. "I think the rest of us should go on, at least. The ferry leaves in an hour."

Molly clasped her hands under her chin. "Please. Please let me take the ferry with you. It's only an hour across the river. If I feel badly when we get to the other side, I'll come back here, and you all can go on. Don't let me be the reason you miss your train."

Clara looked at Elsa. She shrugged. "She *is* eating."

Clara shook her head. She was too tired to fight anymore. "All right."

The ferry left the dock twenty minutes late, and once it reached the Davenport riverbank the women had to run to make their train. Molly clutched Deborah's arm, her face sweaty and pale, and they rushed into the car.

"I'm *fine*," she hissed at Clara.

Iowa stretched on either side of the train like a vast sea, and meadowlarks hopped from one patch of purple prairie phlox to the next. The train chugged over the yellow land. Across the aisle, Elsa stared out the window.

"What do you think of it?" Clara asked. "It's so . . . empty."

"I was just thinking that," Elsa said, a kind of wonder in her voice. "If you got lost out there, how would you find your way back? How would you even know you were *lost*? Every mile looks just the same as every other."

"Are you nervous about meeting Mr. Schreier?"

Elsa shook her head. "I don't have to like him, only work for him. My lot is far easier than what the rest of these young women have to do."

None of the risk, and none of the reward, Clara thought. But none of the suffering either. It seemed like a wise trade.

Halfway through the trip, Clara handed out the sandwiches the farmer's wife had packed for them, ham steaks and salty cheese on thick slices of bread. Deborah unwrapped her own and held Molly's on her lap while Molly slept, her forehead resting against the glass, a shawl draped across her shoulders and tucked under her chin.

"Don't worry," Deborah said when she saw Clara give Molly a worried look. "She's snoring. I can hear her."

But when they arrived in Des Moines, the train a black snake slinking through the darkness, Molly didn't wake up.

Rowena

Of course, it was terribly sad that Miss Zalinski had died. Rowena wasn't arguing otherwise. But what sort of foolish girl would undertake a journey of this length knowing she was ill? She had put them all at risk, the way they were traveling together in such close quarters. Now the brides would all worry over every little sniffle and cough. Miss Bixby should have done something to stop it, Rowena thought, but alas, she did not. They were delayed two days in Des Moines making arrangements for the girl's body to be transported east. Rowena overheard Clara telling Elsa that she was forced to spend much of her remaining funds on their board and on the return fare for Molly. The girl's family was poor and could barely afford to send her father to meet the train in Chicago and bring her body back to New York.

Rowena stood very still just outside the door to the kitchen at the inn so that she could continue to eavesdrop. Clara, it seemed, had agonized about whether to write to the mayor and deliver the bad news, both about Molly and about the fact that she would be delivering far fewer women than promised. She worried all through the night about what would happen when the men learned that some of them would not have wives after all—and that most of their money had been spent. In the end Clara decided not to write ahead. The news wouldn't reach the men much faster than the women would. They would learn of their misfortune soon enough.

Deborah Peale cried through all six hours of the bone-rattling trip by coach from Des Moines to Council Bluffs. She rested her cheek on Miss Bixby's shoulder. The rest of them were quiet, chastened by what they had seen but determined to move forward. Rowena certainly felt determined. Nothing was going to stand in the way of her marriage to Daniel Gibson.

When the coach finally slowed as it approached the Missouri River, the women pressed close to the windows on either side to get a good view—they had seen very little water since Chicago. Both banks were thick with trees that grew right down to the water's edge. The river was low after a dry spring, and the water splashed against a rim of rocks, lacy with weeds and moss.

The coach stopped at a small depot. Passengers continuing west would board the Lone Tree Ferry across the river to Omaha, then file onto another train. From a distance, the river had seemed like an inconsequential ribbon unspooling across the landscape, but from the slow-moving boat it was as wide as a lake, a lake on the move, hightailing it southeast to St. Louis even as they moved west across its belly.

Omaha was nothing more than a grid of several streets and a few dozen identical wood-framed buildings, plenty of horses and wagons, and a smattering of soddy houses on the outer ring of town. Manhattan City had layers of history: an inner core with buildings older than the Republic, dotted and encircled by additions from each new architectural trend. Lanes wound circuitously around ancient trees and ponds and cemeteries; as the city grew, improvements were made to the existing framework, but the original was never usurped, only augmented, like a new layer of shingles hammered over the old. Here in eastern Nebraska was a town built all at once where, ten years before, there had been nothing. It had a sane feeling of absolute utility. It was unencumbered by the past and its mistakes, by sentimentality, by the daunting task of living up to some great man who had lived in your grandfather's time. It was clean and new and simple and yet seemed to be missing something at its core. It didn't yet have a story.

Within minutes they were chugging west and leaving Omaha behind. The land, of course, was as old as any other land, and it seemed to gaze warily back at the people driving railroad spikes into its back. The Union Pacific line followed the westbound course of the Platte River, a tributary of the Missouri, its banks shadowed by cottonwood trees, vines, and shrubs. Treeless land stretched north and south of the river, as flat as a planed board and feathered by impossibly tall buffalo grass. Every ten miles or so they passed a town, if you could call it that, two or three buildings leaning up against each other in the wind. After three hours the train finally slowed to a stop next to a depot with a painted sign that read *Destination*.

At least half the town seemed to have turned out to welcome Bixby's Belles from Manhattan City. The men stood in clusters of three or four, some with their arms crossed, some with their hands in their pockets, shifting from side to side and spitting intermittent arcs of tobacco juice into the dirt. Most needed a haircut and a shave. At first they tried, as men will, to hide their desire to see the women on the other side of the train car windows. But a few couldn't keep from cheering as the engineer hopped down to open the door to the car, unfolding the stairs to the platform.

Rowena stood and touched the back of her bonnet to be sure it was firmly in place. Miss Bixby stepped down first and greeted the men in the front of the crowd, and then Rowena, Elsa, Kathleen, Anna, and Deborah filed out. The six of them blinked in the brilliant sunlight. Eight days ago they had left Manhattan City with crisp ribbons and white gloves; now they were filthy and exhausted from the journey, their dresses rumpled, their cheeks pale. Only Rowena had taken the time to change into a fresh dress and splash water on her face from the fire bucket outside the engine car.

A strange quiet fell over the crowd, especially the eight waiting bachelors as their eyes moved over the arrivals and they wondered whether they might, on sight alone, be able to recognize the woman they had been corresponding with for months. They were so eager for these women it was palpable in the air, thrilling and a little ominous too. But then a few men seemed to realize something was wrong.

They glanced into the train car. "Where's the rest of them?" someone murmured. They glanced at each other, then at Miss Bixby, waiting for an explanation. Perhaps the rest of the women would come out of the train in a minute, or on another train in a day or two? A shipment of supplies from Chicago had come in along with them, and a pair of enormous railroad men were unloading the crates of nails, door hinges, and carpentry tools, as well as a giant spool of chicken wire, onto a wagon to haul it over to the general store. The scraping and clanking of their work, and the huffing of the idle train, were the only sounds anyone heard for a few long moments.

Anna Ludlow was the first to step forward when she saw the reverend in his black garb. Miss Bixby glanced at the cluster of papers she held in her hand. They flapped and curled over her fingers in the wind. "Reverend Crowley, allow me to introduce Miss Ludlow." The reverend was a tall man and seemed to stoop a little at the shoulders as a gesture of good faith to all the shorter men who stood nearby. He took Anna's gloved hand and she made a shade above her eyes with the other. They grinned at each other like schoolchildren, despite the fact that they were both well over thirty years old.

"It's a pleasure to meet you, sir," Anna said, her face full of relief.

Reverend Crowley nodded. "Like meeting an old friend."

Nit LeBlanc, Molly's intended, stood off to the side holding his hat and looking confused. Rowena knew it was him from the large goiter that hung beneath his chin. He had told Molly about it in a letter so that she wouldn't be shocked when she saw him, but Molly was undeterred. "I simply shall not gaze upon it," she had written back, so proud of the dignity in that sentence that she had repeated it to Rowena on the train. Miss Bixby noticed him too, and Rowena could see the dread cross her face when she prepared to tell him the news about poor Molly.

Amos Riddle had not taken the time to bathe before driving his wagon the five miles from his homestead to meet his bride. Rowena watched the expression on Kathleen's face shift like a cloud changing shape in two competing currents. He looked very little like the man in the tintype Kathleen had held on the train—"He said he wanted to send it so I would know what I was in for," Kathleen told her. But now the Irish bride had to look past the dirt on his face and hands, the sweat-stiffened lock of hair that fell over his brow, and discern whether beneath it all he might still be just a little bit handsome. She bit down on her lip, determined, Rowena could see, to be hopeful. Meanwhile, Mr. Riddle looked her over as one examines a horse. Rowena was so caught up in watching the two of them appraise each other that she did not hear Miss Bixby call out her own name and Mr. Gibson's. It wasn't until he stepped close enough to her to cast a shadow on her face that she turned.

"Oh," was the first word she said to her soon-to-be husband.

Daniel seemed momentarily stunned. He had seen her likeness and Rowena understood from his look of surprise that he had prepared himself to greet a young woman with some kind of deformity that lurked outside the edges of the frame. She was beautiful, yes, but it was probable that she had a lame leg, an incongruously fat set of hips, a revolting growth on the back of her head—something, anything, that could explain why such a beautiful woman would have agreed to come here, to marry *him*, sight unseen. Feeling a little amused by this, Rowena twirled and curtseyed with a flourish so he could see that she was hiding nothing. Her small frame was perfectly proportioned, her bust smooth and high with the help of her French corset. She could have sold it back to the dressmaker when her finances contracted and gotten enough money to feed herself for several more months, but she had felt that one couldn't put too high a value on the right foundational garment. Rowena saw instantly that she had been correct to do this. The urge to draw near to the female silhouette resided deep in the ancient center of a man and she had ignited it now in Daniel, not to mention several other of the nearby grooms who gazed jealously on. Rowena felt for a moment like Helen of Troy, capable of setting the entire prairie ablaze.

"It's a pleasure, Mr. Gibson," she said, never breaking eye contact with him.

He shook his head. "Believe me—the pleasure is all mine." He put out his elbow and she took it. He wasn't a bad-looking man, Rowena thought, not that it mattered in the least to the question of whether she would marry him. She felt sure she would have wed a goblin if he had money. He was not as tall as Richard but, still, of decent height, and he wore a well-made suit and hat. As they moved away from the crowd she nosed something slightly off-putting wafting from his dark hair, a rancid smell, like tallow.

"A few of us fellows were overeager to see you ladies, I'm afraid, and we've got a minister waiting inside the depot," Daniel said. The thick rope of his mustache turned up on the ends and wiggled above his lip as he talked. "What do you say, my dear?"

Her hackles raised at the endearment. The only men who called Rowena *my dear* were her father and Richard, and it took her a moment to remember that she probably wouldn't be hearing it from either of them ever again. She tried to consider Daniel's question with a clear head. Kathleen had explained that she would be heading on to the land office in Fremont to put in her claim for acreage adjacent to Amos's land. By law, they would have to wait three months to marry before the land could be combined. But Rowena had no interest in land and supposed she really had no reason to wait. "Mr. Gibson," she said, sidestepping the question. "You spoke of your business interests and clients in your letters, but despite my queries, you've never said precisely what it is you do for a living."

He chewed his lip for a moment, opened his mouth, then hesitated. "I'm the butcher," he said finally, pointing at the shop at the end of the lane with a cow painted on its sign. "I know I should have told you."

Rowena thought back on his enigmatic letters, in which he spoke of great ambition and certainty his business would grow now that products could travel by train to and from Chicago with ease. The way he avoided specifics made her suppose he was a trader of some kind, perhaps involved in something not quite legal that paid handsomely for the risk. But the assumptions had been hers. She saw now that she should have pressed harder, but in truth Rowena had wanted to believe he was what she imagined. She had been staking her entire future on it.

"It's all right," she said, straightening her back. "It's an honest living."

Relief washed over Daniel's face and he held out his hand. "Come on—let's go inside."

Rowena walked beside him into the depot, her chin trembling. She would get used to it, the blood-meat smell of him. She would simply get used to it.

Elsa

Elsa was the last woman to step down from the train car. After she did so, two large men carried the trunks from the train to a spot under the overhang. Miss Bixby moved among the new couples, checking names off her list. Elsa could see that the woman was once again in pain from her headaches. She touched her fingers to her temples as two men spoke roughly to her near the entrance to the depot.

Because Mr. Schreier had not expressed interest in Elsa's appearance, she had not included a likeness of herself in the letter she sent him back in the fall. Neither had he sent one of himself, and as Elsa stood alone next to her trunk under the overhang, she realized that she had no idea who he might be. Fifteen minutes passed. She watched as the crowd thinned. It was a clear, warm day, and the wind skimmed over the land. The horses stood patiently waiting for their masters to return, their manes whipping in the air.

Elsa was seized suddenly by a terrible thought: What if Mr. Schreier did not come? What if something had happened to him in the time that passed between their letters and this journey? Surely someone would have written to Miss Bixby to alert her that Elsa should stay in New York, wouldn't they? Elsa closed her eyes and tried to calm her mind. She was here and she would have to find a way to make the best of it. *I am in the palm of his hand.*

Over the howling of the wind, Elsa heard a creaking sound. She saw the dust cloud up before she saw the small wagon made of sun-baked wood lumbering toward the depot. One slow horse pulled it up the road. After a long time the man driving guided the horse to the edge of the platform and stepped down. He tied the reins to the post and started toward the platform, moving with the uneven rhythm of a limp. With each step, he leaned his upper body forward to compensate for the fact that he could not bend his left knee, then swung the leg forward, hopping to his right foot. He was concentrating so deeply on his movement that he seemed not to notice Elsa, but it soon became clear that he was walking straight toward her.

She took a few steps in his direction and he stopped.

"Are you Miss Traugott?" the man barked. He leaned on his good leg and struggled for breath. With one arm cocked at his hip, he squinted up at her.

Mr. Schreier had a hard, square face and a pinched mouth. Fear froze Elsa's voice in her throat. She struggled to reply. "Yes, sir," came the whisper, but it died in the wind. She nodded her head but couldn't tell if he saw it. His eyes were not focused on her but on something nearby, over her shoulder, and on closer inspection she saw that his right eye was clouded with a cataract.

"Everyone calls me Elsa, sir."

"Well, come on, then. I don't have all day."

He turned and began the slow uneven walk back to his wagon.

"Sir," Elsa said.

"What is it?" He turned angrily back.

"Sir—Mr. Schreier—what will we do about my trunk?"

Mr. Schreier waved and kept on walking. "One of the boys will bring it around later."

Elsa hesitated. In Manhattan City, only a fool would entrust her most precious belongings to a stranger. Thieves lurked in every alley.

Mr. Schreier stopped, waiting for her to follow him without turning around. "No one is going to steal your things, Miss Traugott."

"Yes, sir," she said. She followed him at a polite distance, understanding that though his way could be made much easier by the assistance of her elbow on his left side, it would be unwise to offer. When they reached the wagon, he waited for her to climb up first. There was only one step and Elsa doubted that she could with any dignity raise her knee high enough to get purchase. She reached up and gripped the top of the cart, feeling the seam of her shift stretch dangerously close to tearing. The toe of her boot slipped on the first try, but the second time she placed her foot and heaved up onto the step and then into the front of the cart. Her cheeks were pink from exertion and shame as she thought of the view Mr. Schreier had from down on the ground: his fat new housekeeper's ample behind.

Mr. Schreier freed the horse's reins and pulled himself up to the bench. The horse backed up with slow confidence, her blond tail twitching, then turned to the left and drew them along the main road. It cut straight west between the town's six low buildings, then out across the flat land.

They passed a handful of farms along the way, each with a barn much bigger than the squat sod house or rude cabin of uncut logs that stood alongside it, an uneven fence marking the boundary of the property. The doorway to each window-less structure was draped with a blanket in place of a door. Here and there a single cow cast its mooning gaze at them as she chewed her cud. Elsa took a breath, her body nearly vi-brating with a mixture of relief and fear. The dot on the map she had stared at so many times over the last six months was, truly, a *place*, with houses, with people who lived in the houses. All the while, life had been going on here.

She thought the air smelled strange, then realized she was noticing the *absence* of the scents to which she had grown ac-customed in Manhattan City. Here there was no garbage along the road, no excess of dung, no overflowing privies, no clouds of coal smoke. She smelled the clean, cloying scent of manure spread recently on the fields and the sweetness of the hay lining the cart. That was all.

Mr. Schreier rode silently along, his back curved and his hat pulled low on his head. After a while they turned into a lane on the left that led to a wood-frame house, its planed wood siding whitewashed long ago but now faded to a weath-ered gray. It was the first two-story house Elsa had seen, larger and more permanent looking than any of the others they had passed. He pulled the cart alongside and stepped down. Elsa followed him in through the side door, which led directly into the kitchen. The house had two doors, in fact, made of solid wood and hung on iron hinges in the door frames. It was certainly the finest house in town. And that made what she saw next all the more surprising.

The sink overflowed with dishes, caked hard with food and attended by a colony of flies. A line of empty cans stood on the butcher block, each with a spoon propped up inside it. Something had spilled on the rough planks of the floor and been left to dry into a sticky blob. The table was covered in newspapers.

Mr. Schreier passed through the kitchen without comment and into the sitting room. A bucket of coal sat on the floor beside the hearth, which was covered in a thick layer of dust and ash. Dried scrub leaves had blown in with the wind and settled in the corner. The room's one window was draped with a filthy curtain.

"I know it doesn't seem like much, but I have worked the last ten years and more to make this place what it is." Mr. Schreier set his hat on the table beside the armchair. "I have worked hard for every single thing that I have. I promise you that you will not want for anything—food, clothing, books, if you are interested in books. But the one thing I will not tolerate is dishonesty or theft or furtiveness. If you want something, ask for it. If you take things behind my back, I will have no more use for you here, understand?"

He crossed the room to a door and pulled it open. A rush of warm, stale air came down the stairs.

"Your rooms are up there," he said. "I meant to get up there and air them but . . ." He gestured to his leg.

"Of course," Elsa said.

"Well, aren't you going to have a look?" he said irritably.

She nodded. "All right." She stepped past him and made

her way up the steep staircase. Airing was unnecessary since the wind seemed to be blowing right through the walls. Elsa braced herself for more filth—perhaps a family of mice—but as her head rose above the floor she felt her heart swell with delight.

The room was dusty, yes, but there was, as there had been in her dreams, a large window that looked out over the land. There was a bed piled with quilts that, once laundered, would be cozy indeed. An armchair sat next to a small fireplace and a braided rug. Elsa walked from one end of the long room to the other. It was as large as the quarters for all ten of Mrs. Channing's laundresses.

"Well, is it all right, then?" Mr. Schreier called from the bottom of the stairs.

Elsa had to clear her throat to steady her wavering voice before she answered.

"It's just fine, sir. Just fine."

Clara

The men who had accosted Clara once all the women had left the depot with their partners now ushered her across the street to a building with a sign that announced it was the Town Hall. She might not have known otherwise, given its ramshackle state. With its unfinished wooden steps and porch and grease-clouded windows, it looked just like the tavern next door.

"Miss Bixby," one of them barked at her as they crossed the road, "you need to know you aren't going to get away with running a swindle like this on us. We have the law here, just the same as in New York."

Clara wrested her elbow out of his grip and smoothed the sleeve of her traveling dress. "Sir, you need not rough me up—I told you I'll be glad to go see the mayor and Mr. Drake. And this is *not* a swindle. It's just a big misunderstanding." They reached the double doors and Clara stopped, but neither of the men pulled it open for her. She grabbed the handle and threw the door open, nearly hitting one of them in the face with it. "After you, *gentlemen* of Destination."

The men strode through the small foyer and toward Mayor

Cartwright's office. They hadn't introduced themselves, but Clara felt sure they were Bill Albright and Walther Luft, whose Cynthia and Bethany hadn't made it out of Chicago because of the blasted soup tureens.

Clara's eyes widened when she saw the man sitting behind his desk taking notes on a long document. He was entirely different than she had imagined. His letters were written in such neat, careful script that she had pictured a diminutive man with soft features. But the mayor was enormous, broad-shouldered, with a great wind-tangled mane. His left-handedness had never been corrected, and he wrote with his arm curved awkwardly across the top of the page. Beside the desk, a brown-and-white dog dozed, then cracked one eye when they entered the room.

"Gentlemen," the mayor said, looking up. "I was just about to come to see how you all were getting on over at the depot."

"We're not getting on at all," said the angrier of the two. He stepped up to the front of the desk. "And you need to do something about it."

Mayor Cartwright raised his eyebrows and appraised the man for a minute, then set down his pen. "Now, let's just slow down there, Bill." The mayor put his palms on the top of the desk and stood, slowly. Bill's head seemed to shrink down into his shoulders as Cartwright's full height revealed itself. The mayor had a thick beard and dark blue eyes, which he turned, now, to Clara.

"Hello, there," he said, extending his hand. "I'm Randall Cartwright."

"Yes, sir, I know. I'm Clara Bixby."

He smiled and shook her hand. "It's a pleasure to finally

meet you in person, Miss Bixby. I trust these men have welcomed you to Destination."

Clara bit her lip. "They are understandably distressed, sir."

"And why is that?" Mayor Cartwright asked, turning back to Bill.

"All these months I have been writing to a girl in New York named Cynthia. But there's no Cynthia on this train. I'm starting to wonder if she exists at all."

"Oh, of course she does," Clara spat at him, losing patience. "You think I have time to sit around making up eight different women and keeping them all straight?"

"Not eight—obviously the ones who showed up on the train today are real." Bill turned to Cartwright. "But we're certainly short a few wives." Behind him, Walther Luft nodded, his thumbs looped through his suspenders.

Clara closed her eyes and took a breath, then began again in a softer tone. "Mr. Albright, I am very sorry about what has happened. Miss Ruley was keen to meet you—she told me so herself just a week ago—but when we arrived at the train station in Chicago she had second thoughts about leaving her family and decided to turn around," Clara fibbed. "I'm sure she will write to you to explain." She looked up at the mayor. "Sir, as I'm sure you can understand, there are limits to what I can do to compel these ladies to follow through on their promises."

Bill laughed. "Well, isn't that just what you *would* say, now that things have gone awry. You promised plenty, but now you can't deliver."

Clara heard boots on the wide planks of the floor behind her and turned to find a scowling man with a black mustache.

"Jeremiah Drake," he said with a curt nod. "And you must be Miss Bixby."

Clara tried to straighten her back. "Yes, sir. I am."

"Sorry, gentlemen—I got held up at the brewery." He turned back to Clara. "So what's my bride's explanation? A sick relative? Fear of Indians?"

"Mr. Drake." Clara sighed. "I worked very hard—*very* hard—to find a bride who met your specification for hair color. If you'll recall, you exchanged letters with several young women."

He laughed. "So I was too particular? *That's* your claim now that my . . . what was her name again, Bill?"

"Pauline, sir."

"Pauline. That's right. Now that my Pauline has failed to show up as promised?"

"Mr. Drake, I promise you—there's no deceit here. We've had some bad luck in choosing some young women who have not kept their word. But I certainly never set out to keep you from finding brides."

Drake ignored her and turned to Cartwright. "Mayor," he said, mockery in his tone, "this is *your* fault. You found this woman. You arranged all this. Now I see why you didn't throw your hat in the ring."

Mr. Cartwright's voice was steady. "Drake, you know that's not how it happened."

"Ever since Samuel and Terrance got killed, you've tried to use it for your own gain."

Mayor Cartwright groaned. "Got themselves killed, you mean. And what gain? They made it into newspapers across the country for the spectacle they caused, no disrespect to the dead. They've made Destination the wrong kind of famous. The only good that came out of it is that it brought us to Miss Bixby's attention. You all wanted wives. When Miss Bixby wrote to me, you asked me to pursue it."

Walther had crept toward the door, little by little, as the confrontation thundered on. The mayor's voice froze him in midstep. "You're awfully quiet over there, Walther. I suppose you been left in the lurch too?"

Walther nodded, his hands curling nervously in his pockets. "Seems that way. I'm told Miss Mint stayed behind with Bill's bride."

"What are you going to do, Mayor?" Drake said. "How are you going to fix this?"

Cartwright held up his hands and shook his head. "What do you expect me to do? Gentlemen, I'm sure you understand that life, and, for that matter love especially, offers us no guarantees. Miss Bixby can't be held responsible for the fickle nature of womankind."

"Maybe not," Bill said. "But she *can* be held responsible for taking my money."

The mayor's eyes widened and he turned back to Clara. "Ah. I see. *Now* we're getting down to it."

Clara looked down at her hands.

Drake hooted with laughter. "Boy, you really aren't that bright, are you, Mayor? Did you think we all just had broken hearts?"

Cartwright's cheeks pinkened and he turned to Clara, keeping his voice steady. "It is always, at the last, about the money. Don't you find that to be true, Miss Bixby?"

"I can offer these men about a quarter of what they paid, for it's all I have left. I couldn't recoup the cost of the train and ferry tickets, and there were other . . . complications." Clara thought of Molly's poor father, on his grim errand to meet her train in Chicago today. Molly's intended, Mr. LeBlanc, had gone pale when Clara told him about her passing. He said nothing about the money and Clara felt strange about bringing it up just then, but after expressing her deep condolences, she vowed to call on him soon to discuss what they could do about his situation.

"Why should we accept that mere sum?" Drake said. "She should return every penny."

Cartwright stepped out from behind his desk. "I'd like to speak to Miss Bixby and get this straightened out. Why don't you all go on home and I'll send word about what we're going to do."

"My brewery built this town, and this is how I am repaid?" Drake nearly shouted. He pointed at the mayor. "If you don't do something about it, I will."

"Mr. Drake," Bill said, feigning a realization as they left the office. "Wouldn't you consider this *fraud*, sir? We put men in jail for that, don't we? Why not her?"

"That's a very good point, Albright," Drake said loudly, over his shoulder as he stepped through the door. "A very good point."

The mayor cleared his throat. The angrier he seemed, the softer his voice became in the small room. "Good afternoon, gentlemen," he said as he closed the door behind the departing men.

Clara knew the thwarted grooms were angry, but the way they were acting made it seem to her that it was all a little like a game to them too, something that was between Drake and the mayor that didn't have much to do with her. She stared at a bit of mud on the floor, shaken by their accusations.

Mayor Cartwright gestured to a chair opposite his desk. "Miss Bixby, please have a seat." Once she sat down, he did too. The state of being indoors seemed to make him uncomfortable, as did the tight-fitting jacket that pulled across his wide shoulders. The dog stood up and hobbled over to her, one of its legs not quite falling into line with the others. It sat down in front of her knees. She saw that in addition to its limp, the poor dog was missing an eye and an ear.

"Who's this?" Clara asked, stalling for time.

"That's Sergeant."

Clara smiled at him and patted his head. "A military man!"

This made the mayor chuckle, then sigh. He folded his hands on his desk. "You can imagine that I am in a bit of a difficult spot here."

"Yes, sir," she said. "I understand why these men are angry."

"I should say so. You accepted payment for a service you did not provide."

"Well, that's not exactly the case, Mayor Cartwright. Much of the work required to match these men was completed back in New York, where I had to find suitable brides for them and facilitate their correspondence over the winter. I had to procure travel arrangements in advance, which will not be refunded, even though they've decided not to make the journey. We encountered costly delays. And one of our girls fell ill and died en route."

The mayor's eyebrows shot up. "My God. I'm very sorry to hear that."

"So, you see," Clara said. "It's not as if I have the money

sitting in a purse somewhere." Sergeant pressed his cold nose against the back of her hand, and she rubbed his head. He lay down on top of her boots.

"Businesses take a loss sometimes, but they don't expect their customers to cover it. You take it out of your profits. Out of your capital reserves."

"My reserves," Clara said sheepishly, "were not deep enough, it seems. I imagined that some of the brides might change their minds, and I did plan for that eventuality. But I never could have imagined losing Molly the way we did. Believe me when I say that I am writing to the families of the three who live and breathe to demand repayment. But it is a difficult task. It seems they pledged to go with me against their parents' wishes."

Cartwright's mouth was stern but his eyes couldn't hide his amusement with the whole debacle. "Didn't you ask them to sign any kind of agreement with you, binding their promise?"

"No, sir. I didn't think of it. And I had no one to advise me to do so."

"That you would ever think such a mercurial thing as marriage could be a matter of business!"

"I know," Clara said. "I shouldn't have trusted that they would follow through. But can you help me, sir, at least, to convince those men that I haven't broken any laws? My intentions were honest—you must know that."

"I do," Cartwright said. "But you may have noticed that my position doesn't mean a whole lot to folks around here. Jeremiah Drake runs this town and he does as he pleases. It's unfortunate that he happens to fall into the group of men who have been disappointed."

Clara twisted her handkerchief in her hands. "What am I going to do?"

"Do you have accommodations for yourself, at least?"

"I made a temporary arrangement with someone named Mrs. Healy. She said she rents out rooms. I had planned to stay until the new couples were settled and then I had hoped to have enough profits saved to move on," Clara said, thinking of the little white cottage. "I had a plan for my future, but I see now that I won't be able to achieve it anytime soon."

"Mrs. Healy is the only woman remaining in this town, and only because her husband was killed in a train robbery when they were traveling from Detroit to California. She couldn't afford to go any farther west. I think you had better plan on staying in town until we get this sorted out. Those rooms are above Mrs. Healy's tavern."

A hard laugh escaped from Clara's lungs and she sat for a moment with her mouth open, gaping at Mayor Cartwright. "Above a *tavern*?" she said.

He nodded.

"Above a tavern." Clara repeated the phrase once more, feeling the blood rush to her cheeks and her head begin to throb. She had traveled across five states, through a nightmare and a hailstorm, across a dusty prairie, losing these men's money, as well as the life of one young woman, not to mention thwarting George Bixby, all to find herself living penniless above a *tavern*, just as she had in Manhattan City.

"Are you all right, Miss Bixby?"

Another moment passed before Clara nodded and pulled herself together. "May I ask you, sir—Why *aren't* there more women in this town?"

Cartwright grimaced. "Homesteaders, including my uncle Kellinger, founded this town starting ten years ago, and Jeremiah Drake sank his inheritance into that idiotic brewery. For a while everyone was getting by all right. Making a life out here is no easy thing, you understand, and that was before the railroad. One shouldn't expect comforts or leisure. And the few women who were here surely didn't. But they *did* expect a little Christian civility. Unfortunately for them, when Durant and his ilk decided to run the railroad through Destination, we lost what little bit of civility we had. The workers were rough. They lived a kind of life that the farmers' wives found objectionable. And who could blame them? Drinking, fighting, gambling—the unholy trinity. But, you see, it wasn't the people of Destination who were causing a problem. It was the railroad men passing through. They had a corrupting influence on this town, and they left it forever changed, even though the railroad has brought us some revenue. It certainly fattened Drake's pockets. But the few women who were here and hadn't yet died of fever or childbirth eventually threw up their hands and went back east, or persuaded their husbands to move farther out away from town. I do think most of our men regret letting that happen. Of course, now all those rail jobs have moved west. And here we sit."

Clara nodded. "I really meant to help to change that. I hope you believe me. I promise you, you have my word that I will pay these gentlemen back, sir. I just need a little time."

"I'll try to hold them off," he said. "But Bill is right—should they organize themselves, which, fortunately for you, is doubtful, the law *is* on their side."

Rowena

The new Mrs. Gibson rode beside her husband as they bumped and shimmied down the dusty main road, then turned north on a narrow lane. It was a clear, gusty day. A small dog with a mangled ear came out from behind a tree and trotted happily alongside the wagon. Rowena glanced nervously at Daniel, feeling her confidence suddenly desert her. What was she doing here? Her gaze skimmed the collar of his jacket, then down his arms to his meaty hands, clutching the reins. His fingertips were caked with dirt. She shuddered to think that in a few short hours she might have to see this stranger without any clothes on, might have to feel those grimy hands grope her flesh.

He looked over at her with a shy smile. "I meant to inquire when you first arrived about your father's health."

"Oh, thank you," Rowena said. And right on time, here was a reminder of why she had agreed to this arrangement. "He is doing as well as can be expected. I owe you a great debt for your willingness to see after his care."

"It is the very least I can do, Mrs. Gibson," he said, trying the name out. "I am only honored that *you* would consider *me*."

Rowena felt her dread ease just a bit. Maybe he wouldn't insist that they rush into the nighttime visits. He seemed gentle enough, easily persuaded. She might have the upper hand, and if that was the case, she could bear it all just fine. Perhaps she would find herself even liking him a bit.

The lane wound through a handful of small sod houses near town. Farms spread across the land in the distance. Each house was low to the ground, curved on top like the back of a sleeping dog, and most had a clothesline stretched between the exterior wall and a post driven into the ground two dozen feet away. One had a well with a red-painted bucket on a pulley, which stood out against the palette of gray and brown and the pale green-yellow of the grass. Because the land was so flat, Rowena understood that she wouldn't crest a hill and have something unexpected revealed to her. Yet even as Daniel slowed the wagon in front of one of the soddies, no larger or more distinguished than the others, Rowena expected that the Gibson house was hiding somehow, behind a tree that wasn't there, off much farther in the distance where the view lost its crisp edges in the wavering heat.

"Are we stopping off here first?" she asked.

Daniel stared at her a moment, then broke into a smile. "What a delight you are, my girl. Always full of humor."

"What do you mean?" Rowena glanced at the narrow footpath cutting through the scrub to the low door of the house. On the line hung four sets of men's underwear, each one smaller than the next. A pair of antlers had been tacked over the door. Two of the points on the left one were broken off.

A young man of fifteen years or so came around the side of the house. "*This* is her?" he said.

One by one, three more boys appeared. Each one was six inches shorter than the one who came before, but that was the only variation in their appearance: fair, nearly transparent skin, icy blue eyes, spindly legs and arms that moved with the jerky motion of a jointed wooden puppet.

Daniel nodded, stepping down from the wagon. He crossed in front of the horses and offered his hand to help his new wife down. "Rowena, this is Sigrid. And Gustav, and Odin, and Dag," he said, nodding his head at each one down the line.

Rowena stared blankly at him, refusing to allow the truth to penetrate her mind.

"My sons." He waved his hand at the boys. "Well, come on."

"Wel-come, Moth-er!" the boys shouted in unison, their grins wide and bright. Their lips were a preternatural shade of red too intense for their complexions.

"We practiced that all morning," Daniel said triumphantly. He swept his hand across the general scene, like a magician on stage revealing the prestige of a trick. He was *proud* of all of it, Rowena realized with a growing horror—proud of the bare, scrubby land, the crude house, the ragged children. How was it possible that they could even fit inside the one-room house? Where did they sleep? Eat? Wash? It was a ghastly scene.

The hinge on Rowena's jaw had lapsed and her chin hung down. She stood, frozen, until a gust culled a cloud of dust from the ground and shot it up into her face. Rowena closed her mouth, waved it away.

"What's wrong, my dear?"

"Perhaps," Dag began in a tinny voice as he stepped forward. "Perhaps she is wondering about Ully."

"Of *course*," Daniel cried, jovial. "Sigrid, where's Ully?"

"Inside, Father. Too afraid to come out."

Rowena found her voice. "There's *another one*?"

"Ulrika Eleonora, my only daughter. She's just a tiny thing. Nine years old but kindly stopped growing around age seven." Daniel winked at Rowena as if this were funny. One horror after another seemed to come out of the soddy, out of his mouth, out of the mouths of his . . . *spawn*.

"*Ully!*" Sigrid shouted. "Present yourself at once!"

"Siggy, there's no need to be rude," one of the middle ones said, Odin or Gustav—Rowena couldn't remember which was which. The front door creaked open a few inches and a pale face peeked out.

"Come along, Ully. There's nothing to be afraid of." Daniel's reassurance coaxed her into the light, and Rowena reeled back once again. Oh, she was ugly. She wore a man's shirt belted at the waist with a piece of rope. The shirttails hung to the ground, skimming the top of a pair of enormous boots that must have been stuffed with cotton in the toes to keep them on her tiny feet. Her greasy hair was cropped unevenly at her jaw and parted down the middle, and she had a vulgar, pointed chin, the underbite of a terrier.

"This child is a girl?" Rowena whispered.

Ully clomped slowly, unsmiling, toward Rowena with her hands on her hips, then tipped her head back and looked up at her. "I am Swedish royalty," she said, her voice a squeak.

Rowena looked at Daniel. He shrugged. "She is—well, *named* for royalty, that is. My late wife was very proud of her heritage."

"We try to get Ully to wear dresses but she won't," Sigrid

said. "It was she who cut her own hair too. We honestly don't know what to do about her."

Ully scowled to be discussed as if she weren't standing right there before them. "You came from Manhattan City?" she said to Rowena.

Rowena blinked. What in the world was she going to do? She had prepared herself to accept almost any sort of shortcoming in Daniel because she couldn't imagine anything she wouldn't be able to endure. So what if he was fat or homely or cruel? Rowena could be cruel right back. Nothing mattered but the money he would send to the asylum. It was a business arrangement in which they both would gain. But this—this was too much to bear.

Ully stood expectantly. "Didn't you hear my question?"

"*Ully,*" Daniel reprimanded.

The little girl twisted up her mouth, then raised her leg at the knee and brought the heel of her heavy boot down hard on Rowena's foot. "Rude!" Ully shouted. "I *don't* like her!"

They all seemed paralyzed, waiting to see what Rowena would do. They didn't have to wait long. She turned on her heel and tromped through the grass up to the road, swinging her arms like a Viking. She walked in a straight line back toward the town where she knew she'd find the woman who was to blame for all of this.

Clara

Clara went back to the depot to claim her trunk and paid the porter, Stuart Moran—soon to marry Deborah—to bring it over to her new room and leave it in the hallway. It was after two when she got back to the tavern, and it was empty. She found Mrs. Healy in the kitchen, a plump, friendly woman who thanked Clara for shipping some sense out to the prairie. Clara paid her for the first week's room and board with the last of her money, then climbed the steps to her new home with the key pressed in her hand. She barely looked around the dark room before lying down and closing her eyes in fitful sleep.

She bolted upright and slapped her palm to her chest, gasping for a breath, at the sound of frantic knocking on her door. She understood that the dream had come on again, but her sleep had been shallow enough that she had been able to steer the walking Clara away from the staircase. The knock sounded again. Why wouldn't the porter leave the trunk and go away?

"Miss Bixby, I know you're in there."

It was a woman's voice, a pinched and angry woman's

voice, and Clara knew instantly the grating harpy to whom it belonged. She rose from the mattress and smoothed her hair before opening the door.

Rowena Moore stood in the hallway with her arms crossed, breathing through her nose in short bursts.

"Mrs. Moore," Clara said. "Good afternoon."

"It's no longer Mrs. *Moore*," Rowena said, pushing past Clara and into the room. "Thanks to you, it's Mrs. Gibson. Or as those children seem to have been taught to call me—*Mother!*" Clara closed the door. Rowena spun around on her heel. "How could you do this to me?"

"I don't know what you're talking about," Clara heard herself say. She had noticed upon their arrival that Daniel Gibson met the train with a minister in tow. Smart man, to get that marriage certificate signed before taking Rowena home.

"That is a bald lie, and it will be a judgment on your soul. You *knew* that man had five children. Why didn't you tell me?"

A defensive haughtiness broke over Clara's face. "Why didn't you *ask* him? It seems an awfully important matter to settle before agreeing to marriage."

Rowena held out her hands in a gesture of helplessness.

Clara shook her head, feeling a hint of remorse about her deception but fighting to keep it at bay. "How old are you? Can it *be* that you have not yet learned?"

"Twenty-five. Learned what?"

"That men will always disappoint. Will always fall short."

Rowena opened her mouth to retort, then stopped and pursed her lips. "Not all men," she said quietly. "Not my Richard."

"But," Clara said, softening her tone, "he is *dead*. Had he lived long enough, he would have failed you eventually." Clara had once felt George would be forever steadfast, forever in love with her. But she was wiser now. Perhaps Rowena could be wiser too.

Rowena's nose grew pink and she sniffed, her eyes welling with tears. "You know nothing," she said, her arms rigid at her side, refusing to fish in her pocket for a handkerchief. "If he had lived I would be spending the rest of my life cherishing his every flaw. And, happily, I never would have had to meet you."

So she will be impervious to my advice, Clara thought. "Well, we are all perfect in death, I suppose."

Rowena stared at her. "I don't understand it—why do you hate me so? I've never done a thing to you."

"Hate you? I don't hate you. I have no feeling for you, good or ill." Even as the words formed on her lips, Clara knew they weren't true. She *did* hate this Rowena Moore Gibson, hated everything about her: her foolish youth, the petite frame suited for fine garments and parlor dances. So the girl's beloved husband had died. What of it? Did she suppose her own tragedy was somehow remarkable? It was as common as dirt. Clara refused to feel badly for Rowena just because it had taken her so long to discover how cruel life could be.

Rowena sank down in the chair and put her head in her hands. "What am I going to do?"

"I suppose you could go back to New York," Clara said.

Rowena looked up at her. "Go back to what? I have a tenant in my house now—it's the only way I can pay the taxes. And Daniel is paying for my father's care. He has been paying, if you can believe it, since we first exchanged letters. He is as trusting as I was."

"So you'll stay then," Clara said. "And make the best of it."

Rowena stood and walked over to her. "Yes. But there is no question," she said, pointing her finger very close to Clara's face, "that what you did is *wrong*. And trust me when I say that I will make you very sorry."

Elsa

As soon as she rose on her first morning in Leo Schreier's house, Elsa set to work. The man was fortunate that vermin had not fully claimed the place, the way he let food sit out to rot, left soiled clothes heaped on the floor and stagnant bathwater in the small, round tub. By the end of the day Mr. Schreier's laundry hung on the line, including a pair of overalls that had been so crusted with filth, Elsa had had to boil them for hours. The dishes, too, had been washed, all the surfaces in the kitchen rubbed down with vinegar. Elsa opened the window to air the place, then dragged the one rag rug outside and beat it with all her might. She thought about how pleased Mr. Schreier would be when he saw what a difference she could make with just one day's work.

He stayed out in the fields until the sun was low and orange. It was marvelous to watch the vibrant disk slip over the line of the horizon. In New York there were so many buildings in the way, Elsa hardly ever noticed time passing. But out here there was nothing to keep you from the fact of the heavens doing their work, nothing to shield you from the wonder and terror of the sky's size. A man standing on a prairie in Nebraska could not escape an awareness of his insignificance. For a woman, Elsa supposed, it was slightly less jarring. Most women knew how insignificant they were without an enormous sky to remind them. And, anyway, Elsa liked feeling small for a change.

She heard the sound of Mr. Schreier using the boot scraper, and then the door creaked open. He sniffed as he walked into the kitchen, then froze, gazing around. He hung his hat on the hook by the door and walked into the sitting room, where Elsa had lit a small fire and the lamp next to his armchair. He had yet to bring home groceries or offer to take her to purchase supplies, so she had made do with what she found in the small cellar beside the house: potatoes and sausage. The pot sat on the stove, waiting for him to come in.

Mr. Schreier stared at Elsa. "Where are my newspapers?"

She bit her lip. He didn't seem to notice that his house was spotless. "I thought I would straighten up a little bit, sir. Are you hungry? I've got supper here."

He ignored her and limped back into the sitting room, his eyebrows contracting, his lips pursed. He seemed to be chewing on the inside of his cheek when he came back into the kitchen and stood before her.

"*Where are* my newspapers?"

The ink on some of them had been smudged and smeared beyond recognition. The out-of-date papers came from all over: Chicago, Detroit, St. Louis. In Elsa's opinion, not that she would ever express it, Mr. Schreier was too much interested in the things of this world, in war and politics and commerce, when his own soul should be his object of study.

"Be warned, woman—I'll put you out if anything happened to them. You can walk back to New York, for all I care."

Elsa stepped over to the shelves on the back wall of the kitchen, behind the table. She pulled the basket down from the top shelf and tipped it toward Mr. Schreier so that he could see what was inside: each of the papers, neatly folded.

She heard him swallow, then let out a breath.

Elsa gave him a hopeful smile and he grunted, leaning his cane up against the wall and sitting down at the table.

Earlier that day, Mr. Schreier's farmhand Nit LeBlanc had come up to the house because his arm was bleeding from a cut on a nail. The cut was about four inches long, on the pale, hairless inside of his forearm, but not deep enough to worry about. He sat at the kitchen table pressing a reddening towel against it while Elsa ripped a remnant of linen she found in a sewing basket upstairs into strips to make a bandage.

While she worked on the cut, Nit told her about the farm. Despite the poor condition of his leg, Mr. Schreier kept a hundred acres of wheat and barley and a year-round kitchen garden that by the middle of June should bloom with lettuce if they had enough rain. East of the house were several acres of tall prairie grass, and when the weather was fair the milk cow and sheep and two horses grazed in it. When the cow—Leo called her Honey—lay down on her side, her jaw always working, working in a circle, they knew it was time to get all the animals in the barn. When the rain came, it gushed from the sky, the way feed streamed out of a burlap sack when you ripped your knife through the bottom seam. Too much in one night could wrench the sprouting barley right out of the soil. But Destination and environs hadn't seen rain in weeks. It had been a strange year so far, Nit explained. They expected drought in August, but no one could remember two weeks in May without rain.

The previous season, Mr. Schreier had allowed Nit, whose family had come from Quebec a generation back, to build a soddy on the western edge of his parcel and employed him as a farmhand. Nit intended to put in a claim for the land adjacent to Schreier's, but he had to save up some money first. It cost only ten dollars to file for as much as 160 acres, an unthinkable generosity on the part of the government for anyone who had come from the Old World, but while the land was free, breaking it, making it yield something you could live on, was not. A claimant had only five years to make the land produce. Nit would need tools, a team of horses, and seed, at the very least. In the meantime, he did the work Mr. Schreier could no longer perform.

"Does it hurt an awful lot?" Elsa asked as she tightened the bandage and tucked the ends under the linen.

Nit shook his head. "No, ma'am. I'm busy enough to keep my mind off it. Leo probably told you that he has a ewe we aren't sure about. She got loose twice over the winter, you see, once after Christmas and once at the start of February, and we don't know which visit with Mr. Gade's ram was the, well, *fateful* time. It takes about five months, but we aren't sure when to start the count from. She's always been a shy one—won't let us get near her to see."

Elsa nodded. But Mr. Schreier hadn't told her anything about the sheep, or the existence of Nit. They had hardly spoken at all, in fact. Elsa woke to the sounds of Mr. Schreier working in the barn a good two hours before the sun came up.

At midday he set two pails of milk outside the kitchen door next to a bowl and cloth. The bowl he took over to the pump and filled with water, then plunged the cloth into it and wiped it across his face and hair. He rubbed it vigorously over the back of his neck, up the meaty ridges of his oversized ears. Elsa knew how cold this water was from the first time it splashed over her hands as she tried to learn how to work the pump. It turned her skin white, made her two front teeth ache. But the cold didn't seem to bother Mr. Schreier. He would finish washing up, then splash the water across the lettuce and come silently through the kitchen door, wiping his boots on the mat.

"Do you have any family here, Mr. LeBlanc?" she asked as she wiped the dried blood off his hand with a rag.

He shook his head. "I had my hopes up that a bride might arrive on that train for me." He pressed his lips into a line. "But it was not to be."

Elsa nodded. "I got to know Miss Zalinski a little bit on our journey. She was a kind girl. It's very sad, what happened. For your sake and hers."

"Zalinski," Nit repeated to himself. "Do you happen to know her Christian name?"

"It was Molly," Elsa said. "Margaret, I suppose."

Nit smiled. "She never would tell me herself."

"What will you do about your money? A few of the other men whose brides didn't arrive seem to be fighting awfully hard for theirs."

"It is a loss, surely, but I can't see holding Miss Bixby responsible for the girl's death. It was just God's will. I should have listened to my father and found myself a Québécoise.

Every single one of them is beautiful and devout. But why in the world would any of them leave Montreal to come *here*?"

Elsa thought this over for a moment. "Well, why did *you* come here, Mr. LeBlanc? Sometimes people looking for a fresh start don't care so much about where they go."

"I suppose." He had wiggled his fingers and stood up. "Thank you for the bandage. I should get back to work."

Now she set Mr. Schreier's dinner down in front of him at the table and he nodded his thanks, then bowed his head on his knuckles. He didn't invite her to sit down, and so she stayed over by the cutting board next to the sink and busied herself kneading dough and peeling potatoes for starch. Anything to keep in motion so that he did not have to feel the burden of her.

There were so many things she wanted to ask him. If she needed something from the grocer or Baumann's store, would he take her there in his wagon? Or should she walk over on her own? It was about two miles into town. Elsa didn't mind walking, but she fretted over her slow gait, the hours of work she would miss. And how was she to pay for things? The thought of asking Mr. Schreier for household money filled her with dread.

And then there was the matter of Sunday meeting. She didn't know what she would do if he didn't attend or tried to prevent her from going. He had professed faith of a sort in his letter, but he seemed not to like the reverend. So much of her fate was in this man's hands, and he was an utter stranger to her.

That night, as she pulled the quilt up to her chest—a quilt surely assembled by the loving hands of the late Mrs. Schreier when this home was new and her husband was a younger man—Elsa thought about the shape her life had taken. The robust beginning, in the sweet cocoon of her family; the pinched everlasting middle spent alone in a city completely indifferent to her existence. And now this. What would she be here? What would she do? She had known every shade of loneliness in this world and, yet, the Lord was always nearby, speaking softly in her secret heart. Was he there now? Elsa tried to listen for the murmur but sleep answered first, sweeping over her like a spell.

Summer 1867

Clara

The rented room above Mrs. Healy's tavern was not just as bad as the room at Mrs. Ferguson's—it was worse. In New York, Clara had lived three floors above the men who shuffled in and out of Mr. Rathbone's; here she slept in one of four small rooms directly above the saloon. The cigar smoke wafted up through the floorboards and clouded her tiny window, and each time a man won a game of poker, the boot-stomping was loud enough to fool her into thinking they were playing at her bedside.

For her weekly rent she got the mattress, a table and chair, and a heavy iron pot for boiling water on her flimsy stove. A parade of drifters occupied the room next to hers, each one "just passing though" town, usually on foot or horseback because a train ticket was too dear. Passing from where? Clara thought. Passing *to* where? Where was there to go? More than once she met these men in the hallway or on the stairs, accompanied by a busty woman with a smear of rouge on her cheeks. Reliably, each man introduced the woman as his "cousin from Omaha."

These cousins, Clara knew, lived all together in the long log house at the western edge of town. That first week, for a lark, they went as a group to Cheyenne for a few days to get a relief from Destination's dullness. Clara could tell the cousins had cleared out because the tavern filled to bursting that night and a fight erupted over nothing more than a bit of ale sloshed out of someone's glass. When the cousins returned, they got off the train wearing the same clothes they had been wearing when they left, now filthy, the paint gone from their faces and replaced by the sallow complexion of the ailing. More than one had a fresh purple ring around an eye, a black gap where a tooth used to be. But at least once they were back, things settled down significantly in the tavern for a while.

On the first Monday in June, Clara sat in her chair writing out a list of things Mrs. Healy had asked her to pick up from the store for the tavern kitchen. Clara had explained her situation, how she had to find a way to earn back the money she owed the men, and Mrs. Healy agreed to let her work in the tavern in exchange for room and board and a small wage. She heard a soft knock and opened the door to find Deborah Peale, now Mrs. Stuart Moran, clutching a sodden handkerchief in her fist.

"Deborah," Clara cried. "What's the matter?"

"Miss Bixby, you have to help me." Deborah's hair was parted severely down the middle and pinned behind her ears. Dark half-moons hung beneath her eyes; she seemed to have aged years in the eight days since their arrival.

Clara glanced behind the girl out into the deserted hall-way. "Well, of course, I'll try. Come inside."

She settled the trembling woman in the chair, then sat down across from her on the edge of the bed. Clara patted Deborah's knee. "Now, tell me."

"Miss Bixby, this man's household has nothing in it," Deborah said, her voice wavering. "No kettle, no linens, no soap. Not a single book! Only one lamp, which he refuses to light. No food put up in his pantry. We might as well be living in the woods like Adam and Eve."

"Well, weren't they perfectly happy until they got themselves into trouble?"

Deborah's meek expression turned angry. "This isn't a laughing matter. I can't cook! I can't clean! I'm going to lose my mind."

Clara sighed, weary with her own worries. "I wish I could help you, Deborah."

She shook her head. "He said this would happen, that I was wasting my time running to you. I heard some of the men are trying to have you arrested for swindling them—is that true?"

"Deborah." Clara pressed her lips together. "Do you think you could ask Mr. Moran for a little bit of household money? Just a small amount, to get yourself set up? If you asked very sweetly, I suspect he would find a way."

Deborah sniffed, then shook her head. "I tried. But he says he needs to learn whether he can trust me first."

"Well," Clara thought for a moment. "I was just about to go over to Mr. Baumann's store and buy a few things for the kitchen downstairs. I'll be sure to tell him about the kinds of things some of you may be needing soon: kettles, fabric, needles and thread. And I'll see that he mentions the supplies to your husbands. Perhaps Mr. Moran will be more likely to agree if he hears about it from Mr. Baumann. All right?"

Deborah nodded and wiped her nose, but she didn't get up from the chair. "I miss Molly."

Clara shook her head. "Oh, my dear," she said. "I know it. It's just terrible what happened. If I could go back to that day we left New York, keep her from getting on the train, you *know* I would. But Molly would want us to do the best we can here. Make the best of things."

"It's true," Deborah said. "She would tell me not to worry. Except . . . there's . . . there's something else."

"What is it?"

Deborah wailed into her handkerchief. "It's too awful. Not even Molly would know what to say about this, I don't think."

"Just tell me," Clara said. "Whatever it is, it can't be that bad."

"I believe Mr. Moran is a . . . a deviant."

Clara's eyes widened. "What makes you say *that*?"

"Well, he wants me to . . ." Deborah leaned over and whispered something to Clara, then sat back in the chair and waited for the shock to set in.

But Clara only nodded. "Yes, that sounds about right." She looked the new wife in the eye. "Deborah, how old are you—really? And don't lie to me this time."

She looked at her lap. "Seventeen."

"And your mother? She never talked to you about—"

"She died when I was seven."

Clara bit her lip. "And you haven't any sisters? Aunts? You and Molly never talked this over?"

"Well, yes, but . . . I suppose it was the blind leading the blind."

Clara thought back on the New York doctor's assurance that all the brides were virgins—she had hardly believed it could be true. And now here she was faced with a married woman who didn't know the first thing about what she was in for.

"Deborah," Clara said, patting the girl's knee, "I believe I will make us a pot of tea. We have a few things to discuss."

Three days later Clara walked to the depot to post a letter and as she came back outside she saw a man walking toward her. She pressed her lips into a line; she would have known that gait anywhere.

"Good morning, my darling!"

Clara gave him a wary glance. "Hello, George."

He opened his arms to embrace her, but she stayed put. "Aren't you surprised to see me?"

"I'm only surprised it took you so long." Clara smirked at him. "Why, I've been here nearly two weeks."

"That was an awfully cruel thing you did, Clara, slipping out of town without telling me," he said. "I had to find out where you went from Mrs. Ferguson. It was embarrassing."

"Did you ever think maybe I didn't *want* you to find me?"

He ignored this. "I certainly wouldn't have chosen Nebraska, of all the godforsaken places in this world, but, well, here I am. I suppose it doesn't matter where we are as long as we're together."

"Well, you've come a long way for nothing."

"Don't be silly, Clara."

She sighed. "There isn't any money, George. Not a penny. I'm working at the tavern and everything I make goes to room and board and paying off this trio of dissatisfied bachelors. I'm in a bad way out here. You don't want any part of it."

George's winning smile dropped from his face and he was quiet for a moment. He took Clara's hand and pressed it against his lapel. "Do you really think I would travel this far just to get my hands on some money I *thought* you might have?"

"Without a doubt, I do."

"Leave off the kidding a minute, Clara. I mean it." George set his jaw. "I *know* I haven't been the sort of man I should be. I know I've let you down."

Clara closed her eyes to break from his unbearable gaze. She felt the hair on the back of her neck stand up, as if she were a doe sensing danger in the crack of a twig a mile away.

She tried to pull her hand away but he clutched it tight. When he spoke again, his voice was thick. "I didn't know what to do, Clara. I couldn't face what happened, couldn't face you when M—"

A small moan escaped from Clara's lungs and she shook her head hard. "*No.* Please don't say his name."

"Please," George said. She could see his eyes filling. "We can't pretend this didn't happen."

Clara took a breath. Her lungs felt full of broken glass.

"The only way I can live from one hour to the next is to tell myself that it didn't happen. It was a nightmare from which we've both awoken and now we must go on."

George touched her cheek and she ground her molars down on the pain that surged in her chest, bloomed in her skull like a choking, poisonous weed.

"Oh, Clara," he sighed.

"I mean it, George. Have mercy on me. Or I'm likely to hit you. *Hard.*"

"Fine," he said softly. "We don't have to talk about it. But you have to believe me: I didn't come here for money."

"With all the practice you've had, I should think by now you would be a better liar."

He held up his hand. "All right. I did come hoping you would have *some* money. All my prospects in New York have dried up. But even though I know now that you've fallen on hard times, I'm not going anywhere. I love you, Clara. We should be together. *Please.*"

Clara felt a weariness that threatened to bring her to her knees. How long had it been since a day passed without some crisis or another, without some anguish? How much should one woman have to endure alone? She winced.

"Is it the headaches again?" George asked. "Let me take care of you. Let me make up for what I've done."

She tried to call up her resistance but her body felt as broken as her heart. George put out his elbow and looked expectantly at her, his dark brows raised, his cheeks pink and sure. Clara put her fingertips on his forearm, as if to test it, and it felt as sturdy as a wood beam fixed in place. They shared a secret sorrow and it bound them together. What they had endured was stronger than anything—stronger than love or hate or disappointment or anger—and no matter how she tried to escape, to begin again, the sorrow pulled her back in like a tide.

She leaned against George and he slipped his arm across the small of her back, then helped her across the road and up the stairs to their room.

Clara fell into a deep and dreamless sleep. When she woke, she noticed before opening her eyes that the right side of her body felt hot. She turned her cheek on the pillow and looked out at the room. Inside the stove a low fire glowed. A basket of coal sat beside it on the floor. On the small corner table was a tray with a clay teapot, and steam poured from its spout; beside it was a plate of toasted bread and jam. Clara's gaze turned to the foot of the mattress, covered in a wool blanket she hadn't seen before. George sat in the chair, reading a newspaper. She closed her eyes and opened them once more, certain her dreams had turned to happier but nonetheless fictional matters.

"Rise and shine," George said softly. "How are you feeling?"

"Hot," Clara said, lifting her loose hair off the back of her neck. "It's too warm for a fire, George."

"I know," he said. "But I wanted to make you tea."

She stared at him a moment, then shook her head. "I have been so very tired."

"Well, rest all you like. I've talked to Mrs. Healy and you need not come down today."

"What do you mean, you talked to her?"

"I explained that I've joined you here, that we'll be sharing the burden of the cost for the room between the two of us. In addition to your work downstairs, I've agreed to light all the fires first thing and bring the kegs over from the brewery. That privy out back is likely to fall over any day. I told her I'd build her a new one. Anyway, she won't hear of your coming down until tomorrow. She sends you her best wishes for good health."

Clara eyed him. "She does?" He nodded as he poured her tea into a cup. "George, you should have let *me* tell her about you."

He waved this away. "Nonsense. She didn't mind at all. I believe she's glad to have a little more help."

"Well." Clara shook her head. This was certainly new. She wasn't sure what to make of it.

"Now, I want you to have a little bit of bread to eat, and then it's straight back to sleep."

This wasn't the old George—this was a George she had never seen. No one had talked this way to Clara since she was a child. She did not abide being taken in hand, particularly by this man, but somehow she didn't feel like getting her back up over it. It felt nice, to hand over the reins. Nice but strange.

"All right," she said, sitting up all the way.

He brought the plate over to her and she ate in silence. The bread was fresh and chewy, the jam tart with rhubarb. George stood at her side, patiently waiting for her to finish, then took the plate away.

"All right, then," he said. He placed the cup of tea on the floor near her head. "In case of thirst." Then he sat back down in the chair, snapping open his paper once more.

Clara watched him for a moment, awestruck, but found her lids too heavy to continue.

Later on in the darkness, she felt the blanket shift on her legs. The mattress rustled as George slid close to her, his knee-caps pressing into the back of her thighs, the long bones of his feet sliding beneath her soles. He kissed the back of her head and she allowed herself to revel in the tobacco-spiced scent of him, knowing that, were she to turn and face him now, to run her lips from his mouth to his cheek to the cluster of gray hair that had sprouted recently at his temples, she would taste salt: the remnant of a day's work. He had betrayed her, and she could go on punishing him for it—probably would for a while—but he *was* here now. Perhaps it was possible to begin again in this new place, not quite so wrenched and distorted by grief. With patience, with time. George slid his hand down her arm, across the plane of her small breasts, and Clara felt them pucker, shamelessly, at his touch. She clutched the back of his hand with her fingers and removed it to a cold place on the mattress.

Clara laughed. "Not a chance in hell, Mr. Bixby."

The next day she felt better than she had in months, in a year. Who could have guessed that a simple night of deep sleep was all she needed to repair? The headache still thrummed on but it seemed very far away, like the echo of pain instead of the pain itself. She was hungry and thirsty and ready to work.

Downstairs in the tavern she chopped an onion and carrot and put them in the small kettle with a generous helping of shaved salt pork. There was no shortage of pigs here, and Nebraskans seemed to eat pork with every meal. As she was pulling the crockery down from the shelf, the door creaked open. This one had no bell.

"Anybody here?" a voice called. "Something sure smells good."

Clara leaned out the kitchen doorway with a stack of bowls braced against her middle. "Well, hello, Mayor Cartwright."

His quick smile deepened the lines at his temples. "Miss Bixby. I was hoping it would be you who was banging around back there in the kitchen." He set a large bundle down on the floor. "I was just bringing my laundry to Mrs. Healy. She'll do it for me, but she makes me carry it all the way from my uncle's farm." He wiped his forehead with a handkerchief. "That's the life of a bachelor, I suppose."

"Are you hungry, sir? This stew is just about ready."

"Thank you. I would like very much to have some."

Clara came around to the front of the bar and set a place for him, with a mat and a spoon, at the table under the window. "May I bring you something to drink?"

"Just an ale, if you will."

Clara drew it from the tap and ladled the stew into a bowl.

"Say, Clara," the mayor said. "How are things . . . coming along?"

She pressed her lips together. "Do you mean to ask whether I've yet come up with the money to pay those men back?"

Mayor Cartwright stirred his stew a moment before he replied. "I only ask because yesterday the sheriff for Dodge County, which includes our town, called on me to inquire about the whole matter. It seems those men intend to pursue this as far as they can."

"They do?" Clara asked, her voice full of dread.

"Yes. And if they knew I had tipped you off about that, they would probably run me out of town."

Clara sighed. "Well, I thank you for telling me, though it won't do any good to speed up my plans. Mrs. Healy has me working in exchange for room and board, plus a fair wage, but a small one. At this rate it will take me years to pay them back. I suppose I should begin taking in sewing."

Clara heard footsteps and turned to see George come into the kitchen through the back door with another man. George's shirt sleeves were rolled up to the elbows and his collar was damp with sweat. He had been working to hang a new door on the privy out back.

"Well, sir," Clara said to the mayor. "I'll let you enjoy your dinner."

George took a washcloth and bathed his neck at the wide sink, then strode behind the bar.

"Clara," he said, jerking his thumb at the man who followed him in. "Have you met Tomas Skala? He's a fine carpenter."

Clara shook her head, then extended her hand with a polite smile. "Pleased to meet you, Mr. Skala."

Tomas took it and covered her knuckles with his other hand. "That is my thinking, that *I* am pleased to meet *you*."

George nudged Clara with his elbow. "He's a Bohemian. Fresh off the boat—so to speak. I can't get enough of the way he talks." Tomas winced ever so slightly and Clara felt a pang of embarrassment.

"Are you hungry?" she said to Tomas.

"We're both famished," George said, starting toward a table. "What's for dinner?"

Then he noticed Mayor Cartwright sitting under the window. "Hello, there," he said. Tomas sat down across the room and removed his bowler, wiping his brow with a pressed handkerchief.

"Good day, sir," Mayor Cartwright said to George. He put down his spoon and stood up. "Randall Cartwright," he said.

"*Mayor* Cartwright," Clara said. "Allow me to introduce George Bixby."

The mayor's shoulders softened. "Ah, I didn't know you had a brother. What a pleasure to meet you, sir."

"Brother?" George laughed. "Now, see here. I am this lady's husband."

Cartwright glanced at Clara, confusion clouding his face. "Forgive me, Miss, Mrs.—I wasn't aware—"

"It's all right," Clara said. "You couldn't have known. 'Miss Bixby' is the name I use for business, but in truth I am a Mrs." She put her hand on George's forearm to reassure him, and his jaw softened.

Cartwright extended his hand again and gave George a generous smile. George straightened his back but even then was a good deal shorter than the mayor. "Well, I am very pleased to meet you. Your wife is a remarkable woman, a remarkable woman. She's turned this settlement upside down. And mostly for the better."

He smiled at Clara and she replied with a nervous laugh. George's eyes bounced back and forth between them. She would hear about this later, upstairs in their room. Like most unfaithful men, George had the gall to be jealous of any man who paid his wife attention. The fact that Cartwright was taller, stronger, and smarter only made things worse.

"Husband, let me bring you some stew," Clara said loudly enough for George to know that Mr. Cartwright would hear. What efforts had to be made to protect men's pride! The mayor returned to his stew, and George watched him for a moment, then joined Tomas at his table.

Rowena

"Rowena?" Daniel said, as he slurped his coffee in the most intolerable way.

"Hmm?" Rowena did not turn to face him from where she stood at the sink scrubbing a pot. Lately she was finding it hard to remember what it was she had liked about him that first day in his wagon. Daniel sat in the center of the table, with two boys on either side of him. The quietest part of the day came during the five minutes it took the children to bolt their porridge. It was like the momentary stillness surrounding a company of soldiers as they reload their rifles.

"Leave *off*, Ully," Dag said. He kicked the side of his chair with a thud.

"That's enough now, Ully," Daniel said.

"Pa, she won't stop," said Gustav.

Rowena took a beleaguered breath and glanced back at them. Ully sat cross-legged under the table, untying each of her brothers' boots. Rowena couldn't decide what was worse— that these illiterates covered with mange existed at all, or that the house's dirt floor forced them to keep their boots on morning, noon, and night.

Daniel continued. "Rowena, would you please not wander far today? I am sending a carpenter to start work on the chicken house and you need to be here to show him where to put it."

"Yes, Mr. Gibson," Rowena said absently. She knew it irked him that she still would not call him *Daniel*. But he could hardly complain that she wasn't holding up her end of the bargain. She kept the little hovel as tidy as possible. She hired Kathleen Connolly to come once a week and do the wash—Daniel hadn't dared to assume Rowena would do it herself. She did do all the cooking, though, serving a rotation of the only three dishes she knew how to prepare: chicken pie, chicken on biscuits, and pork stew. That Rowena had not fallen in love with Daniel could not be held against her. Each month since they first exchanged letters in the winter, without fail, he had sent the postal order for the money to cover her father's care.

A small mercy had arrived in a note from Anna Ludlow Crowley, the reverend's new wife, explaining that she wanted to start a school at the church for the Gibson children, and "any other young ones who may come along eventually." Rowena could almost picture the woman winking as she wrote that last part, and it made her shudder. But Rowena was grateful for the respite the school provided. Daniel's children would complete their chores after breakfast and walk straight there for their lessons, guaranteeing Rowena four hours of peace.

"I don't know what we're going to do about this drought," Daniel was saying. "Cows don't get fat off dry grass."

Odin began to whistle a cloying tune and Sigrid joined in, banging his spoon on the tabletop to keep time.

"No whistling at the table," Dag yelled.

"No *yelling* at the table," Odin yelled at Dag.

"Boys," Daniel said. "Enough."

Dag turned to his father. "Ully's still at it, Pa."

Daniel stuck his head under the table. "Ully, I said that's enough."

"No," she said sweetly. "You told the boys it was enough. You didn't say anything about what the girls could do. I suppose that means Mrs. Gibson and me can do as we please."

"Mrs. Gibson and *I*," Sigrid said. The family scholar.

Rowena took a still-wet bowl from the drain board and slammed it against the chopping block. It made a bright crash and the shards of china scattered across the kitchen. All six of the Gibsons stared, openmouthed, at Rowena.

"If you do not become absolutely still this instant, I will poison your food," she said to them in an eerily calm voice. "But you won't know when. You'll never know which bite will be the one that kills you." The boys traded glances, their eyes wide. "I assure you—it's not an empty threat."

Daniel pressed his lips together to keep from breaking into laughter at how well her threat worked on the children. He glanced at his wife to share the moment of triumph, but Rowena had no intention of allowing any kind of alliance to form between them. It seemed impossible now that she could grow to feel anything more than tolerance for him. She couldn't get past the children. This wasn't what she had agreed to.

"Yours too," she said to Daniel, tapping the side of the iron pot with her fingernail. Clara Bixby was to blame for all of this, Rowena reminded herself, as she did at least once a day. And the woman would get her comeuppance.

As soon as Daniel and the children filed out of the kitchen, Rowena tied a light shawl across her shoulders and walked out the door of the soddy to the other end of the main road. Drake's Brewery occupied one of the few wood-frame buildings in Destination. It, along with Mr. Schreier's farmhouse, was among the first to have been built from the few dozen mature trees that once stood on both sides of the Platte River. Clearly no one had thought about how many decades it took for a tree to grow that tall, and that when they used up this wood, there wouldn't be any more to replace it. Probably no one had thought the town would last longer than a few years. If only they had been right.

The heavy door creaked as Rowena pulled it open. The brewery structure resembled a barn, two stories high and open from the floor to the ceiling inside. The sun shone through the spaces between the slats of wood along the walls and cast a lined pattern of light and shadow across the floor. Rowena cleared her throat.

"Good morning," she called into the expansive room. She didn't see anyone, but she could hear the clanking sound of work with a metal tool somewhere. The air was thick with the floral bite of hops. "Good morning," she called again.

The clanking stopped and a pair of men's boots appeared on the ladder that ran down the back side of the enormous copper kettle standing twenty feet high in the center of the room.

"Are you Mr. Albright?" Rowena asked. She had been in Destination for more than two weeks, but had been so overwhelmed with the work in the soddy that she had ventured out little and met almost no one.

"Yes, ma'am," Bill said. She waited for the expression on his face to shift, the light to come into his eyes that would indicate he noticed her beauty. Nothing happened. Rowena stepped farther into the room and threw her shoulders back.

"I understand you and some other men in town aren't very happy with the matchmaker Mayor Cartwright hired," she said.

Bill's eyes widened. He held up his hand. "Look. I understand she may be your friend, but this business doesn't concern you. Your husband may be happy with how things turned out, but that Miss Bixby took our money and didn't deliver what she promised."

"Sounds to me like you're accusing Miss Bixby of fraud. And don't worry. She's no friend of mine."

"At this point, it's only theft. We can't prove that she never *intended* to deliver the brides she promised us. All of us spent the winter corresponding with . . . somebody. As far as we can tell, Miss Bixby is telling the truth: Our girls just changed their minds about coming out here. We can't hold her responsible for their temperaments. But the money is another thing. We intend to get that back."

"I wouldn't be so quick to give up on the fraud charge, Mr. Albright. I have some evidence that I believe could help make your case." She waited for understanding to dawn on his face.

"What are you talking about?"

"Conversations," Rowena said. "Conversations I've had with Miss Bixby, conversations I've overheard."

"But why did she deliver to some of the men and not others? If it really was fraud, why didn't she take all the money and go to California or something?"

Rowena took a breath. Even in her anger at Clara, she knew she was about to do something wrong, something that couldn't be undone. How long would this game continue to go on? The world had put hurt into her and so she wanted to put hurt back into the world, for the sake of equilibrium, for the sake of justice. She had been waiting for someone to say it was all right, to say no one could blame her, but no one would sanction *this*. She went right on anyway, though, caught up in a dare with herself. "You see, Mr. Albright, Miss Bixby has an awfully high opinion of herself and her ability to judge the worth of men. The reason that she delivered wives to some men—like my Mr. Gibson, like Reverend Crowley and Mr. Moran and Mr. Riddle—is that she deemed them the *right* sort of men. Worthy, you see. You, Mr. Luft, Mr. Drake . . . well, forgive me for speaking plainly, sir, but Miss Bixby found you, in her words, 'dim, coarse, and unlikely to be able to earn a living.'"

Bill's jaw tightened. "And what of Miss Ruley?"

"A figment."

"I *knew* it. But why? Why would Miss Bixby go to so much trouble for such a small sum of money?"

"Even a little money is no small sum for a single woman, Mr. Albright. And four brides are missing. But you have to understand that this is not really about the money. This is about Miss Bixby's ambition. She loves the idea that she pulled one over on you. Some people even say she was some kind of crusader for the rights of women back in Manhattan City. I can't speak to that, but . . ."

Rowena had planted plenty of seed now. She waited, as if there were any doubt about what was taking hold in Bill's mind, what would soon take hold in the minds of all three thwarted men. Nothing could raise hackles faster than a rumored suffragette. They might not like to admit it, but Rowena suspected the phenomenon of uppity women was one of the things that had driven these pioneering men from the cities. They felt things were going haywire back east, the government getting involved in all kinds of things it had no business dictating. If you let women march in the street, go to college, vote in elections—what would be next? Rowena knew men like those in Destination believed a man would have a bit in his mouth and the *horse* would be sitting up on the platform, driving the cart, that's what. That part of the country had gone crazy, and she was sure men like Bill had been grateful for a place to come and begin again.

But she also saw that Bill was no fool. He narrowed his eyes at Rowena. "And why would you be so eager to help me, I wonder?"

She turned her calculated glance on the brewer, the eyelashes, the slow smile. "Because, sir—there is an order to things and she has upset the balance. Someone has to stand up for the way things ought to be. Don't you agree?"

Rowena went back to the house and settled in an armchair with a book. She felt all aglow with justice, then slipped into a satisfying sleep until a knock at the door startled her awake. She sat up and listened. It came again, two long knocks and three short, like the rhythm of a tune.

She opened the door to find a young man in a spotless hat and fawn-colored jacket, with boots shined to an impossibly high gloss, given the amount of dust he had had to trudge through to reach the front door.

"Hallo, my name is Tomas Skala." The man put out his hand and Rowena stared rudely at it a moment before consenting to the handshake.

"Good afternoon," she said warily.

"You are thinking, *Who is this man?* No?" Tomas smiled. A carefully groomed beard limned his jaw in copper-colored whiskers.

"I suppose I am."

"I am carpenter. Your husband ask me build house for chickens?"

Rowena raised her eyebrows. "*You* are a carpenter?"

"Yes," Tomas said, nodding vigorously. "Very good one. You not believe me?"

Rowena laughed. "It is only that you aren't *dressed* like a carpenter."

"This is because I always look future. Someday I am becoming man of business."

"Oh. What sort of business?"

"I not know yet, but hey—get clothes right first, rest will follow, yes?"

She laughed again. "I see—well, it *is* said that the clothes make the man."

Astonished delight broke over Tomas's face. "Yes, this is *my* thinking too!"

Rowena stepped outside next to him, feeling the heat of the sun on her bare head, and felt suddenly cheered. "Come with me around back," she said. "I'll show you where I would like you to build it."

"Ah. You want it should be big?"

"Not too big. I plan to keep eight or ten chickens. But it should be well insulated for the winter months." Rowena stopped about twenty feet away from the house on a patch of scrubby dirt on which nothing would grow, and spread her arms. She wouldn't want to walk much farther than that on chilly mornings to gather the eggs. "Right about here should be fine."

Tomas nodded and his gaze lingered on her for a moment. His eyes were a surprising green under the brim of his bowler. "What is your name?"

Rowena gave him a confused look. "Why, it's Mrs. Gibson, of course. My husband is the butcher, the one who hired you?"

Tomas shook his head. "Yes, I know. My meaning is, what is your *Christian* name?"

Rowena's amusement with this man's impervious confidence was starting to fade. "Pardon me, sir?"

Tomas pointed at his chest. "My name is Tomas. What is yours?"

"I *know* what you are asking, but don't *you* know it is impolite to call a woman you just met by her Christian name?"

Tomas shrugged and smiled broadly. "Who say I polite?"

Rowena found she was fairly speechless just then, had to force her mouth closed. Was this how the help talked to their employers in Nebraska? When she spoke her voice was hard. "Will there be anything else? I have work to do in the house."

"You come from New York, yes? I hear about this. They call you—Bixbybelle?"

Rowena nodded. "Yes, I came here with Miss Bixby."

"In New York you have money, yes? Fine house with servants, bring your food?"

"Well, at one time I did."

Tomas nodded. "In New York, I work in factory. My wife sew clothes. We have nothing. Here, I can have land, build things. You know what change?"

Rowena shook her head.

"In New York, you different from me." He pointed at the ground. "Here we are same." Tomas turned back toward the front path. She couldn't tell if he was angry or making a joke. "I go buy wood now and come back few days." After a moment he snapped his finger, then turned back. "Rowena."

She stared at him, her hand at her forehead to shield her eyes from the bright sun. "How did you—"

"I know it already. I want only to see if *you* tell *me*."

"Listen here, Mr. Skala. I won't be disrespected in my own house. And my husband won't stand for it either."

Tomas glanced up at the sky. "We are not inside house."

Rowena's eyes flashed and she turned on her heel and stomped toward the door.

"Rowena," she heard him say to himself as he walked away. "This is pretty name."

Rowena stayed angry all afternoon, whipping through her housework. *Here is a coarse Bohemian*, she thought, as she hacked at an onion on the chopping block. *He may not look it, but that changes nothing. He has set his sights so far above his station as to make a mockery. Why, he barely speaks English!*

Rowena had worked herself into such a state she could not remain in a chair. She passed the hours beating out all the rugs, scouring the already clean pots. The house was aired and sweet-smelling by the time Daniel walked through the door to find his wife pacing back and forth. With each turn she made an aggravated little squeak.

He gazed around and a slow smile spread across his face. He put his hands on his hips and puffed out his chest. "Now this is what a man's home should look like when he walks through the door."

"*Mr.* Gibson," Rowena said, marching in his direction and planting herself only a foot away from where he stood. Her diminutive stature made her seem like an overexcited child. "Wait until you hear what sort of disgrace took place here today."

Daniel's smile faded. "What is it, my dear?" Rowena squeaked again and held up her finger to correct him. "I mean, *Rowena?*"

"Tomas Skala, the carpenter. That is what happened. Need I say anything else?

Daniel laughed. "Ah, he *is* known for humbugging. Did he have a laugh on you?"

"That insufferable man insulted your wife. I ask you, who does he think he is? And will you tolerate it?"

"Now, it can't be as bad as all that. Tell me what happened."

She opened her mouth to speak but hesitated. In truth, it wasn't that bad. So Tomas had found out her Christian name, somehow. Had he stolen from them or cheated them out of money? "He was—he was very rude."

"Oh, you must know, Rowena, the man has a peculiar sense of humor. No one here holds it against him. He is well loved for it, in fact."

"Well, I don't want him coming back here."

"You take things too hard, woman. You have to learn the ways of people out here. This isn't a parlor in a Manhattan mansion. We aren't *refined*."

"*I'll* say."

"But there is a freedom in it, don't you think, my—I mean, Rowena?" He took her hand and led her to the sofa. "We can say what we think, don't have to worry so much about the mincing rules of etiquette. A man can be himself."

"Well, Mr. Skala *certainly* was that."

"He means no harm, I promise you. Did you know he lost his whole family on the journey here?"

It irritated Rowena that Daniel wasn't taking her side. Richard always listened to her frustrations and complaints, never questioning her perception of an exchange in which she felt she had been wronged. He was tender with her, vowing to take action on her behalf. Why was Daniel making this day's events about Tomas, when they was so clearly about *her*?

"He came with his parents and his wife and her brother," Daniel said. "When they were en route from Detroit, the train was robbed by bandits and Tomas's parents and wife were shot in the confusion. Only her brother and Tomas survived. Another man was killed too, Al Healy. His wife runs the tavern now."

"Oh," Rowena said, her hand at her throat. "That's terrible." She knew all too well how quickly the world could take away the thing you loved.

"It was Tomas's father who wanted to come to Nebraska and claim land, not Tomas. But he decided, even after everything that happened, to stay on. To try to make a life for himself."

Rowena clutched her hands in her lap.

"So you see," Daniel said, "not everyone is what he seems. Not Tomas. Not me."

Or me, Rowena thought, but she held the words between her lips.

Elsa

At seven o'clock in the evening Elsa heard the squeak of the pump handle and then the sound of Mr. Schreier's boots. He stepped into the kitchen and placed his hat on the hook, then made his thumping way across the floor.

"Evening, Elsa," he said as he eased himself into the chair and swung his bad leg under the table. He tipped his head back and closed his eyes. "Smells good in here." Even with the sun as low as it was, the air inside the house was sweltering. And that wasn't the only thing that had her on edge. The second Sunday in June had passed and Elsa still hadn't been to church.

"Evening," she said. She filled a plate with pork left over from dinner, then set it down in front of him, along with a glass of ale.

Elsa stood respectfully still while he prayed. He drank the ale down in one long gulp, then took a bite. She watched him chew, his expression stern, the muscle that ran from his jaw up the side of his face moving beneath his skin. His bare head was deeply browned from the sun, speckled pink in places. A fine whisper of yellow-gray hair grew in a horseshoe shape around his scalp.

"How is your work going, sir?" It was her first attempt to make conversation at the end of the day.

Mr. Schreier started, as if surprised to learn anyone else was in the room. He spread a forkful of the meat on a piece of bread and shoved it in his mouth. He grunted, nodding.

"Mr. LeBlanc says that ewe could drop her lamb any day." He nodded again. "Mm-hmm."

"Seems like it's getting late in the season for her not to have gone yet. My grandfather had a farm, near Deggendorf. He always called on us children to help when there was a calf or some piglets coming. I was so frightened of the way the mothers cried through their labor. All that time they were in their travail—it just seemed like so much suffering. I understood about Adam and Eve, and why a woman was charged with knowing that pain. But why a poor old sow, who couldn't sin?"

Elsa shook her head, turning to the sink as the blood rose in her cheeks. She was talking just to talk now. All that time working in the Channing laundry she had hardly talked at all. But she had had plenty to listen to. The other laundresses—especially the young ones who thought they were just biding their time until they found a man to marry—gossiped incessantly. They talked about hair arrangements, slippers with silk ribbons, the benefits and drawbacks to corsets with whalebones, the new collapsible crinoline. As if any of them would ever in their lives own such a thing. They wondered aloud what would happen when one of their friends found out her husband's jacket had been seen hanging on the doorknob of a

room at Libby's, whether she would throw all his belongings
into the snow, whether they should tell the minister and let
him sort it out. Elsa had never realized that in a strange way
she looked forward to the talk. It was the frivolous, vapid
music of the work. It made the hours pass. Here at Mr.
Schreier's it was absolutely silent all day long. There was a
peace in it, certainly, but she found herself longing for something to listen to. Her talk rattled on. "But then those sweet
little piglets came and she forgot all about her pain."

Mr. Schreier stared at her with wide eyes, chewing with
his mouth partway open. He swallowed. "I don't like a lot of
talk at meals."

To Elsa's horror, she felt her eyes welling with tears. She
turned quickly back to the sink and took a shaky breath. Mr.
Schreier's fork continued to clank against his plate. "Yes, sir,"
she whispered. She wiped her hands on her apron and passed
quietly out the kitchen door, the dry grass along the edge of
the barley field rustling beneath her feet. The sun was low
behind her and its glow tinted the sky the color of custard.
Inside the barn she pulled the milking stool down off its hook
and sat beside Honey, pressing her palm gently against the
cow's flank.

What a silly thing to be upset over, Elsa chastised herself. *It
is Mr. Schreier's house to run as he pleases.* It was only that she
had been nursing a small hope, because of the way he had
talked a little bit about himself in his letters, that they might
be some sort of . . . *friends* after she arrived. That they might
talk in German to each other, share stories about their families, how they had come to America. She put her hand on her
chest. "Be still," she said to her beat-up old heart.

Her eyes had adjusted to the dim light and she glanced around the interior of the barn. In the stall next to Honey, the horses nosed their oats, languid tails swishing. Their saddles hung beside them. Every object in the barn had its place, every tool, every bucket. And someone had taken the time to put them where they belonged. Elsa felt envious of them all. On the far side of the barn, the skittish ewe peered at her, then backed into the shadows.

Elsa stood abruptly to shake off the maudlin thoughts. She had been alone since she was sixteen years old. There wasn't a reason under the sun why that should change, and not a thing wrong with it besides. *Earthly things will pass away. They will pass away and what will be left is my Savior.* The sadness receded and she walked back to the house. In the front room, Mr. Schreier sat in his armchair, the newspaper open in front of him. It was a Chicago paper with a headline that read "*Carnage at Antietam.*" *Again with the war,* she thought. *Again he reads about these terrible things, now years in the past.*

Elsa walked by him without a word and into the kitchen. She carried his empty plate to the sink and poured hot water from the kettle into it, then swished in some soap flakes. When the dishes were dry she passed back through the sitting room. The paper lay across Mr. Schreier's chest, his head slung to the side in sleep.

The next day Elsa moved gently and tried to be grateful for the silence while she worked. She had never minded that women were supposed to keep silent in the church, for there was more than one way to speak; why should a house on the prairie be any different? By midmorning, after the breakfast dishes were washed and put away, Elsa straightened up the sitting room. She found that Mr. Schreier was endearingly untidy and left a trail of his activities wherever he went; Elsa knew everything he had done the night before by walking in his footsteps through the house. After tidying, she cooked an *Eintopf* of chicken and noodles for dinner and served it to the men when they came in from the field at midday. She ate her own small portion after they went back out, then washed the dishes yet again and chopped the leftover meat for supper. She slid a plate on top of the bowl to keep the flies out.

Elsa realized that in her silly huff the night before she had forgotten to pull the laundry down from the line. She went out through the kitchen door with a basket on her hip. At the edge of the field, Mr. Schreier walked the rows of sprouting barley, his motions slow and deliberate, his face in shadow. She knew he was worried about the lack of rain. Elsa shook her head, wondering yet again just exactly how old Mr. Schreier was. Fifty? Sixty? How long he planned on working this hard was anyone's guess. She tried not to think about what would happen to her if he died in the field.

Mr. Schreier owned six pairs of thick wool stockings knitted for him by his late wife, and Elsa was careful to wash them last, after the water had gone lukewarm, to keep the wool from felting. Mrs. Schreier had been a good knitter, Elsa could see. There was an invisible join in the toe, a complicated maneuver, but the best sort of seam. It joined the top and bottom of the sock firmly and did not leave a rough selvage on the inside of the toe to rub a blister on the skin. Looking at that seam, Elsa thought she probably would have liked Mrs. Schreier.

She unpinned the kitchen towels, humming a hymn as she rested the stiff linen against her bosom to fold it. She could hear the melody ring through her mind, the way it had sounded in the village church in Deggendorf when she was eight years old, standing beside her mother. Elsa's father had stopped attending meeting, a decision that plagued his wife. Elsa knew her mother prayed every Sunday that he would come back to worship. The austere building allowed only one indulgence in beauty, and that was the organ that sat behind the altar. Its body was carved from walnut and painted with a gold-leaf cross. Elsa's mother loved that instrument. When it came time for the congregation to sing, Elsa's mother would clutch her daughter's hand and smile down at her.

The chorus came back to Elsa through the distance of all those years, and because she knew she was alone, she sang it out loud in a slow, clear voice. *Mein Herz will ich dir schenken.* To thee, my heart I offer. It was a Christmas hymn that marveled at the Lord's decision to give flesh to his son and send him to earth, not as a man but as a *child*; marveled at how, on the day of his birth, this son was *already* full of love for every man. Even though he had straw sticking him in the back and was out in the cold of a barn.

Elsa reached for the bed sheet. When it fell away from the line, she screamed.

"Don't stop," a tiny voice squeaked. It came from a girl sitting on the ground with a large book open on her lap. She stood and brushed the dirt off the back of her legs. "I like that song."

Elsa felt her heart right itself after the somersault. "Child, you startled me. It's not nice to do that to people—hiding and jumping out that way."

The girl chewed her lip. "Sorry," she said, sullen. She was all elbows and knees, this one. Like a sketch of a child without any shading. And someone had *cut* her hair. What a thing to do to a little girl!

"It's all right. Where did you come from?"

The girl chucked her thumb over her shoulder toward town. "Gibsons'."

"Your father is the butcher."

"Yes, ma'am." She kept her eyes on Elsa's shoes.

Elsa nodded. She had heard Mr. Gibson had a handful of sons but hadn't heard a thing about a daughter. *Imagine a butcher's daughter being as skinny as this child!* "What is your name, Miss Gibson?"

"Ully," the girl said.

"Well, Ully, I'm pleased to meet you. My name is Elsa."

Ully tipped her head up finally to look at Elsa, squinting at her through one eye. Her gaze fell down along Elsa's midsection, the girth of her hips. She starred in that transparent way children had, unashamed, the machination of their thoughts laid bare. "You all must have a lot of good things to eat over here."

Elsa laughed in surprise. "Well, that is thanks to Mr. Schreier." She pointed at him out in the distance, a silhouette against the sky. "He works very hard, and the Lord has blessed him with bounty."

"What's *bounty*?"

"Plenty," Elsa said. "Good food, to give us strength, so that our bodies may do our work."

Ully worked her tongue inside her cheek. "I wonder . . . may I have some bounty?"

"Are you hungry?"

Ully nodded. Elsa hesitated for a moment, thinking about what Mr. Schreier would say if he came in at the end of his work day to find this little urchin at his table, eating his food. For all his grumbling, Mr. Schreier *was* a Christian man. And this Ully probably ate like a bird.

"Well, come along, then," Elsa said, turning toward the kitchen door. Ully hurried along behind her. Elsa put her hand on the doorknob, then stopped. She looked down at the greasy part in the girl's hair, the sooty fingernails. "But you're not coming inside," she said, pointing at the water pump, "until you wash up."

Ully scowled, but she went. She gave Elsa her book to hold and took Mr. Schreier's towel off the pump handle, swiping it over her face and neck. "Your hands too," Elsa called to her as she slipped the book in her apron pocket and folded the rest of the laundry. As hot as it was outside, Ully shivered as she rubbed her palms together under the spurt of cold water.

Inside, Elsa pointed to a chair at the end of the table. Ully slipped into it. Her shoulders barely crested the tabletop. "Here," Elsa said. She pulled down a small wooden crate and put it on the seat of the chair for the child to sit on top of. "There," Elsa said. "That's better."

She turned back to the hearth, heating up a bit of pork fat in a pan. Out of the supper bowl, she scooped some of the cold meat, then cut two thick slices of bread. She put everything in the pan and topped it with the lid to warm. She spooned stewed gooseberries into a bowl, then poured cream on top from the tin jug, aware all the while that Ully was watching her every move. When Elsa set the bowl down in front of her, Ully's eyes grew big.

"This looks ex-qui-zette," she said, stretching out the word.

Elsa bit down on the inside of her cheek to keep from smiling. "That's a fancy word. Do you like to read?"

Ully nodded as she leaned her face low over the bowl and shoveled the berries into her mouth. Cream ran down her chin. She swallowed. "I learned that one from Mrs. Gibson. She's our new mother. But she won't let us call her that."

"Well," Elsa said. It was a strange situation, indeed, for the children. "Some people just need a little more time to get used to things." The fat crackled inside the pan and Elsa pulled it off the stove, scraping the food onto a plate. When she turned to carry it over to the table she saw Ully leaning against the back of the chair, tipping the bowl in front of her face with both hands. She slurped the cream.

"My goodness," Elsa said. She held the plate up high, near her shoulder.

"What?" Ully asked, slowly setting the empty bowl down.

She hesitated. It wasn't her place to teach another woman's child—even a woman who wouldn't acknowledge her new responsibility—manners. "It's just that you seem so hungry."

Ully shrugged. "I got four big brothers. Anytime I try to beat them to the table, I get squashed. Or somebody pulls my hair." Ully grinned at this and Elsa saw that she had only one large front tooth, growing in at an angle that was keeping the other one cowering up in her gum. "That's why I cut it off."

"Well, you can have as much as you want here, so there's no need to rush. All right?"

Ully nodded, straining to see what was on the plate. Elsa

set it down and something about Ully's overjoyed expression wrenched the muscle at the back of Elsa's throat. *So much hunger.* Ully reached for the fork.

"Let's say grace first," Elsa said, holding up her finger.

Ully gave her a solemn nod and closed her eyes.

Elsa put her hand on Ully's shoulder. "Lord, we pray that you will impart thy peace and love to each of us through this bread. Amen."

"Amen," Ully said, then went at the food like a wild beast.

Clara

In the pale light of early morning, Clara would not open her eyes. She heard George rise from the mattress and step into his clothes, the snap of his suspenders on his shoulders. He sat back down on the bed and put his hand on her shoulder, waiting to see if she would wake. She was careful to keep her breathing steady so that he would believe she was still asleep. After another moment he sighed, then leaned down and kissed her on the temple where her hair was damp from the heat in the close room. She kept very still until she heard the swish of the door opening and closing.

Gerhard Gade, the farmer on the parcel southeast of town, had asked Mrs. Healy the day before whether she knew of a man looking for work. George would go out there today and help the farmhand build a new barn to replace the one those drunks had burned down. He would come home with a little more money for the fund they kept in a chipped teacup on the high shelf above the stove. Mr. LeBlanc had insisted she remove his name from her list of debts. She still intended to give him something, but at least now she knew he wouldn't join

Jeremiah's Drake's crusade against her. With George's help, it would take all summer and then some, but she would pay those men back what they had lost. She could hardly believe that George would follow through, but he was here and he was working.

Clara rolled toward the wall and pulled the pillow over her face, her eyes squeezed so tightly shut she could feel the ache in her jaw. If she allowed them to open, it seemed, if she allowed even a flash of light to penetrate her lids, the day would begin: June 11. The baby's birthday.

The worst thing about the baby's death—and that was saying something, for there were so many terrible things to choose from—was that Clara herself had been so ill through his five days of life that she had very few memories of him. She had missed the chance to notice everything *specific* about him, everything that made him a Wilson-Bixby in particular and not just one of the millions of babies who had come into the world. She could remember two times emerging from her fever like a person coming up from under the water, to raise herself up on her elbows and glance across the room. Both times the baby was asleep in his cradle; she could see the top of his downy head, the way his pulse fluttered beneath the still-unfused bones of his skull as he breathed.

The longing to hold him was stronger than any urge she had ever felt in her life. In her demented feverish state she came to believe that he was not an independent being but a part of her body she had never noticed before, a little wing of ingeniously compact design that had for years been folded neatly against the skin over her ribs. Suddenly, with his birth the wing had opened, its dense feathers white and gray and sleek blue-black. Clara saw the breeze move through them. And then the breeze became a powerful gust, a gale that severed the wing from her body with a painful crack.

On the third day of Clara's fever, George got the doctor. He had waited because he hadn't known how they would pay for the visit, but soon he didn't care what he had to do. Clara needed help. She had no memory of this day. It was gone from her mind like a page ripped out of a book. George had told her later that the doctor urged her to feed the baby—*urged* was the word he used and it seemed so carefully chosen that Clara imagined the doctor shouting, red in the face, something like, *If you don't feed your baby, he will die.* She couldn't fathom why she hadn't been able to understand what it was she should do. What kind of a mother gives in to sickness and lets her baby starve? Where was her instinct? Where was her strength? But the fever had been so severe, she was making very little milk. She couldn't sit up, couldn't hold him without her arms going slack and the infant in his swaddling rolling down her lap, dangerously close to the edge of the bed, to falling on the floor. So George got the minister, who baptized the child while Clara slept.

It was only after he died, after her fever broke, that her body became the body of a mother. She was alert to the sound of a cry that never came. It seemed she was suddenly producing enough milk for three babies. The weight of her coarse cotton gown on her engorged breasts made tears stream from her eyes. George sat with her, trying to think of something to say. Clara, too, wanted to tell him what she was feeling and wanted to tell him how sorry she was, but there were no words for this kind of regret. It was a bottomless, limitless, world-flooding sorrow that rendered both of them mute.

And then she learned that the cure, or, at least, the thing that might get her through another day, was motion. It didn't matter what kind. Motion was what got her out of that bed. Motion was what kept her from despair when George, undone by grief, drank himself silly and ran off with that Lucia.

Clara was a little bit better now, a little bit further from the precipice because she never allowed herself to think of the baby and his name and because if she was in constant motion, the memories never could catch her.

And so today, for the three-hundred-sixtieth time, Clara chose to get up and go to work.

She was in the tavern kitchen boiling rags and washing glasses when she heard the door open and somebody come inside and walk over to the bar. He sighed a few times before calling, "Hello? Anyone here?"

"Yes, sir," Clara called back. "Just a moment and I'll be out." She wiped her hands on a towel and peeked out through a crack in the kitchen door. The man was about eight inches shorter than Clara and wore a bowler hat one size too large for his head. He had not removed it when he came inside. His thin mustache was like a smudge on his upper lip but by the way he ran his finger absently over it while he waited, she could tell it was a source of pride.

"Good afternoon," Clara said as she stepped out of the kitchen.

He nodded, using the mustache-smoothing finger to poke his hat up off his head for a brief second. "Would you be Mrs. Clara Bixby?"

"Yes, I would," she said, with more than a little regret.

"Well, ma'am, I am Sheriff Brooks, sheriff of all of Dodge County, and it's my duty to tell you that you are the subject of an official investigation."

It was hard to take him seriously. He was so small, like a boy playing dress-up. Any minute, Clara expected him to pull his lapel back to reveal a star-shaped toy badge on his waistcoat.

She must have grinned a little because his lip curled and he barked at her. "This is a serious matter, ma'am. In fact, there's an argument to be made that it is a *federal* matter, as you crossed state lines while committing these crimes. You should thank your lucky stars that we don't make it a habit to call in outsiders to handle our business. You've been accused of fraud by several respected men from this county. A lot of people are willing to vouch for them, but as far as I can tell, nobody around here can speak to *your* character."

This weasel thinks I'm afraid of him! Clara felt like laughing. When the worst thing you can possibly imagine has actually happened to you, it certainly cures you of carefully tiptoeing around your life. Her debt to the men in Destination couldn't feel like a true threat on her dead son's birthday. Everything that once seemed frightening now seemed a farce. What the world could do to her, it had already done, and Clara felt punch-drunk on fearlessness, in the mood to taunt the fates. What did she have left to lose? "I can vouch that they spend plenty of time sitting on their brains in this tavern. And plenty of money on the painted ladies down at the end of the road."

The sheriff's eyebrows jumped slightly in the shadow of his

brim. He set his jaw. "You know, folks have written a lot of stories about what it's like out here, published them in your eastern newspapers and such. People have gotten the idea that this is some kind of lawless territory, where everything is settled with gunfire. I can tell you, ma'am, that in my three years as sheriff, I've never once fired my gun. Do you know why that is?"

"Because you don't know how to use it?"

His nose twitched. "*Because*, the folks in this county respect the law. There's a lot of misconceptions. It's honest people out here just trying to get by, to work their parcels and earn the deeds to their land. I don't like it one bit when somebody comes out here with her head full of ideas about scheming— and trust me, you're not the first to try and *fail*—who thinks she can do as she pleases and make a dollar by breaking the law. I simply do not stand for it, Mrs. Bixby."

Having any more fun at this man's expense was not going to help her situation. "Respectfully, Sheriff, I am sympathetic to all the things you're saying. I don't think it's right either for someone to take advantage of the fine people in this town. I myself never set out to do that. I only wanted to find brides for these lonely men, and in turn, help some of the widows and spinsters of New York find a place too. I only ever intended for it to be a mutually beneficial arrangement. And I'm deeply sorry that some of these matches went awry. But I mean to pay those men back as soon as I can, I hope by the end of the summer. You have my word."

"As Bill Albright had your word, you mean? As Mr. Drake had it? A lot of good it did *them*."

"Sheriff," she said, leaning toward him, "I'd have to be the world's least competent swindler if the result of my efforts had me working in a tavern, don't you think? I have in no way profited from the money those men lost on their intended brides."

"Well, we have reason to believe you *do* have money, which you are hiding."

"If I intended to steal from them, wouldn't I have left town? Don't you think? I mean, I'm not any more familiar with criminal activity than the next person, but it stands to reason . . ."

"A witness has come forward, Mrs. Bixby. This witness has testified to conversations in which you stated that you never intended to provide brides for these men, but intended to take their money all the same. That you intended to deceive them. The law calls that fraud."

Clara's amusement with the situation vanished. There was only one person she could think of who would manufacture these untruths without so much as a ripple of guilt, and that person was as dangerous as the devil. Clara had seen the way men hung on the siren's every word as if they were in a trance. What chaos could be wrought by a pretty face! What evil!

"The end of the summer won't do, Mrs. Bixby," the sheriff said. "You have until the Fourth of July to repay these men, or I am going to take the case before the county judge. We cannot have this matter going unresolved, lest we encourage more of your ilk to travel west. Good day." The sheriff poked his hat once more and strode out of the tavern, using both hands to push open the heavy door.

Clara went back through to the kitchen and stood for a

long moment in the middle of the room, just staring. She put her hands on the small of her back, then sat down on the flour bin and wiped her palm over her face. It was going to be her word against Rowena Moore Gibson's. There was no question about whom they would believe.

She had not stolen from these men. She had not committed fraud. The truth would come out in the end, wouldn't it? Somehow, everything would get sorted out, she would pay the men back, and then she could finally move on. The little white cottage seemed to be receding further from her each time she thought of it, but there was still hope of finding it, and at least now she had George's help. *The truth will come out*, Clara reassured herself, though in all honesty, she put very little stock in divine justice, having seen so little of it in her own life or the lives of the people she knew.

Around seven the men began to file into the tavern, hot, dusty, and tired. Daniel Gibson and Nit LeBlanc sat with Stuart Moran, Deborah's "deviant" of a husband. Clara pressed her lips together to hold back a smile when she thought of the girl's horrified expression as she told Clara what Stuart had asked her to do. Clara thought she might see her own husband come in for an ale but he didn't show. She hoped it meant he was working late, earning them another dollar or two.

Just when each man had a full glass and Clara and Mrs. Healy had a moment to step back behind the bar and take a breath, Jeremiah Drake and Bill Albright walked in and took the table under the window. Clara felt her fists tighten in her apron pockets. Outside the light was fading, and she looked at Mrs. Healy.

"You stay right here," her employer said. "You know they only want to scare you, the fools."

Clara nodded, then busied herself with the broom while Mrs. Healy walked over to the table with two glasses of beer. The next time Clara looked up, Mr. Drake was waving her over, his big jack-o'-lantern grin a sure sign that he'd already had his share of whiskey before coming into the tavern. Clara leaned her broom up against the bar and walked slowly over to them.

"We heard you had a visitor today," Mr. Drake said.

Clara watched him carefully.

"You boys gossip worse than any woman I've ever met," Mrs. Healy said.

Drake drained his glass and handed it to her. "I'll take another. You know I don't like waiting."

"And you know I don't like serving you, but nobody seems to care what *I* like." Mrs. Healy sighed. She looked at Clara, her eyes full of apology.

"Gentlemen," Clara said in the sweetest voice she could muster. "I'll leave you to enjoy your drinks."

But Drake grabbed her wrist before she could walk away. "The Fourth of July is just around the corner, Bill. Isn't it? What do you think we'll do to mark the occasion?"

Clara snatched her arm away from him, clutching the skin where he had touched her. She prayed that the floor would open and swallow her whole, or, better yet, swallow these men right down into hell. She tried to will George to walk through the door and come to her rescue, but the hinges didn't move.

"Oh, I don't know," Bill said, his balding scalp gleaming in the lamplight. "Seems like now that this town's grown a little bigger, we should organize some kind of picnic."

Jeremiah nodded. "That's a fine idea. What do you think, Miss Bixby? We could roast a pig. Bill here will set off some firecrackers."

Clara shook her head, her tongue frozen her in mouth.

"Course," Bill said, shrugging his shoulders, "we're forgetting that she might be on her way to Fremont that day. I doubt they hold many pig roasts up at the jail."

Clara heard heavy bootsteps behind her then, too heavy to belong to George, but she felt she would happily take any man's help at the moment. A cold canine nose brushed the back of her hand and she glanced down. Her eyes welled with tears.

"Evening," Mayor Cartwright's soft voice rumbled. He lifted his hat. "Mrs. Bixby."

"Good evening," she whispered.

"Do you see that this woman has work to do?" Cartwright said to the men. "Why don't you leave her be."

"Happy to," Jeremiah said, swaying a bit in his chair. "I am just trying to help Miss Bixby with her financial predicament."

Mrs. Healy returned with Jeremiah's ale then and set it down in front of him. "That will be the last one you get tonight. You've had enough, Mr. Drake."

Drake ignored her and she walked away. Cartwright cleared his throat. "Drake, this woman is a Mrs., and you know that very well. You'll show her a little respect."

Jeremiah scowled at the mayor and swiped his hand through the air, as if he were brushing a mosquito away from his ear. He leaned on one elbow and turned to Clara. "*Mrs. Bixby*," he said, his voice full of false deference. "It may be that you're going about this all wrong. Have you thought about another line of work? Something that might pay a little more?"

Clara held up her hands. "I'm doing the only thing I can think to do, Mr. Drake." She tried to keep her voice steady. "You *must* see that."

"Why don't you just let her be?" Cartwright said.

Jeremiah shrugged and looked over at Bill. "You know, she's a little old for it, but they're always looking to hire another girl out at the log house."

Before the words could make their way from Clara's ears to her brain, the table tipped forward and glasses crashed to the floor, ale splashing on Bill's boots. The mayor clutched the left side of Jeremiah's collar in his enormous hand, pulling the red-faced man up onto the toes of his boots. The talking at the other tables stopped and Sergeant lowered his head and began to growl. Cartwright tightened his grip and Jeremiah's face turned a deeper shade of red, his eyes bulging.

"I said you'll show her a little respect," the mayor said, his voice even, his shoulder barely straining to hold the entire weight of the man up with one arm. He wrenched Jeremiah's body toward the door and the man's boots dragged across the floor. Mayor Cartwright cast him out the open door onto the front porch. As the door swung closed they heard Jeremiah coughing, gasping for breath.

Bill stood up and rushed across the tavern toward the door. "You saw what he did to Mr. Drake," he shouted, pointing at the other customers as he went out. "You all saw it."

Mr. Cartwright straightened his jacket, then pulled a handkerchief out of his pocket, removed his hat, and mopped his forehead. "Mrs. Healy," he said. "I am so sorry for making a mess."

She laughed. "You cleaned up a bigger mess, as far as I'm concerned." She bent down to pick up the broken glass.

The mayor wouldn't look at Clara. A moment passed and she touched his elbow. "Thank you," she whispered, her voice breaking before the words could make it out.

He nodded once, cleared his throat. "Come on, Sergeant," he said, whistling for the dog. "Let's get you a drink."

After eleven Clara climbed the stairs to her room, but she was restless and not ready to sleep. There was an hour left in this wretched day and still George was nowhere to be seen. She straightened the bedclothes and stacked the mugs next to the stove. Out of habit, Clara checked the teacup that held the Bixby fortune, as she had come, wryly, to think of it. All the money was still there; in fact, there seemed to be a little more than last time. George was to be counted on after all.

Speaking of George, his aroma was strong off the shirt he had worn to work the previous day. Clara took it, along with a stiff set of his underclothes and her own spare shift, down to the tavern kitchen to soak them while she prepared a cup of tea. She boiled the tub of water, then shook each article out before plunging it in with the dissolving flakes of soap. She grasped George's shirt, but something stiff in the breast pocket stopped her from dunking it in the tub. She felt around the object with her fingers, then slid them inside the pocket to retrieve it and stared, openmouthed, at what she found.

The queen of diamonds stared back at Clara. So the sheriff's visit, or Jeremiah Drake's bullying, was not to be the worst news of the day. For at least in the matter of this investigation and trial, there was hope, however small, that things would turn out all right. In the matter of George's gambling, however, Clara knew with absolute certainty that he would ruin them. Where he had gone to find a game was anyone's guess; he couldn't have done it right under her nose at Mrs. Healy's, but there were always other towns, other taverns. The extra money in the teacup showed that he had won a hand or two—cheated, it seemed, from the card hidden in his shirt—but eventually he would lose. And then he would go on losing. Just like before.

Rowena

Four days after he first introduced himself to Rowena, Tomas arrived back at the soddy with another man and a wagon full of wood. Rowena heard their conversation and laughter as they came up the path. Daniel tipped his hat to them as he left for the shop. The children scurried ahead of him on their way to school.

Daniel's words about how the people in Destination had broken from the constraints of New York society had struck a chord with her. Rowena could see that, for someone like her, Nebraska really did offer the chance to forge her own path, to leave behind the failures and embarrassments of the past. The last few years clawing to keep her head above water with Eliza Rourke and her ilk had been exhausting. What was it all for, really? Rowena decided she would talk to Daniel soon about bringing her father west to live with them. If only she could have him near and care for him in his final years, she thought maybe she could be happy here.

Rowena felt her heart was tenderer toward Tomas too, now that she knew they both belonged to the same mournful club. She was determined to begin again with him.

But Tomas did not knock on the door. He and the man went to the spot behind the house that Rowena had shown him and began work. She watched from the window over the sink, careful to stand back far enough from the curtain to be invisible in the dim light of the room. Tomas wore the same clothes as the day they met but removed his jacket as he began and rolled up the sleeves of his shirt. The boots still gleamed. His companion wore a worker's rough clothing, which emphasized just what Tomas had hoped to communicate, that he was bound for greater things than this labor, that he was a man of authority and position. Not once did he glance up at the kitchen window.

By afternoon they had completed the two sets of walls, filled the space between them with straw, and begun construction on the roof. Rowena heaped two plates with chicken and potatoes and poured two mugs full of cool tea from the pitcher she kept under the sink. She waited as long as she could stand it, hoping that Tomas would be the one to ask first for food so that she did not have to lose the upper hand, but he did not stop his work until the sun was well west of the peak of the sky. When she worried, finally, that they would work themselves sick, she opened the kitchen door and called to them.

"Gentlemen, I have some dinner for you." She held up the plates so they could see them. Tomas braced his weight against his knee and sawed into a piece of wood. The other carpenter threw down his hammer and jogged for the door. Rowena had intended for them to come inside and sit at the table, but the man reached out to take the plates from her.

"Don't you want to get out of the heat for a while?"

He glanced back at Tomas. "He will not."

"Well, why ever not?" Rowena called to him. "Mr. Skala? Please come inside."

Tomas continued sawing. "I not hungry."

Rowena shook her head, then looked back at the other carpenter, whose eyes were on the plate. "Well, you're very welcome, if you want to eat."

"Thank you, ma'am." He followed her inside and sat down at the table, taking off his hat and placing it on the seat of the chair beside him. He wiped his brow with his sleeve, then picked up one of the mugs of tea and drained it in a single gulp.

"What is your name?" she asked.

"Radek."

"Well, Mr. Radek," she said. "Would you like to wash up first?"

He colored. "Ah, please forgive." He pushed back his chair and came to the sink, where he lathered his hands and used the cloth to wipe his face and neck with water from the bowl she reserved it in to wash the dishes. The water turned red-brown from the prairie dust. Radek was taller and broader than Tomas, and coarse the way she imagined most Bohemians must be. She suspected he was a young man, but his skin was leathery from so much time outdoors.

As he sat back down at the table and began to bolt the food, Rowena busied herself at the sink. An awkward silence filled the room and she couldn't bear it. She tried to make conversation.

"Have you known Mr. Skala a long time?" she asked.

Radek nodded, though he could not speak with his mouth full of potatoes. His fork scraped the first plate clean and he pulled Tomas's plate toward him and started in on it. "My sister being his wife," he said, then searched for the word. "*Was being.*"

Rowena turned to face him. "My husband told me what happened to Mrs. Skala and Mr. Skala's parents. I am so sorry to hear of it."

Radek nodded. "I thank you."

She hesitated, not sure what she meant to ask. She supposed she felt a little troubled that Tomas didn't seem bereaved in the way she thought he should, or must. "Mr. Skala seems to be bearing up under it all right."

Radek nodded. "I guess his thinking being that life is for the living."

After Radek finished eating he went back outside and took up his tools. The men finished hammering the wood frame as the children, filthy from hours playing in the dusty fields behind the church, rumbled into the house, shoving and shouting and asking for their supper. Tomas and Radek threw all their tools and the leftover wood in the cart and began their slow amble home.

Rowena stood at the front door watching them go. The sun was low and intensely orange, like the round head of a marigold. It seemed almost scented with a marigold's perfume, though nothing was blooming in this dry place. Tomas squinted into the sun and dust, his posture weary but relaxed. He seemed to know something that Rowena had been trying for years to find out, but she feared he wouldn't tell her, even if she asked. She wanted to call out *Thank you* or *Good afternoon*, but her voice stuck in her throat like a thorn.

* * *

When Daniel and the children left after breakfast the next day, the house was finally quiet again. Rowena moved through her morning routine in a steady, deliberate way. She washed each dish carefully and lined them up to drain next to the sink. She opened the small window that looked out on the lane, then closed it again when a cloud of dust coughed into the room. It was even hotter today than it had been the day before, and the sky was clear and pale, a bleached-out blue, not a drop of rain in sight.

When she had done everything she could possibly do to pass the time, Rowena sat down, restless and irritable. It wasn't yet ten in the morning. When the image of Clara Bixby appeared in her mind, Rowena tried not to panic. She let the apparition stand there, Miss Bixby in that drab suit she seemed to think was flattering, leaning against the post on the tavern porch. In the vision she seemed fine. Rowena tried to let her imagination convince her that nothing she had said to Mr. Albright had come to anything. Rowena even felt a little relief, though deep down she knew she had no right to it.

She had come to understand over the last year or so that her temper worked on a kind of cycle, like hunger. First there was the building desire, the planning, the preparation. Then she ate the meal. And for a while she was satisfied, until the desire began again to build. So far she had been following a code that seemed, at least to her, to be consistent—she never set her anger on anyone who didn't have it coming. Mrs. Channing, for example, really had only nefarious aims in the world. Eliza Rourke too. There was no call for guilt, even if the things Rowena said and did to them were cruel. And Rowena had never lied. Until now. This matter with Mr. Albright was new. Her conscience plucked at her.

She stood up. It was no use thinking this way. The house was too quiet—that was all. She had become accustomed to the children's commotion. Her mind was playing a trick on her, drumming up this guilt. She had to remember what Clara had done, how she had turned Rowena's life upside down, deceived her. That was the thing to focus on. There was no question—she had been wronged.

She sighed. Standing in the middle of the kitchen, Rowena closed her eyes and tried to imagine what her life would be like if she had never come here, if Richard never had died. She reversed the events in the years since the war, as if she were flipping back the pages of a book, and took herself back to the place of waiting for him to return, back to the place where there was still hope. In her mind's eye, she put herself in the armchair in the parlor of her father's row house, spread Richard's letter open in her hands. This was a day back before the point where her life diverged in such an unexpected direction, the day *before* she got the bad news. She was still Rowena Moore then, just as frivolous as she pleased, her thoughts foamy with lace and silk and perhaps, in a year or two, a nursery in the upstairs bedroom that would make her friends green with jealousy. A little blond son in her grandmother's cradle. Oh, how delicious it would be to have a party to show him off!

Richard would come to the door, weary, filthy, missing a finger or a hand or a few teeth. Rowena felt herself nodding her head at the vision, lingering over the details to make it as real as she could. From the parlor window she spied him making his slow way up the walk. And an ache thrummed in her chest and she fell into the posture of prayer as she heard his tired feet scrape up the steps. It seemed essential that she not run to him right away but that she keep on praying, *Thank you thank you thank you thank you* crackling on her lips. If only she had been allowed to feel that gratitude, Rowena thought, she could have been so much better, could have *done* better in the world. If God had allowed Richard to come home to her, she would have been the most adoring, serene, devoted wife who ever had walked the earth. But God had not allowed it.

No, she urged herself. *Not yet.* She couldn't return yet to the present day, to the sod house in Nebraska. Keeping her eyes closed, Rowena pulled Richard's letter from the top of her corset. She put her hand out in front of her and groped, blindly, across the kitchen and out the door, the sun bright against her closed lids. The hot air rasped into her lungs, the smell of iron in the dust. She had a notion of getting to the chicken house before she unfolded the letter and opened her eyes. But she couldn't wait. With careful fingertips she unfolded it and sat down on the ground. Finally, when she was sure the letter was the first thing she would see, she opened her eyes.

But it didn't work. She didn't believe the fiction in her mind. The letter was upside down, the words inverted, wrong. Richard was still dead.

She was sitting in that strange pose when Tomas walked up behind her. "Rowena, are you well?"

Her eyes darted up to him.

"Bad news?"

She shook her head. "What are you doing here?"

"I leave my saw. What is this you read, Rowena?"

Her eyes filled with tears. "*Why* won't you call me Mrs. Gibson?"

"Ah, me," he said. "I apologize for this, the other day."

She shook her head.

He looked at her hands, then sat down on the ground beside her. "This is letter? Who send you?"

Rowena continued to stare at the paper. "My husband."

Tomas raised his eyebrows and gave a surprised laugh. "He write you when you in kitchen, he at butcher shop?"

Rowena shook her head. "Not that husband. My *late* husband, the one who died in the war."

Tomas gave her a confused look.

"My *first* love. My only love."

"But war end . . ." Tomas counted on his fingers. " . . . two years past."

Rowena nodded.

"And now you marry Mr. Gibson, but still your heart breaking?"

She sighed and nodded.

"Ah, me," Tomas said again. "My wife die too, you know."

"Yes, I heard about that. I'm so very sorry."

"Only one year past. That is whole reason I come this place," he said, moving his arm in an exasperated arc. "Why else anyone come here?"

"It's awful, isn't it?"

"Yes," he said. "Hot, dry. Nothing to do."

"Do you mind if I ask why you have stayed?" A bubble of mucus descended from her nostril and she sniffed, then wiped her face rudely on her sleeve. She felt strangely about herself at that moment, as if she were watching her body from the outside.

"Saving money. But soon I move on to a city. Somewhere they have opportunity."

She smiled at him. "You'll do well."

Tomas shrugged. "You know, Rowena—forgive, Mrs. Gibson—"

"Rowena's all right," she said. "May I call you Tomas?"

This seemed to please him very much. "Yes. I want to ask you something."

"All right."

"You know what best thing for you could be?"

She shook her head.

"This letter," he said, taking it carefully from her, holding it by the corner with his left hand. "If it burn up." He moved the fingers of his right hand like flames at the bottom of the page, crinkling the paper. She gave him a fearful look and he handed the letter back to her. "Don't worry," he said. "I not going to do it. But you reading it all time and again . . . is like . . ." He searched for what he meant to say. "Is like you not be in love anymore with the *man*, your husband from before he die. Is like you be in love with *losing* the man. You be in love with *sadness*. You see what is my meaning?"

Rowena swallowed. "Yes." Destroying the letter seemed like severing the rope that moored her. Without it, she would be at risk of endless drift. And yet, the thought thrilled her too. To be free of it all, to let it all go. Because Richard never *was* going to come back, no matter what she imagined, and she knew it.

"If this letter burn up, then you have to stop," he said,

making a chopping motion with this hand. "Then you move ahead."

She folded it up and stuck it back in the collar of her dress, not caring that Tomas watched her fingers reach into the gap between the fabric and the top of her breast, that for a split second before the paper slid inside, the fair skin of its curve was exposed. She wouldn't burn the letter yet. But she would allow herself to imagine burning it, the way she had allowed herself, a little while earlier, to imagine Richard's return. We couldn't bridle the world and its tricks, but oh, how the imagined life in our minds' interior could substitute. How real these visions seemed!

She looked up at Tomas, not with a demure tilt of her head, not with the manipulation of lashes swaying down, but simply *looked* at him. His eyes were the blue-green of patina on copper left out in the elements, the particular hue that resulted only from neglect.

"I'm thirsty," she said. "Would you like to come inside for some tea?"

Elsa

Ully came back every day for five days, at the same time in the afternoon. She must have waited to be sure Mr. Schreier was out in the field. Elsa never had to tell her again to wash; she stopped each time at the pump and came inside with water dripping from her chin.

At first Elsa gave the girl only the scraps they could spare from the lukewarm dinner, and she devoured every bite, eagerly. But in the hours after Ully went back home, Elsa began to daydream about the sweets and cakes of her childhood that she had loved: *Marzipan* and *Kreppel* and *Rumkugeln*. She prepared them one by one, disregarding the season. Mr. Schreier finally did go to the grocer, but she didn't want to ask him for ingredients he might think were frivolous. Instead, she gave a coin to Ully and sent the girl to Mr. Baumann or Mr. Wessendorff's in search of the nuts or chocolate or spice. She worried, the first time, that Ully would take off with the money, but she never did. The girl always returned with the ingredient wrapped in brown paper, the change in her moist palm.

"Good afternoon, Ully," Elsa would say, and if the little girl only nodded or shuffled in reply, or said, "Hallo," or "Hey,

Elsa," Elsa would ask her to go outside and come back in to reply, "Good afternoon, Elsa." There were so many things the girl didn't seem to know: how to use a napkin, how to cut her meat with a knife, how to chew without her lips hanging open for all the world to see her cud. Ully was in constant motion at the table, banging and scraping and humming and sighing over the food. She was missing that steadying line that ran between the shoulders of refined girls, kept them still and quiet and straight. Elsa felt at once sad and a little thrilled for her because of it.

"Ully," she said Saturday afternoon as they each ate a slice of *Lebkuchen* as deep as a brick. Christmas in June. Elsa worked the words in her mouth carefully before speaking. "What was your mother like?"

Elsa was glad to see the girl finish chewing, then wipe a dusting of sugar from her upper lip, before she replied. "Nice when I was little. But then she got sad, and then sick, and she was sick for a long time. And then she died. My pa said that she just couldn't cheer up, that some people can't."

Elsa nodded, thinking for a moment about what she could possibly say to this. "Well, she isn't sick anymore. Isn't that so, *Spatzchen?*" Elsa bit her tongue; the pet name had slipped out before she could stop it.

Ully nodded cautiously.

"She is always with you now, looking down, and she isn't sick or sad anymore."

The girl shrugged, then peered suspiciously at Elsa. She had only ever been called names by her brothers, and they weren't kind. "What's a spots chin?"

Elsa laughed. "A sparrow. You remind me of a sparrow, small and full of energy, always moving. It means I am fond of you."

Ully scraped her fork in a slow circle on the empty plate, then looked up at Elsa. She stuck out the tip of her tongue and made a rude sound with her mouth.

Elsa went to sleep that night with the taste of ginger on her tongue. It had been years and years and years since she had experienced these flavors. The fine cloud of powdered sugar, the almond crunch and sleek caramel. Elsa spent every cent of the money she had brought with her from New York on hazelnuts and stewed fruits. When that was gone she began to dip into the wages she had planned to save. It felt reckless, but Mr. Schreier only bought sorghum and she had to have real sugar.

Already the little girl's skin looked brighter, her cheeks a little less hollow. Elsa knew she would soon have to stop. What if Mr. Gibson realized where his daughter was going in the afternoons and said something about it to Mr. Schreier in town? Besides, every day the weather got worse—drier, hotter. Keeping the fire hot enough to bake the desserts made it over ninety degrees in the kitchen. By the time Ully left and Mr. Schreier returned from the field, Elsa's shift and the sides of her dress were soaked with sweat, not to mention growing tighter across her hips every day. She rinsed them out each night in the stifling attic, the air so hot that the clothes dried within an hour. It was insanity to continue.

And yet, as she slipped into the anteroom of sleep, aware of the pressure of the cotton sheet on her bare skin but unable to move her limbs, Elsa knew she would keep on. For she hadn't yet made the *Dampfnudeln*, the sweet dumplings, which she loved most of all, and she just knew in her heart that Ully would love them too.

Elsa woke a few hours later with a rasping breath, her throat dry. She lit a candle and glanced at the clock next to the bed: it was not yet three. Even Mr. Schreier didn't rise this early.

Her feet bare, the ribbons of her nightgown hanging untied at her collar, Elsa crept down the stairs to the kitchen for water. Even in the dark there was no relief from the heat. Everything felt warm to the touch, even the tin pitcher in which they kept the drinking water. Elsa drank the mug down, then set it next to the sink and crept back through the sitting room toward the stairs. Mr. Schreier's bedroom door clicked open, throwing light from his lamp into the room.

"So we're both up, then."

Elsa started. "Oh," she said. "Mr. Schreier." She crossed her hands over her collarbone, her elbows pressing her breasts against her ribs.

"Good evening, or good morning," he said, "since the chances of falling asleep again aren't good." Mr. Schreier limped into the sitting room and eased into his armchair. He looked exhausted. "Do you often have trouble sleeping?"

"Not too much. Sometimes."

She stood awkwardly near the door to the stairs. Mr. Schreier glanced at her, then leaned forward and pulled the blanket from the back of the chair. He handed it to her.

"You know, I was married for an awfully long time." He was trying to put her at ease, she saw. She had nothing he hadn't seen before. But his calling attention to her body at all, her near nakedness, made her feel worse. She felt the blood in her cheeks.

"Sit down," he barked. He shook his head. "I mean, if you'd like."

She draped the blanket over her shoulders and instantly felt the skin on her flanks begin to dampen. She stepped over to the window and pushed it open. The stale air in the room shifted slightly. "I'll fix us some tea," she said.

In the kitchen she put the kettle on the stove. The heat was everywhere, oppressive. The soles of her feet felt hot, her eyeballs roved sweatily in their sockets. She took some lace cookies from the tin and lined them up on a plate. She brought the tray back into the sitting room and poured Mr. Schreier's cup, then sat on the sofa.

"I've never seen so many cakes and sweets as you make," he said irritably, taking a bite of the crisp brown cinnamon cookie. A smattering of crumbs fell in his lap and he brushed them away.

Elsa hesitated, wondering if he was testing her. She folded her hands in her lap. If he knew about Ully's visits, why wouldn't he just *say* so? "I hope you don't mind all the baking, sir."

He waved his hand. "I suppose you mean well."

Guilt plucked at her again. Now was the time to tell him.

"This heat," Mr. Schreier said. He pulled a handkerchief from his pocket and wiped his brow. "We're going to be in for it if we don't get some rain soon."

"It *is* awfully dry," Elsa said. "The kitchen garden is in very poor shape."

"If I put my hand to the barley shoots, they turn to dust. It's all supposed to go to Drake's after the harvest." He put his elbows on his knees and laced his fingers beneath his chin. "That brewery employs four men who'll be out of a job if they can't brew on schedule."

Elsa looked down at her lap.

"Have you ever noticed that all the things that matter in this life, all the things that really matter to other people, I mean, to helping them get by—no man can do a damn thing about them? A man can't make the rain come, can't make the crops grow. Can't make the sick well."

"Is that why you read all those old newspapers? To try to understand these things?" The questions were out before she could stop the words. He grunted in response but seemed to wait for what else she might say. "Sir, I believe we must have faith in the Lord and his plan, that he will provide for us, protect us. That the trials of this life are temporary."

He gave her a stern look. "I find that the folks who say things like that are just the ones who've never seen a trial in all their days."

Elsa bit down on the tip of her tongue. She felt she was at such a disadvantage here in this town, in this house. She knew nothing at all about men, what they thought about, what drove them. In her whole life she had scarcely even been in a room with a man except for her father, and the last time she saw him she was still a girl. Once Mr. Channing had stopped her in the wide, blue-carpeted hallway above the stairs to the laundry to ask her whether she knew where his wife had hidden the bourbon. Elsa had only whispered, *No, sir*, because Mrs. Channing had threatened each laundress with termination if she helped him get his liquor back.

Why did they speak and do as they did? Mr. Schreier, for instance—why did he seem to be all the time so angry? Elsa couldn't begin to think of an answer. And for another—why had he asked her to sit and talk with him if he so disliked her presence? There was no telling. Elsa was growing angry, she realized, for she could name a dozen trials she had known in her life, and Mr. Schreier was arrogant to assume she had known nothing but ease. These trials did not threaten her faith, but strengthened it. The darker things became, the more she knew mercy.

"There are a good many things," Elsa said, steadying her voice as the words tumbled out, painted red with her anger, "that I'm sure you *don't* know about me."

Mr. Schreier looked at her in surprise. His expression changed slightly, as if he were coming to a slow realization about her. When he spoke, his voice was quiet. "I'm certain that's true, Elsa."

She nodded and stood up, folding the blanket and placing it on the sofa. She was no longer self-conscious about him seeing her in the nightgown. "I believe I will try to sleep a little more before the morning," she said. "Good night, sir."

"Good night." Mr. Schreier picked up the now-cool cup of tea and took a sip. She started up the stairs. "Elsa?"

She stepped back down and turned her face toward him.

"I suppose you have been wanting to go to church. I'm sorry I didn't think of it before."

"Yes, sir. I am anxious to go."

"We'll go together then, tomorrow."

She nodded, then started back up the stairs. *After all that harsh talk, a kindness!* Elsa wondered whether all men were so strange.

Clara

Since coming to Destination, Clara hadn't once heard Reverend Crowley's Sunday sermon, but she vowed to start today. She hadn't wanted to subject herself to the harsh judgments of the people in town. Some, like the minister's new wife, felt Clara had done them a great service by delivering them to their husbands. But Albright and Luft, not to mention Mr. Drake and Rowena Gibson, held her in contempt. All the problems in life they'd ever have were somehow Clara's fault. But here Clara was at the church, subjecting herself to it after all, for she found that she needed the guidance of the Lord at this particular juncture—a sad state of affairs, since she was fairly certain he could do nothing for her.

The Methodist Church of Destination was a small A-frame building with a year-old coat of paint now worn through down to the wood by the omnipresent prairie dust. There was no bell, no steeple, no stained glass. It could have been merely one of the finer homes in town (being that it was made from wood and not sod), but for the cross that hung over the door and the graves scattered on the plot of land on the building's east side, surrounded by a fence to keep a wandering cow or horse from befouling the sacred ground. Among those graves, Clara knew, were the eternal resting places of the two drunken men who had burned down Gerhard Gade's barn with his horse roasting inside. Mr. Skala's wife and parents, and Mrs. Healy's husband, all of them killed in that train robbery, were buried here too along with men who claimed land ten years ago or more but hadn't survived, and rail workers lost to fever or injury.

Mrs. Healy had told Clara that the worst part of her husband's death came after the shooting, when the bandits were carted off by the marshals and the train carried on down the line. Mr. Skala and Mrs. Healy, so rattled and disbelieving of what had taken place, had insisted on riding in the half-empty luggage car with the bodies of their loved ones the rest of the way to Destination, a town they had never seen. They leaned their backs against two large crates of nails that had come all the way from Detroit and sipped whiskey from Mr. Skala's pocket flask. Mrs. Healy said she could hear her husband's dentures rattling with the rhythm of the rails from inside the wood crate that served as his makeshift coffin. Somebody had forgotten to take them out.

Clara had dressed for church in her traveling suit and arranged her hair with care. She poked George where he lay in a heap on the mattress. He groaned and stirred but refused to wake up. It was just as well. Clara wanted to go to meeting by herself. Just to be certain she would not be plagued with anxiety while she was gone, Clara tipped the contents of the teacup into her coin purse and stuffed it deep into the pocket of her skirt. As she was leaving, she noticed George peering at her through one slitty eye. Clara had said nothing to him about the playing card she'd found in his shirt pocket. She wanted to believe that he had changed, that the presence of that card was a fluke, an apparition. But she wasn't going to take any chances.

Inside the church, Clara slipped into a back pew, hoping for invisibility. She nearly got it. Bill Albright cut his eyes at her, but that was to be expected. Deborah floated in, clutching her husband Stuart's arm close. She winked at Clara as she passed by, as if to say that certain wifely duties were not quite so burdensome as she had first suspected. Reverend Crowley began his sermon, Mrs. Crowley gazing adoringly at him from her place in the front pew. He read to them from the Scripture. "'Cursed be the man who trusteth in man. He shall inhabit the parched places of the wilderness. But blessed be the man who trusteth in the Lord, whose hope the Lord is. For he shall be as a tree planted by the waters, that spreadeth out her roots by the river, and shall not see when heat cometh, but her leaf shall be green.'"

Clara tried to contemplate these words but found in her heart only skepticism. What good would it do any of them to sit here hoping for rain? She found herself distracted by the presence of one Rowena Moore Gibson, three pews up. The haughty woman sat shoulder to shoulder with her husband, his blond children arranged in order of height on his other side like a staircase leading down to the far aisle of the sanctuary. The littlest one, a girl, kicked the pew in front of her with a continual thudding, then lay down in the aisle with her feet up in the air. Rowena simply ignored this disgraceful behavior.

Clara despaired. The weeks of constant work had allowed her to keep her guilt over what she had done to Rowena at bay. But in the quiet of the church it tumbled in her mind. How had she allowed things to go so far that Rowena would make up this awful story about the fraud? Clara knew she should have apologized right at the start for the deception about Mr. Gibson and should have helped Rowena get back to New York somehow. But Clara had insisted on teaching the young woman some kind of lesson through suffering. As if Clara were in any position to dole out wisdom. And as if suffering ever taught anybody a thing except to thank God when it ended.

"Just as the Lord protected Noah from the flood," Reverend Crowley said. "So will he protect us, his faithful ones."

There was a wager George would be smart enough not to take, Clara thought. The piano started up then and the collection plate bobbed along the pews, lingering for a long moment in Rowena's lap, Clara noticed. Clara bowed her head as the parishioners filed out. But instead of praying she only wished she could go back to November and stop herself from writing that first letter to the mayor. She should have stayed in New York, found another position in another tavern after Mr. Rathbone let her go. She should have kept her head down and saved her money, then gone somewhere sane, western Pennsylvania or Ohio, and found her little white cottage in a small town.

Clara felt a few pairs of vicious eyes on her, then felt them pass. She peeked up over her folded hands to see that the pews ahead of her were empty. Rowena and her brood were now safely out of the church. Clara sighed, the nagging fears about George surfacing once again. What was she going to do if he betrayed her?

Just then, she felt a hand on her shoulder and looked up.

Elsa Traugott stood next to Clara in the pew. Leo Schreier passed behind her and out the door, moving as quickly as his bad leg would let him. He seemed not to be a man for too much chatter.

"Good morning, Miss Bixby. I'm glad to see you," Elsa said.

"You are? How are things going out at the farm?"

Elsa smiled that serene, closed-lip smile that pulled her plump cheeks up high like two apples on a string. "Very well. It has taken some getting used to, but I must say I do not miss the laundry at the Channings'."

"I can't imagine how you would," Clara said with laugh. She remembered that back in New York nothing had seemed worse to her than doing someone else's laundry to earn her bread. Now she would happily do it, would happily do anything to resolve the mess with these men.

Elsa took Clara's elbow. "Let's go outside and talk for a moment." They moved out into the aisle, Elsa's rump brushing the hymnals askew in their slots as she swished past.

Outside, Leo had pulled the wagon around front and held the reins. "Come on, Elsa." His mouth worked impatiently on the hunk of tobacco he had wedged in his cheek.

"Yes, sir. Just a minute." She turned to Clara. "And how do things go for you, *Mrs.* Bixby?"

"Ah," Clara nodded. "So you heard about George finding his way out here, then?"

Elsa nodded. Mr. Schreier's horses shifted out of boredom and the wagon lurched. "Elsa, let's go."

She nodded. "Mrs. Bixby, why don't you pay me a visit sometime?" She put her hand on Clara's arm.

Clara felt her eyes filling with tears and looked away, clearing her throat. She was working so hard to keep everything together that any kindness felt like a threat. She feared, more than anything, coming undone. "This dust is another kind of plague, I swear."

Daniel Gibson approached them on Elsa's other side. "Miss Traugott, I wonder if I could have a word with you."

Up in the wagon, Mr. Schreier sighed dramatically.

Rowena stood off to the side with those seemingly endless Gibson children. She wouldn't look at Clara.

Clara noticed Elsa stiffen and instinctively kept close to her side.

"Of course," Elsa nearly whispered to Daniel. She glanced up at Mr. Schreier.

"Well, I just wanted you to know that *I* know my Ulrika has been coming around your place an awful lot."

"Well, occasionally, yes, sir."

Daniel laughed. "I don't know how *you* define *occasionally*, but it seems like an awful lot to me."

"Yes, sir," Elsa said again.

"I just wanted to thank you for your kindness. That child has been in a terrible way since her mother has been gone. I honestly haven't known what to do with her. And things with the new Mrs. Moore are still . . . settling."

Elsa nodded, then glanced again, nervously, at Mr. Schreier. "Well, it's my pleasure, sir. She is a good girl."

Daniel sighed. "I believe that somewhere deep down she is just that, though she does a remarkable job of convincing everyone otherwise. If it ever gets to be too much, you know, just send her on home. She and Mrs. Gibson are going to have to get used to each other eventually. I've got no energy to deal with the child myself, what with trying to keep my business going in this awful summer."

"I am happy to have her, sir."

Mr. Gibson shook his head, a little amazed at this good fortune. "Well. Good day, Miss Traugott, Mrs. Bixby," he said, tipping his hat. Elsa said good-bye to Clara, then got up into the wagon, and Mr. Schreier took off down the main road so quickly, Elsa's bonnet sailed behind her head, secured by its chin strap. Mr. Gibson and Rowena set off walking too, followed by the children. Everyone in Destination scattered to get home and out of the heat, leaving Clara standing alone in front of the empty church. Showing up for the service hadn't gone as poorly as she feared it might, so with some relief Clara headed back to her room.

When she approached the tavern, Mrs. Healy waved to her from the wooden steps that went up the outside of the building to the second floor. She was taking laundry down from the complicated zigzag of clothesline she had rigged up there, high enough to stay out of the dust. Clara climbed the stairs.

"Good afternoon, Mrs. Healy."

"I don't know about *good*." She and Kathleen Connolly and the handful of Catholics in town had their own church at the other end of the main road, but no priest. Now and then an itinerant came through on the train to hear confession and give communion. What they did in that building on their own each Sunday morning was anybody's guess, but it probably wasn't nearly so interesting or scandalous as the Methodists speculated.

Clara reached for a shirt collar. "May I help you with these?"

"Mayor Cartwright usually comes to pick them up on Saturday evening, but he must have forgotten. I was going to take them over to him."

"What do you know about him, Mrs. Healy? I'm surprised that he is still a bachelor."

"So am I. I suppose it has something to do with choosing to live out here, of all places, where there's nary a woman to be found. He's a good nephew to that ungrateful uncle of his, but it has cost him his youth. I wonder now if he isn't too settled in his ways. After all, he could have asked *you* to bring him a bride."

Clara put her head in her hands. "Thank goodness he didn't. I've got about all I can handle as it is." She folded the last collar. "I don't mind walking the bundle over. I know you've got plenty to do here."

Mrs. Healy leveled her eyes at Clara. "I surely do. You should see the state of the room down the hall from yours. You would think I rented it to a wild hog. Dishes and crumbs everywhere, empty bottles, cigar stubs. I don't know why I bother with any of this. Mr. Healy would have a fit if he knew how I earn my bread these days."

Clara shook her head in solidarity. "I'll get started on the room right away."

Mrs. Healy waved her hand. "I'll do it if you'll take these to the mayor. I can't bear walking anywhere in this heat." She piled the two stacks of folded clothes in the sheet and tied the four corners into a neat bow.

"Of course," Clara said. "And leave the room as it is. I'll clean it up as soon as I get back." It felt good to do something to ease Mrs. Healy's burden, to repay her for her kindness and friendship. Clara had learned the hard way never to take those things for granted.

Mrs. Healy smiled gratefully at her. "You are a dear. I surely don't know why so many in this town speak hard words about you, Clara. To my mind, you are a fine woman."

"Well, they have their reasons, I suppose. It's a long story that brought all of us out here, isn't it?"

Mrs. Healy laughed. "When you get to be my age, there's nothing that *isn't* a long story."

Clara set off back down the main road with the laundry. She was halfway to the mayor's office before she realized that he wouldn't be there on the Sabbath and also that she didn't know where he lived. Just then, Anna was coming out of the front door of the church after sweeping the floor. She gripped the broom with one hand and stretched her back, then saw Clara waving to her.

"Mrs. Crowley, where is Mr. Kellinger's farm?"

She pointed southwest. "If you're looking for the mayor, he'll be out in the barn working on his machines."

"His machines?" Clara asked.

"You'll see. Would you like the reverend to give you a ride? He's around here somewhere."

"No, thank you," Clara said. "I don't mind the walk."

Clara continued to the west end of the main road and then about a half mile across the dusty pasture to Lambert Kellinger's farm. Next to the barn a couple of meager trees clustered together to suck moisture from way down deep in the soil with all their might. Two hot and thirsty cows stood beneath them trying to stay cool.

"Mrs. Crowley said I'd find you out here tinkering," Clara

called to the mayor on the other side of the barn. She set the bundle of laundry down on a chair just inside the doorway.

He glanced up from where he worked, crouched on the floor. His back was as wide and sturdy-looking as the barn door. When he saw her he smiled. "Tinkering? Mrs. Bixby, what you see here is *invention*."

"Hm," Clara said, glancing around at what looked to be nothing more than a big mess. Mr. Cartwright's work was spread on a table. A tan cloth lay draped over one side with oily tools and gears and nuts and bolts of all sizes spread out over it. Around him in the hay were machines in various states of completion, along with metal rods and leather belts. The mayor had traded his waistcoat and cravat for a farmhand's attire: denims and boots and a collarless shirt filthy with smudges of grease.

"Let me show you," he said. Clara crossed over to him. "Here we have a regular old butter churn." The cask for the cream was about waist high and the churn dash, a thick piece of wood, stuck up out of the center. "But where a farm wife would have operated this with her own elbow grease, I have invented an improvement that will save time and effort."

He pulled a tarp off the contraption standing next to the churn. There was a lever connected to the dash, and a set of gears and a conveyor made of wood slats held in line by thick rope. When the conveyor system moved, it turned the gears; the turning gears moved the lever, and the lever turned the agitator in a circle to churn the cream into butter.

Clara laughed at the idea of using so complex a system to perform such a simple task. "So you'd have the farm wife walk on this conveyor all afternoon long, walking and going nowhere? Forgive me, sir, but I don't see how that is any better than simply churning the old-fashioned way."

Mr. Cartwright put his hand over his heart. "It hurts, the way you underestimate me, Mrs. Bixby. But I can assure you that you aren't the first lady to do so." He put two fingers between his lips and whistled. A deep *woof* came from somewhere outside and a moment later, Sergeant kicked up a cloud of dust outside the barn and pranced across the hay with his strange loping limp.

"Mrs. Bixby, I have to give credit where credit is due. This whole contraption was Sergeant's idea."

Clara smiled and looked down at the dog. His one good ear hung properly alongside his face. The mutt tilted his head to the side where his one good eye blinked, black and round. "Can I ask you, sir—what in the world happened to this dog?" Clara crouched down in front of him and scratched his head.

"He was like this when he showed up on my porch last year. But I am almost certain he fought on the side of the Union in the war."

The dog licked Clara's hand, then turned to his master and sat up, waiting for instruction. Mr. Cartwright pointed to the conveyor. Sergeant hopped on and began walking at a steady pace. The dash moved in the churn.

"He'll do this for hours," the mayor said.

Clara clapped her hands. "A dog that churns butter— remarkable!"

Mr. Cartwright laughed and wiped his hands on a rag. "I'm glad to see you, Mrs. Bixby. How are you doing?"

"All right. Sheriff Brooks sure isn't letting up."

"I'm sorry to hear that." Sergeant glanced quizzically up at his master as he continued walking on the conveyor. Cartwright waved him off and he stepped down. The dash slowed to a stop.

"The Fourth of July will be coming around awfully soon."

Mayor Cartwright was quiet for a moment. "Well, do you have the money?"

Clara shook her head. "We have some of it saved," she said, patting her pocket. "But we won't have it all in time."

Mr. Cartwright glanced at her hand. "You carry it on your person? That seems a little dangerous."

"Not more dangerous than leaving it alone with my husband," Clara said. As soon as the words were out she regretted them. Bemoaning George's flaws was second nature to Clara, but it wasn't right to speak of them to another man.

To his credit, the mayor said nothing in response. "Mrs. Bixby, I want you to know that I am fairly close to flat broke myself. The office of mayor in Destination is a sort of honorary position—all of the work and none of the pay. And I have yet to sell any of my machines. But if I had the money, I would gladly give it to you."

Clara colored to the ends of her hair. She shook her head.

"No, I honestly would. You are a fine woman who tried to do something good. It went awry, but it isn't your fault. You don't deserve all this."

Clara couldn't wait to escape. She kept her eyes on his shoulder, too embarrassed to meet his gaze. "I thank you, sir." She pointed to the barn's open door. "Mrs. Healy asked me to bring your laundry. There it is."

"Oh, that's right—I forgot to pick it up."

"Yes," Clara said, nodding stupidly. "Well, I should be off now."

He put his hand on her elbow. "It's not just that I want to help you, Mrs. Bixby. I don't like the sort of man who goes running to the law to solve his problems. Bill Albright is always looking for an angle, a way he can get a leg up on everybody else. And don't start me on the subject of Jeremiah Drake. In a town of this size, we've all got to pull our own weight. And I certainly don't like him bringing Sheriff Brooks over here from Fremont. That man has a tendency to turn a case into a crusade, all for the sake of his own theater."

"He seemed quite impressed with himself, that is certain."

Cartwright gave her an amused smile. His gaze lingered on her face for a long minute. "I have no doubt you'll figure out something," he said finally. "You are very resourceful."

"Only because life has given me no other choice. Let's see . . . perhaps you can build me a press that prints banknotes?"

"I would in a heartbeat, if it weren't for that old tattler right there." He pointed at Sergeant, who lay in the dust on his back, waiting for someone to rub his belly. "I just know he'd go straight to the sheriff, and then we'd be in it up to our necks."

Rowena

Rowena burned the letter, without ceremony, on Monday. She woke up still ruminating on the idea of her life without it, and as she passed the hearth on the way out to the pump for wash water, she cast it into the fire. She didn't pray or say good-bye—just dropped it in. The weight of the act pressed down on her, disguised as the oppressive heat, which was unbearable even at dawn. The sky was wide and a washed-out blue; clearly it would be another day without rain in Dodge County. It was done now. She waited to feel something—remorse, relief—but felt nothing but weariness and hunger, as she did most mornings.

The bill for Rowena's father's care at the Wards Island asylum was again due. She lit the morning fire and prepared breakfast for Daniel and the children: a porridge of barley and salt pork, and stale bread with a jam of gooseberries Elsa Traugott had rescued from the shrubs before they shrank in the heat. Rowena had a vague notion that Ully had been spending time in the afternoons with that woman, Mr. Schreier's housekeeper. She had seen Daniel talking to her after church, wondered what he thought about their strange friendship. Certainly Rowena had no intention of giving the child that sort of attention. She and Daniel seemed to have come to a truce; he was asking less and less of her each day.

It was clear he no longer held out hope that their connection would grow into anything more than an exchange of funds for labor. The pack of children and the dearth of privacy in the one-room soddy had prevented more than a handful of moments when they found themselves alone. Daniel had tried, once, to kiss her, but his determination to win her affection withered beneath her cold gaze. Occasionally he touched her hand, or simply stood near her, hopeful, but she never yielded to it. Though Rowena supposed he was well within his rights to do so, to Daniel's credit, he never once attempted to take his liberties with her in the night. If he had insisted, Rowena knew she would have given in. She was his wife, after all. He occasionally mentioned a "cousin in Omaha," though, curiously, he was never gone long enough to have traveled there and returned in one afternoon. In any case, when he disappeared on such ventures, he seemed to return with his urges sated.

Daniel rose now from the bed and nodded to her as he slung his suspenders up with his thumbs and shuffled to the privy. The spring on the door slapped it closed when he emerged a few moments later. He then stuck his head under the well bucket for a brief splash. They had been told during announcements at church the day before to conserve water as no one knew how much longer they would have to wait for rain. It wasn't just the farmers who were worried. There would be less of everything—meat, milk and butter, tobacco, ale—without healthy crops and verdant pastures. After meeting, Rowena had overheard some of the men talking about leaving town, going east, where the weather was less severe, to find work.

She poured Daniel some coffee when he came back inside and sat down at the table. Water dripped from his beard and he wiped it on his sleeve. "Good morning," he said.

Rowena nodded. "Good morning."

The children were up and moving with their usual commotion. They filed one by one through the kitchen and out to the privy, then back inside to stand near Rowena as she dished the porridge into bowls. They had long since stopped calling her *Mother* but did not like *Mrs. Gibson*, either, and so said nothing at all. The two older boys, Sigrid and Gustav, seemed to have decided something about her, she saw, perhaps that she was not the sort of woman of whom their sainted mother would approve. Rowena had only speculation to imagine the first Mrs. Gibson's appearance as there were no images of the woman anywhere in the house. But she imagined someone sturdy and plain and openhearted. The boys found Rowena pretty, she knew, for she had caught each of them watching her with that furtive look they believed concealed their thoughts, when in fact, the content of those thoughts was as plain as day. She was closer in age to them than she was to their father, so she knew they must notice her. They scraped their chairs up to the table. After all, they were only a few years younger than Radek and Tomas.

"The payment for your father is in the drawer," Daniel said, pointing to the battered writing desk that stood in the far corner. "Would you mind arranging the postal order and sending it off today?"

Rowena had been looking for a way to bring up the subject

of the money, but Daniel had saved her from that indignity. She couldn't say a thing against this man, really. He was kind and honorable, both in his business and at home. He loved his children. He was a man of his word, unwavering, and he trusted someone as unworthy of trust as Rowena. He was a much better person than she was, much better by far, she knew.

"Thank you, Mr. Gibson," she said, and meant it.

When Daniel and the children had cleared out for the day, she composed a letter to accompany the payment, listing her father's name and the period of time for which the funds were intended, then tied on her bonnet and walked down the lane toward the main road and the depot to post it.

She made it as far as the town hall when a little man accosted her in the road.

"Mrs. Gibson?"

"Yes?" she said, startled.

He was even shorter than Rowena. He tipped his hat. "Sheriff Brooks."

Rowena felt dread tighten in her chest. "Hello, Sheriff."

"I've been wanting to speak to you about a conversation you had recently with Mr. William Albright, at his place of employment."

She shifted her weight from one foot to the other with her hand on her hip, then glanced down the length of the road. The sun was so bright she had to squint. "All right."

"Well, ma'am, I need to confirm the statements you made to him, regarding the activities of Mrs. Clara Bixby."

Rowena sighed. "Could you please save us both some time and tell me what it is that you want?"

Sheriff Brooks cleared his throat. "You told Mr. Albright that Clara Bixby never intended to find brides for him and some of the other men who paid for them. And that you know this information because she told you herself of her plans to defraud them. Do I have that right?"

This whole thing had gone too far, and Rowena knew down in her bones that she had to do something to stop it, that she was the only one who *could* stop it. She had maligned an innocent woman. What these men had was bad luck. That was all. And yet, when she glanced down at the envelope in her hand, she hesitated. What if Daniel learned what she had done and cast her out? What if he stopped sending money to help her father?

"Well?" the sheriff asked. "Did you tell Albright these things? Or not?"

Rowena couldn't bring herself to say the words, so she simply nodded once, then a few more times until she was sure he understood.

The sheriff raised his eyebrows, his penchant for intrigue ignited. "I see." He glanced around. "Perhaps you are afraid that someone will hear you." He put his hand on her elbow. "I can assure you, Mrs. Gibson, that I will protect you. No harm will come to you on my watch."

Rowena had to press her lips together to keep from laughing at the thought of this runt defending anyone. All she could do was nod again, sealing Clara's fate and the fate of her own miserable soul.

"I thank you for your honesty, Mrs. Gibson. It feels good to tell the truth, doesn't it?"

She turned away from him then and strode toward the depot, sick to her stomach.

Stuart Moran nodded sleepily from his chair in the corner when she came in. He filled out the form for the money order and she folded it with the letter in the envelope, and set it in the basket of outgoing mail that would travel east on the afternoon train.

When she turned to go, Mr. Moran called her back. "Mrs. Gibson, I almost forgot—you have a telegram. I was just getting ready to bring it down to you."

Rowena pursed her lips. "I'm sure. Well, let me have it, then."

He nodded and stepped behind the ticket counter without looking at her. She had never bothered to be friendly to one person in this town, and they had all responded accordingly.

Mr. Moran passed the paper facedown across the counter to Rowena. She held it by the corner and walked out of the depot without saying good morning to him. Her first thought was that the telegram was from Richard. All this time he had been wandering the demolished towns of the Virginia countryside, sleeping on the bare floors of abandoned homes cleaned out and half burned by Union raiders. He had been living on what he could get selling objects he found along the road: a silver candlestick that fell from a fleeing plantation woman's rucksack, a gold tooth from a dead body. Rowena didn't want to know about the things he had had to do to get by. But all of it was behind him now because once he got his strength up, Richard had walked and hitched his way back to Manhattan City, back to the row house. Only, where was Rowena? Why was there a tenant sleeping in his bed? And when would she be coming back? Burning Richard's letter had summoned this telegram. She felt sure of it.

Rowena turned the message over.

JUNE 17

SORRY TO REPORT DEATH OF RANDOLPH BLAIR AT 3 A.M. TODAY. PASSING WAS PEACEFUL. REPLY WITH BURIAL ARRANGEMENTS. MR. HARRISON, WARDS ISLAND ASYLUM, MANHATTAN CITY.

She stared at the words, stunned, then worked her tongue around the inside of her mouth in two circles, first in one direction, then another, across the tiles of her teeth.

Panic seized her chest and she gasped for breath but none would come. *I made this happen*, she thought. *And I deserve this pain.* Her sweet, addled father, who had done nothing but love her since before she knew the word *love*, since before she could stretch her lips over the sounds its letters made, was gone. She had spoiled the only good thing she had ever tried to do, taking care of him; she had wrecked it.

And yet, that serpentine shade of herself, that tricky little voice that urged her toward all her lies, spoke now in a soothing tone and tried to calm her fears. How foolish it was to be surprised by this news! Her father was an old man, and ailing. This day had been nigh for a long while. Rowena couldn't be responsible for the death of a man so many hundreds of miles away. What would she do now? That was the question that mattered, the scheming voice said. Her whole purpose for coming to Destination, for agreeing to masquerade in what felt now like the desert as a stranger's wife, was to do right by her father, to ensure his continued care.

Of course, Rowena battled with herself, she could have come about the money she needed in any number of ways in Manhattan. It was ridiculous to maintain that coming all the way to this nowhere town had been her only option. That simply wasn't true. It was her pride, her haughty refusal to let the Eliza Rourkes of the world see her laid low. And, to be sure, the promise of escape had thrilled her. She had thought that in leaving Manhattan she could also leave behind widowhood, the responsibilities of taking care of her father, could leave behind her awful self. But all of it had traveled west right along with her, a trunk full of misery she dragged at her heels.

"Ah, me," she heard herself say. And suddenly, she thought, those were the words Tomas would breathe when she told him about her father, though she had no notion of whether she would see the carpenter again. The work on the chicken house was finished. She had no idea whether he lived in town or somewhere else on the trackless prairie, or in a shack on the edge of the ever-shrinking Platte River, beneath a wasting cottonwood tree. He had told her he planned to leave this place. Perhaps he planned to go soon; perhaps he had gone already.

She couldn't give in. That was the main thing. There was, always, a way around, a solution that would allow her to skirt the consequences of what she had done to Clara, to Daniel. Rowena stepped back inside the depot and plucked the letter containing the postal order from the mail basket.

"Mr. Moran, may I reverse this order?" she asked, handing the postal form back. "I made a mistake."

He gave her a curious look, then nodded. He counted the banknotes out and slid them across the counter to her, then tore the form in half.

Rowena marched back to the empty soddy, full of purpose. She stoked the fire in the stove. She set the telegram, along with the letter she had nearly sent to Wards Island, on top of the flames. She folded the banknotes into a neat rectangle and slipped them down into the side of her corset.

Rowena went out the kitchen door and down the narrow steps to the storage shed, where Daniel kept his tools in a wooden crate. She felt in the dark for the cool iron and hooked end of the crowbar. Back outside she glanced in both directions to be sure the neighbors weren't watching. The midday heat had driven every single rational soul inside somewhere. Already, Rowena knew, she would have sunburn on her cheeks, and once that faded, the vulgar freckles her mother had always disdained in common girls. She stepped inside the chicken house, waiting for her eyes to adjust to the sudden shade. Then she pulled out every nail in the south-facing wall and kicked it hard with the sole of her boot. It creaked and teetered, then fell over into the dust.

Elsa

Elsa rose late, well after six, and she knew this meant Mr. Schreier had had to fix his own coffee and breakfast once again. What kind of a housekeeper slept in longer than the man who employed her? She would find herself on the train back to New York in no time.

What was it about this place? She slept so deeply here it was unsettling. Back in the maid's quarters at the Channings', she heard all through the night the sounds of the big old house and people moving within it. There was the occasional bell, one of the children sick in the night or Mrs. Channing awake and wanting a cup of tea. People passed in the hall, talking. Even as she slept, the sounds kept her tethered to the waking world. It wasn't a satisfying kind of sleep, but it was all Elsa had known for a very long time.

But here in the attic of Mr. Schreier's house, Elsa fell into the kind of sleep she enjoyed as a child. She remembered how she felt in the muscles at the back of her knees and in her shoulders, even then soft with pudge, the yearning to run as fast as she could, to feel her ribbon-tied braids undulating behind her. She ran through the wood beside her grandfather's cottage, her shoes thudding against the mossy ground. She ran until someone called her in for the night, and before her head settled against the pillow she had dropped into the inky black cavern of sleep, soundless and still. Elsa had forgotten the sensation until now, for it had come back to her again. Perhaps it was the fresh air here, or the work, or the great quantities of butter and sugar she and Ully had consumed together, but her sleep was like a death—absolute stillness.

Elsa dressed and descended the stairs. She opened the door to the sitting room and hit something she heard swish across the floor. Elsa craned her neck around to see a package wrapped clumsily in brown paper with twine tied in a bow. A scrap of paper tucked under the twine said, "To Elsa" in a shaky hand.

"Now, what's this?" she said to no one.

She sat down in Mr. Schreier's armchair with the package on her lap. Today was indeed her birthday, though she couldn't imagine how anyone—and then she remembered that she and Ully had exchanged this information about each other. The girl's birthday was, fittingly, in the middle of February, when the entire town was encased in ice and the most fun she could have was tormenting her brothers with impunity. Elsa had laughed and confessed that she was luckier; she was born in June, when the fields were thick with edelweiss. Ully had looked wonderstruck by that, but they hadn't talked of it again.

Still Elsa had noticed that the girl had these moments, now, of kindness, of thought for others. Elsa didn't want to take any credit for that, for the urge was always in the girl. Ully was a kind child, really. Elsa was just coaxing her out, like the sprout tucked up inside the acorn. And this thought made her laugh for the seeming lack of trees in the entire state of Nebraska.

Elsa pulled on the twine and opened the paper and her pride in Ully withered. The gift was a silver hairbrush and mirror, decorated with repoussé climbing vines. Elsa passed the bristles of the brush across her palm. The silver was real—Mrs. Channing had had a dozen brushes like this. The child must have stolen the set from Mrs. Gibson, or stolen the money to buy them out of the case at Baumann's store. It wouldn't do to be charmed by the good intentions of this gesture, Elsa knew. Yes, the girl meant well; yes, the girl was trying to repay her for the kindness she had shown. (And how nice it was to be remembered on her birthday—how long it had been since anyone had!) But it wouldn't do. The girl did not fear God the way she should. Or, at the very least, she did not fear the law.

But Ully's newfound trust that perhaps the world contained one or two good things was so new, so fragile. Elsa knew she would have to be careful not to come down too hard on her. She wrapped the set back up in the paper and took it upstairs, pushing it under the head of her bed. When she found out where it had come from, she would give it back.

Elsa tried to put the worries about Ully's conscience aside and get started on her work. By ten in the morning it was so hot, she felt sick to her stomach. She hadn't dared to light a fire in the stove. Dinner would be sausage and hard cheese from the cellar on thick slices of bread, though she couldn't imagine how anyone could eat. While she moved around the kitchen she kept a damp cloth on the back of her neck, but the water in the basin was eighty degrees at least and not a bit refreshing. She went out to the pump to fill it—the water in the well had to be cooler—but when she touched the handle with her fingertips she snatched her hand back. The metal was scalding hot.

Elsa went into the dark sitting room to get out of the kitchen for a few moments and cool off. She fluffed the sofa pillow, then straightened Mr. Schreier's slippers under his armchair. On the table beside the chair was a framed portrait of the late Mrs. Schreier. Elsa picked up the bronze frame. The image was cloudy, the features of her face ethereal, in motion. Almost as if, even in life, she had been a ghost. Elsa felt something rough on the back of the frame with her finger. She turned it over to see the edge of a scrap of newsprint sticking out from behind the matting. Elsa slid it out and opened it. It was a clipping from an Omaha newspaper.

It is our painful duty to report the death of Birgit Lundstrom Schreier, wife of farmer Leopold Schreier, on September 17, 1862, after a long illness, at her residence in the homesteading outpost of Destination, Nebraska. The deceased was born in Munich May 4, 1806, and was married in New York City to Mr. Schreier in 1828. From there the couple established a farm in western New York, and then, years later, in the Nebraska territory. Mrs. Schreier has ever been a faithful Christian and a constant wife, who nobly bore the privations incident to a frontier life. It is reported that Mr. Schreier sat at his wife's bedside in her final hours and told her that when the angels finally came to take her, he understood that she had to go. A service will be held in Destination this Saturday.

September 17, 1862. Elsa stared at the date a moment, wondering. She folded the notice back up and slipped it into the frame, then walked back into the kitchen. Hoisting herself up on one of the kitchen chairs, she lifted down Mr. Schreier's box of old newspapers. It had been a while since she had seen him reading them. Each one—the papers from Chicago and Detroit, Albany and Pittsburgh, and one all the way from New Orleans—was dated the same: September 17, 1862.

Honey roved the pasture looking for a bite of green grass, but there wasn't a blade to be found. She lowed all morning. She too seemed to be going mad from the heat, and Nit and Mr. Schreier ushered her back into the barn before nine. Elsa had been charged with the task of using her milk as soon as they brought the pails up to the house, for there was no way to keep it cool. She had made more puddings and quark cheese than they could possibly eat.

At the pump she wrapped the towel around the handle and filled her pail halfway. She glanced out at where Nit and Mr. Schreier stood on either side of the thresher, Nit with an oil can in his hand. Heat rose in waves from the tall brown grass and made it seem for a moment that they were teetering on their feet. Then Nit's body steadied but Mr. Schreier continued to move, wavering, then sinking into the grass.

Elsa put the pail down and started in a hobbled run toward them. She felt the dry stalks crunching beneath her feet, swishing under her dress against her calves like the bristles of a broom. She seemed to be moving with unbearably slow speed. The sun was just west of the apex of the sky and its bright glare made her eyes water.

"Mr. LeBlanc," Elsa cried, when she had nearly reached the place where the grass was matted beneath Mr. Schreier's body. She gasped for breath. "What is it?"

Mr. Schreier's head was wrenched to one side so that his cheek touched the ground. A yellow foam trailed down his lips and chin and his hat had fallen off, exposing the tender, spotted skin of his scalp. Elsa crouched between the sun and Mr. Schreier, casting her ample shadow across the top half of his body. As she settled onto her knees she heard the stitches breaking, one by one, along the seams of her shift.

Nit crouched at Elsa's right elbow. "He said he felt dizzy. I asked him when was the last time he had something cool to drink and then he just went down." Nit wore a handkerchief tied around his throat, the broad triangle of fabric protecting the back of his neck from sunburn. He untied it now and tipped water from his canteen onto the cotton, then handed it to Elsa.

Elsa's hands shook as she pressed it to Mr. Schreier's cheeks and brow. "No one should be out working in this heat. No one." She felt a surging anger, though she knew it wasn't Nit's fault. Elsa hadn't known Mr. Schreier long, but what she did know was that he would have it his way or nothing.

"I tried to tell him," Nit said, his voice pleading. "But he is stubborn about the crops. You know he's lost half the barley already."

Elsa nodded. She glanced up at the dull, cornhusk yellow of the eastern sky with the question in her mind: *Why is this happening?* But Elsa knew better than to succumb to the small-mindedness that was particular to the faithful, the mistake of putting herself at the pinprick center of the sphere of God's creation, so that everything that happened, bad or good, could be explained by her actions alone. Perhaps the drought had something to do with her, perhaps it did not. She couldn't ask God to change the world on her behalf—and anyway, he would do it or not do it for his own complex host of reasons.

Mr. Schreier's eyes fluttered open. "What happened?" He wiped his sleeve across his mouth.

"Sunstroke," Elsa said. "We need to get you inside."

Nit helped him sit up, then got Mr. Schreier's arm up over his shoulder so he could stand. "Where's Honey? And the sheep?"

"You put them back in the barn, Leo—remember?" Nit said. "You said it was too hot for them to be out."

"That ewe is going to drop her lamb any day." Mr. Schreier turned his head to the side and spat on the ground.

"Yes, sir."

"This is the worst month of June I have ever seen."

They helped him through the kitchen door and into his bed, and Nit went to get Dr. Owen. Mr. Schreier seemed lucid, but Elsa couldn't get him to drink anything, even plain tepid water. One sip of it had him trying to bring up the contents of his empty stomach all over again. She helped him unbutton his shirt and pull it down his shoulders. He didn't bother pulling it all the way off and it ringed his waist like a cummerbund.

Mr. Schreier tried to get Elsa to leave him alone in his room. "I'm fine now," he barked, even as he vomited again into the bowl she had brought him and slumped against the wall.

Elsa shook her head. She pulled a kitchen chair into the room at the left side of his bed and settled in to wait for the doctor. Mr. Schreier slept for a half hour. Elsa watched him carefully. His forehead was shiny with sweat, his eyes roving beneath their lids. With a sudden jerk of his body he tossed to one side and whispered to her, his eyes still closed, "Would you read something to me? If I'm going to die, I'd rather not spend my last moments in boredom."

Elsa hesitated. There was only one book she could read, would read. "Yes, sir," she said, then moved quickly across the sitting room to the stairs to retrieve the Bible from her room.

When she returned to his bedside his breathing had steadied. His bare chest rose and fell, revealing, on the exhalation, the hard lines of his ribs. She sat quietly a moment, clutching the book. She had decided he had fallen back to sleep when he sighed. "Well, then?"

He didn't want her to know that he was afraid, but fear emanated from his pores. Elsa plunged her index finger into an arbitrary place in the center of the book. She began to read the psalm she had marked with a penciled star. "'As the hart panteth after the water brooks, so panteth my soul after thee, O God.'"

Mr. Schreier soon slept. It was two hours before Dr. Owen came, and Elsa left the bedroom then, fixing a plate of food for Nit in the kitchen. Nit ate while Elsa stood at the sink. She closed her eyes and tried not to think about anything at all. Leo Schreier had been, in his own way, kinder to her than any man ever had been. Than any person. In all of her life.

Finally, Dr. Owen came out. He gave Elsa a glass bottle

containing an amber tonic. "Give this to him three times a day for three days. And be certain he eats. Meat."

She slipped the bottle into the pocket of her apron and nodded. "Yes, Doctor."

Nit stood up and walked the doctor to the door. "Will Leo be all right, sir?"

Dr. Owen gave them a confused look. "Why, yes, of course." He laughed. "You didn't think he was dying, did you? That man's only ailment is foolishness."

"Oh," Elsa sighed softly, though neither man heard it. Her heart dipped back down into place, like that thirsty deer in the psalm, lowering its mouth to the stream.

I never pegged you to be an ungrateful sort of woman," Mr. Schreier said to her when she came back into the room. He had put on a clean shirt and was sitting up in bed.

Elsa blinked at him and sat down. Perhaps he was not all right after all. She wondered if that red dust that had caked in the fibers of the laundry was caked in his brain too. Or was it Ully he was asking about—had he discovered her visits? "Mr. Schreier," she said, shocking herself by touching his forearm with her fingertips. "Please rest, sir. I beg you."

He glanced at her hand and she quickly pulled it away. "But you haven't told me whether you like it. I've given you plenty of time to say something. You haven't said thank you."

"Like it? Why, of course, you must know that I like it here very much." Her chest tightened. If he told her now that she was fired, would the order stand? Was he delirious? "You don't know what my life was like before I came here. Each day I was in a sea of people but I was utterly alone. Your letter to me asking me to come west—that letter changed my life."

The stern lines in his brow that pointed like arrows to his nose shifted into an arc of surprise and he said nothing but watched her for a moment. Elsa's hands remained in her lap, her fingernails caked with dust.

"I meant the hairbrush, the mirror," he said. "You didn't find them outside your door this morning?"

Elsa pressed her lips together. "Those were from you?"

Mr. Schreier laughed. "Why, yes. Did you think they came from Nit?"

"No, sir," Elsa said. She covered her face. Embarrassment whisked over her entire body. Mr. Schreier's hoarse laugh continued, then became a hacking cough. He leaned over to the other side of the bed and spit into his handkerchief, then laughed some more. When Elsa's eyes filled with tears, he stopped.

"Elsa, I'm not laughing at you. It's only that I am surprised. I didn't know you had other suitors."

She spread her fingertips so that she could peek out at him. What a word for him to use! *Suitors.* He had with one sentence, she felt, made her the most ridiculous woman in the world. She wanted nothing more than to get up and leave the room, but she felt bolted to the chair.

"I think you are very cruel," she said.

Mr. Schreier grinned at her. "Cruel is withholding an answer from me while I'm lying here, near death!"

"I don't think you are so near death as I did a few minutes ago."

"Nonsense, woman. I am as old as the dirt—I could go at any minute."

"You want to make a fool out of me. Well, I won't let you do it." She stood up and pointed an accusing finger at him. "This earthly life is only a season. Soon I'll cast off all the shame of it, all the degradation, and meet my Lord in heaven."

"Indeed," Mr. Schreier said. "Some day you will, I have no doubt of that. I wonder, though, if, in the meantime, we could walk together in the evenings?"

Elsa grew silent. She turned to the window and smoothed her hair, then untied and retied her apron strings with a firm tug. "It's the heat. You've lost your senses, Mr. Schreier."

"It's not the heat, Elsa. I'd like you to call me Leo now."

She stood next to the bed with her hands on her hips. "I can't imagine why I would do that," she whispered.

"Just consider me, is all I ask," he said. "I know I am hunched and irritable. I know I have a face like an old shoe."

Despite herself, Elsa laughed.

"Well, I'm sorry to say it wasn't any better when I was a young man. Always have been ugly."

"That's not true," she whispered.

"So your eyesight is bad too? I have always looked for that quality in a woman."

She shook her head.

"Will you consider me, Elsa?"

Her right hand was still on her hip. She covered her mouth with her left, so the smile starting there wouldn't betray her.

Rowena

Someone vandalized my chicken house," Rowena told Daniel the night she learned of her father's death. She was splitting a chicken carcass into pieces to stew overnight for broth.

Daniel nodded behind his newspaper. "I saw that one of the walls came down."

"You will have to ask that carpenter to come back, I suppose," Rowena said, careful not to look up from her work too quickly and give herself away.

"How do we know it was vandalism? Perhaps the chicken house was poorly constructed. Perhaps Mr. Skala is not a very good carpenter."

She felt Daniel's eyes on her, probing. "There was a crowbar on the ground," Rowena said. "The nails were pulled out one by one."

"Really." Daniel grunted, then set down his paper, rubbing his eyes with the heels of his hands. "Who would do such a thing?"

"I don't know," Rowena said, working her way around to

the explanation she had dreamed up. "And I would never point a finger at anyone without proof. But it is a fact that Sigrid and Gustav do not care for me. And they see that project as *my* chicken house. Perhaps . . ."

Daniel stood up abruptly and his chair scraped the floor. He crossed the tiny kitchen and stuck his finger in Rowena's face. "The Lord knows I have put up with an awful lot from you, but I *won't* put up with that. My sons would not steal from me, which is what has been done in destroying that carpenter's work. They are good boys. Their *mother* saw to that."

"I'm sure she did," Rowena said quietly. "I'm sure she was a wonderful woman. I wish she were still here to take care of you all. I wish that I had never left Manhattan."

Daniel sighed. "Well, she *was* wonderful. Until her mind got sick. She wasn't perfect, Rowena, though she tried to be." He folded his hands in his lap and looked down at them, worked his jaw as if he were working up his nerve. "But I haven't been completely honest with you, or with the children, about her."

"What do you mean?"

"She didn't die. She ran away."

Rowena's eyes widened. "Oh, my. Where did she go?"

"Memphis. Maybe New Orleans. She got it in her head that she was meant to work on one of those riverboats. As a singer. I don't really know where she may have ended up. She may not know herself. There were times when she didn't recognize me or the children—she lived a lot inside her own head."

"Will you ever tell them the truth?"

Daniel shrugged. "I know I should, but what difference would it make? I'd rather let them go on believing it wasn't her choice."

"But what if she comes back?"

Daniel shook his head. "She won't. I'm certain of that. She believes we're all part of a dream she has woken up from."

Rowena put the last of the chicken in the pot and came over to the table, wiping her hands on a towel. "That's terrible. No man's wife should do that to him, no mother to her children."

Daniel shrugged. No woman should, he seemed to be saying, but this woman had. "May I ask you something?"

Rowena nodded.

"Why are you so determined not to like any of us, not to like me? I know we aren't what you expected," Daniel said. "But I do believe I have some things to offer you. We could be happy here together, if you would just give us a chance."

Tell him, Rowena thought. *Tell him what you did to Clara, to the chicken house. Tell him about Father.* She didn't want to be irredeemable, but everything seemed so far gone.

Rowena thought for a long moment about what to say. She knew she didn't deserve his kindness. If he knew who she really was, he wouldn't want anything to do with her. Besides, though it made no earthly sense, she could think only of Tomas, of seeing him once more before he went away forever. "You have been very good to me, Mr. Gibson, and I'm sorry if I have seemed ungrateful. I will try to do better. And I'm sorry for what I said about your sons."

Daniel cocked his mouth to the side. "Oh, hell—who

knows? Perhaps they did do it. I can't think of anyone else who would. I will have Mr. Skala come out to make the repairs."

Rowena waited inside the house when she saw Tomas coming up the path two days later, but instead of coming to the door he went around back without knocking and started in on the work. The walls of the chicken house consisted of two sections separated by eight inches of space filled with hay for insulation. She watched from the kitchen window as he hoisted the heavy wall and propped it onto his knees, then pushed it back into place. His jacket was draped over the fence and his shirt collar was unbuttoned, wilted from the heat. He drove a few nails in from the outside to hold it in place, then went around to the small open doorway and stooped to step inside and secure the interior boards.

In the kitchen, Rowena touched her hair, running her finger along the bumps in her braid. She sighed. She clasped her hands behind her back, then put them on her hips, tied and retied her apron strings. She tapped her boot on the floor of the soddy, as if to mark the passing seconds, each one a victory of restraint.

But there was nothing she could do to stop it.

She went out the kitchen door and crossed through the dust of the yard to the chicken house. With her hand on the top of the door frame, she lowered her head and passed inside the eight-by-ten-foot space, the dim light striped with rays that pierced the spaces between the boards. Dust swirled in the light. Tomas had his back to the door and held a fistful of small nails. He hammered each nail into place with one careful blast of the hammer. There was nothing clumsy or inexact about him. Everything in his domain—his tools, his clothing, his conversations—was completely under his control. He didn't seem at all, even, to be working; only the damp hair around the back of his ears, over his collar, betrayed him. He hesitated for a moment when he heard Rowena's footsteps, but he didn't turn around or greet her.

"Good morning, Tomas," she said.

He nodded once in acknowledgment but still did not turn around. "How this happen, I wonder?"

"We aren't sure. Perhaps one of the Gibson boys . . ."

He nodded again with a curt jolt of his head that told her he didn't believe that theory. She was manipulating him and he knew it and it made him furious.

The rest of the nails went into the wood like gunshots. *Bang. Bang. Bang.* Tomas pushed on the wall with his open palms. It gave a small creak but stayed firmly in place. The structure was sound, warm.

Rowena took a small step toward him in the space. She could see Tomas's face in profile. His eyes looked tired, the corners turned down, and this surprised her. His joviality was gone, his playfulness worn away. He seemed to be holding his jaw carefully; Rowena saw it move under his cheek. She took a breath, then touched his elbow.

The space between them disappeared. His right hand went to the back of her head, pulling almost painfully on her hair as he yanked her mouth to his. His left hand was on her neck, then her shoulder, then her waïst, then her hip. He pressed her so hard against him she felt everything—his collarbone digging into her shoulder, the hard buckle of his belt, his knee at the bottom of her thigh.

His mouth roved over her mouth until it felt raw. The wiry hairs of his beard prickled the skin around her lips, and Rowena felt tears spring to her eyes, moved her face to the side to suck in a breath. His hair was so soft beneath her fingertips, the salt scent of him so marvelous and real. Tomas ran his lips down her neck and over to her ear, taking the lobe into his mouth. He bit down on it, and a small whimper escaped her lips. He pushed her away, roughly, stood panting.

"I am hurting you?" he nearly snarled.

Her heart was bashing against her ribs like an animal in a cage. "Yes," she said, then moved toward him again.

He held up his hand. "Why you are doing this?" he asked, then moved farther away from her, his back up against the wall in the small space, and gave her a desperate look. "Nothing good coming from this."

She shook her head, angry now. She could be haughty, at least, if he tried to deny that he had wanted this too. "Oh, don't behave as if you haven't thought of it."

Tomas hit the wall with his fist and the little house shuddered. "*Damn it.* I thinking about it all the time, Rowena."

All at once she understood that it wasn't about her. "You're feeling badly about your wife," she said stupidly.

He held up his palm again, looking away. "I betray her *never*, not once. I am faithful always."

"Of course you were," Rowena said, speaking more softly now.

The ferocity in his eyes was shifting into something tenderer, more afraid.

Rowena chose her words carefully. "But you were right in what you said to me the last time you were here. We can't bring them back. Your wife is never coming back. My Richard is *never* coming back." Though she was resigned to this, the words still wounded her. Tomas rubbed his face and sighed. "And time only stops for the dead."

He looked at her for a long moment, the tension easing from his shoulders. She moved cautiously toward him again, and he pulled her, gently this time, to his mouth. He kissed her forehead, then her cheeks, then her chin. Their mouths moved together gingerly, as if they were sheltering their bruises.

In pursuing this, in allowing another man to touch her, she was casting Richard off forever. Her whole body ached as she felt him slip away. As Tomas pulled her dress away from her shoulders, she felt grim and sad but very much alive, aware of the breath coming in and out of her lungs, aware of her heels on the hard-packed ground. Like a soldier planting a flag on a hill, she was staking her claim in the world of the living.

They passed an hour in the chicken house. Now Rowena leaned back against the shelf she planned to line with hay for the chickens to make their nests. With the drought it almost wasn't worth bringing them in now until the spring. The spring! It seemed so impossibly far away. How would she survive here until then? Tomas lay on the ground with his head in her lap. Rowena drew circles in his hair with her fingers.

"Rowena?"

"Hmm?" she said sleepily.

"When you marry Mr. Gibson, he agree to send money for your father, no?"

"That's right," Rowena said.

Tomas looked up at her through his pale lashes. "And how he is doing now, your father?"

Her eyes flicked away, up to the ceiling. "Oh, better than he has been in years."

"And that is because . . ." Tomas whispered.

"He is dead," she said flatly. "How did you know?"

"When telegram come in, I am there at depot. Stuart Moran is not most discreet man in Destination."

Rowena sighed.

"So your thinking is you not tell Mr. Gibson about this? Keep taking his money?"

"I'm not going to talk about this with you."

"You need to talk about it with someone. You not think he find out about your father?"

"The telegram listed him by name—it didn't say he was my father. Could have been my uncle; could have been a neighbor." Rowena rattled off this explanation, which she had prepared the day the telegram arrived, in case Daniel should confront her. It was the key to telling a convincing lie. Think of everything, anticipate it before it happens.

"But it is *not*. It is your father."

Rowena shrugged.

"Ah, me," Tomas said. He sat up, his legs crossed in front of him. "Let me ask you: Mr. Gibson, he treating you badly, ever?"

"No."

"And you not angry with him about something?"

"No."

Tomas waited for his words to have an impact but they

did not seem to break through. "So *why* you are doing this to him?"

"I'm not doing anything *to* him. This has nothing to do with him."

"But you take his money and lie about why."

"I'm doing everything I told him I would do. I am cooking for the children, cleaning the house, hiring out the laundry, seeing about improvements—like this chicken house."

Tomas gestured to Rowena's dusty, rumpled skirt. "I not thinking *this* is what he have in mind."

She blushed. "Of course not. But it's none of his concern."

"How long you plan to keep doing this?"

Rowena hadn't let herself think more than a week or two ahead. "Until I have enough money to start over somewhere new without having to marry again, I suppose."

"So you never wanting marry again? My meaning is, after Mr. Gibson?" Tomas looked away as he said this. "This is not real marriage."

"It's real enough for me. For now." But of course, Rowena suddenly realized, the marriage was not real, not to God or Rowena or Daniel, and certainly not to the state of Nebraska. Daniel's wife was still alive, still out in the world somewhere. Rowena and Daniel had no claim on each other.

"And you not wanting . . ."

"No. Never." She knew what he was getting at, what he felt: that snap of recognition, his skin touching the skin of the person, maybe the only one in the whole world, who could truly see him. And because that person existed, the lead weight of loneliness in his lungs lifted for a time. And he could breathe.

She felt the same for him, of course, but she'd be damned if she would let him know.

"Well, then." He paused, smart enough to know not to argue with her. "How much is enough, so that you not have to marry?"

"Quite a bit," Rowena said. "It's going to take a while."

Tomas stood up and tucked his shirt back into his trousers. "This that you are doing is wrong. I not being part of it."

Rowena gave him an unconcerned gaze. "You don't know anything about it."

Tomas groaned. "I not understand why, but for some reason I like you. Why you not willing to listen to me?"

"Because my financial situation does not concern you."

"When wrong thing being done to you, Rowena, like your husband dying, you not fixing it by doing wrong thing to someone else. You not knowing this?" He looked beseechingly at her. She did know it, in theory, but she wasn't sure whether she believed it to be true. After all, wasn't this exactly what she was trying to do, to fix one wrong with another wrong, to even the score? If he only knew about everything else: the way she treated Daniel's poor children, what she had done to Clara Bixby, all the money she had stolen from Manhattan City to here. The ability to keep those secrets, the ability to resist succumbing to the weak need to confess, felt like all Rowena had left.

When she didn't answer, he sighed. "Time for me to go." He screwed his bowler hat on over his hair. "Probably, you not seeing me again, Rowena. I leave Destination soon. Go somewhere they are having jobs for men like me."

She did not react to this. "I know, Tomas. You will do very well there."

They stared at each other in silence.

Just then they heard the *clunk, clunk, clunk* of something against the wall. Rowena sniffed the air for the scent of rain but there was none and no one had seen a cloud in the sky for weeks. They peeked out the door.

One by one, two-inch-long grasshoppers sailed against the side of the chicken house and fell to the ground, gathering and milling in the dirt. Soon there were dozens, crawling over each other's backs.

The sunlight's glare seemed to dim and Rowena looked up at the sky. A cloud of grasshoppers moved across the sun, an ominous gray swarm.

Elsa

Elsa stayed at Leo's bedside all through the first night and the next day. He had moments of lucidity but then sank into sickness again, uncomfortable, thrashing, fitful. It was sunstroke, severe, and he could recover from it, but only if they could find a way to get him to eat something and drink water.

At dawn on the third day she took the big tin pitcher out to the well. As she stepped out the kitchen door, she glanced down, as was her habit, at the vegetable garden. In the last few weeks the plants had wilted some, but enough green remained to reassure her that the root vegetables, at least, were coming along in the still-damp soil six inches deep.

But now, the little plot was absolutely bare. No evidence remained that a single thing had ever grown there, only dime-sized holes in the caked soil. Elsa stooped down and dug her fingers into one of them, pulling out an aborted onion. The top third was missing its brown paper and the outer layers of white flesh. It was not so much severed as *gnawed* away.

"What in the world?" she whispered.

Then she heard the roaring vibration, like the sound of rushing water, and glanced up. The sound came from a haze in the sky, growing nearer, and then dropping down en masse. One member of the horde broke away and flew toward her, nearly as big as a dragonfly. It landed near the onion hole and rested for a moment, its wings spread and glittering in the sun, then flew off to join the rest, dropping down into the barley field and across the dry pasture like a brown, crawling carpet.

On the other side of the field, Nit came out of his house and looked wonderingly at the rows of barley, then Elsa, and started toward her. The whole prairie was full of the whirring sound of the grasshoppers' wings.

Before they could eat the rest of her vegetables, Elsa dug up the remaining onions and carried them to the kitchen. She cleaned and sliced them thin enough to see the light through. On the board she mixed flour and water with a bit of oil, kneading it until the dough was smooth, then pressed it flat on the baking stone. She melted butter in the frying pan and cooked the onions on a very low fire until they were like caramels. When they were nearly done, she chopped two slices of bacon as thick as her finger and added them to the pan. She spread the butter and onions and bacon on the dough, then slid it into the brick oven. The sweet-salt smell filled the entire house. When it cooled a bit, she would spread the tangy quark cheese on top. She knew she should be outside helping Nit, but Elsa was determined to get Mr. Schreier out of bed, and this tart could make a dead man's mouth water. Her *Tante* always claimed it had made at least three men fall in love with her.

Just then the shadow of the man appeared, hunched, in the kitchen doorway. "Is it time for dinner already?"

Elsa smiled to herself and said a silent thank you to Tante Gretchen, then brought the tart to the table and cut Mr. Schreier an enormous slice.

Later, after Mr. Schreier had gone back to bed with a full belly, Elsa joined Nit in the field to survey the damage. Within a few hours, the grasshoppers had destroyed at least half of the crop and they showed no signs of slowing their devastation. Elsa and Nit swung a pair of rakes through the rows to shake the insects from the stalks, then tried to rake them into large piles. The hoppers crawled over each others' backs in a heap six inches deep. Nit tried setting one of the piles on fire but a couple of flaming hoppers took flight and spread the fire into the farthest row of dry barley. He and Elsa stamped the fire out quickly, the squashed hoppers forming a slime on the ground, before they burned the entire field and barn and house down. Elsa and Nit stared openmouthed at each other, at a loss for what to do to overpower them.

"Elsa!"

She recognized the squeaking cry as Ully came around the side of the house. The girl ran to her and hugged Elsa around her middle.

"Hi, *Spatzchen,*" Elsa said. She picked a few hoppers out of Ully's hair. "Seems like a long time since we've seen each other."

"Mrs. Gibson told me I wasn't to come bothering you because she heard in town that Mr. Schreier is sick. Is it true?"

"Yes, my dear, it is," Elsa said. "We are hoping he is on the mend." She hesitated about inviting Ully in. The girl had never come around when Leo was inside the house. *He probably is sleeping deeply*, Elsa thought. *If he wakes up and sees her, I'll tell him he's dreaming.* She grinned at her friend. "Come on inside. I have something for you to eat."

Nit told Leo about the seeming plague of hoppers and that persuaded him, finally, to stomach the water with honey that Elsa prepared for him each morning. Within a day, he was better. He was slow and irritable, but he had been slow and irritable before. He said nothing to Elsa about what he had asked her to do, to call him *Leo* and walk with him in the evenings. She wondered whether she had imagined the whole thing. She did take to calling him *Leo* in her head, but said nothing at all to him in person when she could help it, for fear of the shame of having misunderstood him.

Leo really didn't believe them until he dressed for the first time in three days and went outside to see the destruction for himself. He confessed that in his fitful dreams he had thought they were under a hailstorm, but it was only the sound of the hoppers banging against the outside of the house. He had seen something like this once before, he told Elsa and Nit, about ten years back when he had first come to Destination with Birgit. But not nearly as bad as this and much later in the summer. What would they do if this went all through July? They would have to abandon the town, every single one of them. The place would be uninhabitable. If the trains couldn't pass on the tracks, thick as they were with these roaming tormentors, then the town would be truly cut off from the basic supplies, from food. They would have to flee or starve.

Leo and Nit took the wagon into town to get feed, much to the horses' horror. They stamped and shuddered, shimmying down the lane like something possessed. The trip would be a slow one, Elsa could see.

By the afternoon, the heat had ebbed by a few degrees—though it was still as dry as a bone. Elsa glanced out the kitchen window to see Ully running at top speed, her awkward legs like miniature windmills churning behind her, her cropped hair spreading out like a fan. When she got to the kitchen door, she shouted to Elsa that she was coming inside.

"No, you don't!" Elsa shouted back, wiping her hands on her apron and coming to the door. "Not until we get those filthy things off you." She stepped outside and swatted at the back of Ully's dress, gave the girl's hair a vigorous rub, then ushered her into the kitchen.

"My word," Elsa said, and Ully sat down at the table. Elsa poured her a mug of lukewarm tea. "You drink this now, and then you're going to have another."

Ully scowled. "How many times you want me in the privy today?"

Elsa gave her a warning look. "First of all, young ladies do not speak about those sorts of things. Second, Dr. Owen says we must all drink plenty in this heat. Understand?"

"Yes, ma'am," Ully said sweetly.

They sipped their tea in silence. Elsa glanced out the window. All day long the blue had been fading from the sky. There were no clouds, but everything had dulled. The sun was worn out from shining.

As soon as Ully drained her mug, she burst out with a

surprising piece of news. "I think Mrs. Gibson is going to leave," she said, glancing carefully at Elsa.

"What do you mean?"

"She's been gathering up her things, packing them in her trunk."

"Now, Ully, let's not start rumors."

"Elsa, she pressed the good dress she hasn't worn once since she arrived, and packed away the little Bible she keeps near her bed."

That Rowena Gibson kept a Bible near her bed! Would wonders never cease? Elsa thought for a moment. "Well. What does your father say about it?"

"Not a word. He told me to go out and play. I think he forgot that our whole town is under siege."

Something about this phrase made Elsa smile. It was no exaggeration, of course. The grasshoppers were a true plague. But it was a colorful sort of thing to say, something a reader would say, an educated woman full of wit, which was what Ully really could grow into being, if she wanted to. If she had someone to help her.

"And what do you say about it? About Mrs. Gibson's leaving?"

"Good riddance is what I say," Ully answered, her eyes darting down to the table. "I never liked her and she never liked me."

Elsa saw it at once: Ully's feelings were hurt. She had never been able to win Rowena over. *Don't do that to yourself, Spatzchen,* Elsa thought. *The world is full of Rowenas, women who could cut you to the quick with their cruel appraisals of what they think you are. You have to know your own sacredness in order to endure them. You have to know that you have been created for a reason that has everything to do with what is good and what is righteous. And no one can ever take that away from you.* How could Elsa make her see?

"Leaving, just like that," Elsa said, thinking, watching Ully carefully. "Well, I suppose not everyone is cut out for life on the prairie."

She slid a slice of the leftover tart onto a plate and set it down in front of Ully, then refilled the mug of tea and opened a tin of chocolates. "But some of us are."

"Yes," Ully said, looking up at her. "Some of us are."

Clara

In times of trouble, small kindnesses could come to mean everything.

The sheriff let Clara alone, didn't come around checking up on her every few days as she had feared he would. That was a small kindness, even if kindness wasn't what he intended. Mrs. Healy found more little jobs for Clara to do and paid her generously for them. She didn't make her wait for the end of the month to get her money either. That, too, was a kindness.

Despite what she was up against, Clara found herself growing strangely fond of Destination. This town and its terrible weather, the feeling that it was so far removed from the rest of the world that even God had forgotten about it—somehow the place was growing on her. It was just awful enough to have potential, nowhere to go but up. Albright, Luft, and Drake weren't backing down, but not everyone had it in for her. Some were happy with their new wives; Clara could take a small amount of credit for her part in that.

And Mr. Cartwright nearly felt like a friend. Most days he sent Sergeant trotting over from the town hall at least once to say hello to her in the tavern. Sometimes the hound carried a note of encouragement in his teeth. *In spite of rock and tempest's roar, in spite of false lights on the shore*, one read, *Sail on, nor fear to breast the sea! Our hearts, our hopes, are all with thee.* Clara pressed the notes into her apron pocket and sent Sergeant back to his master with a bone in his teeth. When she asked the mayor about it later on he said he didn't have a thing to do with the note. It was probably Sergeant up to his old tricks, wasting lamp oil in the night on Longfellow.

It wouldn't do to dwell on any fleeting good fortune, lest she tempt her miserable destiny to find her, Clara thought sharply but too late. It was only one day later when she climbed the stairs to find that George had ransacked their room and taken all the money. The drawers hung open like wagging tongues; the mattress drooped halfway off the bed. He had rifled through Clara's trunk, ripping the seam on one of the silk pockets. What a fool he was, Clara thought, not to have first checked the most obvious place, the basket of soiled laundry where the money waited in yesterday's apron. He could have saved himself all that effort of tearing the room apart before he found it. That George was far from clever made it all worse somehow. It didn't take long for her to hear what people were saying, that Stuart Moran had seen him leave Destination on the eastbound train. George had left her again, without a penny.

Clara was so tired, so worn out from worry, that the prospect of jail began to seem like a solution to her life's troubles. She tried to picture her cell—a narrow, windowless room with a small bed and nothing else to speak of. Perhaps it made no difference whether she wound up in her much-dreamed-of white cottage or a jail cell; the outcome would be the same.

Peace. Time. Distance from this sorrow that never left the two of them, a sorrow she wouldn't acknowledge, a sorrow George couldn't *stop* acknowledging, over and over and over again. She saw for certain that he wasn't going to come back this time.

In a haze, Clara found her way to Elsa out at Leo Schreier's farm. The land looked as if it had been burned. The tall ribbons of yellow-green grass were long gone, the cottonwoods stripped bare as in the deepest phase of winter. But somewhere, still, the grasshoppers were eating. Clara could hear the low buzzing that was a permanent fixture across the prairie.

The sun was just breaking the horizon when Clara arrived. She stood outside the kitchen door, peering in at Elsa sitting at the table with Mr. Schreier. Their empty dishes sat beside them and he was reading something to her from a book with his glasses down low on the bridge of his nose. Clara couldn't make out his words but Elsa suddenly giggled, her hand flying to her mouth. Mr. Schreier looked up at her. Then his eyes caught Clara's figure in the doorway.

"I believe you have a visitor," he said.

Elsa turned in her chair to look, then stood and came to the door. "Miss Bixby—what a surprise!" Clara stepped into the light of the kitchen. Her face must have revealed her state of mind, for Elsa took her hand. "Is something the matter?" she whispered. "I've heard in town that the sheriff is not letting up."

Mr. Schreier could sense that a long feminine conversation of the sort he dreaded was imminent. He finished tying his boots in the corner, then slipped by the women and took his hat from the hook. "Good day, ladies."

When the door closed behind him, Clara sat down at the table before Elsa had the chance to offer her a chair. She folded her hands beneath her chin. "Mr. Bixby has taken his leave of me once again."

"Oh, dear," Elsa said, sitting down across from her.

"He took every penny I saved this last month." Clara explained about Rowena's testimony, the sheriff's plans for a hearing. "I have twelve days left until I must pay those men in full. It's impossible. It seems I will be going to jail."

Elsa sat up very straight and shook her head. "Nonsense. We aren't going to let that happen."

Clara smiled. "Well, the only way to avoid it is to come up with a great deal of money. Do you happen to have that pressed between the pages of your Bible?"

"I do not," Elsa said, her tone grim. "You could leave town—surely we could scrape the funds together to put you on a train."

"But where would I go? What would I do? I don't have the energy for it. And I didn't do anything wrong—not intentionally. The things Rowena Gibson is saying are *not* true. I didn't pick and choose whom to help. Everything would have come out all right if I had steered clear of George." Clara put her face in her hands. "Oh, why did I ever take that man back?"

"Because you were trying to honor the union in which the Lord joined you."

"I wish I could say that were the reason. But I think it was loneliness, pure and simple. I had the chance of having him back again, and I took it, however unlikely it was to endure."

Elsa nodded. *"To the hungry soul, every bitter thing is sweet."*

"Indeed, *every* bitter thing. More, even, than you know."

With George gone, Clara couldn't bear to be the only one in the world who knew. She looked at Elsa. Elsa waited patiently with her hands in her lap.

When Clara was a young girl, spending afternoons combing out the yarn hair of her dolls with her sisters, playing jacks on the floor of the pantry, she felt quite literally that if she didn't tell her sisters about a thing, it just hadn't occurred. The neighbor's dog had growled at her in the alley only after it scared Maura to hear the story. A rich lady smiled and waved at Clara from a passing carriage and Clara knew it was so when Frances got dreamy-eyed hearing the tale of it. The things she kept from them, the things she forgot to tell, evaporated into nothing like the bits of a dream. The *telling* was what made it real.

So Clara began to tell it. "There was a baby," she said.

Four simple words. She had finally uttered them aloud now, and in doing so made the fact of him, and the fact of his wrenching unmaking, a real, true thing, forever.

Elsa took a sharp breath. "A *baby*," she whispered. She took Clara's hand and pressed it between her palms, then held it as the long, sad tale unfolded.

"His name was Michael." Clara spoke in an even tone, as if she were talking about someone else, a woman in a myth from long ago. She told Elsa everything—meeting George and getting into trouble, about how it felt to be so big she could no longer hide it, how she didn't mind. God had never answered a single one of Clara's prayers all her life, but the promise of that baby felt like one big belated answer. She felt maybe he had been listening all along, felt he was finally going to give her something precious, something true. Clara counted the days and she sewed and sewed, waiting. It made the terrible shock of it all going wrong so much worse, that hopeful feeling she had for a while. When the labor finally began, it surged ceaselessly for days. The pain, bashing in her back like a hammer, knifing all the way down from her neck to her knees, was unbearable. By the time Michael slid into George's arms at last, Clara was at the bottom of the fever's deep cavern, too ill and weak to put the baby to her breast.

Clara began to cry now, and Elsa cried too. There was nothing to do but split the sorrow between them, break it in half. That was what a friend could do, Clara saw. She could help you carry it.

After a while, Elsa sighed. "We are all such secrets from each other, aren't we?"

"Yes," Clara said, letting the truth of those words rest between them in the room for a while. "It was my fault, you see."

"No! What could you have done? It was not in your hands."

"Perhaps, if I had tried harder to shake off the fever, if I had just *tried*, I could have fed him, helped him survive. I won't ever know for sure."

"You *must*. You must know it. You cannot blame yourself just because there's no way to understand it."

"I just can't help it. I think about it all the time."

Elsa set her jaw, her face as stern as Clara had ever seen it. She seemed to sense a dangerous kind of desperation in Clara's voice, that she might now be willing to do anything to escape her misery for good. "You *will* go on, just as you have always done. And we will find you that money."

Clara gave her a wry smile. "If there's any paper money left in this county, the grasshoppers will find it before we do."

"No," Elsa shook her head. "Don't do that. Don't make it a joke."

"Elsa, I have to face the truth—there is no more hope for me."

"There is always, always hope. In the darkest corner of the world."

"I cannot wait around for the Lord to come save me, Elsa, as much as I *do* admire the strength of your belief."

"I'm not talking about the Lord," Elsa said. "You're going to save yourself. We'll think of something."

Rowena

It had been a week since the grasshoppers descended on Destination, and everyone in town had been driven just about out of their minds. Mr. Gibson was keeping limited hours at the shop because few people were willing to leave the shelter of their homes and venture out into the ravenous swarm. The idea of hitching up the wagon was inconceivable; the horses simply could not tolerate the hoppers crawling around their flanks, diving to and fro before their eyes. Lambert Kellinger, the mayor's uncle, had told Daniel that he tried once on the first day of the hoppers' arrival to saddle his horse out next to the barn and before he could climb on, the insects had devoured the leather harness and the wool blanket that hung beneath the saddle.

If Rowena had not seen it with her own eyes, she would not have believed it possible. The biblical proportions of the episode made it seem like the sort of exaggerated story a city girl might find in *Peterson's*, a vague warning against—what? Marriage to a westerner? The godless pioneer life? She could picture Eliza Rourke tucked up in her Manhattan City parlor, reading the article with a silver tea tray at her elbow.

Mrs. Crowley canceled school after the flag outside the church had been gnawed to shreds, so all of the children were home and inside, restless and irritable and trying to read their books. They probably could have gone out into the yard for a while—the hoppers seemed to ebb and flow throughout the day—but Rowena couldn't bear how, every time they opened the soddy door, a dozen of the insects buzzed in and the Gibsons had to scurry around to clobber them with the heels of their shoes and the dictionary. So she had decreed that the doors would stay closed. Laundry hung all around the sitting room, from the curtain rods and on the backs of the kitchen chairs, for Rowena didn't dare hang it outside. As Daniel and Rowena sat at the table drinking coffee, astonishingly, someone knocked on the door.

Daniel's eyes widened and he stood, crossing the room. Rowena followed and stood behind him. The children clustered around her. He pulled the door open only a crack. Stuart Moran stood in the shadow of the house. Hoppers dived and sailed through the air around his head, landing on his hat. Once one of them found a place to land, it seemed to send a signal to its friends, for soon there would be two, then eight, then twenty clustered together on the perch. Stuart removed his hat and shook off the insects. Two of them leapt into his thick black hair. He had a wild look in his eyes like he might lose his mind right then and there.

"Afternoon, Mr. Gibson, Mrs. Gibson," he said. "May I please come in?"

"Of course," Daniel said. He ushered Stuart inside.

"Children?" Rowena said, and they sprang into action with the frying pan, the old boot someone had outgrown. Ully seemed to take particular pleasure in wielding the giant dictionary over her head and bringing it smashing down. She looked a little like a grasshopper herself, Rowena thought, with her scrawny arms and oversized eyes.

Stuart laughed. "They are getting pretty good at this. How much longer do you think it will last, Daniel?"

"I talked to Leo about it. He says they will just keep coming until they eat everything up or it rains, whichever comes first. I can't see that there's much left for them to eat."

"Well, they aren't very discriminating, that's for sure." Suddenly Stuart yelped and began to thrash around. He dropped his hat on the floor and yanked the right side of his shirt free from his waistband, shaking it violently. A single hopper dropped to the floor, stunned, then buzzed off toward the kitchen. Ully followed it with the dictionary, howling like a banshee.

"My heavens!" Rowena said.

Stuart shook his head. "God deliver us."

"You're welcome to stay as long as you like to get some relief, Mr. Moran," Daniel said as a way of finding out about Stuart's business.

"Apologies," Stuart said. "I thank you, but I came just to deliver this to you, Mrs. Gibson. We've had it at the depot for two days now but you haven't come for the mail—I mean, no one has. It was late coming today anyway, what with the train delay. These infernal insects have gummed up the track. The letter looked important, so I thought I'd bring it over." This statement was an inquiry from the nosy man, Rowena knew. He waited to see whether she would offer up something he could gossip over later on.

"Well, thank you, Stuart," she said. She looked at the letter. It had come from the Dodge County courthouse in Fremont.

Stuart sighed. "Well, I guess I'll be going." He took a deep breath and replaced his hat, then nodded to them both. With a swift motion he opened the door and exited, closing it behind him as quickly as possible. They watched at the window as he hurried down the lane. He waved his arms and swatted at the tormentors, which were invisible in the dusk. From the distance of the house, he looked like a lunatic.

The letter explained that on July fourth a judge was coming to Destination to hear evidence against Miss Clara Bixby on the charge of fraud leveled against her by a group of concerned Destination citizens. Rowena was ordered to appear in "court"—to be held in the tavern—to give testimony about what she had told Bill Albright at the brewery. This testimony would be given under oath.

The enormity of what she had started pressed down on her and she heard her father's voice. *Oh, this is quite a mess you have made, Rowena.*

Daniel, may we speak for a moment?" Rowena asked a week later, on the morning of the Fourth of July. He was on his way out the door, into the infestation, with a flour sack wrapped around his collar and over his shoulders to keep the grasshoppers from crawling down his shirt. He had tucked the edge of it into the back of his hat so that it looked like a long curtain of burlap hair. The children blew by him and out the door, like shots from a cannon. Rowena was so tired of having them underfoot she had told them to go out and play in the swarm.

"All right," he said, and stepped back into the kitchen.

"Why don't we sit for a moment?" Rowena eased into a chair.

Daniel appraised her face, winced, and sighed. "This doesn't sound like good news."

"Daniel," she said, taking a breath. "I'm going to take the train back to New York. Today."

"*Today?*" He removed his hat and the flour sack flopped over the back of the chair. "Why do you have to go today?"

"Because my mind's made up."

"It's not because today's the day you're supposed to go speak in front of those men about Clara Bixby?" Daniel asked.

"How do you know about that?" Rowena whispered.

Daniel sighed. "This is a small town, Rowena."

She shook her head. "You don't have to worry about that. The reason I'm leaving is that it isn't fair to you for me to keep staying on."

He threw up his hands in exasperation. "Well, then why even *tell* me, Rowena? Why not just pack your bags and go, since you *will* do as you please?"

"Because . . ." She stalled. She had determined to come clean. She pressed herself on. "Because I owe you an apology. You have been so good to me and I haven't treated you very well."

Daniel shook his head. "It was a doomed arrangement from the start, I suppose, built as it was on near total misunderstanding."

"My father is dead, Daniel."

His face changed then because he was a compassionate man, a good man. Indeed, watching Daniel now, Rowena's definition of a *good man* shifted. It no longer had to do with Richard's fearless gallantry, a tireless hero on a quest to defend a noble set of ideals. She wasn't even really sure if Richard had embodied all those things or whether she had merely ascribed them to him because she saw in him the potential to become them, to grow into them, given enough time—time of which they were robbed. Love hadn't made her blind. It had given her a far-sightedness she never had before, an ability to look down to the end of a long road and see how they would stand there together, side by side, improved by life. But they never even began their journey.

A good man, Rowena thought now, was a man who moved through the world careful not to do others harm. That was it, simple as it seemed, but it was a profound and essential thing upon which to build an entire life, a succession of lives. Daniel Gibson was *this* sort of good man. Rowena didn't love him, but she wished mightily that she could. Whoever did love him—and someone certainly would—was a blessed woman indeed.

"Rowena, forgive me for being cross just then," he said. "I didn't know the reason for your journey."

"No, Daniel. You don't understand. My father died weeks ago."

His eyes widened, but still he did not suspect her of dishonesty. His goodness benefited Rowena in many ways, but it certainly did Daniel himself no favors. "Word took so long to reach you!"

Rowena put her head in her hands, then took a breath,

determined he should know the breadth of her crimes. "I've known for some time, but I didn't tell you so that you would continue to give me money. I've been saving it so that I could leave you. And now I'm going to do it."

He nodded, then looked down at his hands and said nothing. She couldn't have been more clear.

"Do you see *now*? I've lied to you, I've stolen from you. I'm no *good*, Daniel. I don't know if I ever will be."

He nodded again, his eyes still on his hands in his lap. He chewed his lip. He scratched his beard on the side of his chin, and finally he looked up. "It's all right."

"What do you mean, it's all right? It's *not* all right!" She felt like throttling him. Here she was, trying, finally, to make her confession, and he wouldn't accept it.

He held out his palms. "The money is yours to do with as you wish."

She had hoped in her secret heart that he might shove her into the wall, strike her, curse her name for all the neighbors to hear. She deserved at least that much. But he did none of those things. She felt worse than she had before, more hopeless for herself. "But you *must* be angry that I lied," she whispered.

"Rowena, I am only disappointed that, try as I might, I could not offer you the sort of life that would make you happy. You owe me nothing." He stood and picked up the flour sack from the back of the chair. "We'll be all right. They're my children, and I'll see to them. I should have been doing a better job of it all along." He sighed. "You'll be gone, then, when I return home this evening?"

She nodded.

"All right. I ask that you say nothing to the children, and that you take nothing else from this house, besides the money, which is yours to keep."

She nodded again. It was mortifying. Of course, she wouldn't *dream* of—and then she remembered the strand of the former Mrs. Gibson's pearls she had tucked into the pocket of her trunk. She shuddered with surprise at her own deceitfulness. Daniel stood there, stupidly refusing to punish her. Would he never leave for the shop? It was unbearable.

"You say you aren't good, Rowena, but that just isn't true. You could be good, if you *chose* to be. That's all it is, a choice."

"I haven't done one good thing in a very long time."

"But just now you turned the tide. You told me the truth, you honored me enough to tell me the truth."

"So that *I* would feel better, so that *I* would not have to carry guilt. It's really only for myself, you see."

He shook his head. "You feel remorse about what you did *because* you are good. And you could keep being good, if you wanted to." He nodded at her and strode toward the door. "Good-bye, Rowena," he said.

She sat at the table for a long time after he left, wondering whether what he said was true.

Clara

Sheriff Brooks had decided to hold the hearing in the tavern as it was the only place in town, besides the Methodist church, with enough chairs for everyone. The church certainly smelled better, but it was in constant demand lately from people coming to pray for rain.

Mrs. Healy knocked on Clara's door at seven that morning and brought in a tray of coffee and toast. She came back a while later and helped Clara dress. Clara felt perspiration pool in the cleft above her lip but the black cape she wore over her shoulders made the worn dress somewhat respectable, and she could use every advantage she could get. She braided her stiff incorrigible hair into two plaits, then wound them together and pinned them in a low bun at the nape of her neck. Mrs. Healy tied the plain black bonnet beneath Clara's chin.

"You look like a widow," Mrs. Healy said.

"All the better," said Clara.

Mrs. Healy wanted to pray and Clara didn't object. She began with the *Ave Maria*, and though Clara had been taught from an early age to rebuke Mary worship wherever she heard it, she found the meaningless Latin words soothing, like an incantation against whatever awful outcome awaited her down-stairs. There was nothing Clara wanted to say about it in any language.

Just before nine, Mrs. Healy hugged her and Clara de-scended the stairs, Mayor Cartwright's laundry brushing over her cheeks and shoulders as she passed through it. The sky was a dull gray-white; grasshoppers bobbed in the air all around.

Clara had taken special care to clean the tavern thoroughly before she went to sleep the previous night. The floor was tidy and the surface of the tables gleamed. Sheriff Brooks was moving them off to the side of the room when she stepped inside.

"Good morning, Sheriff," Clara said.

He nodded at her. Two tables remained at the front of the room, with chairs behind them, and the remaining chairs faced these in four rows. The sheriff adjusted the one on the end so that it was evenly spaced from the rest, and Clara was again struck by the notion that this small man was only pre-tending the way a boy pretends, with toy soldiers and a rifle made out of a tree branch.

"Sir," Clara said, sitting down in one of the chairs in the first row. "Is all of this really necessary?"

He pursed his lips. "Today is July the fourth, is it not?"

"Yes, sir."

"And you have not met the condition of repaying the men whose money you stole?"

"Sir, I did not *steal*—"

The sheriff cut her off. "Have you repaid the money? Yes or no."

"No."

"Then all of this is *indeed* necessary. Quite necessary. Judge Tharp is on his way here now, in fact. He is old and a bit infirm. I wouldn't summon him here if it weren't important. And I expect Mrs. Gi—that is, our *witness*, any minute now."

Clara laughed. "Sheriff, there is no need to shroud this in mystery. I know that Rowena Gibson is your witness."

He ran his finger over his mustache. "You do?"

"Heavens, Sheriff—this is a pretty small town. And there's only one person in it as conniving as she is."

He held up his hand. "I won't hear disparagement of Mrs. Gibson. I won't hear it. She is a fine, upstanding woman—*citizen* of this county."

"Oh, my," Clara said, folding her hands in her lap. Another man with nothing but cobwebs between his ears at the sight of a beautiful woman.

There was the sound of a horse outside and the sheriff went to the door. A few minutes later he came back holding an old man by the elbow and helping him step unsteadily over the threshold. "Judge Tharp, this here is the accused."

The judge squinted in Clara's general direction, his rheumy eyes clouded and useless. "Ma'am," he said, lifting his hat to the empty coat tree that stood behind Clara. The sheriff helped him into a chair.

"Where is everybody?" the judge asked. He was a portly, red-faced man and he wore a rumpled jacket with old food crusted on the lapel. He cleared his throat with a sudden violence that made the sheriff jump.

"They should be along shortly, Your Honor."

"Nothing starts on time anymore. This country is going straight to perdition. Don't you agree, Mrs. Bixby?"

"Yes, I do," Clara said.

The judge slammed his fist down on the table for emphasis. "That's right." He turned his head and looked at the room out of the far corner of his left eye. "And why in the Sam Hill have you got the chairs arranged thusly, Brooks? Do you think this is some kind of theater?"

The sheriff's eyes darted around. "We're expecting some members of the community, Your Honor."

"No, we are not. It will be myself, the accused, the accusers, and the witness—that's it. This is not a trial." Clara felt relieved that she hadn't told anyone—Elsa, the mayor—about the hearing. Though they were sure to have heard about it somehow.

The sheriff hesitated. "And *I* may stay, of course?"

The judge turned the corner of his functioning eye on the sheriff. He cleared his throat again, and the sound was like a cross between a cough and a gunshot. "I suppose. If you keep your trap shut." Clara tried to hide her amusement with this exchange.

Bill Albright and Walter Luft arrived next and settled into the chairs opposite Clara, but both of them refused to look her in the eye. Bill was a fine-looking man, Clara thought, with a respectable job. Why didn't he just give all this up, go find another girl to marry in Omaha or Chicago or Cheyenne? He couldn't really have been in *love* with Cynthia Ruley after so short a time writing letters—could he? And even if he was, what sort of a justification was *love*? Why did we allow love—fickle, mysterious, fleeting—to be the explanation for such bad behavior as was on display here today in this tavern? Or was it all just about their pride?

Jeremiah Drake arrived then and took the chair next to the other two men. Clara hadn't seen him since the night the mayor almost strangled him to death in the tavern. He pursed his lips and stared down at his hands folded in his lap.

The phlegm bedeviling the judge was on the move again and he cleared his throat once more. It was the only sound in the tavern, aside from the sheriff's fidgeting. For some reason he refused to sit down. He stood by the door, waiting for Rowena, Clara supposed, with his hat in his right hand, then in his left, with his right boot crossed over his left and his hand on his hip. He shifted his weight from one side to the other, as if he were stretching out his legs after a day's ride. The judge pulled his watch out of his waistcoat pocket and stretched the chain to its limit, pulling it close to his eye.

Clara had decided that morning while she dressed in her room that she would not be going to jail merely to appease the wounded pride of these foolish men. If she were guilty, it would be another thing altogether. But Clara knew for certain she had done nothing wrong, save holding on to a naïve belief that the young women in Manhattan City would be true to their word, that people would do their duty *because* it was a duty. Clara had tried her whole life to be a good person and she had succeeded, though it seemed she was being punished for it every time she turned around. But Clara was strong too. She was much stronger than George, she saw now. He couldn't endure, but Clara would. If the judge was convinced by Rowena's testimony today, or, more likely, if the judge was as entranced by her looks as the rest of these men had been, and declared that the county would organize a trial, Clara would get herself on the next train to Anywhere before the judge could swing his leg over his horse's back. Mrs. Healy already had agreed to lend her the money for the ticket.

It was strangely quiet in the road outside the tavern. An occasional horse passed—which caused the sheriff's ears to perk, caused him to shift his weight once again, despite the fact that Rowena would be arriving on foot. But something was missing. With a flash, Clara realized what it was: the hoppers had gone silent. Perhaps they had finally run out of food.

After a half hour had passed, the judge slammed his fist down on the table and glared at all of them through the corner of his eye. "Sheriff, where *is* your witness?"

Rowena

Rowena was walking down the road with a small case containing the money and her Bible—she had decided to leave behind the trunk and most of her clothes, as well as the former Mrs. Gibson's pearls, of course—when a possibility for atonement struck her so hard it almost knocked her down. It was big, it was good, and, oh, it was *awful*.

Rowena shook her head. There was no way she was going to do it. She would rather lie down in the dusty road in her one dress and wait for a horse to run her over. She would rather scrub Eliza Rourke's kitchen floor with all of Manhattan society assembled to watch. She would rather pull the five Gibson children to her bosom and sing them a sweet lullaby. No way. Nohow.

Rowena stamped the heel of her boot into the dust, once, then several times, harder and harder. She made that growl-squeal that the Gibson children had learned to fear, then balled her hands into fists and pounded them against her thighs. But despite how she thrashed and raged, the certainty, the inevitability of what she would do wouldn't go away.

She stood in the lane that curved toward the main road between the Methodist church and the town hall. They would be assembled in the tavern together; in fact, they would be there now waiting for Rowena to arrive. She had only so much time before they dispersed or sent someone to look for her.

First she went to the log house, her shoulders squared. Everyone in town knew what those women were. Rowena saw them from time to time, walking to the train or picking up a package from Baumann's store. She was in no way naïve about the needs of men or the ubiquity of women who would make a living satisfying them. It was only that their dresses were far finer than any belonging to the legitimate women in town. It hardly seemed fair.

Rowena raised her hand and knocked on the heavy oak door. She felt suddenly nervous, afraid of what she might encounter inside. Before she could retreat the door swung open, revealing an old woman.

"Oh," the woman said, straightening up and drawing her mouth into a line. "Good morning."

"Good morning," Rowena said, pushing past her into the parlor.

"Excuse me, madam," the woman said, spinning around on her heel. The door slipped from her hand and closed. "I don't believe I invited you in. What's your business here?"

The question hung in the air for a long moment as Rowena stared around the parlor, her mouth hanging open like a trout's. Silk upholstery and mahogany furniture. Velvet drapes. A stone hearth with silver candlesticks.

"I don't *believe* it," Rowena said.

"Now listen here, madam. I'm very sorry if you think your

husband's been coming here, but you'll have to take that up with him. We don't get involved in—"

Rowena laughed. "Is that what you're worried about?"

The woman gave Rowena a confused look. "Well, yes. You can imagine unhappy wives call on us from time to time."

Rowena waved her hand. "I couldn't care less about what my husband does—he's no longer my husband, anyway. I was only thinking I'd like to live here."

"Oh, I see," the woman said, nodding. "I misunderstood. If you'd like to come back this evening to speak with one of our regular girls, she can tell you about how much our proprietor charges the girls to rent a room and—"

Rowena's eyes widened and she shook her head. "Oh, no— that's not what I meant either. But I would like to talk with . . . one of the girls, as you say."

"Now? It's so early in the day. They are resting."

"I would be so grateful if you could wake one for me. I promise you have no cause for worry."

The woman peered at her a moment longer, then nodded. "Wait here."

She walked down the hallway. Rowena felt nervous again, like her presence here and her purpose were ridiculous. A few minutes later the old woman came back followed by a dark-haired woman with bright green eyes. She didn't smile.

"My name is Mariah," she said. "What can I do for you?"

"I'm Mrs. Mo— Mrs. Gib—" She sighed. "I'm Rowena. I wonder if we might speak in private."

The young woman nodded. "Come on." Rowena followed her back to her room, trying not to notice the mussed bed-clothes and undergarments strewn over the back of her chair and the door of the armoire. She found herself wondering just how much money Mariah's services brought in.

Mariah sat down on the bed and gestured toward the bench in front of the vanity. Rowena sat down.

"I won't take up too much of your time," she said. She opened the latch on her case and drew out a small bundle. "I was wondering if you might be interested in purchasing this."

Mariah took it from her and unwrapped it. Inside was Eliza Rourke's diamond brooch, gleaming against the red cloth. "It's beautiful," Mariah said.

Rowena nodded.

"But why would you think that I would want to buy it?"

"I don't know that you do," Rowena said. "But I need to sell it. And there isn't anyone else in town who would have a use for it. Or keep quiet about where she got it."

Mariah twisted up her mouth. "How much do you want for it?"

Rowena told her the price. Mariah kept her expression absolutely still and Rowena knew from this that the woman understood she was asking far less than what the piece was worth. If nothing else, Mariah had to be shrewd in matters of business. "You could resell it in Cheyenne," Rowena said.

Mariah shrugged. "Maybe I'll keep it." She went over to the vanity and opened the bottom drawer, then pulled a stack of banknotes from the jewelry box and handed them to Rowena. "I suppose I'll be seeing you around, then," she said.

"No, you won't," Rowena said. "But I hope you enjoy the brooch."

She left the log house and walked east down the main road where the butcher shop stood, and passed around to the back of the building, careful not to linger in front of the small side window where Daniel might see her and have his nose rubbed in the fact of her leaving.

She moved between the scrubby yard and the train tracks, averting her eyes and nose from the pile of carcasses and parts too far gone to be useful. Daniel would bury them at the end of the day. It seemed even the hoppers knew better than to eat from that poisoned meal. Their reverberation was noticeably absent from the whole main road. Perhaps they had gathered somewhere west of town, in a field that had some green thing left in it. They had come to Destination when it suited them and taken everything they wanted without so much as a thought about who might miss the things they took. Rowena felt a sickening sense of recognition in that behavior. Next door to the butcher shop was Baumann's general store, and after that the depot. Its two back doors were open wide, twine looped between the door handles and the iron boot scrapers on either side of the entrance to keep the doors from slamming closed in the wind.

Rowena went inside. Stuart Moran stood with the newspaper spread on the counter. He was eating a small peach so soft it was more liquid than solid. The juice dripped down his forearm from wrist to elbow, where he had pushed up the cuff of his shirt. He licked it off, the half-devoured fruit held aloft in his palm, its dark pit lodged in the deep pink center. She couldn't blame him for the uncouth act. The perfume of the fruit seemed to fill the entire depot. Whatever this desiccated and dusty and abandoned place was, that peach seemed to be its antithesis: luscious with flavor and color, vivid and sweet and relentlessly alive.

"Where did you *get* that?" Rowena asked.

Stuart blushed at the mess he had made, then wiped his wet chin on his sleeve. "They came in on yesterday's train. From Illinois. They don't have the drought there. Wessendorff's got them over at his store, but I have a couple extra. Would you like one?"

"Yes, please," she said, though she had meant to decline the offer. He handed it to her and she held it to her nose with her eyes closed. The peach smelled heavenly. All of a sudden Rowena felt she was going to begin to cry.

"Hey," Stuart said, watching her. "Ain't you supposed to be over at the tavern for the—"

"Oh, but you wouldn't gossip, would you? You wouldn't speak about things that don't concern you?" The wave of emotion passed. Rowena kept her voice sweet, like the peach, but her eyes were as hard as pits, her brows stern and flat. If this nuisance of a man had a notion of making trouble for her, God help him.

"No, ma'am," he lied. "I would not."

"Well," Rowena said. "That *is* a relief, for I was afraid you were about to do just that." She fixed him with a stare that made his head sink into his collar.

"No, ma'am," Stuart said again, his eyes skittering this way and that.

"Very well. Now. I'm here to see about the eastbound train."

He peered curiously at her. "Well, that one has been delayed, Mrs. Gibson. An engine blown just east of Julesburg. We had the telegram this morning."

Rowena sighed. It *had* to be today. She had to go *today*.

Stuart watched her. "If the object is *departure*, without so much concern for the *destination*," he said, choosing his words carefully, "then perhaps you would consider the westbound train. It's due within the hour."

So it would be the West, then, Rowena thought. It wasn't New York that she had planned on, of course, despite what she had told Daniel, but Chicago. Her mother's cousin was there. They hadn't spoken since her condolence letter after Rowena's mother had died. But Rowena knew the cousin would take her in, out of duty if nothing else. It was the only plan Rowena had, but it seemed now that it was not to be. She would go west, as far as the train would take her, then farther still by coach. What mattered was that she be anywhere else but here.

"Yes, I'll take it," she said, and handed him the money for the ticket.

"You have about twenty minutes," Stuart said. He was showing remarkable restraint, though she knew he was bursting to tattle to someone the moment she stepped onto the train. "Safe travels."

"Thank you for the peach."

As she left the depot, she thought she saw a man around the corner wearing a brown bowler hat. When she looked again, he was gone. Rowena sighed. It seemed her mind was playing tricks on her. Tomas was sure to be gone by now. She wondered where he had finally decided to go. Across from the depot was the brewery and she crossed the main road and circled behind that building, then around the back of the tavern, careful to cut a wide path so that she would not be seen from its windows. With the peach in one hand and her case in the other, she climbed the exterior stairs, ducking to avoid the flapping laundry. At the depot, passengers lingered as they waited for the train to arrive. She tried to stay out of sight. She felt as though an invisible hand at the small of her back pushed her to the second-floor hallway, to the rented rooms above the tavern. She stepped carefully, knowing that the people gathered for the hearing downstairs could hear her footsteps across the creaky floor.

Rowena crouched down, set the case on the floor, and opened the latch. She removed a stocking and dropped the peach into it, wrapping the silk around the fruit to keep it from bruising, then tucked it into the lining. Then she removed the envelope of money. There was all the money Daniel had given her plus the things she had managed to steal. Rowena counted out the sum owed to the thwarted bachelors, then added most of the rest of what she had. She began to wrap it in her handkerchief, but paused. That Rowena would give this money to Clara was no longer in question—she had succumbed to whatever relentless force, fate or conscience, was propelling her. But the notion that Clara would feel victorious, that somehow Clara's drab and uninteresting ways had triumphed over Rowena's beauty and cunning, was too much for Rowena to bear. She might try to be better, but the Lord knew she could never stop being herself.

She put her handkerchief back in the case, then glanced around. Back out on the stairs, a row of handkerchiefs undulated in the breeze. Rowena scurried over, plucking one of them off the line, then quickly folded it over the bundle of money, with the monogram *RC* in the center.

Then with one motion, Rowena snapped her case closed, shoved the money under the door, and stalked down the stairs. In the distance she heard the *chhh-chhh-chhh* of the train.

Clara

Rowena Moore Gibson never showed up at the hearing. That was the first good thing to happen on what would prove to be a very good day indeed.

"Well, Sheriff," Judge Tharp said as he put his palms on the table and pushed himself out of his chair. "You've wasted just about as much of my time as I'm willing to forfeit today." The judge stood up and buttoned his coat over his expansive belly, then grunted to the room at large, "Now, somebody needs to see about my horse."

Sheriff Brooks stood at the tavern door and held up his hand. "With respect, Judge, I'm sure Mrs. Gibson is going to be along any minute now."

Clara shifted restlessly in her chair. Across the main road at the depot, a handful of people gathered, waiting for the train. Though she had felt too worn down all these months— and too sure of her own innocence—to try to plan any kind of escape, Clara wished now that she had. She imagined slipping in among the passengers, boarding the train, and saying good-bye to Destination and these hateful men forever.

She recognized one man who was waiting by the tracks in

a brown bowler hat, Mr. Skala, the carpenter who had worked with George. Though all the others were looking down the line, waiting to see the engine puffing smoke in the distance, Mr. Skala looked at something off to the side of the tavern. Clara heard the old wooden stairs creaking under footsteps. Probably just Mrs. Healy, taking the mayor's laundry down from the clothesline. But Mr. Skala didn't wave to her; instead, he pulled the brim of his hat down lower and slipped inside the depot.

The judge turned toward her accusers. "Gentlemen, do I have it correct that Mrs. Gibson's testimony comprises the whole of your evidence to support a charge of fraud against this woman?" The judge pointed again to the coat tree behind Clara. She wondered whether he thought her particularly tall and thin and *inert* for a woman of her age and station.

Bill sighed. "Yes, Your Honor, you are correct."

"Well, then, I see no reason why Dodge County would proceed any further with this matter. The inevitable separation of a fool from his money is of very little concern to the law of this land."

Jeremiah flew to his feet. "But this woman swindled us, Judge!"

"In this country, we prosecute crimes based on evidence, not rumor. Which is lucky for you, Drake, as I've heard plenty of ugly rumors about you. Crooked business deals in Cheyenne, bribery of officials from the land office. And just generally being a pain in the ass—my apologies, ma'am," he said, turning to Clara.

"Please don't worry," she said.

"—which is not illegal, but probably should be. If I were you, I don't believe I'd be casting stones."

Jeremiah eased slowly back into his chair.

"Why don't you all try finding a wife the usual way? There's a lot of girls over in Omaha now. A lot of church dinners and other nonsense of that kind. How do you think I found Mrs. Tharp?"

"Yes, Your Honor," Bill mumbled. Walther nodded his head.

"No, I am asking you a question—how do you think I found her?"

"I don't know, Your Honor," Bill said.

"I was in *Chicago*," he said, striking the table with his fist. "Had two good eyes then too, thank the Lord. Mrs. Tharp—she was just Lucinda, then—was pouring lemonade for the men. It was a *picnic*." His fist hit the table once again. "So what do you think, boys? Did I write her letters for six months, hoping to speak with her someday far in the future?"

"I imagine not, Your Honor."

"You're out of your deuced mind if you think I did that."

"I *said* I imagined not." Bill slumped in his chair.

"That's right. I walked right up to her at the table and said, 'You're the prettiest girl in Chicago, and someday I'm going to be rich, and it only makes sense for us to pair up now.' And what do you think she did?"

"Fell madly in love with you, of course," Bill said miserably.

"That's right. Of course, I was wrong about getting rich—we've rarely had two pennies to rub together. She was pretty, though—I wasn't wrong about that."

"Your Honor," Clara ventured. "Does this mean I am free to leave?"

The judge turned to the coat tree and opened his mouth to respond. Just then, the sheriff shrieked in a most unmanly way. The men bolted from their chairs to join him at the door.

The judge sniffed the air. "Now just what in the Sam Hill is going on out there?"

Rowena

An engineer reached for Rowena's elbow to help her step up from the platform into the car.

"Good day, madam. We are quite full this afternoon," he said.

Rowena nodded as she passed by him and walked slowly up the long car, glancing from side to side at the backs of the passengers' heads. The reason the train was so full, of course, was that no one was getting off at Destination, or anywhere else in eastern Nebraska, for that matter. The passengers were men, mostly, wearing brand-new gray and brown coats over crisp white shirts, but there were a few women travelers, their enormous brightly colored skirts cascading into the aisle. Many of them clutched cases on their laps and gazed out the window at the desolate main road. Rowena wondered what those cases contained. A letter of introduction to a music school, where this traveler might teach piano lessons to young children? A platinum letter opener with a line of diamonds down the handle, the last vestige of a family's long-faded wealth, brought to be sold? So many hopeful, clean, brightly dressed people! The train seemed to be fueled not by coal but by optimism itself, the self-sustaining energy source of Americans moving west to begin again or *yet again*, after the last failed beginning. It was impossible that every person on this train would accomplish the thing he or she set out to do—the music school might be shuttered, the diamonds might be glass—and yet each face radiated the signs of the belief lodged in the ribs: that *he* would be the one to succeed, that Providence would make the ways straight and somehow fill her coffers. It was dizzying and troubling all at once, this fearlessness, this foolishness. Rowena clutched her case closer, thinking of the peach nestled in her underthings, the shrewdest cargo of all. For it promised nothing more than itself, plotted nothing but a few moments' indulgence that would quench hunger and thirst for a brief time. Everything that came after that peach would have to be earned.

An elderly man struggled to push himself up on his cane. He had a shock of white hair that reminded Rowena of her father and she thought of him sitting on the bench on Wards Island, looking out at gulls swarming the East River, with his weathered hands stacked on top of his cane. But then she remembered that he was no longer there, was instead in the damp asylum cemetery ground, or that his *body* was in that grave but that the rest of him was nowhere, or everywhere, loosed and scattered through the world. How many particles did a dead man become?

"Madam," the old man croaked. "You are welcome to this seat." He gestured with a palsied hand toward the place where he had been sitting and she smiled at him, still imagining her father, disassembled, swirling around the train. And then Randolph Blair shocked her to her center by hurtling himself against the glass—*thwop, thwop, thwop*. Rowena gasped and her left hand flew to her throat. She closed her eyes, then opened them. Of course, it was not her father, but only the grasshoppers swarming back into town, the train colliding with the hard shells of their bodies.

"That is so kind of you, sir, but I couldn't take your seat," Rowena said, and pushed on down the aisle. Her heart pounded. She watched the glass, waiting to see the mangled insects appear in clumps, but instead she saw clear, crooked rivulets distorting the image of the world.

"Could you take *this* seat, madam?" a voice behind Rowena asked.

"It's raining!" a woman cried somewhere in the car, and the passengers began to chatter, then cheer. Some of the men got out of their seats, crowding toward the windows. The downpour was fierce and deafening; a clap of thunder added to the marvelous chaos.

Rowena turned around to see the last empty seat on the train and the man who sat beside it, with his hat in his hands.

She nodded slowly, her nose filling with the earthy scent of the rain. "Yes, I could," she said, smiling.

"That is what I am thinking you say," Tomas replied.

Elsa

The Independence Day rain began with a sound Elsa had never heard the rain make: It began with a hiss. The first uncertain droplets evaporated before they even hit the rock-hard ground, hot to the touch. The water vapor formed a kind of rolling fog over the prairie and when the air was saturated, the rain began to fall in earnest. It rang on the metal cistern out by the barn like a peal of church bells calling the people to worship.

"Ully, come on!" Elsa said, pulling her to the open kitchen door to see. It seemed impossible that the sky could contain this much water. It poured violently down, the caked soil unable to absorb it, and ran in a hundred rivers across the land. The tributaries met in the narrow lane that led to town, tamping down the clouds of dust that had lingered there beneath the cottonwoods since the day Elsa had arrived in Destination.

"Do you think it's raining where Pa is?" Ully cried. "I can't *wait* for him to see it."

"Oh, yes, *Spatzchen*—it's raining everywhere in this county right now, I'd wager." Ully made a move to run out the door, but Elsa held her arm. "Ully, look at that road—you'll be washed away. Stay with me until it dies down some."

The girl scowled but relented easily. Elsa was glad they could share watching the rain come down, that they had been together, standing next to each other in the kitchen side by side, the moment when the fortunes of everyone in the town might change.

Just then, Leo and Nit exploded out of the barn, each carrying a stack of milk pails. They barred the door behind them. Nit waved to Elsa with his arm stretched high over his head. They began to arrange the pails on the ground in a line to catch the water. Together they tipped the horse trough to dump the fetid water on the ground and let it fill up with fresh water from the rain.

"Come on—let's help them," Elsa said. She took the girl's hand and they ran across the field, raindrops the size of pennies exploding on their shoulders. Elsa glanced at Ully. Her hair was plastered to her cheeks and the nape of her long neck. Her thin dress sculpted the lines of her shoulder blades. She loped like a rabbit, focused and beautiful, as she ran.

When they reached the barn, Nit looked questioningly at the child but Leo seemed not to notice her at all. Leo explained quickly what they had to do, shouting to be heard over the rain. The animals were the most important thing—what was left of the crop would be lost now to the flooding. Whatever stalks of barley the hoppers hadn't eaten were being wrenched out of the soil by the rushing water. Inside the barn, Honey and the sheep were kicking the walls with their hooves, anxious to get at the fresh water. They could smell it, the hot muddy froth sending its aroma under the barn door, through the cracks in the walls.

The pails filled quickly and they carried them in to the animals to drink. When the horses as well as the rest of them had each drunk a full bucket, Leo seemed to relax. As long as the roof on the house held, they would be all right. With a sponge, he spread the cool water over the horses' backs and down their flanks. They nickered with satisfaction, their lips curling back to reveal straight, flat teeth. They dipped their heads and nuzzled against Leo. Elsa watched him carefully as he closed his eyes and pressed his cheek into the horse's mane. Two weeks ago, she had wondered if he might die.

The old griping would save him from too much mooning over his close call, though. "Nit, that's enough," Leo barked at him as he brought yet another round of buckets into the barn. "They'll just keep drinking it until they make themselves sick."

Ully veered from where she played in the corner to Elsa's side, frightened at Leo's harsh tone.

"Yes, sir," Nit said, and set the buckets down in the corner. Leo's tone seemed not to bother him in the slightest. There was too much relief in the room, in the whole of the town, Elsa was sure, and it cushioned Nit against Leo's prickly nature. When a person has held that muscle of worry clenched for so long, letting it lapse can make him feel a strange lightness, a floating, an easy rotation of the shoulder in the socket. Nit sat down on a crate and leaned his head back against the wall, water running in rivers between the planks. After a moment, he stood. "I had better go check on my own roof, see what I can do to shore it up." He took one of the horse blankets off the hook by the door and held it over his head as he ran across the sodden field.

The three of them sat for a long time, listening to the rain. The ewe, still heavy with her lamb, ambled quietly over to the buckets and began to drink. She lapped, moving her head in a small circle so that her tongue could touch the whole surface of the water in the pail. Then she lifted her head and held very still. One of her back legs kicked out slightly. She breathed through her muzzle, then let out a low bleat. Her flank clenched and unclenched like a fist.

Leo glanced up and looked at Elsa, his eyebrows raised. "Must have been the drought that kept her waiting so long," he said.

Elsa nodded.

"Come on," Leo said. "Let's leave her to it."

"What's happening?" Ully whispered to Elsa.

Elsa took her hand and held her close to her skirt in a ridiculous attempt to keep her hidden. If Leo minded the girl's presence, she supposed he would have said something by now. "That ewe has got some work to do," Elsa said. She chose her words carefully, not wanting to call the lamb a baby just yet. The birth was so awfully overdue that there seemed to be a good chance things wouldn't go well. "And we should leave her to it."

Ully agreed without an argument. They all left the barn. The rain had slowed to a steady, pleasant shower. "Hey," Ully said, spreading her fingers in the water. "The hoppers are gone."

The sky was dark and they were exhausted by all the commotion. Leo insisted on staying outside and checking the roof and foundation for leaks. He kept saying how much there was to do now that they finally had rain. Elsa and Ully went into the kitchen and Elsa put Ully to work peeling potatoes for supper. She knew the girl should go home to be with her father. He would be worried about her out in this weather. But Elsa didn't want her to leave. She got the fire going in the stove, then melted butter in the cast-iron pan and arranged the potato slices in the sizzling fat. She took a handful of salt from the crock and sprinkled it on top.

Ully was arranging the strips of potato skin into four even piles, her brow drawn in concentration. "Elsa, what kind of work does the ewe have to do?"

Elsa rolled her lips together. "She is birthing her lamb, *Spatzchen*."

Ully looked up, surprised. "She is?"

"Mm-hmm." Elsa kept her eyes on the pan. The potatoes popped and hissed. It wouldn't do to make a big thing out of it. But then she wondered whether Ully even understood what she meant by *birthing*. "Do you know how that happens?"

Ully rolled her eyes. "Yeah. I know." She was quiet for a long moment as she moved some of the strips from the middle pile to the one on the left, using her index finger to measure the height and ensure that the piles were absolutely equal. "Do you think," she said carefully, "that it will hurt her?"

Elsa moved the pan off the heat with the wooden spoon leaned against the pan's handle. She sat down in the chair across from Ully. "It will hurt her some, but her body's made to do it. She'll be all right." Elsa didn't know whether she had just told the girl a lie.

"Here, have some potatoes." Elsa arranged a few slices on a plate and fished a fork from the drawer. "And then it's time for you to go home. You know your father is probably worried sick about you now."

"Gustav will tell him where I am. He can come get me if he needs me. Which I'm sure he doesn't."

"Of course he does," Elsa said sternly. There was a time for sweetness and a time to tell this child where she stood. "Now, eat your potatoes."

After Ully had wolfed them down, she lifted the plate to her face and licked the salt off it.

"Ully!" Elsa cried. "Don't do that!"

The girl giggled.

Elsa knew she did things just to get a rise out of her. Just then, Leo banged into the kitchen, casting water all over the floor.

"Elsa, I need your help," he said. "Nit must have had trouble with his roof. I've been yelling for him for ten minutes, but I don't have time to run over there."

"What is it?"

"The ewe's having trouble. I can't crouch down low enough with this damned knee to help her."

Elsa nodded and wiped her hands on her apron, then followed him back out into the rain, with Ully trailing behind her. Her still-damp dress soaked all over again on the jog back to the barn. They would all have head colds before this was over, she thought, her brain trying to distract her from the worry of what they might see, of what Ully might see.

She grabbed the girl's shoulder. "*Spatzchen*, go on home."

Ully shook her head.

"No, I mean it," Elsa said, making her voice hard. "You need to go on home now."

"I want to see that lamb," Ully said.

Leo was already at the barn door. "Elsa, *come on*."

Elsa shook her head at Ully and hurried into the barn. The ewe lay on her side, scraping her cheek in the hay. Her rump was bright pink and swollen. At the opening, a translucent membrane expanded and contracted like a soap bubble.

"She has been laboring hard," Leo said. "She should be further along than this."

"How many lambs are there?" Elsa asked.

"Just one, thank the Lord for small mercies."

"What can we do for her?"

"When the sac breaks, I want you to get down and pull on the legs."

Elsa nodded. She saw in the periphery that Ully had slid inside the door and stood in the shadow, her back against the wall of the barn. The sac expanded even larger this time, becoming transparent and revealing the lamb's hooves for a moment as if behind a clouded pane of glass. Leo leaned over the ewe's rump, peering down. "*Damnation*. It's turned the wrong way."

Elsa felt her throat tighten. *Please Lord*, she prayed. *Please don't let this child see something terrible.*

The ewe grunted and the sac broke then and fluid sluiced out in a wave. Elsa heard Ully take a breath in the silence that followed and Leo touched Elsa's shoulder. She nodded and crouched down. The back legs poked out of the opening and the ewe moaned, her eyes rolling back in their sockets. Elsa took a breath and grasped the legs with her hands. They were wet and slippery, but she gripped tightly, digging her nails into the fleece.

"Now I should pull?" she asked, looking up at Leo.

He held up a finger. "Wait—" He watched until the ewe's belly clenched again. "Now."

Elsa pulled, but the lamb didn't budge.

"Harder," Leo barked. He sat down on the hay but couldn't bend his leg to get close enough.

"I'm afraid I'm going to hurt her," Elsa cried.

Ully was very quiet over in the corner.

"She has to get the lamb out *now*."

Elsa got up on her knees, her legs parted a little so that she could brace her weight. She leaned forward and took hold of the legs again, then inhaled and pulled as hard as she could. The ewe made a terrible low sound, an almost human keening. If she were a young woman in her travail, she might have cried that sad psalm, *Why hast thou forsaken me? Why art thou so far from helping me, and far from the words of my roaring?* Elsa pushed her hands inside the hot birth canal to grip around the lamb's hips. She felt the tiny creature's legs would break, but she kept on pulling. The suction inside gave way, finally. The lamb slid into the hay, long and lean. It did not move.

Elsa looked at Leo. He scooted closer to her. Even in the dim light of the barn, Elsa could see that the lamb was blue around its eyes and mouth. The rain pounded on the roof, relentless.

"Rub her," Leo said.

Elsa nudged the lamb gently, moving her hand in more vigorous circles on its sticky fleece.

Leo reached over and rubbed too. "Come on, little one,"

he said in the tenderest voice she had ever heard him use. "Wake up."

The mother lifted her head and looked down the line of her body at them. She bleated, desperate to see her baby.

Leo winced as he put his weight on the bad leg and hoisted himself up over the lamb. "Come on," he said. He put his hand on the lamb's belly and moved it in the hay.

Elsa felt her own lungs were made of stone. She felt she couldn't breathe until she saw the lamb breathe.

Just then, the ugly, slick mess twitched and lifted its head. Its flanks expanded with breath and on the exhale it made a tiny whine. The ewe's body relaxed and she called out to her baby. The lamb took another breath, pinkening, and then stood up and limped toward its mother. The ewe began to lick it all over its face, then shoved it down to feed.

Elsa sat back on her heels and watched, wiping her eyes on her sleeve.

Leo sighed, then pushed himself up. "Thank you, Elsa. I don't know what I would have done if you weren't here."

Elsa swallowed. Everything seemed very quiet for a moment and she stared at Leo, this hard, humorless, difficult, precious man. She felt she had been waiting her whole life for someone to say those words to her.

A wail broke the silence and Elsa looked up in surprise. Ully, crying, rushed to Elsa and climbed right into her lap, Elsa's dress still wet with fluid from the birth. Ully buried her face in Elsa's chest and cried and cried. Elsa rocked a bit from side to side, kissed the top of Ully's head and rubbed her palm in circles on the girl's back.

"I thought that lamb was going to die," Ully said, her voice thick with anguish.

"Oh, my darling. But look—she's just fine."

"But I *thought* she was going to die," Ully insisted, trying to get Elsa to understand. And Elsa did understand. That things had turned out all right almost didn't matter at all; if you got what you wanted, if you let yourself love something, all that meant was someday you would lose it. The threat of that loss loomed over you always.

Ully tucked her head under Elsa's chin and Elsa ran her hand along the scraggly line of the girl's lopped-off hair. There was nothing to say. It was an awful thing for a nine-year-old girl to know about the world, but it wasn't untrue.

"My mother died," Ully whispered.

"Oh, my Ully," Elsa said. "I know. And it is so sad." The Lord felt very near, just then. He had brought this child to Elsa's doorstep and asked her what she might do to be of use, to soothe Ully, to soothe them both, in some small way. Elsa hoped she had not failed.

Leo cleared his throat. "Elsa, who is this child?"

Elsa laughed a loud, honking laugh. She pushed Ully to her feet. "Mr. Leonard Schreier, allow me to present Miss Ulrika Eleonora Gibson."

Ully took the long, sputtering breath that came after crying, then wiped her nose on her sleeve before extending her hand. "Pleased to meet you, sir. I'm sorry for all the carrying on."

Leo took Ully's hand, glanced down at her short, dirty fingers.

"I'm sorry, too, sir, about all of my visits. I hope I haven't eaten too much of your food."

Leo looked at Elsa. She held her breath, then gave a tentative little shrug. "Ully has been keeping me company in the afternoons."

Leo frowned at her. "And here I thought you were doing all that baking for me." He turned back to Ully. "It's all right, Miss Gibson. Miss Traugott and I have plenty to share. And something to celebrate now that the lamb made it through, and we have our rain. I wonder if there's any cake left inside."

Elsa nodded and Leo stepped out of the darkness of the barn with his palm up. He led the three of them through the drizzle to the house. Ully doubled her steps to walk beside him and grasped Leo's fingers. To Elsa's surprise, he allowed the girl's hand to hang there beneath his own. Ully was patient with his slow gait, not rushing him or pulling him along. After that cake she absolutely had to go home. Daniel Gibson would be worried.

Elsa wondered, though, as she watched them walking together, if the next time she saw Daniel she might not ask whether Ully could come to live with her for a while. It was what Elsa had been wanting all along, she realized. Not to have her come and go—to have her *stay*. Leo would be all right with it, she thought. He might even be glad. They had yet to take that walk he'd asked her for, but she saw now that they would. For the first time since coming to Destination, she saw that her life would never go back to the way it had been. She wouldn't be alone anymore. In the fall they would celebrate *Erntedankfest*. Perhaps she could get some apple wine from Omaha.

They tromped inside, peeling off their wet shoes and stockings. Elsa got the fire going in the stove because, even though it was still hot outside, the rain made you crave something hot to drink. After she washed up, she put the water on to boil, cut the cake, and slid the slices onto plates. When she turned to the table, Ully was sitting beside Leo watching him unfold his napkin and put it on his lap. Elsa noticed that Ully's hair had grown down just a bit at the back of her neck, a stiff fringe. By winter it would be long enough to braid, and that was what Elsa would do.

Clara

For once, the mayor was in his office. Clara stood in the hallway, suddenly shy, and watched him working at his desk, the pen clutched in his enormous paw of a hand. Outside, the rain hammered the windowpanes, and she could see that Mr. Cartwright had recently come in from it. His hair was matted and wet along his neck, his shirt cuffs soaked transparent, making a mess of the papers he dragged his arm across as he wrote. Clara leaned her umbrella against the wall and took a step toward his desk.

"Good morning," she said, uncertain where to begin.

The mayor looked up. "Oh, Mrs. Bixby—just the woman I have been wanting to see."

"Mr. Cartwright, I hardly know what to say."

"Well, that's because I haven't yet told you of my business proposition."

"It's such a grand gesture, sir, that no respectable person could *accept* it."

"But how did you know?" He shook his head. "You must misunderstand my idea—"

"But I came to say that if you gave it only as a gesture, believing that I would, as decorum demands, return your gift, I am sorry to disappoint you, sir. For I am *keeping* this money. Every penny."

Mr. Cartwright's bushy eyebrows drew together. "What money?"

"Experience has taught me that when someone offers to help you, you should take their help. Especially when you have no hope of fixing the problem on your own. So I am keeping the money. I don't even feel any guilt about that," Clara said in astonishment, almost to herself. "You shouldn't have offered to give it if you didn't think I would accept."

The mayor held up his hand. "Mrs. Bixby—I honestly do not know what you're talking about."

Clara smiled and shook her head. "If you didn't want me to know where it came from, why did you wrap it in your own handkerchief?"

The mayor shook his head.

"All right, I'll play along," Clara said. "My hearing was this morning. Judge Tharp came from Fremont."

"It was this morning? Why didn't you tell me?"

"I didn't want to worry you. You've already done so much to help me, to take my side against these men. I couldn't ask for anything more."

"And? Where does the matter stand?"

"Mrs. Gibson never appeared to give her so-called testimony. The judge let me go."

"So it is finished then? You are free?"

"It wasn't finished until I went upstairs to my room to find a great sum of money wrapped in your handkerchief, slipped under my door. As you know, I have always intended to pay these men back."

"Yes, I do know *that*," Mayor Cartwright said. "But Mrs. Bixby, you have to believe me—that money did not come from me."

Clara stared at him a moment, dumbfounded. Why would he lie?

"Don't you think if I had the money all along, I would have offered it to you sooner and settled this matter?"

"But who else could it be?"

Cartwright shrugged. "Perhaps it came from . . . your husband?"

Clara replied with a halfhearted laugh and then a sigh. "You must know that Mr. Bixby has been gone for some time."

"I had heard something . . ." Cartwright said, pretending to look through the papers on his desk to save her from the awkwardness of a direct gaze.

Clara saw then: He was embarrassed to have done so grand a thing for another man's wife, absent as her husband might be at the moment. Perhaps he had believed she would take the money and leave town, that he could know she was all right but wouldn't have to face her again. She would pretend to speculate for his sake about who else could have given her the money, but she would never doubt that Randall Cartwright thought she was worth something, worth helping, that he saw what she could be if sorrow and debt and George released their hold over her.

"Maybe Mrs. Healy?" Clara said, watching his face for a sign of relief.

He shrugged again. "Anything is possible in this town." He laced his fingers together on top of the desk. "I wanted to come find you today to tell you some things. The first is that my uncle Kellinger has finally gone home, as they say."

"Oh!" Clara said. "By train?"

Cartwright shook his head. "Home to his final rest, that is—not to Missouri. In his sleep last night."

"Oh, Mr. Cartwright, I'm so sorry to hear it."

He gaped at her. "I'm not. *You* met the man—he was the most miserable, profane, ungodly man west of the Mississippi. I believe this rain is a direct result of his wickedness finally taking leave of the county."

Clara laughed. "Well, I'm sure he had his reasons."

"I think he took great joy in making others miserable." Cartwright shook his head and pressed his thick fingers against his eyes. "That was the first thing I wanted to tell you. The second is that I have decided I have had quite enough of everyone coming to me with their problems."

"Oh," Clara said, feeling her blood rise to her cheeks. "Of course you have—and I am one of the worst offenders."

He waved his hands. "No, no—that's not what I meant. What I'm saying is, I don't want to be the mayor anymore. I never should have done it in the first place—it was a fool idea." He stood up, his great towering height always a bit of a shock. "Mrs. Bixby—or what shall I call you now?"

Clara shrugged. She really didn't know anymore. "How about plain Clara?"

He nodded. "Clara, do you know much about the Roman Empire?"

Her eyes widened. The conversation was beginning to feel like an overturned nest of snakes, slithering this way and that. She furrowed her brow. "I can't say that I do, sir."

Cartwright clapped his hands. "Precisely. I don't either. But I *could*, if I had any blasted *time* to read a book now and again. And I'd like to do that."

"Well, then you should, Mr. Cartwright."

"And I want to learn to play the fiddle. I have always wanted to learn to do that, but would the dim minds of this town tolerate a fiddle-playing mayor, do you think?"

Clara began to laugh. "No, sir, I suppose not."

He was pacing now. "Of course they wouldn't—why are you laughing?"

Trying to stop only made Clara laugh harder. "I can't help but picture you trying to dance a jig."

"Cruel woman! A man confesses his meager little dream and you greet it with ridicule!"

Mr. Cartwright laughed now too, opening his great red mouth to roar. The room swam and Clara felt she had to sit down. Everything in her whole body felt loose for the first time in her life. All the weight she had been carrying for years lifted up and sailed away. She felt like she might break out into a jig herself, any minute. Cartwright sat down across from her behind his desk.

"Well, I certainly have no reason now to share what I had planned to tell you." When he smiled, it showed in every feature of his face: the pink slopes of his cheeks, his upturned eyes.

Clara clamped her lips together, then said, "Please tell me. I *promise* not to laugh."

"I'd like to take over my uncle's claim. Make that land yield something for the first time."

"I think that's wonderful, sir." She *did* think it wonderful. She loved the image of her friend working in the red afternoon sun.

Cartwright nodded. "I have come into a little money from the old man. Not much, but it seems he held on to a good portion of the proceeds from the sale of his house in St. Louis. I don't know why he didn't put it into the land out here."

"Perhaps he was saving it for you."

"Perhaps. Of course, we may not need it now that you have come into your own small fortune."

"We?" The room rushed back into focus.

Mr. Cartwright fixed her with that smile again. "Strictly business," he said, holding up his hand. "I wanted to propose the idea that, now that you are the head of your own household, you might claim the adjacent parcel and we might combine our efforts. We can hire out the work, grow more, sell more, and split the profits down the middle. I'll even help you build a home for yourself—we can design it however you please. A *business* venture."

"Business," Clara whispered, watching him across the desk. She thought of the little white cottage, its shabby nobility, and the vision plucked at her heart, like seeing the face of a lost friend. It had been a long time since she had let the dream of it wash over her, a long time since she had felt it would ever be more than just a dream.

Cartwright nodded. He reached over and placed her right

hand on his palm, then lifted it to his lips. Clara felt the bristles of his mustache rustle over the thin cotton of her glove. He rested his cheek on her knuckles, and all the while he kept his eyes on her.

"Unless I can convince you otherwise," he said.

ACKNOWLEDGMENTS

I am grateful to my editor, Claire Zion, for seeing the possibilities in this story, and my agent, Marly Rusoff, a true advocate and source of support. Thank you to Michael Radulescu for his tireless efforts on many fronts, and to Julie Mosow for editorial wisdom, friendship, and tiny sundresses. Thank you as well to the team at Berkley: Leslie Gelbman, Leslie Worrell, Erica Martirano, Lara Robbins, Amy Schneider, Laura Corless, Jhanteigh Kupihea, and the sales reps who fight for books every day. And true admiration goes to the dedicated, passionate, *irreplaceable* independent booksellers we readers and writers depend on.

In order to create the fictional town of Destination and the fictional people who live there, I relied on primary accounts written by women settlers Rachel Calof, Elinore Pruitt Stewart, and Mollie Dorsey Sanford. Mari Sandoz's *Old Jules* was also helpful, as was *Hearts West: True Stories of Mail-Order Brides on the Frontier* by Chris Enss, *Midwest Heritage* by John Drury, *Nebraska: An Illustrated History* by Frederick Luebke. *Law and Order in Buffalo Bill's Country* by Mark Ellis, *Empire on the Platte* by A. Richard Crabb, and the Library of Congress American Memory archive on prairie settlement. J. C. Furnas's *The Americans* and Jane Nylander's *Our Own Snug Fireside* were once again invaluable. And, in that underground-river sort of way, so was Marilynne Robinson's *Gilead*, which might have been Elsa's second-favorite book, if she had really lived and was born more than a few years later.

Thank you to my friend Lara Zielin for the writing retreat where I wrote the first three chapters about Clara, Rowena, and Elsa. Birgit Kobayashi, co-owner of Café Selmarie in Chicago's Lincoln Square, provided Elsa's German recipes. To Jaralinn De La Ossa, much appreciation for your help understanding migraines from the inside; I am only sorry you have to know these facts. Laura Rodgers, an honest-to-goodness shepherd, helped this city girl understand a little bit about lambing. But any mistakes I've made in rendering the details of this story are mine alone.

I am lucky to have the friendship of wise and wonderful writers Kelly Harms Wimmer, Eleanor Brown, and Lori Nelson Spielman. Thank you to fellow authors Robin Oliveira, Katrina Kittle, Kristina Riggle, Stephanie Cowell, Susan Gregg Gilmore, Tasha Alexander, Rebecca Rasmussen, Wendy McClure, Nancy Woodruff, Joe Wallace, Sandra Gulland, M. J. Rose, and the members of the Fiction Writers Co-op. Thank you to my parents and family, for being you; to Ruth Mills, for counsel; to Kate Malloy, for compassion and care, and to Amy Henriott, whose hands gave us our baby in the middle of all this. We love those hands!

Finally, to Bob: We began this year on the precipice of a great adventure. Thank you for dangling your toes over the edge with me.

AUTHOR'S NOTE

The story of *In Need of a Good Wife* was brewing in the back of my mind for years before I knew what shape the novel would take. For as long as I can remember, stories of settlers traveling west, leaving behind a predetermined fate to build a new life from scratch, have captivated me. Like many young readers, I discovered this genre through Laura Ingalls Wilder's *Little House* books and Patricia MacLachlan's hushed and beautiful *Sarah, Plain and Tall*. Later I came to love Alexandra Bergson, of Willa Cather's *O Pioneers!*, a sort of grown-up version of Laura Ingalls, determined to make her farm flourish on the land her father had claimed a generation before. The men and women (fictional *and* historical) who made new lives in the West seemed to have two things: immense determination and vision. They could see something remarkable in a plot of dust and they were willing to do the work necessary to bring that vision into existence. In other words, they had the makings of irresistible characters.

In search of what my westbound story might look like, I stumbled on a book called *Hearts West: True Stories of Mail-Order Brides on the Frontier*. The vignettes in this slim volume told the stories of all sorts of arranged marriages across the West in the second half of the nineteenth century. The matches met with

varying degrees of success. Some produced loving, or at least
friendly, marriages. Other prospective spouses weren't as lucky.
In 1873, a woman named Eleanor Berry began a correspondence
with a man she met through a San Francisco newspaper. When
he proposed, she traveled by train to his town to meet him for
the first time and marry him. En route, the train was robbed by
armed bandits. Eleanor arrived to what was to be her new home
empty-handed, only to recognize her intended husband as one of
the robbers.

I couldn't get enough of these stories. Another told of Asa
Mercer, who thought of himself as a "bride entrepreneur." He
published an advertisement in the *Puget Sound Herald* in 1860
about a community meeting for bachelors interested in the "much-
needed and desirable emigration" of eligible women to the town.
Mercer determined he would travel east, collect a group of willing
brides, and simply import them to the bachelors in Washington
State. For a price, of course. Things did not quite work out as
Mercer hoped—some of the brides had a change of heart before or during the four-month journey by ship. Some died along
the way. In the end, Mercer delivered far fewer young women
than he had promised, and his customers were so dissatisfied that
a riot broke out at the seaport.

The fiction writer in me began to speculate. What if the person hired to match bachelors and brides was not a wily businessman but a woman, a woman at the end of her rope, who needed
a way to get out of New York City? Naïve but determined, Clara,
as I began to think of her, would be intrigued by the advertisements plastered all over New York by the Union Pacific Railroad
in the 1860s, promising cheap farms and free homes in eastern
Nebraska. The newly completed eastern segment of the Trans-

continental Railroad promised a fairly easy journey across New York state and Michigan, through Chicago and across Iowa to the Missouri River, where Omaha was growing on the opposite bank.

In 1866, the Civil War was over, but its consequences still echoed throughout the country. Many eastern cities like New York, Boston, and Philadelphia were teeming with widows who had lost their soldier husbands and single women who had never had the chance to marry before the men went away. The fate of many of these women was in jeopardy; marriage represented their only hope for avoiding poverty. Meanwhile, many young men had traveled west during and after the war to claim land through the Homestead Act, which made 160 acres available very cheaply to citizens who would settle and work the land. After five years, the government would turn over the deed to the settler. For immigrants coming from European countries where land ownership was the exclusive privilege of the wealthy, the Homestead Act was a remarkable gift. But settlers found that the backbreaking work was lonely. They longed for wives and children to help them fulfill their vision of a new life.

Once these single men and women knew of each other's existence, letters, I realized, would play a central role in their relationships. I found inspiration for what these letters might contain in *Hearts West* and the Library of Congress archive on prairie settlement in Nebraska. One letter in particular, from Uriah Oblinger to the woman he hoped to bring to his settled land as his bride, moved me. "Until I receive *your* reply," he wrote, "I shall write to no other lady."

I began to imagine a particular town full of men, northwest of Omaha on the Platte River. I had read about the "Hell on wheels towns" that sprang up in Nebraska, where rail workers would hastily assemble villages—usually little more than a boardinghouse and a tavern—to sustain them while they worked a segment of the line. When they moved west to continue work, the town would be either dismantled or abandoned. But sometimes people stayed behind and developed those towns further. Destination, the town of my story, would be that sort of place, abused by rough, transient men, but enduring because of the efforts of some to make it a respectable place.

Clara would set her sights on this town. And the women who accompanied her—a cast of characters that soon included Rowena, a war widow, and Elsa, a laundress who expected very little from the world—would bring with them the stories of their lives, their pain and longing, their hopes for what the future might bring. When they arrived in Destination, nothing would work out quite the way they had imagined. And the real story would begin.

In Need of a Good Wife

DISCUSSION QUESTIONS

1. The concept of "going west" figured large in late nineteenth-century American culture. Enthusiasm for the opportunity to leave the comfort of the eastern cities and forge new settlements embodied both pragmatic ambition and a kind of mythology about freedom and self-reliance that often fell short of hopes. What does going west mean to each of the main characters in *In Need of a Good Wife*? How are their expectations confirmed and upended?

2. Friendship plays an important role for the characters in this novel, both among the women and between the women and the men. What does friendship have to offer that love and marriage cannot provide?

3. Names are important in *In Need of a Good Wife*. Some characters change their names for various reasons (the new wives, Clara, and Ully); others are uneasy with the names they've been given (Rowena as "Mother" and Randall as "Mayor"). Even the name of the town requires an explanation. What do names signify for these characters?

4. What were some of the reasons the brides had for pursuing the mail-order bride experiment? What do those reasons say about the kind of people who built the West in this country? About the kind of country the women settlers were hoping the United States would become?

5. As Clara narrowed down the list of potential brides early in the story, she seemed to be screening for a particular type of woman. What kind of character traits was she looking for? What was she hoping to avoid? What do these criteria say, if anything, about Clara herself?

6. How would you describe Elsa's faith? Is it different from the sort of faith espoused by either of the two Manhattan City ministers who appear in the first chapter? What role does faith play in Elsa's experience of the journey west?

7. How does the birth of the lamb take on significance for Elsa throughout the story? What has changed for her by the time the lamb finally comes?

8. Do you find Rowena to be a likable character? Why or why not?

9. Why is Rowena drawn to Tomas? How does their relationship change her and the path she is on?

10. Mayor Cartwright is preoccupied with the need to "be of use," a tenet that has been for him both a saving grace and a source of frustration and disappointment. How does the

need for purpose drive the mayor and the other characters in this story? How does it get them into trouble?

11. The novel contains this description of the loss Clara and George suffered: "They shared a secret sorrow and it bound them together. What they had endured was stronger than anything—stronger than love or hate or disappointment or anger—and no matter how [Clara] tried to escape, to begin again, the sorrow pulled her back in like a tide." How does loss and grief affect the characters in this story? How do varying responses to loss impact what happens to them?

12. What do you think will happen with Randall and Clara after the story ends?

NOTES